Ellie I █████████████████
romance ██████████ ██████

Royal Rebels

Royal Rebels: A Convenient Marriage

ELLIE DARKINS

ALLY BLAKE

REBECCA WINTERS

MILLS & BOON

First Published in Great Britain 2021
By Mills & Boon, an imprint of HarperCollins*Publishers* Ltd
1 London Bridge Street, London, SE1 9GF

www.harpercollins.co.uk

HarperCollins*Publishers*
1st Floor, Watermarque Building,
Ringsend Road, Dublin 4, Ireland

ISBN: 978-0-263-30241-7

MIX
Paper from
responsible sources
FSC™ C007454

FALLING FOR THE REBEL PRINCESS

ELLIE DARKINS

For Mike and Matilda

CHAPTER ONE

'NOT YET!' CHARLIE GASPED, willing herself to be dragged back under.

In her dream her skin was hot and damp, on fire from his touch.

Awake, her tongue felt furry.

In her dream her body hummed, desperate for the feel of him.

Awake, her eyes stung as she peeled them open.

In her dream she begged for more, and got everything she didn't even know she needed.

Awake, she needed to pee.

She admitted defeat and stretched herself properly alive, wincing at the harsh Nevada sunlight assaulting her in the hotel room. As her toes encountered skin she flinched back, realising that she did have this one, small reminder of her dream. The man who'd taken the starring role was beside her on the mattress, his face turned away from her, his arms and legs sprawled and caught in the sheets. She looked away. She couldn't think about him. Not yet.

Easing herself out of bed, she willed him not to wake. And worked her thumb into her waistband, rubbing at her skin where her jeans had left a tight red line. The T-shirt she'd slept in was twisted and creased, and she glanced around the room, wondering whether her luggage had been transferred when the hotel had upgraded them to a luxury suite. She shuddered when she caught sight of herself in the mirror and tried to pull her hair up into some sort of order.

It had started out backcombed and messy, and her eyeliner had never been subtle in her life—but a couple of hours' sleep had taken the look from grunge to tragic. She wiped under her eyes with a finger, and the tacky drag of her skin made her shudder. And desperate to shower.

A glint of gold caught her eye and stopped her dead.

No. That had been the dream. It had to be.

She went over her memories, rooted to the spot, staring at the ring, trying to pull apart what was dream and what was real. After eighteen hours travelling and many more without sleep, the past twenty-four hours barely felt real, images and memories played through her mind as if they had happened to somebody else.

The thrumming, heaving energy of the gig last night. That was real. The music capturing her senses, hijacking her emotions and pumping her full of adrenaline. Real.

Hot and sweaty caresses just before dawn. Dream.

Dancing with Joe in the club, trying to talk business, shouting in his ear. Moving so closely with him that they felt like one body. Feeling the music play between them like a language only they spoke. Maybe that was real.

The slide of his bare skin against hers. So, so dreamy.

Him talking softly as they lay on the bed, trading playlists on their phones, sharing a pair of headphones, until one and then both of them fell asleep. God, she wished she knew.

But as she raised her left hand and examined the demure gold band on her third finger, she was certain of one thing.

Vegas chapel wedding. Real.

She banged her head back against the wall. Why did she always do this? She was losing count of the number of times she'd looked over the wreckage of her life after one stupid, impulsive move after another and wished that she could turn back time. If she had the balls to go home and tell her parents that she didn't want their royal way of life and everything that came with it, maybe she'd stop hitting the self-destruct button. But starting that conversation would lead to questions that she'd never be prepared to answer.

Thinking back to the night before, she tried to remember what had triggered her reaction. And then she caught sight of the newspaper, abandoned beside the bed. The slip of the paper under her fingertips made her shiver with the memory of being handed one like it backstage in the club last night, and she let out a low groan. It had been the headline on the front page: Duke Philippe bragging about his forthcoming engagement to Princess Caroline Mary Beatrice of Afland, otherwise known as Charlie. It was the sort of match her parents had been not so subtly pushing on her for years, the one she was hoping that would go away if she ignored it for long enough. She knew unequivocally that she would never marry, and especially not someone like Duke Philippe.

She'd left the cold, rocky, North Sea island of Afland nearly ten years ago, when she'd headed to London determined to make her own way in the music business. Her parents had given her ten years to pursue her rebellion—as they put it. But they all knew what was expected after that: a return to Afland, official royal duties, and a practical and sensible engagement to a practical, sensible aristocrat.

So there was nothing but disappointment in store for her family, and for her.

She shrank into the bathroom and hid the newspaper as she heard stirring from the bed. Perhaps if she hid for long enough it just wouldn't be true—Joe Kavanagh and their marriage would fade away as the figment of her imagination that she knew they must be.

Marriage. She scoffed. This wasn't a marriage. It was a mistake.

But it seemed as if her body didn't care which bits of last night were real and which were imagined. The hair on her arms was standing on end, her heart had started to race, and she felt a yearning deep in her stomach that seemed somehow familiar.

'Morning,' she heard Joe call from the bedroom, and she wondered if he'd guessed that she was hiding out in there. 'I know you're in there.'

The sound of his voice sent another shiver of recognition. British, and educated. But there was also a burr of something rugged about it, part of his northern upbringing that felt exotically 'authentic', when compared to the marble halls and polished accents of her childhood.

She risked peeking round the bathroom door and mumbled a good morning, wondering why she hadn't

just left the minute that she'd woken up—running
had always worked for her before. She'd been running from one catastrophe to another for as long as
she could remember. Because this was her suite, she
reminded herself. They'd been upgraded when the
manager of the hotel had heard about their impromptu
wedding, and realised that he had royalty and music
royalty spending their wedding night in his hotel.

The only constant in her life since she'd left the
palace in Afland had been her job. She'd worked from
the bottom of the career ladder up to her position as
an A&R executive, signing bands for an independent
record label, Avalon. And that was the reason she had
to get herself out of this room and face her new husband. Because not only was he a veritable rock god,
he was also the artist that she'd been flown out here
to charm, persuade and impress with her consummate
professionalism in a last-ditch bid to get him to sign
with her company.

She held her head high as she walked back into the
bedroom, determined not to show him her feelings.
The sun was coming in strong through the windows,
and the backlighting meant that she couldn't quite
see his expression.

'How's the head?' he asked, his expression changing to concerned.

She wondered whether she should tell him that
she'd only had a couple of beers at most last night.
That her recklessness hadn't come from alcohol, it
had been fuelled by adrenaline and something more
dangerous—the destructive path she found herself on
all too often whenever marriage and family and the
future entered the conversation.

Had Joe been drunk last night? She didn't think so. He'd seemed high when he'd come off stage, but she had been at enough gigs to know the difference between adrenaline and something less legal. She remembered him necking a beer, but that was it. So he didn't have that excuse either.

Why in God's name had this ever seemed like a good idea—to either of them?

'I've felt better,' she admitted, crossing the room to perch on the edge of the bed.

Up close, she decided that it really wasn't fair that he looked like this. His hair was artfully mussed by the pillows, his shirt was rumpled, and his tiny hint of eyeliner had smudged, but the whole look was so unforgivably sexy she almost forgot that whatever had happened the night before had been a huge mistake.

But sexy wasn't why she'd married him. Or maybe it was. When she went into reckless self-destruction mode, who was to say why she did anything?

Even in this oasis in the middle of the desert, she hadn't been able to escape the baggage that came with being a member of the royal family. The media obsession with royal women marrying and reproducing. Someone had raised a toast when they had seen her, to her impending marriage, asked her if she was up the duff and handed her a bottle of champagne. She'd been tempted to down the whole thing without taking a breath, determined to silence the voices in her head.

'So,' she said. 'I guess we're in trouble.'

Trouble? She was right about that. Everything about this woman said trouble. He had known it the minute that he had set eyes on her, all attitude and eyeliner.

He had known it for sure when they'd started dancing, her body moving in time with his. So at what point last night had trouble seemed like such a good idea?

When they'd left the dance floor, in that last club, their bodies hot and sticky. When she'd been trying to talk business but he'd been distracted by the humming of his skin and the sparks that leapt from his body to hers whenever she was near. When Ricky, the drummer in his band, had joked that he needed to show some real rock-star behaviour if they were going to sell the new album, and Joe had dropped to one knee and proposed.

He hadn't thought for a second that she would go along with it.

But Charlie had stopped for a moment as their eyes had met, and as everyone had laughed around them he had been able to see that she wasn't laughing, and neither was he. The club had stilled and quietened, or maybe it was just his mind that had, but suddenly there had been just the two of them, connected through something bigger than either of their bodies could contain. Something he couldn't pretend to comprehend, but that he knew meant that they understood each other.

And then she had nodded, thrown back her head and laughed along with everyone else, and they had been carried on a wave of adrenaline, bonhomie and contagious intoxication into a cab and up the steps of the courthouse. Somehow, still high from their performance and bewitched by the Princess, he hadn't stepped out of their fantasy and broken the spell.

They'd been cocooned in that buzz, carrying them straight through the ceremony. Such a laugh as they'd toppled out of the chapel. Right up until that kiss. Then it had all felt very real.

Did she remember that feeling as they had kissed for the first time? He knew in his bones that he could never forget it, as they were pronounced husband and wife.

'Are you going to hide in there all morning?' he asked.

In the daylight, she didn't look like a princess any more than she had the night before. Maybe that was how he'd found himself here. He'd expected to be on edge around her, but as soon as he had met her... Not that he was relaxed—no, there was too much going on, too much churning and yearning and *desire* to call it relaxed. But he'd been... He wasn't sure of the word. Her boss had sent her out here to convince him that their label was a good fit—and he'd been right. They had... Maybe fit was the right world. They'd just understood each other. She understood the music. Understood him. And when they had started dancing, there had been no question in his mind that this was important. He didn't know what it was, but he knew that he wanted more.

And marrying her—it had been a good move for the band. You couldn't buy publicity like that. He must have been thinking about that, must have calculated this as a business move. It was the only thing that made sense.

But was she expecting a marriage?

Because she came with a hell of a lot of baggage. Oh, he knew which fork to use, and how to spot the nasty ones in a room of over-privileged Henrys. He'd learned that much at his exclusive public school, where his music scholarship had taken him fee-free. But the most important part of his education had been the invaluable lesson he'd got in his last year—everyone was out to get something, so you'd better work out what you wanted in return.

The only place he felt relaxed these days was on the road, with his band. They moved from city to city, sometimes settling for a few weeks if they could hire some studio space, otherwise going from gig to gig, and woman to woman, without looking back. Everyone knowing exactly what they wanted, and taking what was on offer with no strings attached.

'Come on,' he said, reaching for her hand. As his fingertips touched hers he had another flash of that feeling from last night. The electric current that had joined them together as they had danced; that had woven such a spell around them that even a visit to a courthouse hadn't broken it.

'I can't believe we got married. This was your fault. Your idea.'

Was she for real? He shrugged and reminded her of the details. 'No one forced you. You seemed to think it was a great idea last night.'

So why was she looking at her ring as if it were burning her?

'Wh…?'

He waited to see which question was burning uppermost in her mind.

'Why? Why in God's name did I think it was a great idea?'

'How am I supposed to know if you don't? Maybe

you were thinking it would be good publicity for the album.'

He looked at her carefully. Yes, that was why they had done it. But also…no. There was more to it. He couldn't believe that she was such a stranger this morning. When they'd laughed about this last night, it hadn't just been a publicity stunt—that sounded too cold. It had been a joke, a deal, between friends. A publicity stunt was business, but last night, as they'd laughed together on the way to the courthouse, it had been more than that.

And maybe that was where he had gone wrong, because he knew how this worked. He knew that all relationships were deals, with each partner out to get what they wanted. He had no reason to be offended that she was acting like that this morning.

'I'm not sure why you're mad at me. You thought it was a great idea last night.'

'I hadn't slept for thirty-six hours, Joe. I think we can say that I wasn't doing my best reasoning. We have to undo this. What are my parents going to say?'

Her parents, the Queen of Afland and her husband. He groaned inwardly.

'Last night you said, and I quote, "They're going to go mental." As far as I could work out, that was a point in the plan's favour.'

In the cold light of morning—not such a good idea. Bad, in fact. Very bad.

He had married a princess—an actual blue-blooded, heir-to-the-throne, her-mother's-a-queen *princess*.

He was royally screwed.

'Look,' Joe said. 'I'm hungry, too hungry to talk

about this now. How about we go out for breakfast and discuss this with coffee and as much protein as they can cram on a plate?'

CHAPTER TWO

CHARLIE GAZED INTO her black coffee, hoping that it would supply answers. Her memories had started to filter back in as she'd sipped her first cup; shame had started creeping in with her second. She hoped that this cup, her third, would be the one that made her feel human again.

'So how do we undo this?' she said bluntly. 'This is Vegas. They must annul almost as many marriages as they make here. Do we need to go back to the courthouse?'

She looked up and met Joe's eye. He was watching her intently as he took a bite of another slice of toast. 'We could,' he said. 'If we want an annulment, I guess that's how we go about it.'

'If?' She nearly spat out her coffee. 'I don't think you understand, Joe. We got *married*.'

'I know: I was there.'

'Am I missing something? The way I see things, we were joking around, we thought it would be hil*ar*ious to have a Vegas wedding, and we've woken up this morning to a major disaster. Aren't you interested in damage limitation?'

'Of course I am, but, unlike you, I think the reasons we got married were sound. Not necessarily the *best* reasons to enter into a legally binding personal commitment, but sound nonetheless.'

She raised her eyebrows. 'Remind me.'

'Okay, obvious ones first. Publicity. The band needs it. The album is almost finished, we're looking for a new label, and there is no such thing as bad publicity, right?'

'Mercenary much?'

'Look, this isn't my fault. You were good with mercenary last night.'

She snorted. 'Fine, publicity is one reason. Give me another.'

'It shows you're serious about the band.'

She crossed her arms and sat back in her seat, fixing him with a glare. 'I've signed plenty of bands before without marrying the lead singer. They signed with me because they trust that I'm bloody good at my job. Are you seriously telling me that whether or not I would marry you was going to be a deal-breaker?'

He leaned forward, not put off by her death stare. In fact, his eyes softened as he reached for her hand, pulling her back towards him. She went with it, not wanting to look childish by batting him away.

'Of course it wasn't,' he said gently. 'But breaking the marriage now? I'm not sure how that's going to play out. I'm not sure what our working relationship could look like with that all over the papers.'

She shook her head, looking back into the depths of her coffee, still begging it for answers.

'All of which I have to weigh against the heartbreak of my family if we don't bury this right now.'

She avoided eye contact as she tried to stop the

tears from escaping. But she took a deep breath and when she looked up they were gone. 'Do you think anyone knows already? The press?'

'We weren't exactly discreet,' he said, with a sympathetic smile. 'I'd think it's likely.'

'And that can't be undone, annulment or not.'

He leaned back and took a long drink of his orange juice. 'So let's control the narrative.'

'What do you mean?'

'What story would hurt your family more—a whirlwind romance and hasty Vegas marriage, or a drunken publicity stunt to further your career? Because that's how the tabloids are going to want to spin it.'

'What's your point, Joe?' She'd taken her hand back and crossed her arms again, sure that this conversation was taking a turn that she wasn't going to like.

'All I'm saying is that we can't go back in time. We can't get unmarried, whether we get an annulment or not. So we either dissolve the marriage today and deal with the fallout to our reputations…'

'Or…?'

'Or we stay married.'

Her breathing caught as just for a second she considered what that might mean, to be this man's wife.

'But we're not in love. Anyone's going to be able to see that.'

He scrutinised her from under his lashes, which were truly longer and thicker than any man's had a right to be. 'So we're going to have to work hard to convince them. You can't deny that it's a better story.'

'And you can't deny that it means lying to my family. Ruining all the plans they were making for my life.

I don't know what your relationship with your family is like, but I'm not sure that I can pull it off. I'm not sure that I want to. Things are diffi—'

She stopped before she revealed too much. Joe raised an eyebrow, obviously curious about why she had cut herself off, but he didn't push her on it.

'Would you rather they knew the truth?'

Of course not. She had been hiding the truth from them for years, ever since she'd found out that she could never be the daughter or the Princess that they needed her to be.

'Are we seriously having this conversation? You want to stay married? You do know that you're a rock star, right? If you were that desperate for publicity you could have found a hundred girls who actually *wanted* to be your wife.'

'Wow, you're quite something for a guy's ego. For the record, this isn't some elaborate ruse to get myself a woman. I don't have any problems on that score. All I'm doing is making the best of a situation. That's all.'

Charlie took a big bite of pie, hoping that the sugar would succeed where the coffee hadn't. 'Well, I'm glad to hear that you're not remotely interested in me as a woman.'

He fixed her with a meaningful stare, the intensity of his expression making it impossible for her to look away.

'I never said that.'

Heat rose in her belly as he held the eye contact, leaving her in no doubt about how he thought of her. She shook her head as he finally broke the contact. 'I can't believe that I'm even considering this. You're crazy There's no way we can keep this up. What happens if we slip? What happens when someone finds out it's not for real? What happens when one of us meets someone and this marriage of convenience isn't so convenient any more?'

He reached for her hand across the table, and once again there was that crackle, that spark that she remembered from the night before. She saw him in the chapel, eyes creased in laughter, as he leaned in to kiss her. Those eyes were still in front of her, concerned now though, rather than amused.

'It doesn't have to be for ever. Just long enough that it doesn't look like a stunt when we split. You weren't planning on marrying someone else any time soon, were you?'

'Never.' Her coffee cup rattled onto the saucer with a clash, liquid spilling over the top.

'Wow—that really was a no.'

She locked her gaze on his—he had to understand this if they were going to go on. 'I mean it, Joe. I didn't want to get married. Ever. I'm not wife material.'

'And yet here I am, married to you.'

He held her gaze and there was something familiar there. Something that made her stomach tighten in a knot and her skin prickle in awareness. With all the unexpected drama of finding themselves married, it seemed as if they'd both temporarily forgotten that they had also found themselves in bed together that morning.

Perhaps he was remembering something similar, because all of a sudden there was a new fire in his eyes, a new heat in the way that he was looking at her.

Her memory might be a bit ropey, but between the caffeine and the sugar her brain had been pretty much put back together, and there was one image of the night before that she couldn't get from her mind.

You may now kiss the bride.

They'd all burst out laughing, finding the whole thing hilarious. But as soon as Joe's hand had brushed against her cheek, cupping her jaw to turn her face up to him, the laughs had died in her throat. He'd been looking down at her as if he were only just seeing her for the first time, as if she had been made to look different by their marriage. His lush eyelashes had swept shut as he'd leaned towards her, and she'd had just a second to catch her breath before his lips had touched hers. They had been impossibly soft, and to start with had just pressed dry and chaste against hers. She'd reached up as he had and touched his cheek, just a gentle, friendly caress of her finger against his stubbled skin. But it had seemed to snap something within him; a gasp had escaped his lips, been swallowed by hers. His mouth had parted, and heat had flared between them.

She'd closed her eyes, understood that she was giving herself up to something more powerful than the simple actions of two individuals. As her eyes had shut her mouth had opened and her body had bowed towards her husband. Her hips had met his, and instantly sparks had crackled. His hands had left her face to lock around her waist, dragging her in tight and holding her against him. His tongue had been hot and hungry in her mouth; her hands frenzied, exploring the contours of his chest, his back, his butt.

And then the applause of their audience had broken into her consciousness, and she'd remembered where they were. What they were doing.

Blood had rushed to her cheeks and she could feel them glow as she'd broken away from Joe, acknowledging the whoops with an ironic wave.

'All right, all right,' she'd said, a sip of champagne helping with the brazen nonchalance; she'd hoped that she was successfully hiding the shake in her voice. 'Hope you enjoyed the show, people.'

She'd looked up at Joe to see whether she had imagined the connection between them, whether he'd still felt it buzzing and humming and trying to pull their bodies back together. By the heated, haunted look in his eyes, she wasn't alone in this.

He was worried, and he should be, because this marriage of convenience had just got a whole lot more complicated, for both of them. It had been a laugh, a joke, until their lips had met and they had both realised, simultaneously, that the flirting and banter that had provided an edge of excitement to their dancing that night would be a dangerous force unless they got a lid on it.

In the cold light of the morning after, she knew that they needed to face the problem head-on. She broke her gaze away from him, trying to cover what they had both clearly been remembering.

'Ground rules,' she said firmly, distracting herself by taking another bite of pie. 'If we do this, there have to be ground rules to stop it getting complicated.' He nodded in agreement, and she kept talking. 'First of all, we keep this strictly business. We both need to keep our heads and be able to walk away when the time is right. Let's acknowledge that there is chemistry between us, but if we let that lead us, we're not going to be objective and make smart decisions. And I think we both agree that we need to be smart.'

'People will talk if we don't make this look good. It has to be convincing.'

'Well, duh.' She waved to the waitress for a coffee refill. 'You're really trying to teach me how to handle the press? Obviously, in public we behave as if we're so madly in love that we couldn't wait a single minute longer to get married. We sell the hell out of it and make sure that no one has a choice *but* to believe us. But that's in public. In private, we're respectful colleagues.'

He snorted. 'Colleagues? You think we can do that? You were there, weren't you, last night? You do remember?'

Did she remember the kiss? The shivers? The way that she could still feel the imprint of his mouth on hers, as if the touch of skin on skin had permanently altered the cells? Yeah, she remembered, but that wasn't what was important here.

'And that's why we need the rules, Joe. If you want to stay married to me, you'd better listen up and pay attention.'

'Oh, I'm listening, and you're very clear. In public, I'm madly in love with you. Behind closed doors I'm at arm's length. Got it. So what are your other rules?'

She resurrected the death stare. 'No cheating. Ever. If we're going to make people believe this, they have to really believe it. We can't risk the story being hijacked. Doesn't matter how discreet you think you're being, it's never enough.'

'I get it. You don't share. Goes without saying.'

She dropped her cup back onto her saucer a little

heavier than she had planned, and the hot, bitter liquid slopped over the side again. 'This isn't about me, Joe. Don't pretend to know me. This is about appearances. I've already told you, this isn't personal.'

'Fine, well, if you're all done then I've got a rule of my own.'

'Go on, then.' She raised an eyebrow in anticipation.

'You move in with me.'

This time, the whole cup went over, coffee sloshing over the side of the table and onto her faded black jeans. At least she'd managed to miss her white shirt, she thought, thanking whoever was responsible for small mercies. She mopped hastily with a handful of napkins, buying her precious moments to regain her composure and think about what he had said. Of course she understood deep down that they would have to live together. But somehow, until he'd said it out loud, she hadn't believed it.

They would be alone together. *Living* alone together. No one to chaperone or keep them to their 'this is just business' word. Watching him across a diner table this morning, it wasn't exactly easy to keep her hands off him, so how were they meant to do that living alone together?

But she knew better than anyone that they had to make this look good. If her parents knew that she'd only done this to get out of the marriage to Philippe they would be so disappointed, and she didn't know that she could take doing that to them again.

Separate flats weren't going to cut it. By the time she looked back up, she knew that she seemed calm, regardless of what was going on underneath.

'Of course, that makes sense. Are you going to insist on your place rather than mine?'

'I'll need my recording studio.'

She nodded. 'Fine. So that's it, then? Three ground rules and we're just going to do this?'

'Well, if you're going to chicken out, you need to do it now.'

'I'm not eight years old, Joe. I'm not going to go through with this because you call me chicken.'

'Fine, why *are* you going to do it?' Nice use of psychology there, she thought. Act as though I've already agreed. He really did want this publicity. But it didn't matter, because she'd already made up her mind.

'I'm doing it because I don't want to hurt my family any more than I have to, and because I think it'll be good for my career.' And because it would save her from being talked into a real marriage, one which she knew she could never deserve.

'As long as you're doing it, your reasons are your own business,' Joe replied. She felt a little sting at that, like a brush of nettles against bare skin. Her own business. Damn right it was, but the way he said it, as if there really were nothing more than that between them… It didn't make sense. She didn't want it to make sense. She just knew that she didn't want it to hurt.

'So what are we going to tell people?' she asked after a long, awkward silence. 'I guess we need to get our stories straight.'

He nodded, and sipped at his coffee. 'We just keep it simple. We were swept away when we met each other yesterday, knew right away that it was love and decided we needed to be married. The guys in the band will go along with it. You don't have to worry about that.' Somehow she'd forgotten that they'd been there, egging them on, bundling them in the cab to the courthouse. When she thought back to last night, she remembered watching Joe on stage, sweat dripping from his forehead as he sang and rocked around the stage. Him grabbing her hand and pulling her to the dance floor when they'd gone on to a club after the gig, when he hadn't wanted to talk business.

She remembered the touch of his mouth on hers, as they were pronounced husband and wife.

But of course there had been witnesses, people who knew as well as she did that this was all a sham.

'What if they say something? They could go to the press.'

'They won't. Anyway, to everyone else it was just a laugh. And if anyone did say something, it'd be up to us to look so convincingly in love that no one could possibly believe them.'

'Ah, easy as that, huh.'

As they sat in the diner she realised how little thought they'd actually given this. She didn't even know when she would see him again. Her flight was booked back to London that night. She'd only been in Vegas to take this meeting. Her boss had sent her on a flying visit, instructed to try anything to get him to sign. She'd given her word that she wouldn't leave without the deal done. Would he see through them when they got back? Would he realise how far she had gone to keep to her promise?

'I'm flying home tonight,' she said.

He raised an eyebrow. 'You were pretty sure you'd

get me to sign, then. Didn't think you'd have to stick around to convince me?'

'I thought you'd be on the move, actually. I was told that you were only in Vegas for one night.' She knew that the band were renowned for their work ethic and their packed tour schedule, moving from city to city and gig to gig night after night. This had been her only chance for a meeting, her boss had told her as he'd instructed her to book a flight.

If he was always on the move like that, perhaps this would be easier than she thought. It could be weeks, months, before they actually had to live together. And by then, maybe... Maybe what. Maybe things would be different? There was no point pretending to be married at all if she thought that they would have changed their minds in a few weeks. They had to stick it out longer than that. If they were going to do this, they had to do it properly.

'I am, as it happens. I'm flying back to London tonight too.'

Why had he said that? They were meant to be in the States for two more weeks. Their manager had booked them into a retreat so that he could finish writing the new album. It should have been just a case of putting the finishing touches to a few songs, but he had an uneasy feeling about it this morning. He needed to go back and look at it again. There were a few decent tracks there, he was sure. But a niggling voice in his head was telling him that he still hadn't got the big hitters. The singles that would propel the album up the streaming charts and across the radio waves.

There was studio space booked for them in London in two weeks' time and it had to be fixed before then.

Their manager was going to kill him when he told him he wouldn't be showing up.

He could write in London; he had written the last album in London. It had nothing to do with Charlie. Nothing to do with her feelings, anyway. As she kept saying, this was just business. But it would look better for them to arrive home together.

Nothing to do with their feelings. Right. He would make her believe that today. Because her memory might be fuzzy but he could remember everything. Including the moment that they'd been on the dance floor, him still buzzing from the adrenaline of being on stage, her from the dancing and the music and the day and a half without sleep.

They'd moved together as the music had coursed through him, the bass vibrating his skin. She'd been trying to talk business, shouting in his ear. Contracts and terms, and commitment. But he hadn't been able to see past her. To feel anything more than the skin of her shoulder under his hand as he'd leaned in to speak in her ear. The soft slide of her hair as he'd brushed it off her face. 'Let's do this,' she'd said. 'We'd be a great team. I know that we can create something amazing together.'

She'd reached up then, making sure she had his attention—as if it would ever be anywhere but on her again. And then Ricky had said those idiotic words, the ones that no judge could take back this morning.

She'd laughed, at first, when he had proposed, assuming that he was joking. It had had nothing to do with the way she'd felt when his arm was around her. The way that that had made him feel. As if he wanted to protect her and challenge her and be challenged by her all at once.

He could never let her know how he had felt last night.

It was much better, much safer that they kept this as business. He knew what happened when you went into a relationship without any calculation. When you jumped in with your heart on the line and no defences. He wouldn't be doing it again.

And then there were the differences between them. Sure, it hadn't seemed to matter in that moment that he'd asked her to marry him, or when they were dancing and laughing and joking together, but a gig and a nightclub and beer were great levellers. When you were having to scream above the music then your accent didn't matter. But in the diner this morning there was no hiding her carefully Londonised RP that one could only acquire with decades of very expensive schooling, and learning to speak in the echoey ball-rooms of city palaces and country piles.

He'd learnt that when he'd joined one of those expensive schools at the age of eleven, courtesy of his music scholarship free ride. His Bolton accent had been smoothed slightly by years away from home, first at school, and then on the road, but it would always be there. And he knew that, like the difference in their backgrounds, it would eventually come between them.

His experiences at school had made it clear that he didn't belong there.

And when he'd returned home to his parents, and

their comfy semi-detached in the suburbs, he had realised that he didn't belong there any more either. He
was caught between two worlds, not able to settle
in either. So the last thing that he needed was to be
paraded in front of the royal family, no doubt coming into contact with the Ruperts and Sebastians and
Hugos from his school days.

And what about his family? Was Charlie going to
come round for a Sunday roast? Make small talk with
his mum with Radio 2 playing in the background? He
couldn't picture it.

But he would have to, he realised. Because it didn't
matter what they were doing in private. It didn't matter that he had told himself that he absolutely had to
get these feelings under control, their worlds were
about to collide.

It wasn't permanent. That was what he had to remind himself. It wasn't for ever. They were going to
end this once a decent amount of time had passed,
and in the meantime they would just have to fit into
each other's lives as best they could.

Just think of the publicity. A whirlwind romance
was a good story. No doubt a better one than a drunken
mistake. But since when had he allowed the papers
to rule on what was and wasn't a good idea for him?
No, there was more to it than that. Something about
waking up beside her in bed that he wasn't ready to
let go of yet.

'I have an album launch party to go to first,
though,' he said at last. 'What do you say to making
our first appearance as husband and wife?'

CHAPTER THREE

CHARLIE ADJUSTED THE strap on her spike heels and straightened the seam of her leather leggings. As soon as the car door opened, she knew there would be a tsunami of flashes from the assembled press hordes. She was considered fair game at the best of times, and if news of the wedding had got out by now, the scrum would be worse than usual.

These shots needed to be perfect. She wasn't having her big moment hijacked by a red circle of shame.

It was funny, she thought, that neither she nor Joe had called his manager, or her boss yet, and told them about what had happened. Not the best start to a publicity campaign, which was, after all, what they had agreed this marriage was. It was more natural, this way, she thought. If there was a big announcement, it would look too fake. Much better for them to let the story grow organically.

As the limo pulled up outside the club she realised that no announcement was necessary anyway. Word had obviously got around. The hotel had arranged for them to be picked up from a discreet back door, an old habit, so she hadn't been sure whether there had been photographers waiting for her there. If there had, they'd taken a shortcut to beat them here. There were definitely more press here than a simple album launch warranted. The story was out, then.

Without thinking, she slipped her hand into Joe's, sliding her fingers between his. The sight of so many photographers still made her nervous. It didn't matter how many times she had faced them. It reminded her of those times in her childhood when she'd been pulled from the protective privacy of her family home and paraded in front of the world's press, all looking for that perfect picture of the perfect Princess. As a child she had smiled until her cheeks had ached, dressed in her prettiest pink dress, turning this way and that as her name was shouted. It had been a small price to pay, her parents had explained, to make sure that the rest of their lives were private. But as she'd got older she'd resented those days more and more, and her childish rictus grin had turned into a sullen teen grimace.

And then, when she was nineteen, and had realised that she would never be the Princess that her family and her country wanted her to be, she'd stopped smiling altogether. She remembered sitting in the doctor's office as he explained what he'd found: inflammation, scar tissue, her ovaries affected. Possible problems conceiving.

She might never have a baby, no chubby little princes or princesses to parade in front of an adoring public, and no hope of making the sort of dynastic match that would make her parents happy.

Her most important duty as a royal female was to continue her family's line. It had been drummed into her from school history lessons to formal state occasions from as far back as she could remember. Queens who had done their duty and provided little princes and princesses to continue the family line.

And things hadn't changed as much as we would all like to think, she knew. The country had liked her mother when she was a shining twenty-something. But it was when she'd given the country three beautiful royal children that they'd really fallen in love with her, when she had won their loyalty. And that was something that Charlie might never be able to do. She might never feel the delicious weight of her child in her arms. Never breathe in the smell of a new baby knowing that it was all hers.

What if she never made her parents grandparents, and saw the pride and love in their eyes that she knew they were reserving for that occasion?

And as soon as she'd realised that, she had realised that she could never make them truly proud of her, somehow the weight of responsibility had fallen from her shoulders and she'd decided that she was never going back. If she wanted to roll out of a nightclub drunk—okay. If she wanted to disappear for three days, without letting anyone know where she was going—fine. If she wanted to skip a family event to go and listen to a new band—who cared?

Her mother insisted on a security detail, and Charlie had given up arguing that one. Her only demand was that they were invisible—she never looked for the smartly dressed man she knew must be on the row behind her on the plane, and so she never saw him. And the officers didn't report back to her mother. If she thought for a second that they would, she would have pulled the plug on the whole arrangement. That was why they'd not intervened last night: they knew she had a zero-tolerance approach to them interfering with anything that didn't affect her physical safety.

She was never going to be the perfect Princess, so why build her family's hopes up? She could let them down now, get it out of the way, in her own way, and not have to worry with blindsiding them with disappointment later.

Except it hurt to disappoint them, and it didn't seem to matter how many times that she did it. Every time, the look on their faces was as bad as the time before.

What would they say this time, she wondered, when they realised that she had married someone she had just met—so obviously to scupper the sensible match that they were trying to make for her? And she had married a rock star at that, someone who couldn't be further from the nice reliable boys that they enjoyed steering her towards at private family functions. What was the point of going along with that? she'd always thought. Entertaining the Lord Sebastians and Duc Philippes and Count Henris who were probably distant cousins, and who all—to a man—would run a mile as soon as they found out that they might not be needing that place at Eton or Charterhouse, or wherever they'd put their future son's name down for school before they had even bagged the ultimate trophy wife.

Joe leaned past her to look out of the window, and then gave her a pointed look. 'I guess our happy news is out.'

'Looks that way,' she said, with a hesitant smile. 'Ready to face the hordes?'

'As I'll ever be.' He looked confident, though, and relaxed. As if he'd been born to a life in front of the cameras, whereas she, who had attended her first photo call at a little under a day old, still came out in a sweat at the sight of a paparazzo.

But she stuck on what she'd come to think of as her Princess Scowl, in the style of a London super-model, and pressed her knees and ankles together. It was second nature, after so many hours of etiquette lessons. Even in skin-tight leather, where there was no chance of an accidental underwear flash. She ran a hand through her hair, messing up the backcombed waves and dragging it over to one side in her trade-mark style. A glance in the rear-view mirror told her that her red lip stain was still good to go, managing to look just bitten and just kissed. She took a deep breath and reached for the door handle.

Joe stopped her with the touch of his fingertips on her knee. 'Wait.'

It was as if the leather melted away and those fin-gertips were burning straight into her skin. Wait? For ever, if she had to.

But before she could say, or do, anything, they were gone, as was Joe. Out of the door and into the bear pit. Then her door was wrenched open and his hand was there, waiting to pull her out into the bright des-ert sunshine. She gripped his hand as he helped her from the car, and the flashbulbs were going off before she was even on her feet.

Shouts reached her from every direction.

'When was the wedding?'

'Was Elvis there?'

'Were you drunk?'

And then there it was, the question that she'd never

anticipated but that she realised now had been inevitable from the first.

'Are you pregnant?'

She stumbled, and it was only Joe's arm clamping round her waist and pulling her tight that stopped her falling on her face in front of the world's press. And then she was falling anyway, because Joe's lips were on hers, and her heart was racing and her legs were jelly and her lips…her lips were on fire. One of his hands had bunched in her hair, and she realised that this, this look, this feeling, was what she'd been cultivating in front of the mirror for more years than she cared to think about. Just been kissed, just been ravished. Just had Joe's tongue in her mouth and hands on her body. Just had images of hot and sweaty and naked racing through her mind. He broke away and gave her a conspiratorial smile. She bit her lip, her mouth still just an inch from his, wondering how she was meant to resist going back for more.

And then the shouts broke back into her consciousness. 'Go on—one more, Charlie!'

And the spell was broken. She wasn't going to give them what they wanted. She turned to them, scowl back in place, though there was a glow now in the middle of her chest, something that they couldn't see, something that they couldn't try and own, to sell for profit.

She grabbed Joe's hand and pulled him towards the door of the venue, ignoring the shouts from the photographers.

She dragged him through the door and into a quiet corner.

'So I guess we survived our first photo call.'

She had hoped the relative seclusion of this dark corner would give her a chance to settle her nerves, for her heartbeat to slow and her hands to stop shaking. But as Joe took another step closer to her and blocked everything else from her vision, she felt anything but relaxed.

'Are you okay? You look kind of flushed,' he asked.

'I'm fine. I just hate…never mind.' Her voice dropped away as her gaze fixed on his lips and she couldn't break it away. This wasn't the time to think about what she hated, not when she was so fixed on what she loved, what she couldn't get enough of. Like the feeling of his lips on hers.

'Joe, I thought I saw you come in. And the new missus!'

Ricky, the drummer from Joe's band, Charlie recognised with a jolt.

More flashbacks of the night before: the band laughing with them in the taxi cab to the courthouse, joking about how they were going to have to sign with her now she'd done this. She had to convince them that they'd been mistaken last night. That she'd married Joe for love at first sight, before they started talking to journalists. If it wasn't already too late.

She reached for Joe's hand and gripped it tightly in hers, hoping that it communicated everything that she needed it to.

'Hi, Ricky,' she said, plastering on a smile that she hoped broadcast newly wedded bliss and contentment.

'So your first day as husband and wife, eh. How's it working out for you?'

She tried to read into his smile what he was really saying. If only she could fake a blush, or a morning-after glow. But in the absence of that, she'd have to go on the offensive.

'Pretty bloody amazingly, actually,' she said, leaning into Joe and hoping that he'd run with this, with her.

'Really?'

Ricky gave Joe a pointed look, and it told Charlie everything that she needed to know. He had thought last night that this was all a publicity stunt, and nothing that he had seen yet had changed his mind.

'Well, I'm just glad that you both decided to take one for the team.' He grinned. 'It was a brilliant idea. I wish I'd thought of it first.'

She opened her mouth to speak, but Joe got there first.

'I'm not sure what you mean, Ricky. We're not doing this for the team. I admit it was a bit hasty, but we really meant it last night. We wanted to get married.'

'Because you're both so madly in love?'

She felt Joe's hand twitch in hers and tried not to read too much into it.

'Because it was the only thing we *could* do,' he said. 'I don't care what we call it. Love at first sight. Or lust. Whatever. I just knew that once I had Charlie in my arms there was no way I was going to let her go. And if that meant marriage, then that's what I wanted.'

Bloody hell, maybe he should have been an actor rather than a singer. He certainly gave that little speech more than a little authenticity. She leaned into him again, and this time he dropped her hand and wrapped his arm around her shoulders. She looked up at him, and there was something about the expression in his face that forced her up onto her tiptoes to kiss him gently on the lips.

'Wow, okay,' Ricky said as she broke away. 'I guess I missed something last night. So, someone wants to chat with us about the new album, if you've got a minute.'

'Okay,' Joe replied, 'but you do remember what we decided last night. We're going to say yes to Charlie's label. I'm not going back on my word.'

'A bit early in the marriage for those sorts of ructions, is it?' Ricky looked at them carefully, and Charlie knew that they hadn't dispelled all of his doubts, regardless of how good an actor Joe was. 'Either way, we still need to speak to them. Until this deal is signed, we schmooze everyone, as far as I'm concerned. I know the others feel the same.'

She *had* to call her boss. She couldn't think why she hadn't done it before now. She'd do it on the way to the plane. She glanced at her watch. They couldn't stay long if they were going to make the flight. For a second she thought wistfully of her family's private plane, and how much easier life had been when she'd been happy to go along with that lifestyle, to take what she didn't feel she had earned. But it had got to the point where she simply couldn't do it any more. If she was never going to be able to pay her parents back with the one thing that everyone wanted from her, she couldn't use their money or their privilege any more.

She had some money left to her by her grandparents—despite her protestations, the lawyers had told her that it belonged to her and there was nothing that she could do about it—and her salary from the record label.

'I'm sorry, do you mind if I talk to them?' Joe asked, turning to her.

'Of course not.' She forced a smile, trying to live in the moment and forget all of the very good reasons she should be freaking out right now. 'Go on.'

But Joe turned to Ricky. 'You go ahead,' he said. 'I'll be there in a second.'

'You all right?' he asked, when they were alone. 'Still happy with everything? Because if you're going to change your mind, now's the time…'

She drew away from him and folded her arms. 'Why would I have changed my mind?'

She didn't understand what had happened to cause this change in mood. His shoulders were tense, she could see that.

Was it because he'd just reminded Ricky of their deal to sign with her the night before? The thought made her feel slightly sick, reminded her that whatever they might say to his band, whatever story they might spin for the papers, when it came down to it, this really *was* just a publicity stunt, or a business arrangement or…whatever. Whatever it was, she knew what it wasn't. It hadn't been love at first sight. It wasn't a grand romance. It wasn't a fairy tale, and there was going to be no happy ending for her. Well, fine, it wasn't like she deserved one anyway.

But now that they were married, they had to make it work. They had to appear to be intoxicated with one another. Luckily, intoxicated was one of her fortes. She forced herself to unfold her arms and smile. 'Of course I'm all right.'

Taking a deep breath, she stepped towards him, and with a questioning look in her eye snaked her arms around those tense shoulders. She placed another chaste peck on his lips, and smiled as she drew away. 'See? Picture perfect. Everything's as we agreed. Let's go say hi to everyone.'

Under the pressure of her arms, she felt his shoulders relax and his face melted into a smile. 'Well, we could give them something to talk about first.'

His arms wrapped around her waist, and she was reminded of the rush of adrenaline and hormones that she had felt outside when he had kissed her in front of the cameras. Her breath caught as her body softened into his hold. This time when his lips met hers, there was nothing chaste about it. Her arms tightened around him as he lifted her just ever so slightly, rubbing her hips against his as she slid up his body. His arms wrapped her completely, so that her ribs were bracketed with muscular forearms, and his hands met the indents of her waist. She was surrounded by him. Overwhelmed by the dominance of his body over hers.

His mouth dominated her too, demanding everything that she could give, and it was only with the touch of his tongue that she remembered where they were. She pushed both hands on his chest, forcing him to give her space, to unwind his arms from around her waist.

She smiled as she looked at him, both of them still dazed from the effect of the kiss. 'Do you think they bought it?' she asked, remembering that just a few moments ago they had been discussing the fact that this relationship was just a business deal—that the purpose of the kiss had been to keep up appearances. But Joe's face fell, and she knew that she had said the wrong thing.

'I think they bought it fine,' he said. 'It was a winning performance.'

Through the bite of his teeth, she knew that it wasn't a compliment.

She shook her head, then reached up and pecked him one last time on the cheek. 'Whatever it was, it blew my mind.' She met his eyes, and she knew that he saw that she was genuine. Whatever else might be going on, there was no denying the chemistry between them. It would be stupid to even try.

But beyond that, beyond the crazy hormones that made her body ache to be near his, was there something else too? A reason that the disappointment in his eyes made some part of her body hurt? She slipped her fingers between his and they walked over to where Ricky was holding court with a woman that she recognised from another record label, her competition, and a music journalist.

'So here's the happy couple,' the hack said with a smile, raising her glass to toast them. Charlie spotted a waiter passing with a tray of champagne and grabbed a flute for herself and one for Joe. She saw off half the glass with her first sip, until she felt she could stare down the journalist with impunity.

She watched Joe as they chatted, her hand trapped within his, and tried not to think about whether the warm glow of possessiveness she felt was because she'd bagged him as an artist, or a husband.

As they walked through Arrivals at Heathrow Airport, Joe felt suddenly hesitant at the thought of taking Charlie back to his apartment, definitely not something he was used to. It wasn't as if he were a stranger to taking girls home. Though in fairness home was more usually a hotel room or their place. But now that he and Charlie were back on British soil, he realised how little they'd talked about how this was going to work.

'So we said we'd stay at my place,' he reminded her as they headed towards the end of another endlessly long corridor.

'We did,' she agreed, and he looked at her closely, trying to see if there was more he could glean from these two words. But he had forgotten that his new wife was a pro at hiding her feelings—she'd had a lifetime of practice. Charlie offered nothing else, so he pushed, wanting the matter settled before they had to face the press, who were no doubt waiting for them again at the exit of the airport. Airport security did what they could to push them back, but couldn't keep them away completely. Not that he should want that, he reminded himself. They wanted the publicity. It was good for the band. It was the whole reason they were still married.

But even good publicity wasn't as important as finishing a new album would be—that thought hadn't been far from his mind the last few days. He couldn't understand how he had thought that it was nearly finished. He'd played the demo tracks over and over on the plane, and somehow the songs that he'd fine-tuned and polished so carefully no longer worked when he listened to them. They didn't make him *feel*. They had a veneer of artifice that seemed to get worse, rather than better, the more that he heard them.

His first album had come from the heart. He shuddered inwardly at the cliché. It was years' worth of pent-up emotion and truths not said, filtered through his guitar and piano. It was honest. It was him. This latest attempt… It was okay. A half-dozen of the tracks he would happily listen to in the background of a bar. But it was clean and safe and careful, and lacking the winners. The grandstanding, show-stopping singles that took an album from good to legendary.

He was still writing. Still trying. But he was out of material and out of inspiration. His adolescent experiences, his adult life of running from them had fed his imagination and his muse for one bestselling album. But he couldn't mine the same stuff for a second. It needed something new. So what was he meant to write about—how ten years on the road made relationships impossible? How his parents kept up with his news by reading whatever the tabloids had made up that week? That his only good friends had spent most of that time trapped with him in some mode of transport or another for the last decade? It was hardly rousing stuff.

'Do you want to go back there now, then?' he asked Charlie.

How was this so difficult? Was she making it that way on purpose?

She looked down at her carry-on bag. 'This is all I have with me.'

'We can send someone for your stuff.'

'No.' She didn't want anyone riffling through her things. Occasionally she missed the discreet staff from her childhood home in the private apartments of the palace, who had disappeared the dirty clothes from her bedroom floor before it had had a chance to become a proper teenage dive, but she loved the freedom of her home being truly private. That the leather jacket that she dropped by the door when she got home would still be right there when she was heading out the next morning.

She stopped walking and looked up at him. 'Okay, so we go back to yours tonight. Tomorrow we go to my place and pack some stuff. Does that work for you? Or I could go back to my place tonight. Sleep there, if we don't want to rush into—'

'You sleep with me.'

He couldn't explain the shot of old-fashioned possessiveness that he had felt when she suggested that they sleep apart. Except… The bed share of the previous night. That was a one-off, wasn't it? He supposed they'd find out later, when she realised that his apartment's second bedroom had been converted to a recording studio. Leaving them with one king-sized bed and one very stylish but supremely uncomfortable couch to fight over. He was many things, but chivalrous about sleeping arrangements wasn't one of them. He couldn't remember the last time that he had slept eight hours in a bed that wasn't hurtling along a motorway or through the clouds. So he could promise her a chivalrous pillow barrier if she absolutely insisted, but there was no way he was forgoing his bed. Not even for her.

'For appearances' sake,' he added to his earlier comment. 'What would it look like if we spent our first night back apart?'

CHAPTER FOUR

'WHEN ARE WE going to tell our families?' Joe asked as the driver slid the car away from the kerb, and the throng of photographers who had been waiting for them grew distant in the rear window.

He was probably just hoping to fill the awkward silence, Charlie thought, rather than trying to bait her. But the niggle of guilt that had been eating away at her turned into a full-on stab. She really should have called her parents before she had left the States, but she had just kept thinking about how disappointed they were going to be in her—again—and she couldn't bring herself to do it.

But now they had another load of morning editions of the tabloids to worry about, full of their red-carpet kisses from the night before. Or was it two nights? Losing a day to the time difference when they were in the air hadn't helped her jet lag, or her sense of dislocation from the world. Whenever it was that those kisses had taken place, somehow, she didn't think that they were going to help matters.

'When we get home,' she said, cracking open a bottle of mineral water and leaning back against the leather headrest. In theory she had just had a eleven-hour flight with nothing to do but catch up on missed sleep. And it wasn't even as if she and Joe had spent the time chatting and getting to know one another. He had pulled out noise-cancelling headphones as soon as he was on board and she'd barely heard a word from him after that.

She'd shut her eyes too, pulled on a sleep mask and tried to drift off. But sleep had been impossible. First her mind had run round in circles with recriminations and criticisms; then slowly, something else had crept in The scent of Joe's aftershave, the drumming of his fingers on the armrest as he got into whatever he was listening to. Her body remembered how she had felt that morning waking up next to him, after her dream filled with hot, sticky caresses. Before her memory returned and she remembered the idiotic thing that they had done. When he was just a hot guy in her head and not the man she had married in a fit of self-sabotage. Lust, pure and simple.

Things were anything but simple now. Attraction could be simple. A marriage of convenience could be simple too, she supposed. She was the product of generations of them. But she and Joe had gone and mixed the two, and now they were paying the price. As Joe shifted on the seat beside her she opened her eyes and watched him for a few moments.

Their late night followed by a long, sleepless flight had left him with a shadow on his jaw that was more midnight than five o'clock. She could almost feel the scratch of it against her cheek if she shut her eyes again and concentrated. She snapped herself out of it. Too dangerous. *Far* too dangerous to be having those sorts of feelings about this man. They had made this arrangement complicated enough as it was. Attraction made it more complicated still. Acting on that attraction anywhere but in the safety of the public gaze was complete madness. No, they were just going to have to get really, really good at self-restraint. She was so looking forward to shutting her bedroom door on Joe and the rest of the world and finally being able to relax and sleep off the jet lag.

Their driver hauled their bags up the stairs to his first-floor warehouse conversion, and Charlie breathed a sigh of relief when they shut the door on him. Home and private at last, all she wanted to do was sleep.

'Do you mind if I just crash?' she asked Joe. 'Which is my room?'

He looked suddenly uncomfortable. 'About that, there's actually only one bedroom.'

Determined not to lose her cool in front of him, she forced the words to come out calmly. 'What do you mean there's only one?'

She crossed the huge open living space and stood on the threshold of Joe's bedroom, her mouth gaping at what he had just told her. He was the one who had suggested they live at his apartment. He couldn't have mentioned he didn't have a guest room?

'You can't think that I'm going to sleep with you.'

'As if, Princess. You're not that irresistible, you know.' Way to kill an ego. Not that she cared right now. All she wanted was to sleep. No, she corrected herself. She needed privacy to call her parents and let them know that she'd messed up—again. And then she needed to sleep. Probably for about three days straight.

'Look, Charlie. I'm tired, I'm grouchy. I have to go call my mum and explain why I decided to get married without her there, and then I'm sleeping. The mattress is big enough for us both to starfish without getting tangled. So you do what you like, but I'm going to bed.

He was tired? *He* was grouchy?

She stood for a moment in the doorway, and could almost feel the delicious relief of slamming it shut with her on the inside. Instead, she pulled herself up to her full five feet ten inches, turned on the spot and stalked off with a grace that her deportment coach had spent months all but beating into her.

Charlie plopped down onto the couch with significantly less grace—no way was she contorting on there to sleep—and pulled out her mobile. She dialled her mum's private number, and heard her voice after a single ring. She could picture so clearly the way the Queen would be working at her desk with her phone beside her blotter, just waiting for her to call.

'Caroline.'

So much said in just one word. She'd been worried about disapproval, disappointment. But the heartfelt, unreserved concern in her mother's voice was the killer.

'Hi, Mum.'

'Charlie, are you okay?'

She dropped her forehead into her hands and wished for the first time that she had gone to do this in person. Surely it was the least her mother deserved. But—like so many of her other mistakes—it was done now, and couldn't be undone.

'I'm fine, Mum. I'm sorry, I know I should have called earlier...' Her voice tailed off and she held her breath, waiting for forgiveness.

'I'm just glad to hear from you. Are you going to tell me what happened?'

She wanted to tell the truth. To confess and tell her that she had messed up again. Her mum would forgive her...eventually. But that wouldn't stop her being disappointed. Nothing could do that. So she steeled herself to lie, to trying to cover up just how stupid she had been this time.

'I met a guy, Mum, and I don't know what happened, but we just clicked. It was love at first sight, and we wanted to get married right away.'

The long pause told her everything she needed to know about how much her mum believed that story.

'If you've made a— I mean if you've changed your mind, Charlie, we can take care of this, you know.'

It was the air of resignation that did it—the knowledge that her mother had been anticipating yet another catastrophe that strengthened her resolve.

'It wasn't a mistake, Mum. It's what I wanted. What we both wanted.' Another long pause, followed by the inevitable.

'So when do we get to meet this young man and his family?'

Her heart kicked into a higher gear as she worried what her mother was expecting—how formal and official was this going to get?

'I was thinking family dinner this weekend. Fly in and stay Friday night—how long you stay is up to you. I've already told your brother and sister. My secretary will ring with the details.'

Charlie couldn't speak. So this was real. She was going to bring Joe to meet her family, pretend that they were crazy in love. She nodded, then realised what she was doing. 'Okay, Mum, we'll be there.' Because when your mum was the Queen it was hard to say no, even more so when you had just done something you knew must have bruised her heart, if not broken it completely.

'I can't wait, darling.' The truth she could hear in her mum's voice broke her own heart in return.

She hung up and for a second let the tears that had been threatening fall onto her cheeks. Just three. Then she drew a deep breath, wiped her eyes and set her shoulders. She had, once again, got herself into an unholy mess and—once again—she would dig herself out of it. There was one other call that she knew she had to make—to her boss, Rich. But she had just disappointed one person whose approval she actually cared about. She didn't have it in her to do the double. She'd need at least a couple of hours' sleep before she could think about that.

She scrubbed under her eyes with a finger, determined to show no signs of weakness to her new husband. This was a professional arrangement and she had no business forgetting that.

As she opened the bedroom door she squared her shoulders. For just a few more hours it was just her and Joe, before the lawyers and managers and accountants wanted to start formalising everything at work. Damned right she was going to enjoy the calm before the storm.

The door opened and she looked over to the bed. *Holy cra—*

She was never going to be able to sleep again. At least not while she was pretending to be married to this man. He hadn't been lying when he'd said that there was room for the two of them to sleep side by side. It was an enormous bed. But the man she had decided to marry had chosen to starfish across it diagonally. There was barely room for a sardine either side of him, never mind anyone else.

And space wasn't the only issue. She'd assumed no naked sleeping, but maybe this was worse. The white T-shirt he must have pulled on before climbing between the sheets hugged tight around his biceps, revealing tattoos that swirled and snaked beneath the fabric, tempting her to follow their lines up his arms. The hem of the shirt had ridden up, showcasing a strip of flawlessly tanned skin across his toned back. And, just to torture her, the sheets had been kicked down to below his tight black boxers—the stretch of the fabric leaving nothing to the imagination. For half a second she thought about sleeping on that back-breaking couch. Or even calling a cab back to her own flat. But the lure of a feather mattress topper was more than she could resist. She kicked off her jeans, noting that her black boy shorts underwear was more than a little similar to her husband's. Luckily *her* white shirt covered her butt.

She crawled onto the mattress beside Joe, trying to keep her movements contained and controlled. Waking him would open the door to a host of possibilities that she didn't want to—couldn't—contemplate right now. Lying on her side on the edge of the bed, she tried to ignore the gentle rhythm of Joe's breathing beside her. She balanced on her hip, the edge of the bed just a couple of inches in front of her. So much for a deep, relaxing sleep. There was no way that was going to happen with her frightened of hitting the floor on one side or Joe on the other. No, she had to start as she meant to go on, and there was no way she was enduring marriage to a man who thought she would perch on the edge of the bed.

She snuck out an experimental toe and aimed at the vicinity of Joe's legs. When her skin met taut, toned muscle, she wasn't prepared for the flash of warmth that came with it. For the memory of the night that flashed back with it. Of her and Joe heading for the bed in their suite, high from champagne, the roulette wheel and the new and exciting gleam on the third fingers of their left hands.

She'd jumped back onto the mattress, the bemused bellboy still standing watching them from the doorway. As Joe had approached her, the look in his eyes like a panther stalking its prey, the bellboy had withdrawn. Her eyes had locked on Joe's, then, and her breath had caught at the intensity in his gaze. And then he had tripped on the rug and fallen towards the bed headfirst, breaking the spell. She'd collapsed back in a fit of giggles, and as her eyes had closed she had been overtaken by a yawn.

She'd fallen asleep so easily the night before. Maybe she could kick him out completely. That might be the only way she was going to get to relax enough to fall asleep. She remembered the look on his face, though, when he'd told her he wasn't giving up his bed for her. She didn't think he'd take crashing to the floor well. And, really, they had enough troubles at the moment without him being any more annoyed with her. She braced herself for the heat that she knew now would come and pushed at his leg again. Success. He shifted behind her and she shuffled back a few inches on the bed. She could hear Joe still moving, but she lay stiff and still, determined not to give up her hard-won territory.

With a great roll Joe turned over, and their safe, back-to-back stand-off was broken. His breath tickled at the back of her neck, setting off a chain reaction of goosebumps from her nape to the bottom of her spine. Maybe she had been better off on the edge of the bed, because her body was starting to hum with anticipation. Her brain—unhelpful as ever—was reminding her of how good it felt to kiss him. How her body had thrummed and softened in his arms. She reached down for the duvet and tucked it tightly around her, though she didn't really need its warmth. But with her body trapped tight beneath it she felt a little more secure. As a final defence, she shoved in her earphones and found something soothing to block out the subtle sounds of a shared bed, and shut her eyes tight.

Joe stood in the bedroom doorway, surveying the scene in front of him. A pair of black skinny jeans had been abandoned by the bed, and silver jewellery was scattered on the bedside table. Dark brown hair was strewn across the pillow and one long, lean calf had snaked out from beneath the duvet. Along with the jeans on the floor, it answered a question that he'd been tempted but too much of a gentleman to find out for himself.

His wife. He had to shake his head in wonderment of how that had happened. A simple kiss from her did things to his body that he had never experienced before. He'd woken with his arms aching to pull her close and give her a proper good morning. And she was the one woman he absolutely couldn't, shouldn't fall for. They had gone into this marriage with ground rules for a good reason. They couldn't risk their careers by giving in to some stupid chemical attraction, or, worse still, by getting emotionally involved.

He'd made the mistake before of giving his heart to someone who was only out to get what she wanted. He'd learnt his lesson, and he wouldn't be making the same mistake again. And of all the women he could have married, it had to be her, didn't it? One who would throw him back into that world of privilege and wealth.

He'd spent just about every day since he was eleven years old feeling like the outsider. And now he had gone and hitched himself to the ultimate in exclusive circles. Once he and Charlie were married, there was no way of getting away from them. But he had learned how to deal with it a long time ago. Keep his distance, keep himself apart, to prevent the sting of rejection when he tried to fit in. The same rule had to apply to Charlie. It didn't matter what she had told her parents, how real they were going to make this thing look—he couldn't let himself forget that it was all for show.

He placed a cup of coffee down among her earrings and bracelets, and from this vantage point he could see the chaos emerging from her suitcase, where more shirts were spilling from the sides.

Charlie jerked suddenly upright, knocking his arm and sending the coffee hurtling to the floor.

'Crap!'

He jumped back as the scalding liquid headed for his shins. Charlie was scrambling out of bed, and grabbed her jeans from the floor to start mopping up the coffee from the floorboards. 'What the hell?' she asked, crouching over the abandoned coffee.

'I thought I'd bring you a cup of coffee in bed, you ungrateful brat.' She sat back at the insult and crossed her arms across her chest. 'I suppose I ought to expect the spoilt little princess routine,' he continued, and they both flinched at the harsh tone in his voice. 'Sorry. Look, you wait there. I'll grab a towel.'

He retreated to the kitchen and took a deep breath, both hands braced palms-down on the worktop; then grabbed some kitchen roll and headed back to the bedroom. Charlie was crouched like a toddler, feet flat on the floor, attacking the coffee with a hand towel from the bathroom. She took a slurp from the cup as she worked, swishing the towel around ineffectually, and chasing streams of coffee along the waxed floorboards and under the bed.

'Here,' he said, taking the sopping towel from her and holding out a hand to pull her up. 'I'll finish up. You drink your coffee.'

'Thanks,' she said, relinquishing the towel with a look of relief. 'And for the coffee. Sorry, I was just a bit disorientated.'

'Forgot you picked yourself up a husband in Vegas?'

'Something like that.' She grabbed her watch from the bedside table and shook off the coffee, leaving flecks of brown on the snowy white duvet cover.

'Ugh. I've got to be at work in an hour.'

She walked over to the bathroom, and he directed his gaze pointedly away from the endlessly long legs emerging from beneath that butt-skimming shirt. He had no desire to make this arrangement any more dif-

ficult than it undoubtedly was. Keeping it strictly business was the only way that it was going to work. She
eyed her suitcase uncertainly. 'I've got more jeans, but
I'm all out of clean tops. Can I raid your wardrobe?'

'Go for it. I'm jumping in the shower. We'll need
to leave at quarter to if we're going to walk.'

She stopped riffling through the rails in his dressing room for a second.

'We?'

'I think I'd better come talk to Rich. There's a lot
to go through before we can sign anything.'

Of course she hadn't forgotten that Rich had sent
her out to Vegas with a job to do. So why wasn't she
exactly thrilled about the prospect of going in and
seeing him this morning? Because this hadn't been
what he'd meant, she knew. It hadn't been what she'd
wanted either. If this was a casting-couch situation
she wasn't sure which of them had been lying back
and thinking of the job, but she knew that she was
good at what she did. She knew that she could have
bagged this signing without bringing her personal
life or family into the picture. But who was going to
believe that now?

Her face fell, and somehow he knew exactly what
she was thinking.

'You think he's going to be pissed at you?'

'Why would he be? He sent me out there to close
this deal. Job done, mission complete. He's going to
be thrilled.'

'Really? So why don't you look happy about it?'

'It's nothing.'

'It's clearly something.'

He sat on the edge of the bed as she turned back to

the wardrobe and started looking through his shirts again. Sliding them across the rail without paying much attention.

'I'm just not sure how he's going to react to…this.' She waved a hand between them so he understood exactly what 'this' was. His hackles rose.

'You told me you weren't involved with anyone. Are you telling me you and he are…a thing? Because that would be a major problem. I can't believe you'd—'

'It's nothing like that.' She grabbed hold of a shirt and pulled it from the hanger. 'God, why does everyone assume that any professional relationship I have is based on sex?' He lifted one eyebrow as he took in her half-dressed form and the unmade bed.

'Oh, get lost, Joe. This is nothing to do with sex. This was *your* idea. I'd have got you to sign anyway.'

'Really? Why did you say yes, then?' She had been starting off to the bathroom, but she stopped halfway across the room, his shirt screwed up and crumpled in her hand.

'Oh, why does a party girl do anything, Joe?' Her smile was all public, showing nothing of the real woman he had spent the last couple of days with. 'I'm an idiot. I was drunk. It was a laugh.' It was what everyone would assume, there was no doubt about that—but what was most shocking to him was that she didn't believe that any of those statements were true. So if it hadn't been just for a laugh, and it wasn't about her job either, then why had she done it?

He waited for the water to shut off and for Charlie to emerge from the bathroom before he grabbed his wash bag from his suitcase. She kept her back to him as she emerged and headed straight into the dressing room. Respecting her obvious need for privacy, and reluctant to continue their argument, he went straight into the bathroom and locked the door.

So what was the deal with her boss if she wasn't sleeping with him? Why was she so bothered about what he would think about their marriage? Their reasons for staying together were still good. The papers had been full of stories about the two of them, and there had been talk about the anticipation of their new album. It was exactly the sort of coverage that you couldn't buy. Her boss would be able to see that. He should be pleased that she'd got the job done and with a publicity angle to boot.

He stepped under the spray of the shower and let the water massage his shoulders. Maybe he should let her go and deal with her boss on her own. But he was keen to get this contract signed. He had meant what he had said. He'd been impressed with what the label had pitched to him—he would have signed even without Charlie turning up in Las Vegas.

He followed in her footsteps to the dressing room and wasn't sure whether to be disappointed or relieved that the towel had been discarded on the floor and she was fully dressed. One of his shirts was cinched in at the waist with a wide belt of studded black leather. A pair of black leather leggings ended in spike-heeled boots and she was currently grimacing into the mirror as she applied a feline ring of heavy black eyeliner.

'Walk of shame chic,' she said as she met his eye in the mirror. 'What do you think?'

'I think that now you're a married woman we can't call it the walk of shame. This is home. If you want it to be.' He leaned back against the wall as she paused with a tube of something shiny and gold in her hand. His eyes met hers in the mirror, and he gave a small smile. Relaxing in that moment, he enjoyed their connection— the first since they had woken up that morning. And he remembered again that feeling when he had first met her. When he had glanced across the stage and seen her in the wings, watching him. How they had danced and felt so in tune, so together, that the idea of marriage had seemed inevitable, rather than idiotic.

He laughed as she broke their eye contact to apply a coat of mascara, complete with wide open mouth.

'Come on,' he said, heading to the kitchen. 'I'll make another coffee.'

She glanced at her watch, returning his smile.

'We might have to drink on the go.'

He couldn't deny that he was startled. Princess Caroline all worried about being late for work the morning after bagging the biggest signing of her career. She was just full of surprises.

In the kitchen he set the coffee machine going and grabbed his only travel mug from a cabinet. 'Okay, but we're sharing, then,' he shouted back to her as he added frothy steamed milk.

By the door, he grabbed wallet and keys from the tray on the console where he'd dropped them the night before. Waiting for Charlie, he had an unimpeded view of her kicking her coffee-stained jeans towards her suitcase, and swiping some of the jewellery from the bedside table, but knocking the rest of it under the bed. Spot the girl who'd grown up with staff, he thought again to himself. They were going to have to talk about this at some point, he realised. He wasn't going to pick up after her like some sort of valet.

Was that how she saw him, he wondered—on a par with the staff? Barely visible in a room? She swept past him and out of the door; then drew up short in the corridor, clearly surprised that he wasn't just following in her wake.

'Are you coming?' she asked over her shoulder.

Slowly, Joe turned his key in the lock and then walked towards her. He took a long sip of coffee from the travel mug and then met her eye.

'You're not a princess here, sweetheart,' he told her gently. 'Home means you do your own fetching and carrying.'

Her brows drew together and he knew he'd pissed her off. 'I'll start by carrying this, then, shall I?' She took the coffee from him and walked into the lift, letting the door close in his face behind her.

Charlie swiped them into the office with her key card and waved at the receptionist on her way past. Avalon Records was based in a rundown old Regency villa on a once fashionable square. The grandeur of the high ceilings and sweeping staircases was in stark contrast to the workaday contents. Laminate wood desks had been packed into every corner of the building, and tattered swivel chairs fought for space with stacks of paper and laser printers.

She headed to her desk with eyes forward, intent on not letting anyone—especially Joe—see how nervous she was. Not that she needed to worry about that. She had been so keen to get into the office early that the place was practically deserted. She reached her desk and stashed her bag in a drawer, making herself busy for just a few more moments, turning on the computer and getting everything straight in her head so that the minute Rich arrived she could sell the hell out of this situation.

This was a good day, and there was no way she was leaving Rich's office until he agreed with her. Not only had she closed the deal that Rich had sent her out there to do, she had tied Joe and The Red Kites to their future in the closest way possible. Rich should—and he would—be eternally grateful. This was a massive coup for their indie label, tempting the hottest band of the year away from the big multinationals. She grabbed a couple of files and a notebook from under a pile of papers and then turned back to Joe.

He was staring at her desk with a mixture of shock and despair.

'What?' she asked, alarmed by his expression.

'Oh, my God. You're a slob.' He laughed as he spoke, his eyes wide. She leaned back against her desk and crossed her arms across her chest.

'I am so not.'

'You totally are. I thought maybe back at my place it was because we were both still living out of our cases. I need to clear you some space in the war...' His voice drifted and a shadow crossed his expression before he shook it off and got back to the point. 'But this proves it. I mean...how do you find anything?'

She waved the files in her hand at him.

'Because they're exactly where I left them.'

He shook his head again. 'But wouldn't they also be exactly where you left them if they were...say... filed neatly in a drawer?'

She raised her brows. 'You wouldn't by any chance be interfering, would you, Joe? Because this is my desk, and my office, and my job, and you don't get to boss me around here.'

He snorted out a breath. 'Oh, right, because at home you're so biddable and accommodating.' He laughed again, taking a step closer until she was trapped between him and the desk. She could smell his shower gel, the same one that she'd borrowed that morning, knowing even as she'd done it that she was going to be haunted by this reminder of him all day. She looked up at him, enjoying the novelty of a man who was still a smidge taller than her, even when she was in heels.

'I'm not interfering. I'm just getting to know you. We can talk about this more at home.' He took another half-step closer and she hitched a butt cheek onto her desk, looking for just a little more space, a little more safety. Breathing space for sensible, professional decision-making.

Then Joe lifted his hand and even without knowing where it was heading—hair, cheek, lips—she knew it would be more than her self-control could stand. She grabbed his hand mid-air, but that didn't help. It just pulled him closer as their linked hands landed on the desk by her hip. The front of his thighs pressed against hers, long and lean and matched so perfectly to her body he could have been made for her. She could feel the gentle pressure of his breath on her lips, and her eyes locked on his mouth as she remembered the times that they had pressed against hers. Her brain was desperately trying to catch up with the demands of her body. Remember the agreements they had made. They were meant to be madly in love in public. They were business associates when they were home. But what

were they to each other here? In this public place, but
with no one there to see them.

She dragged her gaze away for a moment, over
Joe's shoulder to the still-deserted office. She had
wanted to be in early. To show Rich that she was still
as committed—as professional—as ever. But it had
left her and Joe dangerously secluded.

His fingers untangled from hers, and she was hit
with syncopated waves of regret then relief. But neither lasted long as his hand completed its original
journey and landed this time on her cheek. His palm
cupped her face as he tilted her head just a fraction.
The sight of his tongue sneaking out to moisten his
lips set off a chain reaction from the tight, hard knot
low in her pelvis to the winding of her arms around
his shoulders to the low sigh that escaped her throat
as she closed her eyes and leaned in, waiting for the
touch of his mouth.

A door slammed behind her and she jumped back,
whacking her thighs against her desk in the process.
She pushed at Joe's chest, knowing even before she
turned to look at Rich's office what she was going
to find.

Her boss was standing in front of the closed door
to his office, leaning back against it with his arms
crossed. Proof that the slam had been entirely for effect. Bloody drama queen, Charlie cursed him under
her breath.

'The lovebirds return,' Rich said, leaning forwards
and extending his arm to shake Joe's hand. 'It's good
to see you again, Joe. We weren't expecting you. Are
you just seeing the wife to work, or…?'

'Actually, Rich, we have good news.' Charlie

watched her boss's face closely, trying to judge his
reaction. 'Joe and the rest of the guys are all in agreement. They want to sign with us. Joe wanted to come
and give the good news in person this morning.'

Rich's professional smile didn't give anything
away, but she knew him well enough to see the slight
hint of tightness around his eyes that told her that this
wasn't unmitigated pleasure.

'That is great news,' he said, clapping Joe on the
back. 'I guess this is a pretty good week for us all,
then. Congratulations to you both. Married? Love at
first sight, the papers are saying. I have to admit, I
was surprised not to hear it from the horse's mouth.'
He gave Charlie a pointed look and she pulled herself up to her full height, determined not to act like a
chastised teenager. She had every right to do just what
she wanted. She didn't need Rich's permission, or his
approval, to marry whomever she chose.

'You know how it is, Rich. The papers knew what
was happening almost before we did. We didn't have
a chance to tell people ourselves.'

'Funny how that happens, isn't it?' Rich said with
a quirk of his eyebrow. So he definitely wasn't going
to buy 'love at first sight' then. Time for Plan B.

Joe looked from her to Rich, and must have picked
up on the atmosphere between them.

'Look, we just wanted to give you *this* news in person,' Joe said. 'I know that there's loads to work out
with the lawyers and stuff so just let me know when
you want to start.' He leaned forward to shake Rich's
hand again before turning back to Charlie. She waited
to hear Rich go back into his office, but the click of

the door handle didn't come. Was this a test? Was he trying to see if this was all for show?

She didn't have time to worry about it as Joe's lips descended on hers. His hands framed her face, his fingertips just teasing at her hairline. His lips were warm and soft as they pressed against her mouth, full of promise and desire. But then his hands dropped to her shoulders as he broke away, and when she opened her eyes she was met by a twinkling expression in his. 'See you at home, love.'

He swept out of the office with a final wave at Rich, and she fought the urge to lean back against her desk to catch her breath.

Instead her hands found the files that she'd grabbed before Rich had arrived, and she stalked into his office with her head held high.

'Are you ready to get started? We've got a lot to cover.'

Rich stood in the doorway, not joining her at the table as she pulled out a chair and sat. Then shook his head as he took in her determined glare. 'I'll be with you in a second.'

Five minutes later he returned with two cups of coffee and a look of determination that matched her own.

She was reading through a boilerplate contract, making notes in the margin with a red pen, and Rich waited for her to finish scribbling before he sat.

'Here, have a caffeinated peace offering. Have you slept at all since you left for the airport? I'm betting your body has no idea what time zone it's in right now.'

'Thanks.' She took the coffee and realised that he was right. She should be exhausted, but she wasn't.

Something to do with having a brand-new husband she wasn't sure if she was meant to be keeping her hands off or not, she supposed.

'So are you going to tell me what happened?'

'I thought you said you already knew.'

'I told you I'd read the papers. I want the real story. From you, preferably. I think I deserve that. This affects us all. This is work. When I sent you out there to seal the deal, I didn't mean do *any*thing. I thought maybe... I don't know. The Princess thing: sometimes it works. I never expected you to... Just... What happened, Charlie?'

She looked him in the eye, still trying to work out her angle. How much she should share. How much she should hide. But Rich was right. This went beyond her personal life. She and Joe had made a calculated business decision—he couldn't expect her to keep it from the head of the business.

'We got carried away. Vegas, you know.' She gestured vaguely with her hands. 'We'd had too much to drink. We thought it would be funny. And that, you know, the publicity wouldn't be a bad thing for the band.'

'So it wasn't...' He hesitated, and Charlie just knew he was trying to find the right words. The ones that would annoy her the least. She prayed he wasn't about to ask the question she knew deep down was coming. 'It wasn't a quid pro quo deal. Nothing to do with the contract.'

She bristled, even though she'd been expecting it.

'What are you implying, Rich? Because if you think that I would do that—that I would need to... There's nothing I can say to that.'

Rich held out his hands for peace.

'I'm just trying to understand here, Charlie. I wasn't implying anything. So you thought it was a laugh, to celebrate the deal, and the publicity wouldn't exactly harm the band. But…now? What's going on now? You're living together?'

'We thought it would look better if it was love at first sight rather than a Vegas mistake. We're both committed to keeping up the pretence until the publicity won't be as harmful.'

'And it's all for show?' Rich asked. She nodded. 'So that little moment I walked in on earlier?'

'All part of the act.'

Rich sighed, non-committal. 'Okay, all of that aside, this is an amazing opportunity for us. Great job on getting the signing. I knew that I could trust you to take care of it.'

Charlie straightened the papers in front of her, enjoying the warm glow of Rich's praise for her work. She'd survived the first meeting: it could only get better from here.

'So how did it go with your boss after I left?' Joe asked when she arrived home that evening. 'It looked like things were about to get heated between you.'

She crossed to the fridge and surveyed the contents as she thought about it.

'It was a bit hairy at first,' she admitted as she grabbed a couple of beers and waved one in Joe's direction. He took them both from her and reached behind him into a drawer to find a bottle opener.

'Does he always get so involved in his staff's personal lives?'

'Only when they go around marrying potential clients.'

He raised his eyebrows in a 'fair enough' expression, pulling out the bar stool next to him at the kitchen island.

'Why do you care so much what he thinks anyway? If you're so adamant that there's nothing going on between you.'

'Jealous again, darling?' She threw him some serious shade while taking a sip of her beer and resting her hip on the stool. The hardness of his gaze drew her up short. 'Don't be an idiot, Joe. I'm not impressed or in the least turned on by the jealousy thing. Drop it.'

'Okay,' he conceded. 'So there's nothing romantic going on between you. Tell me what that weird vibe was, then. Why were you afraid of disappointing him?'

'He's my boss. I'd quite like to not get fired. Are you so much of a celeb these days that you don't remember what it's like to hold down a job?'

'Said the Princess.'

'You wanted to know why I don't want to disappoint Rich? Because he's the only one who doesn't call me Princess. Even when others aren't doing it to my face, they still treat me differently, and it drives me crazy. Rich is the only person who doesn't make exceptions or allowances. He's the one person who treats me like a normal goddamn human being and expects me to act like one. If I stepped out of line he'd fire me in a heartbeat.'

'And you'd walk straight into another job.'

She resisted the urge to throw her beer at him. 'Maybe I would. But not one that I deserve. Not one that I could do as well as the one I have now. Rich has made me work my arse off for every achievement. Every signing. Every bloody paycheque has been in exchange for my blood, sweat and tears. He's the only one who could see that I can do it. I work hard, I earn my keep. When I let him down, I'm proving them right. All the people who just expect the world to fall into my lap.'

Which was why there was no way that she was walking away from the life that she'd built for herself, just because she'd promised her parents she'd come home at some fixed point in time.

'I'm sorry, I didn't mean to.'

'It's a sore point, okay. Because I have let him down. This whole thing is stupid. It's beneath me. I messed up, and I don't like having it pointed out to me by the people whose opinion I value.'

He gave her a long, assessing look. 'We never talked about how it went with your parents, did we?'

She knocked back another long glug of beer.

'They want to meet you.'

'Mine too.'

She caught his eye, and managed a tentative smile. 'How do you reckon that's going to go?'

'My mum asked if she needed to wear a hat.'

Frothy beer hit her nose as she snorted with laughter.

'What did you tell her?'

'That I had no idea. I have no idea how this works.' The laughter died in his eyes and he looked suddenly solemn.

'Are you freaked out by it? The royalty thing? Because I thought you went to Northbridge School. My cousins are there. And you didn't seem all that impressed when I arrived in Vegas.'

He hesitated; the last thing that he wanted was to talk about his school days. He'd been awkward enough there, the scholarship kid from up north. And that was before the school's very own Princess—she didn't need the royal blood to call herself that—had used and humiliated him. 'Yeah, I knew your cousins at school,' Joe said, 'but we weren't friends. I didn't exactly click with my classmates.'

'School can be a cruel place.'

'I guess.' He took another swig of his beer and thought back. It had been a long time since he'd really thought about that part of his life. After he'd been ignominiously dumped in front of half his school year, he'd taken the lesson, moved on, and tried to forget about the humiliation. 'There wasn't any bullying or anything like that. The masters would never have stood for it. It's just, I didn't fit in, you know.' There was no need to tell her the whole ugly story. It had been embarrassing enough the first time around.

'And you're worried it's going to be like that with my family?' Charlie leaned forward and rested her elbow on the bar and her chin on her hand as she asked the question. 'They're really nice, you know,' she said earnestly. 'Well, my brother's an idiot, but every family has one of those.'

'I'm sure they are nice, Charlie. But they're different. We're different. And that's not something that we can change.' The last time that he'd been around people who moved in royal circles, the fact that he was different had become a currency in a market that he hadn't understood. Luckily, he was older and wiser now. He knew to look out for what people wanted from him, and to make sure he was getting a good deal out of it too. He also knew that no one was ever going to see their match as a marriage of equals.

'It's a good job that this is just all for show, then,' she added. 'So my family won't be making you uncomfortable for long.'

A look of pain flashed across her face, and he wondered what had caused it. It was too deep, too old to have been caused by this argument.

'It doesn't matter,' she said after a long pause, turning away from him almost imperceptibly. 'I'm never going to marry, so you don't have to worry about some future husband being trapped in that world.'

'I hate to break it to you, but it's a bit late for never.' He leaned in closer, nudging the footrest of her stool, trying to bridge the gulf that had suddenly appeared between them.

'Well, except this isn't real, is it?' she said.

He nodded, trying to hide his wince at the unexpected pain her statement had caused. Time for a change of subject, he thought. 'So why are you never getting married? Well, getting married again.'

'It's just not for me.' She shuffled to the back of her stool, reinstating the distance that he had tried to breach.

'Wow. That's enlightening.' She was hiding something from him, he knew it. Something big. And while she could keep her secrets if she wanted—it worried him. Because how was he meant to know how to handle this situation if he didn't have all the information? With all the women that had come before her, he knew exactly what they wanted, and they knew what he wanted in return.

With Charlie, despite their best efforts to keep this businesslike, he knew that everything she said carried shades of meaning that he didn't understand. It made him nervous, knowing that he was making calculations without all of the information he needed.

'Look, what does it matter, Joe? I wouldn't make a good wife, it wouldn't be fair for me to get married—not to someone who actually wanted to be my husband. But you'll have a chance to see them all for yourself. When I spoke to my mother yesterday she invited us over for dinner with the family on Friday. We'll need to stay. It's too far to fly there and back in an evening.'

'Yeah, great,' he said, though he knew that his lack of enthusiasm was more than clear.

'Anyway, I don't want to talk about this any more. How about we go out? I'm not sure what's going on with the jet lag, but I'm not sleeping any time soon. We could go get a drink—I know a place not far from here.'

'Like a date?' he asked, uncertainly. Had she suddenly decided that that was what she wanted?

'Like a chance for the press to see us as loved-up and glowing newly-weds.'

He nodded, trying to work out whether he was relieved or disappointed that it was all part of the act. 'Wouldn't newly-weds be more interested in staying home and getting to know one another?'

She spoke under her breath so quietly he could barely hear her reply: 'All the more reason to go out.'

CHAPTER FIVE

SHE PULLED THE front door closed behind them while she smudged on a bright red lip crayon. The bar was a ten-minute walk away. She'd been to their open mic night a few times, looking out for artists that she'd seen online but wanted to check out playing live before she decided if she was interested. As they turned the corner by the bar, though, she realised that this wasn't going to be one of those nights where she struck professional gold. And when they walked in and saw the screens showing lyrics, her worst fears were confirmed. It was no-holds-barred, no-talent-required, hen-parties-welcome karaoke. A trio of drunk students were belting out a rock classic, spilling pints of beer with their enthusiasm. Well, at least their taste in music couldn't be faulted, Charlie thought, boosting the roots of her hair with her fingers in honour of her spirit sister.

'Well, they're certainly going for it,' Joe said with a grin that slipped slightly as they hit a particularly painful note. 'This your usual kind of place?'

She looked around. The place itself was great: a shiny polished wood bar, real-ale pumps gleaming and—importantly—well stocked with decent beer.

Plus there was plenty of gin on the shelves, and good vodka on ice for later in the evening. But most importantly of all, the manager, Ruby, had her number and would call with any hot tips for new acts she might be interested in.

'Charlie!' Ruby greeted her with a smile. 'Don't usually see you here on a Tuesday. Don't tell me this is your honeymoon. That would be too tragic.'

Charlie forced a laugh at this reminder of her newly married status.

'I wish. No time for a honeymoon. But Joe—or we, now, I guess—live just round the corner and we fancied a quiet drink. I'd say you'd be seeing more of me, but...' She looked over at the singing students.

'Wanted to try something new. Don't worry, I won't be repeating the experiment.'

They all watched the tone-deaf trio with similar expressions of amusement.

'Sorry,' Charlie added, realising that she hadn't introduced Joe. 'Joe, this is Ruby, she runs this place. Ruby, this is Joe, my...er...'

'Her husband,' Joe filled in, sliding one arm around her waist and with the other leaning over the bar to shake Ruby's hand.

'I read about your news. Congrats! Vegas, huh. You guys have a wild time?'

'"Wild" is one word for it.'

'The best.'

Charlie, remembering her part, relaxed into Joe's arms. Ruby was watching them carefully, and Charlie wondered what she was thinking. Was she trying to judge whether they were for real? Were they going to face this scrutiny from everyone they met? She might not count Ruby as quite a friend, but Charlie would normally have at least considered her an ally. Well, they would just have to convince her, she decided. Because they were going to make this pretence of a marriage work. The alternative was to disappoint her family even more than she already had.

She just had to remember that it was all make-believe. She didn't get to be the glowing newly-wed in real life. Being a wife, like being a princess, came with certain responsibilities, certain expectations that she knew she couldn't fill. There was no point letting herself fall for a guy only to have him up and leave when he found out that she might not be a complete woman.

Charlie ordered a couple of beers and led Joe over to one of the booths in the back of the bar. It was comfy and private, upholstered in a deep red leather, and just the sort of spot that a loved-up couple would choose, she thought.

'They're really going for it, huh,' Joe said, indicating the girls on the karaoke, who had moved on from rock to an operatic power ballad. He took a swig of the ale, and Charlie watched as his throat moved. His head was thrown back, so he couldn't see her watching him. From inside the sleeve of his tight white T-shirt she could see half a tattoo, weaving and winding around his arm. She was concentrating so hard on trying to trace the pattern that she didn't notice at first that his eyes had dropped and she'd been totally busted.

'Looking at something you like?' It could have sounded cheesy. It *should* have sounded cheesy. But somehow the sincerity in his gaze saved it. 'You wanna see the rest of it?'

Okay, so that was definitely flirtatious. She looked around quickly to see if anyone was eavesdropping. Surely if they were already hitched she should know what his tats looked like.

Ruby was serving at the bar, the drunk girls were still singing enthusiastically, and most of the other customers had been scared off.

She slipped off her bench and darted round the table, sliding in beside Joe until her thigh was pressed against his.

'All yours,' he said, lifting his arm. Her fingertips brushed at the edge of the cotton T-shirt, which was warm and soft from contact with his skin. She traced the band that wound around his bicep, looking up and meeting his eye when he flinched away from her touch as she reached the sensitive skin near his underarm.

'Ticklish?'

'Maybe.' One side of his mouth quirked up in a half-smile, and she filed that information away, just in case she should ever need it.

She shouldn't ever need it, she reminded herself.

This was just an arrangement, and she had no business forgetting it. No business exploring his body, even something as seemingly innocent as an arm. Her body remembered being in bed with him. It remembered those kisses. The way that she had arched into him, desperate to be closer. She shot off the bench, diving for safety on the other side of the table.

'It's nice. I like it.' She tried to keep her voice level, to prevent it giving away how hard she was finding it to be indifferent to him.

'Well, there's plenty more. But maybe we should keep those under wraps for now.' She nodded. Not trusting herself to reply to that statement. She took a sip of beer, hoping the chilled amber liquid would cool her blazing face.

'So the open mic here's usually good?' Joe asked, and she jumped on the change of subject gratefully.

'It is,' she said. 'Very different from tonight. It's normally pretty professional. I've found a couple of great artists here.'

'You like to find them when they're still raw?'

'Of course. I mean a fully formed band with a track record is pretty great too.' She inclined her head towards him and he smiled. 'But there's something about finding raw talent and helping it to develop. It's… It's what gets me to work on a Monday morning when sometimes I'd rather drag the duvet over my head.'

'Must be tough to stay motivated when you don't really have to work.'

She dropped her bottle on the table a little harder than was strictly necessary. 'And why do you think I don't have to work?'

'Oh, I don't know, royal families are all taxpayer-funded, right?'

She placed both palms face down on the table, forcing herself to appear calm, not to slam them in a temper. 'The *working* royals are taxpayer-funded. Yes. And the key word there is "working". Do you know what the royal family is worth to my country's economy in terms of tourism alone? Not that it matters, because I opted out. I don't do official engagements and I don't take a penny.'

'Come on, though. You've never had to struggle.'

'Oh, because a wealthy family solves all problems. We all know that.'

She wished it were true. She had asked the doctor when she had first got her diagnosis whether there was anything that could be done, and the answer was a very equivocal 'maybe'.

Maybe if she threw enough money at the problem, there might be something they could do to give her a chance of conceiving. But it wouldn't take just money. It would take money and time and invasive procedures. Fertility drugs in the fridge and needles in her thighs. It could mean every chance of the world discovering she was a failure on the most basic level, and absolutely no guarantee that it would even work. No, it was simpler to accept now that marriage and a family weren't on the cards for her and move on.

'Where did you pick up this chip on your shoulder, anyway?' Charlie asked. 'I thought your education was every bit as expensive as mine.'

He looked her in the eye, and for a moment she could see vulnerability behind his rock-star cool.

'I had a full scholarship,' he said with a shrug.

'Impressive.' Charlie sat back against the padding of the bench. 'Northbridge don't just hand those out like sweeties. Was it for music?'

She was offended by his expression of surprise. What, did he expect her to recoil at the thought that he didn't pay his own school fees? God, he really did think that she was a snob. Well, it was high time she straightened that one out. Finishing her beer in one long gulp, she slid out of the booth and held out her hand to pull Joe up.

'Somehow,' she said, when he hesitated to follow

her, 'you seem to have got totally the wrong idea about what sort of princess I am. We're going to fix that. Now.'

His expression still showing his reluctance, he allowed her to pull him to standing, but leaned back against the table, arms folded over his chest.

'How exactly do you plan to do that?'

'We, darling husband, are going to sing.'

He eyed the karaoke screens with trepidation.

'Here?'

'Where else?' But he still didn't look convinced.

'Are you any good?'

'I'm no music scholar, but I hold my own. Now, are you going to choose something or am I?'

She grabbed the tablet with song choices from Ruby at the bar, who looked eternally grateful that someone would be breaking the students' residency.

'Are you going to help choose? Because I'm strongly considering something from the musical theatre oeuvre.'

That cracked his serious expression and he grinned, grabbing the back pocket of her jeans and pulling her back against the table with him, so they could look at the tablet side by side.

'As if you'd choose something that wasn't achingly cool.'

She swiped through the pages in demonstration.

'Hate to break it to you, but there's a distinct lack of "achingly cool". The only answer is to go as far as possible in the other direction. We go for maximum cheese.'

'I was so afraid you were going to say that.'

'Come on.' She swiped through another couple of

choices until she landed on a classic pop duet. 'It's got to be this one.' She hit the button that cued up the song and bought another round at the bar to tempt the drunk girls away from their microphones. With another couple of beers for her and Joe in hand, she stepped up onto the little stage.

She glanced around the bar—the girls had done a good job of emptying the place, but a few tables had stuck it out, like her and Joe, and now had all eyes on her. She could see the cogs whirring as they tried to place her face. Obviously not expecting to see a princess at the karaoke night. Even one with her reputation.

'It's a duet!' she shouted to him from the stage. 'Don't you dare leave me hanging!'

She held out her hand to him again and this time he grabbed it enthusiastically, pulled himself up to the stage beside her and planted a heavy kiss on her lips.

The surprise of it stole her reason for a moment, as her breath stopped and her world was reduced to the sensation of him on her. She lifted her hands to his arms, bracing herself against him, feeling unsteady on the little stage as one arm slid around her waist and his hand pressed firmly on the small of her back, pulling her in close.

Her fingers teased up his bicep; though her eyes were closed, her fingers traced the pattern of his tattoo from memory, nudging at the hem of his sleeve as they had earlier, keen to continue their exploration.

A wolf whistle from the crowd broke into their little reverie, and Charlie looked up, only to be greeted with the cameras of several phones pointing in her direction. Well, they'd be in the papers again. She shrugged mentally and reminded herself that that was the whole idea of this marriage.

That was why he'd kissed her.

It took a few moments for reality to break through. For her to remember that of course he'd only kissed her because they had an audience. This wasn't real— they just had to make it look that way. And just as her confidence wavered, and she wondered why that thought hurt so much, the music kicked in and Joe passed her a microphone.

'Come on then, love. Show me what you've got.'

She pulled her hair to one side, puckered up her finest pout and prepared to rock out.

They made it through the first verse without making eye contact, never mind anything more physical, but as they reached the chorus Joe reached around her waist and pulled her back, so her body was pressed against him from spike earrings to spike heels. She faltered on the lyrics, barely able to remember how to breathe, never mind sing.

She looked round at Joe to see if it had had the same effect on him, but when she saw his face she knew that he wasn't feeling what she was feeling. He was just feeling the music: every note of it. His throaty, husky voice giving the pop song a cool credibility it had never had before.

She pulled away to see him better, and though she picked up the words and joined in, it was only a token effort. Backing vocals to his masterful performance. This was why she'd agreed to marry him. The man Joe became on stage was impossible to refuse. She had kicked herself every minute since she'd woken up with a Vegas husband she no longer wanted, asking how she could have been so stupid.

But she hadn't been stupid, she realised now. It was just that they had been so magnetically drawn to one another because of his passion for music—any music—that it would have been pointless even trying to resist. Joe's eyes opened as the song slowed, and their gazes met, freezing them in the moment.

Does he feel it too? she wondered. Or had he just been so high on the adrenaline of performance that he would have agreed to marry anyone who had crossed his path?

She could see his adrenaline kicking up a notch now. His gestures growing more expansive, his grin wider, his eyes wilder.

She sang along, trying to keep pace with his enthusiasm, but whatever performance gene he'd been born with, she was clearly lacking.

The song finished with an air-guitar solo from Joe, and a roar of applause from the bar. She'd been so intent on watching him that she hadn't noticed the place fill up. From the many smartphones still clutched in hands, she guessed that they were about to go viral.

Joe grabbed her around the waist, and before she could stop him, before she could even think about whether she wanted to, his mouth was on hers, burning into her body, her mind, her soul, with his intensity. His hands were everywhere: on her butt, in her hair, gently traipsing up her upper arm. His lips were insistent against hers, demanding that she gave herself to him with equal passion. And his tongue caressed hers with such intimacy that it nearly broke her. Soft and hard, gentle and rough, he surprised her with every touch.

When, finally, he pulled away, they both gasped for air, and she was grateful his arms were still clamped around her waist, keeping her upright. And that she'd turned so that her back was to the bar, so no one would be able to see her flaming red cheeks or the confusion in her eyes.

'Uh-oh. Looks like we've got an audience,' Joe said, and Charlie registered that the surprise in his voice seemed genuine. Had he really not noticed that they were being watched? Because if not, that kiss needed an explanation. The knowledge that it was all for show had been the only thing keeping her from losing her mind. He couldn't go and change the rules now.

'Are you up for another?' Joe asked.

Another song? Another drink? Another kiss? None of the options seemed particularly safe after that performance.

'I think my singing days are done,' she said with a smile, jumping down from the stage and heading back to the relative safety of their booth.

'Where did they all come from?' Joe asked, drinking the beer he'd abandoned when he'd gone into performance mode.

'Happened quickly, huh.'

'So fast I didn't even notice.'

Then why did you kiss me? The question hung, loud and unspoken, in the air.

'So what's your family like?' Charlie asked, suddenly desperate for a change of subject. 'You're from up north, right?'

Joe nodded, and named a town near Manchester. Of course she already knew where he'd grown up from her research into the band, but small talk seemed the safest option open to them at the moment. 'They must have been proud of you. For the scholarship. For everything since.'

'Of course. They were chuffed when I got into the school. It was their idea, actually. My mum was a gifted pianist but never had the opportunity for a career in music. They wanted me to have the best.'

'Sounds like a lot of pressure.' If there was one thing she understood it was the heavy weight of family expectation. But Joe shrugged, non-committal.

'Their motives were good. Still are.'

'But you weren't happy?'

'It was an amazing opportunity.'

'That's not what I asked.'

He sighed and held up his palms. 'I don't like to sound ungrateful. I have no reason to complain. The school funded me. My parents made sacrifices.'

'You remember who you're talking to, right? I do understand that having the best of everything doesn't always make you happy. It doesn't make you a bad person to acknowledge that. It makes you human.'

He was quiet for a beat. 'So what's making you unhappy, Princess Caroline?'

'Oh, no. You are so not changing the subject like that. Come on. Mum and Dad. What are they like? How did they react to…' she searched for the words to describe what they were doing together '…to Vegas?'

He grimaced; she cringed. 'That bad?'

'They weren't best pleased that we did it without them there. They're hurt, but happy for me. I don't

know, but I think that made me feel worse.' He was
silent for a moment, fiddling with the label of his beer
bottle. 'They want to meet you.'

And she was every bit as terrified of that as he was
about meeting her family. She knew that she had a
reputation that was about as far as you could get from
ideal daughter-in-law. 'I could ask my mother to invite
them this weekend? Face everyone at the same time?'

He choked on his beer, caught in a laugh.

'That's sweet, Charlie, but how about we start with
introducing them to one royal and go from there. Not
everyone is as super cool as me when it comes to
meeting you and yours.'

'Oh, right,' she laughed. 'Because you were so ice-
cool you practically dropped to one knee the night
that we met.'

She wondered whether her tease had gone too far,
but his mouth curved in a smile. 'What can I say? You
give a whole new meaning to irresistible.'

She could feel herself blushing like a schoolgirl
and incapable of stopping it. 'So we see my parents
Friday night. Do you want to see yours this weekend
too? If you wanted to go sooner I guess I could talk
to Rich. Work remotely or something.'

He shook his head. 'Don't worry. I think this weekend will be plenty soon enough. We can fly into Manchester on Saturday. Be back home by Sunday night.
No need to miss work.'

'Actually, I could do with stopping by a festival on
Sunday, if you fancy it. There's a band I'd like to see
perform, and try and catch them for a chat.'

He nodded, and then Charlie glanced at her watch,
realising with surprise that over an hour had passed

since they had left the stage. The bar had thinned out a little again, leaving the atmosphere verging dangerously on intimate.

'Speaking of work, I've a fair bit to catch up on. I need to be in the office early tomorrow. Mind if we call it a night?'

He swigged the last of his drink and stood, reaching for her hand as she slipped off the bench. 'I like that you're tall,' he said as they left the bar with a wave to Ruby. 'As tall as me in those shoes.'

'Random comment, but thanks,' she replied, trying to work out if there was a hidden message in there that she wasn't getting. 'Are you just thinking out loud? Is this going to be a list?'

'I'm just… I don't understand. You're right. I didn't play it cool, that night. I didn't play it cool on stage just now. I'm just trying to figure this out. Maybe it is the royal thing, but I didn't struggle not to kiss your cousins when I was at school with them.'

'So you think it's because I'm tall?' Really thinking: What are you saying? Are you saying you like me? That this is real for you?

'I'm thinking about everything. I just figure that if I can work out what it is…you know…that makes us crazy like that, we can avoid it. Stop it happening again. Keep things simple.'

Her ego deflated rapidly. So it didn't matter what he was feeling, because all he wanted was a way of not feeling it any more. After their madness on stage, they were back on earth with a crash, and she had the whiplash to prove it.

'Well, I'm sorry, darling, but I'm not losing the heels.'

'God, no. Don't,' he said with so much feeling it broke the tension between them. 'I love the heels.'

Which was meant to be a bad thing, she tried to remind herself, but the matching grins on their faces proved it would be a lie.

'Or maybe it's the hair,' he came up with as they walked back to his flat, their fingers still twined. 'There's so much of it. It's wild.'

She tried to laugh it off. 'So we've established you have a thing for tall women with messy hair. I guess I was just lucky I fit the bill.' She turned serious as they reached the front door of the warehouse and stepped into the privacy of the foyer. 'Are your parents going to hate me?'

'Why would they hate you?'

'Notorious party girl seduces lovely northern lad into hasty Vegas marriage. Am I not the girl that mothers have nightmares about?'

'Is that how you see what happened? You seduced me? Because I remember things differently...'

'It's not about what I remember. It's about what your mum will think.'

'My mum will think you're great.' But his tone told her that she wasn't the only one with reservations about the big introduction. 'You'll mainly be busy with dodging hints about grandchildren.'

Her stomach fell and she leaned back against the wall for support while the rushing in her ears stopped.

'She won't seriously be expecting that, will she?'

'She's been bugging me for years about settling down and giving her grandkids. Isn't that what all mums do?'

Apparently they did—that was why she made a point of seeing hers as little as possible.

She drew herself up to her full height again, not wanting Joe to see that there was anything wrong.

'Well, we'll just have to tell her that we don't have any plans.'

Joe was looking at her closely, and she wondered how much he had seen. Whether he had realised that she had just had a minor panic attack.

'It's fine; we'll fend her off together. Are you sure you're okay?'

So he had noticed. She pasted on a smile and pushed her shoulders back, determined to give him no reason to suspect what was on her mind. 'Of course. Just tired. That jet lag must be catching up with me after all.'

It wasn't until she reached his front door that she remembered the whole bed situation. How was she meant to sleep beside him after a kiss like that? After he'd all but told her that he was finding it as hard to resist her as she was to resist him.

She dived into the bathroom as soon as they got into the apartment, determined to be the first ready for bed, and to have her eyes closed and be pretending to sleep by the time that Joe came in. Or better still, actually *be* asleep, and not even know that he was there. She pulled a T-shirt over her head, still warm from the dryer, and gave herself a stern talking-to. She couldn't react like that every time someone mentioned babies or pregnancy. There were bound to be questions after the hasty way that they had got married, and she was going to have to learn to deal with them.

CHAPTER SIX

THERE WAS DEFINITELY something that she wasn't telling him. Something to do with the way that she'd reacted just now when he'd warned her that his mum would probably be hinting about grandchildren.

What, did she already have an illegitimate kid stashed away somewhere? No. It couldn't be that. There was no way that she'd be able to keep it out of the papers. What if she was already pregnant? That could be it. After all, she had accepted a completely idiotic proposal of marriage from a man that she barely knew. Was she looking for a baby daddy, as well as a husband?

And how would he feel if she was? That one was easy enough to answer: as if he was being used. Well, there was nothing new in that. He'd learnt at the age of eighteen, when it transpired that the girl he had been madly in love with at school was only with him for the thrill of sleeping with the poor northern scholarship kid, and bringing him home to upset her parents in front of all their friends, that women wanted him for *what* he was, not who.

And after years on the road, meeting women in every city, every country that he had visited, he knew that it was true. None of them wanted him. The real him. They wanted the singer, or the writer, or the rock star, or the rich guy.

Or—on one memorable occasion—they wanted the story to sell to the tabloids.

Not a single one of them knew who he really was. Not a single one of them had come home to meet his parents. And that was fine with him. Because he knew what he wanted now too. And more importantly he knew that relationships only worked if both of you knew what you wanted—and didn't let emotions in the way of getting it.

But it didn't mean anything, he told himself, Charlie coming home with him at the weekend. Like all the others, she was just using him. He provided a nice boost to her career, and a new way of causing friction with her family, though he couldn't pretend to know why she wanted that. And he was using her to get exposure for his band, and sales for his new album. If he ever finished it.

He tidied up the bedroom while he waited for her to finish in the bathroom, chucking dirty clothes in the laundry hamper and retrieving the rest of Charlie's jewellery from under the bed. They would have to pick up the rest of her stuff from her flat at some point. He'd clear her a space in the wardrobe. Of all the things that he'd thought about that night that they got married, how to manage living with a slob hadn't been one of them. He surveyed the carnage in his apartment, and shrugged. Lucky his housekeeper was going to be in tomorrow. He'd leave a note asking her to clear some space in the drawers and wardrobe.

The thought of it was oddly intimate. Strange,

when they were already having to share a bed. Sharing hanging space should have been the least of their worries. But there was something decidedly permanent, committed, about the thought of her clothes hanging alongside his.

It wasn't permanent.

They'd both known and agreed from the start that this wasn't real, and it wasn't going to last. They just had to ride out the next year or so. Let the press do their thing, and then decide how they were going to end things in a way that worked out for both of them. It was as simple as that.

Joe waited outside Charlie's office, wondering whether she'd be pleased or not if he went in. Somehow, over the past three days they'd barely seen each other. That night after the karaoke she'd been asleep by the time that he'd got out of the bathroom, lying on her side on the far side of the bed, so far away that they didn't even need a pillow barrier as a nod to decency. Then she'd been up before him the next morning, though she had said that she had a lot to catch up on. The pattern had stayed the same ever since. She was in the office before he'd had his breakfast every morning, and came home late, clutching bags and suitcases from her flat.

The only sign that they were living together at all was the increasing chaos in his apartment. His housekeeper did her best in the daytime, but once Charlie was home she was like a whirlwind, depositing clothes and hair grips and jewellery on every surface. Leaving crumbs and coffee rings all over the kitchen and the coffee table. He wasn't even mad: he was amused.

How had the prim and proper royal family produced such a slob?

It wasn't as if she were lazy. The woman never stopped. He knew that of her reputation at work. That she worked hard to find her artists, and then even harder to support them once they were signed. She was on the phone to lawyers, accountants, artists all day long, and then out at gigs in the evening, always looking for more talent, more opportunities.

Perhaps that was it, he thought. Why waste time picking up your dirty clothes when there was new music to be found?

The pavements started to fill with knackered-looking workers as the clock ticked towards six. As East London's hipster types exited office buildings and headed for the craft-beer-stocked pubs as if pulled by a magnet.

She'd told him she'd arranged for a car to collect her from work and swing by the apartment to pick him up, but as the hours after lunch had crawled by he'd realised that sitting and waiting for her was absolutely not his style.

He strode into the building, mind made up, and smiled at the receptionist.

'Hey, Vanessa. I'm Charlie's husband. Okay if I go straight through?' There. He made sure he sounded humble enough not to assume that she'd know who he was—though he would hope that the receptionist at his own label would recognise him—but confident enough to be assured that he wouldn't be stopped. He breezed past her, wondering why he felt so nervous. All right, he hadn't even visited Afland before, never mind the private apartments at the royal palace, but he had met a fair few royals, between his posh school and attending galas and stuff since his career took off. Deep down, he knew it wasn't who her family was that was making him nervous. It was the fact that he was meeting them at all.

He'd not been home to meet the family for a long time. Not since the disaster with Arabella.

That weekend when he was eighteen, he'd thought he had it made. His gorgeous girlfriend, one of the most popular girls in school, had invited him and a load of their friends to a weekend party at her parents' country house. For the first time since he had started at the school he had felt as if he had belonged. And more importantly had thought it meant that Arabella was as serious about him as he was about her. He'd been on the verge of telling her that he loved her. But as soon as he'd arrived, he'd realised that there was something wrong. She'd introduced him to her parents with a glint in her eye that he knew meant trouble, and had stropped off when they'd welcomed him with warm smiles and handshakes.

Turned out, he wasn't the ogre she'd been expecting them to see. And if he wasn't pissing off her parents, he was no use to her at all. So she'd broken it off, publicly and humiliatingly, in front of half the school and their parents.

Was Charlie doing the same thing? Perhaps marrying him was just one more way for her to stick her middle finger up at her family. Another way to distance herself from her royal blood. But instinctively he felt that wasn't true. Whenever they'd discussed her family, she'd made it clear that she didn't want to upset them. That had been the main thing on her mind that first morning in Vegas. But she hadn't been so concerned about it that she hadn't married him in the first place.

He showed himself through the office, over to where he remembered Charlie's desk was. She couldn't see him approach, her back to him, concentrating on her computer. Her hair was pulled into a knot on the top of her head, an up-do that could almost be described as sophisticated, and a delicate tattoo curled at the nape of her neck. He'd never noticed it before—and that knowledge sent a shudder of desire through him. How many inches of her body were a mystery to him? How many secrets could he uncover if they were to do the utterly stupid thing and give in to this mutual attraction?

They couldn't be that stupid. *He* wouldn't be so stupid. Opening up to a woman, especially a woman like Charlie, was like asking to get hurt.

By the time that he reached her desk, she still hadn't looked up. He couldn't resist that tattoo a moment longer. He could feel the eyes of her co-workers on him, and knew that they were watching, knew that they had read the gossip sites. It was all the excuse he needed, the reminder that he had a part to play.

He bent and pressed his lips to the black swirl of ink below her hairline.

The second that he met her skin a shot of pain seared through his nose and he jumped back, both hands pressed to his face.

'What the h—?'

'What the h—?'

They both cried out in unison.

'Joe?' Charlie said, one hand on the back of her

head as she spun round on her chair. 'What were you *thinking*?'

He gave her a loaded look. 'I was thinking that I wanted to kiss my wife. What I'm thinking now is that we might need a trip to A&E.' She looked up then, clocked the many pairs of eyes on them, and stood, remembering she needed to play her part too.

'Oh, my goodness, I'm sorry, darling.' She reached up and gently took hold of his hands, moving them away from his nose. 'Does it still hurt?'

She turned his head one way and then the other, examining him closely as she did so.

'Not so much now,' he admitted, finally making eye contact with her. It was the truth. With her hands gently cupping his face like that, he could barely feel his nose. Barely think about any part of his body that didn't have her soft skin against it.

'No blood anyway,' she added.

He smiled. 'Can't meet the in-laws with a bloody nose and a black eye,' he said. 'Not really the best first impression.'

'They'll love you whatever,' she said, returning his grin, but he suspected it was more for their audience than for him.

She was wearing a black dress, structured and tight, giving the illusion of curves that her tall, athletic figure usually hid. Was this what her parents wanted of her? he wondered. For her to tone herself down and wear something ladylike?

Her phone buzzed on the desk behind her, breaking the spell between them. 'That'll be the car,' she said, gathering up her stuff and shutting down her computer. As she grabbed her purse off the desk she sent a glass of water flying, soaking a stack of scrawled notes.

'Argh,' she groaned, reaching into a drawer for a roll of paper towels. 'Last thing we need.'

'It's fine,' he said, grabbing a handful of the towels. 'Here.' He mopped up the puddle heading towards the edge of the desk and spread out the soggy papers. 'They'll be dry before we're back on Monday. No harm done.'

She blotted at them some more with the paper, glancing at her phone, which was buzzing again on the desk.

'Is it time we were going?'

'Mmm,' she said, non-committal, silencing it. 'It's okay, we've got time.' She started straightening up another stack of papers, and throwing pens in a cup at the back of the desk.

'Wait a minute. Are you tidying?'

She shrugged. 'It's happened before, you know.'

'Maybe, but right now you're stalling, aren't you?'

She stopped what she was doing and looked him straight in the eye, leaning back against the desk with her arms crossing her chest. 'Says who?'

'Well, you just as good as admitted it, actually. What's going on? Ashamed to introduce me to your family?'

She started with surprise. 'Why would I be ashamed?'

'Because you're nervous. Why else would you be?'

'Maybe I'm desperate for them to fall in love with you.'

'Maybe.' He watched her with a wry smile. 'I guess we're going to find out. Are you ready?'

She sighed as she pulled on her jacket and swung her bag over her shoulders. 'Ready.'

As the car pulled through the gates at the back of the palace a few hours later, Joe took a deep breath. He might have been all blasé with Charlie, but now that he was here at the palace, with its two hundred and fifty bedrooms and uniformed guards and a million windows, perhaps he was feeling a little intimidated. Regardless of what he'd thought earlier, his brief brushes with royalty before he had met Charlie hadn't left him at all prepared for this.

Throughout the short flight to the island, he'd been making a determined effort not to feel nervous—forcing his pulse to be even and his palms dry.

And now, as they stepped out of the car and through the doors of the palace, perhaps if he closed his eyes, shut out the scale of the entrance gates, the uniformed staff in attendance, and the police officer stationed at the door, he could almost imagine that this was just any other dinner.

Eventually, following Charlie into the building and through a warren of corridors, he had to admit to himself that there was no escaping it. 'The private apartments are just up there,' Charlie told him as they rounded yet another corner.

He nodded, not sure what the appropriate response was when your wife was giving you the guided tour of the palace she had grown up in. In fact, he'd barely spoken a word, he realised, since the car had pulled through the gates.

The uniformed man who had met them at the door faded away as the policeman ahead of them opened the door. He nodded to them both as Charlie greeted

him by name, and Joe followed her through the door.
Unlike the corridors they'd followed so far, the interior
of the private rooms was simple. Plush red carpets,
gilt and chandeliers had fallen away, leaving smart,
bright walls, soft wood flooring and recessed lighting.

'It's like another world in here,' Charlie said with
a smile. 'My parents had it renovated when we were
small. They were doing big repair work across the
whole palace, so they took the opportunity to mod-
ernise a bit.'

'No chandeliers, then?'

'Not really my mother's style. They keep them in
the state rooms for the visiting dignitaries and the
tourists. But my parents have always preferred things
simpler.'

He followed her down the corridor, and she paused
in front of a closed door. 'Ready?' she asked.

He took her hand in his and squeezed. 'Let's do it.'

She opened the door into a light-flooded room.

Her parents were seated on a sofa to one side of a
fireplace, what looked like gin and tonics on the coffee table in front of them.

'Oh, you caught us!' said Queen Adelaide, Charlie's mother. 'We started without you. I know, we're
terrible.' She stood and kissed Charlie on the cheek.

Joe just had time to register the stiffness in Charlie's shoulders before her mother, Her Majesty Queen
Adelaide of Afland, was stepping around her and
holding out her hand.

He held his own out in return, but couldn't find his
feet to step towards her. Was it because she was the
head of state or the head of Charlie's family that was
making him nervous?

'You must be Joe,' Queen Adelaide said, smiling and filling the silence that was threatening awkwardness. 'How do you do?'

Charlie's father stepped forward and shook his hand too, but he wasn't as skilled as his wife at hiding his feelings, he noted. And in his case, his feelings appeared to be decidedly frosty.

'Joe. How do you do?'

He wasn't the only frosty one, Joe realised, watching Charlie as they took a seat on the sofa opposite her parents. Her shoulders were as stiff as he had ever seen them, and her back was ramrod straight. She reached for one of the drinks that had appeared on the coffee table while they were getting the formalities out of the way.

They sipped their drinks as silence fell around them, definitely into awkward territory now. And still a distinct lack of congratulations. Perhaps they were waiting for the others to arrive.

Just as he was taking a deep breath, preparing to dive into small talk, he heard a door open, and the apartment filled with the noise of rambunctious children.

'Grandma! Grandpa!'

The kids barrelled into the room with squeals of excitement. The tense atmosphere was broken, and Queen Adelaide and Prince Gerald beamed with proud smiles and stood to scoop up their grandchildren. But Charlie stayed seated; though she smiled, the expression seemed forced.

Three adults followed the kids into the room. Joe recognised Charlie's sister and brother-in-law, and a second woman who he guessed must be the nanny.

She drifted out of the room after seeing the children settled with book and toys, and Joe shook hands with his new in-laws.

'So, Vegas!' Charlie's brother-in-law said as they all sat down. 'Wish we could have done that. Would have given anything to avoid the circus that we had to endure.'

'Endure?' Charlie's sister, Verity, slapped her husband's leg playfully. 'If that was a circus, I don't know how you'd describe our life now, chasing after these two.' But she smiled indulgently as she said it. Charlie leaned forward and helped herself to her sister's drink, uncharacteristically quiet.

'It was definitely low-key,' Joe said. 'Just us and a couple of friends.' He took hold of Charlie's hand, wondering whether she was planning on checking back in to this conversation again at any point. He withheld the details of the kitschy chapel they had chosen: it had seemed so funny at the time, but less so now that they were facing the consequences of their actions. He looked across at Charlie, and saw the tension in her expression that revealed how uncomfortable she was.

Isn't that what I'm meant to be feeling? he thought. You're back in the bosom of your family. This is meant to be your home, so why are you so uncomfortable?

He was so distracted by wondering what was preoccupying her that he forgot that he had been nervous about meeting the family. Her family were half of the reason he was so sure that this relationship wouldn't work so if it wasn't her family causing the problems, then where did that leave them?

Using one another—that was it. And he knew that

he had to keep his head if he was going to stay ahead of the game, make sure that she was never in a position to hurt him.

His thoughts were interrupted by the arrival of Charlie's brother, Miles, who bowled into the room wearing an air of privilege that outshone his exquisitely tailored suit. He greeted Charlie's brother-in-law with hearty slaps on the back—they'd been friends at school, Joe seemed to remember—and then doled out kisses on the cheek to his female relatives.

'So you're the guy who seduced my sister,' he said when he reached Joe.

He gave Miles a shrewd look. Was he trying to get a rise out of him? Well, he'd have to try harder than that.

'I'm Joe,' he said, standing to shake his hand. 'It's good to meet you.'

Charlie had risen beside him and he wrapped an arm around her waist. She seemed calmer with her brother than with her sister. Interesting, Joe thought. Because so far, her brother seemed like a bit of an ass. But families were strange, he knew. Maybe she'd always been closer to her brother. He tried to push it from his mind as they all sat down again. The nanny came back in, then, and the room was suddenly in chaos as toys were put away, negotiations for 'just five more minutes' were shut down and a pair of desultory kids doled out goodnight kisses.

When they got to Charlie, that stiffness came back to her shoulders, and she straightened her spine, sitting beside Joe on the sofa as if she were in a job interview. She sat deadly still as the children climbed up onto the couch, still offering kisses and messing around.

In contrast to all of the other adults in the room, who were joining in with the kids' silliness, Charlie pretty much just patted them on the head and dodged their kisses.

What was her issue with the kids?

There was no getting away from the fact that there *was* something going on. Joe looked over at Charlie's mum and sister to see if they had noticed—looking for any clues to what was going on—but their attention was completely on the children. Joe's earlier suspicion came back to him. Could she be pregnant? Did that even fit with what he was witnessing?

It did if she was in denial, he supposed. If she was pregnant and didn't want to be. Or didn't want to be found out.

Finally, the kids were bundled out of the room by the nanny, and a member of staff appeared with a silver tray bearing champagne flutes and an ice bucket.

'Ah, perfect timing,' Adelaide declared as the glasses were handed round and champagne poured.

The tone of her voice shifted ever so subtly, from relaxed and convivial to something more formal. Maybe more rehearsed. Charlie was close by Joe's side still, and this time it was she who took his hand, and ducked her head under his arm as she wrapped it around her shoulders and turned in towards him, until she was almost surrounded by his body. He tried to meet her eyes, but she evaded him. He couldn't be sure with her avoiding eye contact, but if he didn't know better he'd say that she wanted him to protect her. From her own family? Who seemed—to his surprise—a bunch of genuinely nice people who cared about one another. Her slightly annoying brother aside. It just didn't make any sense. Not unless she was keeping all of them—him included—in the dark about something.

'Joe and Charlie,' Adelaide began, 'I'm so pleased that we are all together this evening. While we can't say that we weren't surprised by your news...' her raised eyebrows spoke volumes about how restrained she felt she was being '...your father and I are delighted you have found someone you want to spend your life with. Now we didn't get to do this on your wedding day, so I'm going to propose the traditional toast. If you could all charge your glasses to the bride and groom. To Charlie and Joe.'

Queen Adelaide took a ladylike sip, while Charlie polished off half her glass and pulled Joe's arm tighter around her.

'Joe, we're absolutely delighted to meet the man who wants to take on, not only our wonderfully wild Caroline, but also her family, with everything that entails. We're always so happy to see our family grow, and, who knows, perhaps over the next few years it might be growing even further.'

From the corner of his eye he saw Charlie flinch, and he knew exactly how she had taken that comment of her mother's, whether it had been meant as a jibe about grandchildren or not. He sipped at his champagne, having smiled and nodded in the right places during Queen Adelaide's speech.

'Are you okay?' he whispered in Charlie's ear when the toasts were done and attention had drifted away from them.

She nodded stiffly, telling him louder than words that she absolutely wasn't.

'Want to try and make a break for it?'

She cracked half a smile. 'We'd better stay. I'd never hear the end of it.'

He wondered if that were true. Charlie's parents looked delighted to have her home. But were they really the types to nag and criticise if she left? They'd welcomed him with good grace in trying circumstances. Perhaps they deserved more credit than Charlie was giving them.

But there was no getting around the fact that she was still on edge, even after all the introductions were out of the way and they were all getting on fine. Which meant there was more to this than just her worrying whether they were going to buy their story.

What if he was right? What if she was pregnant, and was using him? Would he walk away from her? From their agreement? How would that look to the press…?

He suspected there was nothing worse as far as the tabloids were concerned than walking away from a pregnant royal wife.

He still had his arm around Charlie's waist, but he could feel a killer grip closing around him, making it hard to breathe. He'd thought that he'd gone into this with his eyes open. He'd thought he'd known what she wanted from him. Had he been duped again? Was he being used again, without him realising it?

'So, Joe, you were at school with Hugo and Seb, is that right? At Northbridge?' Charlie's brother had come to sit beside them, dragging his thoughts away from his wife.

'Yeah, they were a year or two ahead of me though. You know what it's like at school. A different year could be a different planet.'

'They remembered you, though.'

He heard Charlie move beside him, and, when he glanced across at her, she looked interested in the conversation for the first time since they'd arrived.

'What did they tell you?' she asked, a glint in her eye. 'You have to share. Don't you dare hold out on me, big brother.'

'Oh, you know, the usual. Ex-girlfriends and kiss-and-tells. God, you've let your standards slip, getting yourself hitched to this one.'

'Standards? Really? Who did he date at school?'

'You really want to know?' Miles laughed and rolled his eyes. 'Masochist. Fine, it was Arabella Barclay,' Miles said.

He watched Charlie's reaction from the corner of his eye. It was clear that she knew her, or knew of her.

'Wow. Miles is right, Joe. Blonde, skinny, horsey. If you've got a type, I'm definitely not it.'

Her brother laughed, and Joe resisted the urge to use his fists to shut his mouth.

'Thank God I came to my senses and left all that schoolboy rubbish behind,' he said. Trying not to think of that leggy, horsey girl. Or maybe he *should* be thinking about her. Really, looking back, he owed Arabella a big thank you. She'd done him a favour, teaching him about how relationships *really* worked, rather than the schoolboy idealism he'd had at eighteen.

'Trust me,' Joe said, dropping his arm from Charlie's shoulders to her waist, 'you were everything I didn't know I was looking for.' He closed his eyes and leaned in for a kiss, thinking that a peck on the lips would finish off their picture of newly wedded

romance nicely. And banish bitter memories of Arabella into the bargain.

How could he have forgotten? Perhaps his brain
erased it on purpose, in an attempt to protect him? The
second his lips met Charlie's a rush of desire flooded
his blood, and he clenched his fists, trying to control
it. To control himself. Was this normal? This overwhelming passion from the most innocent of kisses?
He pulled away as Charlie's lips pouted, knowing that
another second would lead them to more trouble than
he could reasonably be expected to deal with.

Her eyes were still closed, and for the first time
since they'd arrived at the palace her features were
relaxed. A hint of a smile curved one corner of her
lips, and the urge to press just one more kiss there was
almost overwhelming.

'Okay, you've proved your point.' Miles laughed.
'I will never mention Arabella again. Or the fact that
she's still single and still smoking hot.'

Charlie opened her eyes to roll them at her brother.

'Do you think we can stop trying to set my husband up with his ex?'

Miles held up his hands. 'You're the newly-weds.
Your marriage is your own business. I was just providing the facts,'

'Well, as helpful as that is, darling,' Charlie's
mother interjected, 'I think we can leave gossip about
school friends for another time.'

Joe glanced at Adelaide, and as she met his eye he
realised that he had an unexpected ally. He smiled back,
curious. Charlie had been so worried about how her
parents were going to react that it had never occurred
to him that they'd actually be pleased to meet him.

They sat down for dinner in one of the semi-state-rooms, and Joe looked around him in awe. Away from the modest private apartments, it struck him for the first time that this really was Charlie's life. She'd grown up here, in this home within a palace. Her life had been crystal and champagne, gilt and marble and staff and state apartments. Carriages and press calls, church at Christmas and official photographs on her birthdays. And she'd walked away from all of that.

She'd chosen a warehouse apartment in East London. A job that demanded she work hard. A 'floor-drobe' rather than a maid. A real life with normal responsibilities. It occurred to him that he'd never asked her why. He'd mocked the privileges that she'd been born with, but he'd never asked her about the choices that she'd made.

As the wine flowed and they settled in to what to Joe seemed like a banquet of never-ending courses, Charlie relaxed more. He watched her banter with her brother and sister, and marvelled at the change in her since they had first arrived. When her hand landed on his thigh, he knew that it was all for show. Part of appearing like the loved-up new couple they were meant to be. But that didn't stop the heat radiating from the palm of her hand, or the awareness of every movement of her body beside him.

It didn't stop his imagination, the tumble of images that fell through his mind, the endless possibilities, if this thing weren't so damned complicated.

He wanted her. Could he have her? Could they go to bed, and wake up the next morning and *not* turn the whole thing into a string of complications? Could they both just demand what they wanted, take it, and then agree when it needed to be over?

They shouldn't risk it. He looked down at her hand again and caught sight of the gold of her wedding ring. It would never be that simple between them. They were married. They worked together. There was unbelievable chemistry between them, but that didn't mean that a simple night in bed together could ever be on the cards. They'd acted impulsively once, when they'd decided to get married, and that meant that the stakes were too high for any further slips on the self-control front.

Work. That was what he should be concentrating on. Like the fact that he still hadn't managed to write anything new for the album. He'd told Charlie and her boss that it was practically finished when he'd agreed to sign the contract. It *had* been finished. It still was, he supposed, if he was prepared to release it knowing that it wasn't his best work. What he really needed was to lock himself in his studio for a month with no distractions. Unfortunately, the biggest distraction in his life right now was living with him. And then there was the fact that if he was holed up in his studio, then where was the inspiration supposed to come from? What he'd end up with was an album about staring at the same four walls. What he needed was a muse. A reason to write.

Taking Charlie to bed would give him all the material he needed. He was sure of that. But at too high a cost.

They left the drawing room that night and headed to bed with handshakes and kisses from Charlie's family. Charlie stiffly accepted the kisses from her mother, and she climbed the stairs stiff and formal with him.

Joe watched her carefully as she led them down corridor after corridor, low lit with bulbs that wouldn't damage the artworks. He was vaguely aware of passing masterpieces on his left and right, but his attention was all on Charlie.

'Did you have a good time?' he asked. 'I thought it went pretty well; I liked your family.'

She nodded, staring straight ahead instead of at him. 'They liked you. Even Miles.'

'That's how he acts when he likes someone?'

She huffed an affectionate laugh, and turned to face him. 'I know. He's an idiot. We keep hoping he'll grow out of it.'

'Do you think they bought our story?' he asked. Her eyes seemed to turn darker as she looked ahead again. The sparsely spaced lights strobed her expressions, yellow and dark, yellow, dark.

'I'm not sure,' she admitted. 'But I don't think they're going to call us out on it. My mum already—'

She stopped herself, but he needed to know. 'What?' he asked.

'When I first called and told her what we'd done, she told me that she'd take care of it. If we wanted this marriage to go away.'

'And you didn't take her up on it?'

'We'd already talked about why that would be a bad idea. We made an agreement and I'm sticking to it.'

Her face was still a mystery. She was hiding something else. He knew that she was. Something that meant she was happy with their lie of a marriage rather than the real thing. Maybe he'd shock it out of her with some brutal home truths.

'Charlie, I want you. I know we said that sleeping together would be a disaster. But what if it wasn't?'

She turned to him properly now, her eyes wide with surprise. 'And where the hell did that come from?'

'It needed saying. Or the question needed asking. Maybe it could work. Maybe we could give it a go. I mean, we're acting out this whole relationship, so why not make it that bit more believable?'

'Why not? Do you really need me to list the million reasons it's a horrendous idea? As if our lives weren't complicated enough—you want to add sex to the mix?'

'But that's what I'm saying. Maybe it doesn't have to complicate things. Maybe it would simplify them. We're living together. We're married. We're making everyone believe that we're a couple. I mean, how would sex make any of that more complicated?'

'Because you forgot the most important thing we're pretending. Yes, we had a wedding, but this isn't a marriage. We're not a couple. We're doing this for a limited time only, and mixing sex in with that would just be crazy.'

'So you don't want to. Fine, I just thought I'd ask the question. Clear the air.'

'Whether I want to or not isn't the issue, Joe.'

'So you do.'

'Urgh.' She threw her head back in frustration. '*Totally* not the point. And to be honest I'm surprised you're asking, because we both know that there's some crazy chemistry between us. We've talked about it before. And at no point has either of us thought that doing something about it was in any way a good idea. I don't know why we can't just drop it.'

'Maybe I don't want to.'

They stopped outside a door and Charlie hesitated with her hand on the doorknob, a frosty silence growing between them. Joe decided to take a punt, knowing that he could be about to set a bomb under their little arrangement. But if she wasn't going to volunteer all the facts, he had to get them out of her somehow. A pregnancy wasn't the sort of thing you could ignore for ever.

'How are you planning on passing me off as your baby daddy, then, if we're not sleeping together?'

Charlie took in a gasp of a breath, and as he watched her straighten her spine he realised that he'd been right about one thing—this was going to be explosive. But a shiver ran through him as Charlie walked into the room and he wondered whether he had just made an enormous mistake.

CHAPTER SEVEN

CHARLIE KEPT WALKING, calm and controlled, past the four-poster bed, trying to cover the typhoon of emotions roiling through her. She stopped when she reached the bathroom, an island of cool white marble after the richness of the bedroom.

'What are you talking about, Joe?'

Her teeth were practically grinding against one another, and she didn't seem to be able to unclench her fists.

'You're pregnant, aren't you?' His voice faded towards the end of the sentence, as if he were already regretting asking. But she didn't care about that, because the grief and pain that she had been holding at bay all night, seeing her sister's happiness with her children, her easy contentment, broke through the dam and flooded her. Winded, as if she'd been punched in the gut, she turned. She retched into the sink, as a week of new pain caught up with her. This had been building since she'd seen the newspaper headline announcing her own imminent engagement. She'd held it at bay, distracted herself with her stupid Vegas wedding and then burying herself in her work. But with Joe's crazy, heartless words—his absolutely baseless accusation—the pain had gripped her and wouldn't let her go.

Joe caught up with her and leaned against the bathroom door frame as she retched, hoping that she wasn't going to get a second look at her dinner.

'Are you okay?'

She threw him the dirtiest look that she could muster before hanging her head over the sink.

'Is it morning sickness?'

It took every ounce of self-control she possessed not to howl like a dog and collapse in a heap on the floor. Instead she forced herself upright, regaining control over her body.

'I. Am. Not. Pregnant.'

She forced the words out as evenly as she could, determined not to give him the satisfaction of seeing how he was hurting her, driving the knife deeper and twisting it with everything that he said.

'Are you sure? Because—'

She broke.

'I'm infertile, Joe. Is that sure enough for you?'

Her spine sagged and her legs turned to jelly as she spoke the words that she'd buried for so many years. She didn't even put out her hands to break her fall. There was no point—what could hurt more than this?

But instead of hitting cold marble, she landed on soft cotton, hard muscle. Joe's arms surrounded her, and her vision was clouded by snowy white shirt. She pushed away, not wanting him here, wanting no witnesses to her despair. But his arms were clamped around her, his lips were on her temple and his voice was soft in her ear.

'God, Charlie, I'm so sorry. I never would have said that if... I didn't know. I'm sorry.'

More murmurs followed, but she'd stopped listening. The tears had arrived. The ones that she'd kept at bay since she was a teenager. That she'd forced down somewhere deep inside her.

They tipped off the mascaraed ends of her lashes, streaking her cheeks, painting tracks down Joe's shirt as he held her tight and refused to let go, even as she struggled against him. Eventually, she stopped fighting, and accepted the tight clamp of his arms around her and the weight of his head resting against hers. She listened to the pulse at the base of his throat, heard it racing in time with her own. And then, as her heaving sobs petered out to cries, and then sniffs, she heard it slow. A gentle, rhythmic thud that pulled her towards calm. They'd slumped back against the claw-footed bath, her legs dragged across Joe's when he'd pulled her close and she'd fought to get free. The shoulder of his shirt was damp, and no doubt ruined by her charcoaled tears.

'You know,' he said eventually, 'we'd be more comfortable in the other room.' Their conversation in the corridor, when he'd oh-so-casually asked if she wanted to sleep with him, felt like a lifetime ago. Surely he couldn't be suggesting...

But he was right. The floor was unforgiving against her butt, and as comfortable as the bath probably was once you were in it, it didn't make for a great back rest.

She stood, pulling her dress straight and attempting something close to dignity.

'Let's just forget this whole conversation. Please,'

she added, when he stood behind her and met her gaze in the mirror.

He crossed his arms.

'I'm not sure that I can.'

'Well, I'm sure that if I can manage not to think about it, you can too.' She didn't care that he'd just been gentle and caring with her. Spiky was all she had right now, so that was what he was going to get. She walked through to the bedroom, her arms crossed across her chest and her hands rubbing at her biceps. She was cold, suddenly. Something to do with sitting on a marble floor perhaps. She climbed under the crisply ironed sheets and heavy embroidered eiderdown, pulling it up around her shoulders in a search for warmth. She figured she didn't need to worry about Joe's suggestion about sleeping together. There was no way that he was going to be interested in her now, with her messed-up mascara and malfunctioning uterus. When she looked up he was still standing in the doorway of the bathroom, watching her. She pulled the sheets a little tighter and sank back against the padded headboard, wondering if he was going to drop the subject.

'So how's that going for you?' he asked eventually. 'Not thinking about it, I mean.'

She shut her eyes tight, trying to block him out. She didn't need him judging her on top of everything else. But he wasn't done yet. 'Because it looks to me like burying your feelings isn't exactly working.'

Throwing the sheets down, she sat up, and met Joe's interested gaze with an angry stare. 'Just because you catch the one time in goodness knows how many years that I let myself think about it and get upset—all of a sudden you're a bloody expert on my feelings.'

'You might not think about it, but that doesn't mean that it's not hurting you.' His voice was infuriatingly calm, just highlighting how hard she was finding it to keep something remotely close to cool. If she didn't get a handle on her feelings, she was heading for another breakdown, and that little scene in the bathroom did not bear repeating.

'God, Joe. Stop talking as if you know me. You know *nothing* about this.'

He came to sit beside her on the bed, and his fingertips found the back of her hand, playing, tracing the length of her fingers, turning them over to find the lines of her palm. 'I know that it's getting between you and your family,' he said at last. 'I know that it hurts you every time you see your niece and nephew. Every time your mother casually mentions grandchildren.'

She looked up from their joined hands to meet his eye. He'd seen all that? 'You think you're so insightful, but an hour ago you thought that I was pregnant,' she reminded him.

He boosted himself up on the bed, and with a huff she scooched over, making room between her and the edge of the bed. He picked up her hand again, and focussed intently on it as he spoke. 'So I misinterpreted the reason you were acting funny. That doesn't mean I didn't see it. That I don't understand.'

'You don't. How could you?' She tipped her head back against the headboard and closed her eyes, wishing that he would just drop this. It wasn't as if it really affected him. He had no vested interest in whether she could procreate. It wasn't fair that he was pushing this when she so obviously didn't want to talk about it.

But if she could admit it to herself, perhaps talking felt almost…good. She realised that there had been a heavy weight in her stomach, sitting there so long that she'd forgotten how hard it had been to carry at first. Over time, she had got so used to the pain that she had lost sight of how it had felt not to have it there.

'I know that you let it push you into doing stuff that you regret. What happened that night in Vegas. Was it something to do with this?'

'I was just letting off steam. Having fun.'

'I don't believe you. I've not known you long, Charlie, but I can see straight through you. If I'd known you better that night I'd never have gone through with it. If I'd been able to see how you were hurting.'

'Hurting? I was enjoying myself. I got carried away.'

'For God's sake. Can you still not be honest with me, even now? I'm trying to tell you that you don't have to bury this any more. That if you want, we can talk about it. But you're trying to tell me you don't even care and I know that that isn't true. This is why you said you never wanted to get married, isn't it?'

She rolled her eyes, and tried to fake a snort of laughter. 'As if I even have to worry about that. Who would marry me if they knew?'

'Is that really what you think?' Pulling back, he put some distance between them so he could look her in the eye.

'It doesn't matter, Joe. I came to terms with it a long time ago. But yes, it's what I think. What would be the point of getting married?'

'I don't know. Speaking hypothetically here…isn't it usually something to do with spending your life with someone that you love?'

She snorted. 'Who knew you were such a romantic? But in a real marriage, sooner or later, kids always come up. Everyone's expecting it. Everyone's waiting for it. When you come from my family, especially.'

'And you're going to let that dictate what you do— who you date. What the great unwashed masses expect of you?'

'It's not just them, though. You don't understand. You don't understand my family. It only exists to perpetuate itself. To provide the next generation.'

'And that's the sort of person you'd want to marry, is it? The sort of person who sees you as a vessel for the next generation? If someone's looking at you like that, Charlie, you need to run, as fast as you can, and find someone who deserves you.'

The fire in his voice and in his expression was disconcerting, so much so that she found that she didn't have a counter argument. Because how could she argue with that? Of course she wanted someone who saw her as more than just a royal baby maker, but that didn't mean that he existed.

Joe's arm came around her shoulders, and she turned in to him, accepting comfort from the one person who could truly offer it. The one person who knew what she was going through—even if he couldn't really understand.

Listening to the rhythmic in–out of his breathing, she gradually felt her muscles start to relax. First her shoulders dropped away from her ears as her own breaths deepened to match Joe's. Then her fingers unclenched from their fists, her back gave out as she let Joe's side take her weight, and then her legs, bent at the knee and pulled up to her chest, tipped into Joe's lap, and were secured by the presence of his hand tucked in behind her knee.

With everything that had been said and revealed in the course of a night, there was no danger of things turning sexy. Charlie could feel that her eyes were swollen, and her skin felt red and tight from tear tracks. She felt anything but desirable. Burying her face in Joe's shirt, she tried to decide what she *did* feel.

Secure.

Anchored.

Not that long ago, an emotional night like this one would have seen her out on the town, running from her problems, looking for a distraction. But tonight, with Joe's solid presence beside her, she was exhausted. And where had running got her over the years anyway? Right back here in the palace, with her problems exactly where she'd left them.

She took a deep breath in, and as she let it go she released the remaining tension in her arms and legs, concentrating on loosening her fingers and toes. Her eyelids started to droop, and she knew that there was no point fighting it. She was going under, and she didn't want to go alone.

CHAPTER EIGHT

CHARLIE SNORED.

As in she was a serious snorer.

As in it sounded as if he were sharing a bed with a blowing exhaust pipe.

It seemed there was no end to the ways that this woman kept on surprising him.

Not that the snoring was bothering him, particularly. After all, there was no way that he was ever going to be able to get back to sleep. Not with the way that she had turned her back to him and scooted in, tucked inside the circle of his arms, and pressing back against him. Every time that he moved away, she scooted again, fidgeting and squirming in a way that was just…too good. So he'd stopped fighting it and pulled her in close, where at least she kept still, and his self-control had half a chance of winning out over his libido.

When they had fallen asleep last night they had been sitting against the headboard, one of his arms draped loosely around her shoulders. She had been curled up and guarded. Forcing herself into the relaxed state that she couldn't find naturally. He'd felt protective. As if he wanted his arms to keep out all the hurts that seemed to be circling her, waiting to strike. And he'd wanted to get into her head, to show her that the way she saw herself wasn't the way the rest of the world saw her. He certainly didn't see her as damaged goods. As being less than a woman whose insides happened to work differently. But he knew she wouldn't believe him if he told her that.

And more to the point, he didn't want her to think that he had some vested interest in the matter. He'd crossed a line yesterday by suggesting that they sleep together, and, now that he knew how narrow a tight-rope she was walking, he felt like kicking himself for adding more uncertainty and confusion into the mix. They weren't going to sleep together. She had been right—it would make an impossibly complicated situation even worse. He didn't want to lead her on. This was a limited-time deal, and it would end when they thought the timing was right for both of their careers. He wasn't getting involved emotionally—he had known all his adult life that relationships worked best when both parties knew exactly where the boundaries were, exactly what they wanted to get out of it. They would be crazy to go back on those agreements now.

He just had to remind himself that she didn't want that either. She wanted this marriage for what it could do for her career. For the ructions it would cause with her family. And, in light of recent revelations, perhaps she wanted it as a hide-out. An excuse not to meet some suitable guy who might have marriage and babies on his mind.

But that was last night. This morning, 'protective' had well and truly taken a back seat. There were more pressing things on his mind, like the way that her legs fitted so perfectly against his: from ankle to hip they were perfectly matched. Or the way that his arm fitted into the indent of her waist.

Or the fact that if she were to wake up this minute, she'd know exactly how turned on he was, just by sharing a bed fully clothed.

How had his life got so complicated? In bed with a woman he wanted desperately—whom he had already married—but whom he knew he absolutely couldn't have. He cursed quietly, trying to pull his arm out from under her. If he wasn't getting back to sleep, he could be doing something useful, like taking a cold shower and then trying to write.

They were due to fly back to the UK and be up at his parents' house by tea time—they'd made no plans for the rest of the day, and he wondered whether he might be able to find some time alone to work. Last night, Charlie had promised to show him the music room, and the urge to feel the keys of a beautiful grand piano beneath the pads of his fingers had been niggling him since he'd woken. But every time he'd tried to make his escape, Charlie had pressed back against him again and he'd thought...not yet. Just another few minutes.

When she settled, he went for it again, this time pulling his arm out firm and fast, determined not to be seduced into laziness another time. His arm was free at last, and Charlie rolled onto her front, a frown on her face as she turned her head on the pillow first one way and then the other. He felt bad, seeing her restless like that. She had had too little sleep since her overnight stop in Las Vegas, and he knew that for once the black rings under her eyes had nothing to do with eyeliner. He stood watching her for a moment, reminded of that first morning, another night where they had collapsed into bed fully clothed.

He pulled off his T-shirt as he headed for the bathroom, and turned on the shower. He let it run cool before he climbed underneath, concentrating on the sensation of the water hitting his head and shoulders, trying not to think of the beautiful woman lying in his bed.

He wished that they could get out of their second trip this weekend. He wasn't sure that there was a good time to introduce your parents to your fake wife, but he guessed that the morning after a huge row and a heartfelt confession was pretty low on the list. Would Charlie be funny with him this morning? He tried to guess how she would act—whether she'd want to talk more, or pretend that it had never happened and she had never said anything—but had to admit to himself that he didn't even know her well enough to predict that.

By the time that he got out of the shower, she was sitting on the edge of the bed, rubbing at her eyes. So much for some alone time. He secured his towel firmly around his waist before he called out to her.

'Morning.'

Really, was that the best he could come up with? he asked himself.

'Hey,' she said back, tying up her hair and stretching her arms up overhead. 'Have you been up long?'

'Just long enough to shower. I was going to take you up on the offer to play in the music room. Have you got stuff you need to do this morning?'

She frowned, and he realised how that had come

across. But was it really so unreasonable of him to tell her that he needed some space? She had no problem with staying at the office late when she didn't want to see him—this was practically the same thing.

'I was just going to chill. Maybe hang out with Miles for a bit. I've not had a chance to do that since we got back.'

He nodded, trying not to show how claustrophobic he was starting to feel. Was this a normal part of newly married life? he wondered. This discomfort with sharing your personal space?

He crossed to the bureau, where he'd discovered their clothes had been unpacked, and pulled on a T-shirt and a pair of jeans. He'd wondered when he first woke up that morning whether she'd be uncomfortable with him today, he'd not expected when he'd been lying next to her that he would be the one trying to put space between them.

But it wasn't about her, or even about him. It was about feeling inspired to write for the first time all week, and wanting to make the most of it before the motivation deserted him again.

'You don't mind, do you, if I go?'

He was already halfway out of the door as he asked the rhetorical question, hoping that he remembered how to find his way back to the room she'd pointed out to him the day before.

When he eventually saw the piano in front of him, he let out a long sigh of relief. Then sat on the stool and let his fingertips gently caress the keys, pressing first one, then another, and listening to the beautiful tone of the instrument. One to one with a beauty like this, he could forget that he had a wife somewhere in this maze of a palace. Forget all of the complications that she had brought into his life.

He ran up and down a few scales, warming up his hands and fingers, trusting muscle memory to conjure up the long-memorised patterns. He'd been no more than a baby the first time he'd played the piano, he knew. Remembering family photos with him perched on his mother's knee as they picked out a nursery rhyme together.

These scales and arpeggios had taken him through recitals and grade exams. From his perfectly average primary school to the most influential and exclusive private school in the country.

They never changed, and he never faltered when he played them. From the final note of a simple arpeggio, his fingers automatically tipped into a Beethoven piece. His mother's favourite. The one that he'd practised and practised until his hands were so sore they could barely move, and he could see the notes dancing before his eyes as he tried to get to sleep. It was the piece that he'd perfected for his scholarship interview. The one that had opened up a new world of possibilities in his career—and had eventually taught him the truth about human relationships. Okay, so he wasn't writing any new material. Not yet. He let the thought go; saw it carried away by the music. Because this was important too, these building blocks of his art and his craft.

He let his hands pick through a few more pieces, and he stretched his fingers, feeling the suppleness and strength in them now that they were warmed up. He placed his tablet on the music stand, flicked through folders, looking for where he'd jotted down ideas for new lyrics and melodies, stored away for future development.

There'd been nothing new added for a while. Lately, when he'd been working on songs for the album, he'd been much further down the line than this. It was ages since he'd been at square one with a song.

He listened to a few snippets of audio that he'd recorded. A few odd words and phrases that had struck him. None of it was working. He'd been right the first time around when he'd chosen other ideas over these. He shut off his tablet and returned his fingers to the keys. It was only since he'd met Charlie that he'd been so dissatisfied with the songs that he'd written before. Why should that be? He tried to reason it out logically. Because maybe if he could work out why he suddenly hated those songs, he could work out how to write something better. He let his fingers lead, picking out individual notes, and then chords, moving tentatively across the keyboard as he experimented with a few riffs.

A combination of chords caught his ear, and he played them back, listening, seeing where his fingers wanted to trip to next. Maybe that was something…it was something for now, at least. He grabbed a guitar from beside the piano and tried out the same chords. Then picked a melody around them. He turned on the recorder on his iPad. He wasn't in a position to risk losing anything that might be any good. He turned back to the piano and tried the melody again, tried transposing it down an octave, shifting it into another key. He crashed his fingers onto the keyboard harder. There was something there, he knew it. Some potential. He just couldn't crack it. He needed to get through to the nub of the idea to find out what made it good. How to work with it to make it great.

He'd just picked up his guitar again, determined to at least make a start on something good, when the door opened behind him. He spun round on the stool and threw an automatic glare at the door.

Charlie drew up short on the threshold.

'S-sorry,' she stammered, and he knew his annoyance at being disturbed must have shown on his face. 'I brought you a coffee.'

He noticed the tray in her hands and thought twice about his initial instinct to kick her straight out. Maybe he could do with the caffeine, something to get his brain in gear.

'Thanks,' he said grudgingly. 'You can come in— you don't have to stay in the doorway.'

He set the guitar down and turned back to the piano, hoping that she would get the hint, but, instead of hearing the door shut behind him, he was being not so gently nudged to the side of his stool while Charlie held two cups of coffee precariously over the keyboard.

'That sounded interesting,' she said. 'What was it?'

He fidgeted beside her, wishing she'd just go and leave him to it.

'It's nothing. Just playing around with a few ideas. Trying to generate some inspiration.'

She plonked herself down beside him and he held a breath as the hot dark liquid sloshed dangerously close to the piano. Somehow, miraculously, the coffee didn't spill. 'What for?' she asked. 'I thought the songs for the album were all done.'

He shrugged. He really didn't want to go into this now. 'They were.'

'Were?' She finally placed the drinks down on the top of the piano and turned towards him, trying to catch his eye. 'Are they not any more? What happened to them?'

He kept his eyes on the keyboard, his fingers tracing soundless patterns in black and ivory. 'Nothing happened to them. I'm just not sure that I want to include all of them. There's one or two I'm looking at rotating out.' He kept his voice casual, trying not to show the fear and concern behind this simple statement. It didn't work. Charlie's back was suddenly ramrod straight.

'And you're telling me this now? How long have you been thinking this?'

'Are you asking as my wife or as a representative of Avalon?'

'I thought they were the same thing.' The monosyllables were spoken with a false calm, giving them a staccato rhythm. But then she softened, leaned forward and sipped at her coffee, looking unusually thoughtful before she spoke.

'What can I do to help?'

His first instinct was to tell her to leave him in peace—that was the best thing she could do for him. But the timing of this creative crisis suggested that she was in some way to blame for his current dissatisfaction with his work. So maybe she could be the solution too. 'What about a co-writer? I can call a couple of people. Maybe someone to bounce ideas off.'

'I'm not sure,' he said eventually. 'I was happy with

everything before we went to Vegas. I didn't feel like
I had to do anything more to it.'

'And now?'

'I don't know. I listened to the demo when we were
on the plane. I reckon half the tracks need to go.'

She visibly paled. But to her credit she clearly tem-
pered her response. Regardless of the fact that losing
half the tracks would throw a complete spanner into
the plan that she and Rich had been working on for
recording and releasing the album.

'Can we listen together?' she asked. 'You can talk
me through what you're worried about.'

He hesitated. No one outside the band had heard the
new tracks. The record companies that had been so
keen to fight over them had taken their history of big
sellers, and not insisted on listening to the new material. Letting his songs loose on the world was hard
enough when he was happy with his work. Letting
someone listen to something he knew wasn't right…
It was like revealing the ugliest part of his body for
close inspection.

But this was what Charlie did. He knew her reputation. He knew the artists and albums that she had
worked on. She got results, and her artists trusted her.
Maybe he should as well. He'd spent the last week with
his head buried in the sand, trying to ignore the problem. It was time to try something different.

He reached for the tablet, ready to cue up the demo,
but Charlie stopped him with a hand on his arm.

'Why don't you play?' she asked, nodding at the
piano keyboard in front of them. 'One-man show.'

He shrugged. It didn't make much difference to

him. The songs weren't good enough, and it wouldn't matter how she heard them.

He rattled through the first bars of a track he picked at random. Trying to show her with his clumsy hands on the keys how far from good the song was.

She didn't say a word as he played, but her knee jigged in time with the music, and as he reached the middle eight her head nodded too.

He reached the end and looked over at her—ready for the verdict. 'I don't hate it,' she said equivocally. 'Are there lyrics?'

'The chorus maybe. The verses are definitely going.'

She nodded thoughtfully.

'Well, let's hear it before we do anything drastic.'

He returned his hands to the keys and took a deep breath, straightening his back until his posture rivalled hers. He'd been taught to sing classically at school, and there was a lot to be said for getting the basics right.

It had been a long time since he'd sung to someone one-to-one, with just a piano for company. In fact, he couldn't remember ever sitting like this with someone. With so much intimacy.

A lump lodged itself in his throat. Was he really nervous? He'd sung to her the first night that he'd met her. Spotted her on the side of the stage halfway through the gig and made eye contact. Had that been it? The moment that everything had changed for them?

There had been thousands in the audience that night. He'd played at festivals where the audience stretched further than he could see. Just a couple of days ago he'd sung with her in front of a growing crowd of Londoners. It hadn't occurred to him that day to be nervous.

But the thought of singing with her sitting beside him at the piano was bringing him out in a sweat.

She waited, letting the silence grow. Waiting for him to fill it. He pressed a couple of keys experimentally then worked his way into the intro.

Her thigh was pressed against his leg; he felt the pressure of it as he worked the piano pedal. He closed his eyes, hoping that banishing her from at least one of his senses would get his focus back where it needed to be.

He took a deep breath and half sang the first words of the verse. His hands moved without hesitation and he felt his voice grow stronger as he moved from verse to chorus and back again. He winced as he sang the second verse, aware that the lyrics were trite and cliché.

He'd written about love. Or what he thought love might feel like as a thirty-something. The more he thought about the only time he'd thought he'd been in love, the more uncertain he was that that was what he had really felt for Arabella. Sure, it had been intense at the time. There were songs that he'd written then that still tugged at the heart strings. But something told him that love was meant to be...bigger than that. The connection he felt with Charlie right this second, for example. That was big. In fact, he couldn't quite decide if it was warm and enveloping big, or heavy and suffocating big. All he knew was that it was scary big. And a million miles from what he had felt for Arabella when he was eighteen.

And of course all that was seriously bad news—

because big scary feelings did not make for a happy marriage of convenience. He tackled the middle eight with energy, abandoning his original lyrics, and just singing what came into his head. Trying to lose himself in the notes and not overthink.

He sang the last chorus as if there were no one else listening, new lyrics streaming through him as if he were a vessel for something greater than him.

He let his hands rest on the keyboard when he finished, and kept his eyes locked on them as well. He couldn't let her see. It was too dangerous. Too risky to the arrangement that they had both agreed to. He waited until he could be sure his expression was neutral before he picked up his mug from the table beside the piano and took a sip.

'So?' he asked, not sure that he wanted to know what she thought of it.

'Please, please tell me that's not on the cull list.'

He took a second to really look at her. Her eyes were wide, almost surprised. Her bottom lip was redder and fuller than the top, as if she had been biting on it and had only just let it go. He imagined that if he looked hard enough he would be able to see the shadowed indentation of her top teeth still there. That if he leaned down and brushed his own lips against it it would be hot and welcoming.

'I'm not sure about the first half,' she went on at last, 'but the lyrics in the second? The bridge? That last chorus. That's winning stuff, Joe. That's straight to number one and stay there. That's break the internet stuff. I can't believe you were going to toss that.'

'The first half though.'

'The first half we can fix. Anyone who can write the second half can fix the first, I promise you that.'

He stayed quiet for a long moment. He could ask himself what had just happened, but the truth was that he already knew. She had happened. She was what was different about his writing. He finally had the inspiration that he needed.

He had no doubt that he still had a lot of work to do, but maybe working with Charlie would be a good thing. It had certainly helped with these lyrics; they'd worked their way into his brain as he was singing, reaching his lips as if he were channelling them, not writing them.

He launched into the opening chords of another song. One he was more sure of. He tweaked the words as he sang, reaching for more unusual choices, to pinpoint emotions he'd only been able to sketch before.

He glanced across at Charlie and she was smiling. A weight of pressure lifted slightly; a measure of dread fell away. They could fix this. Together.

More than anything, this was what really brought it home to him what they'd done. They had tied themselves together in every possible way. His career and his personal life were indivisible now.

For so long 'personal life' had been synonymous with 'sex life'. When Charlie had stipulated *no cheating* he'd known that it was a no brainer. Of course he wouldn't sleep with anyone else. But had he really thought it through? He'd voluntarily signed up for months of celibacy. Maybe years. Perhaps he had assumed unconsciously that 'no cheating' and celibacy weren't necessarily the same thing.

Everything seemed to keep coming back to that

question—even though they had agreed right from the start that that wasn't going to happen. And now he had acknowledged that his feelings for her were so much more serious than he had originally thought. Had he really thought the word 'love' earlier?

He finished the song on autopilot and knew from Charlie's expression that she could feel the difference. Her smile was more polite and that sparkle had gone from her eyes.

'Lots of potential in that one,' she said diplomatically. 'Definitely one we can work on.' She glanced at her watch and had a final sip of her coffee.

'I should let you work. Are you sure I've packed the right stuff for your parents' house? Because I can go out and pick something up if I need to.'

'Well, you probably can leave your tiara here,' he said with a smile, so she knew it wasn't a dig. 'Just something for dinner tonight. Doesn't need to be as fancy as at your place.'

Had he really just referred to the palace they were sitting in as 'your place'? Perhaps he was getting more used to this royal thing than he had thought. Getting used to her.

It was getting harder and harder to remember they were only in this to forward both of their careers. The lines between business and personal were blurring to the point that he couldn't see them any more. And that was dangerous, because the further they moved away from that simple transactional relationship, the more at risk his heart and his feelings would be.

'And make sure you've got something you don't

mind getting dirty if we're going to that festival. I'm not going to spend the whole time in VIP.'

She rolled her eyes.

'You so don't need to worry about that.'

CHAPTER NINE

CHARLIE CRAWLED UNDER the duvet and across the tiny double bed until she was almost pressed against the wall. Really, the sleeping arrangements in this marriage kept going from bad to worse.

'Do you think they liked me?' she whispered as Joe unbuttoned his shirt and pulled it back over his shoulders, revealing those tattoos she was still getting to know. He pulled a T-shirt from his bag, and then they were covered again. She almost spoke up and asked him not to, but stopped herself. Cosy sleeping arrangements or not, she had no rights over his body. No authority to ask for a few more minutes to look at his skin.

'They loved you,' he replied, sitting on the side of the bed and pulling off his jeans. 'Of course they did. What did you expect?'

'You know what I expected,' she said, tucking her hand under her pillow and turning on her side to face him. He slid between the sheets and lay beside her, mirroring her posture until they were almost nose to nose in the bed.

'And I told you that you didn't have to worry,' he said, though she didn't quite remember it that way.

Why should she care anyway? In a few months these would be her ex in-laws. She wouldn't ever see them again.

He wondered whether his parents had suspected that there was something off about their relationship. But they had been so distracted by Charlie, and protocol and the whole Princess thing that they hadn't seemed to notice anything.

He could feel the warmth of her under the cool sheets, and for a second was flooded by the memory of waking up with her that morning, with her legs fitting so closely to his. Did she even know what she had done?

'Did you know you're an aggressive spooner?' The question just slipped out of him. She looked shocked for a second, but then had to stifle a laugh.

'What's that meant to mean?'

'It means you were grinding into me like a horny teenager this morning. I didn't know where to put my hands.'

Her mouth fell open. 'I did not.'

He couldn't resist smiling. 'You so did. Forced me out of bed.'

Not strictly the truth, of course. He'd lain there so much longer than was a good idea, just soaking up the feel of her.

'A gentleman would have moved away,' she said.

'A lady wouldn't have reversed straight back in again every time I did.'

She kicked out at his leg. 'You're totally making this up.'

'Why would I do that?' he asked.

'I don't know. Maybe you want me to do it again.'

'Would you?' The very air around them seemed to be heavy with anticipation as he waited for her to answer.

'I asked first,' she said at last, deliberately not answering his question.

Was she serious? Were they really talking about this as if it might happen? She looked as if she wanted it. Her eyes were wide, her lips moist and slightly parted. One hand was tucked under her cheek and the other below her pillow. He didn't dare look any further down. He'd seen her pull on a pyjama top and shorts earlier, and he knew that gravity would be making the view south of her throat way too distracting. Too tempting.

'Maybe,' he replied at last.

Such a simple word. Tonight, such a dangerous one.

She turned her back to him but didn't make any effort to come closer. Was she testing him? Seeing if she came halfway whether he would come forward the other half.

With her back to him it was safe at last to look down. From where she'd tied her hair in a messy knot, the ink at the nape of her neck, down the length of her long, elegant spine. The tapering of her waist disappeared into the shadows under the sheets.

If he reached for her, would that be the point of no return?

Would the touch of his hand on her waist be the same as telling her that he wanted a relationship? That he loved her?

Were those statements true?

He wanted her. He knew that. That was the easy question. But how many times did he have to tell himself that having sex with the woman pretending to be his wife was a bad idea? That it could never be just sex, because it was already so much more than that.

What would she want from him in return? More than sex meant thinking with his heart, rather than his head, and that had got him badly hurt—and embarrassed—before.

He had tried his hardest to learn his lesson after Arabella, but even that humiliation hadn't been enough for him to spot the woman who was only with him so she could sell his secrets to the highest bidder.

Could Charlie really want him for who he was, rather than what he could do for her?

He couldn't remember ever being more turned on, more tempted than he was right now, but he had to be smarter than that.

Taking what he wanted came with a price tag. But tonight he couldn't be certain what the price was, or whether he would be willing to pay. And so as much as it killed him to do it, he turned over, pulled the duvet high on his chest and squeezed his eyes shut.

He heard a rustle behind him and tried not to imagine Charlie lifting her head from the pillow and looking over at him, wondering what had happened. He didn't want to see her confusion as he cut dead their flirtation. Her head hit the pillow hard, and the duvet pulled across to her side of the bed.

'Night, then,' she said, nicking territory and duvet as she spread out her limbs.

He was so tempted to retaliate. Almost as tempted as he had been to kiss her. To be pulled back into their banter. But he kept silent and still, feigning sleep.

* * *

Had she imagined it, last night? she wondered, trying to decide if she should be blaming Joe or her over-active imagination for what had happened. Why, oh, why had she had to be so insistent that they didn't have sex? Because that was where this relationship had been heading, before they were so stupid as to get married.

If they'd done the sensible thing and had a one-night stand that first night, like any self-respecting party girl meeting a rock star, they could be thousands of miles apart and a week into forgetting it all by now. Instead she had been shacked up at her new in-laws', trapped in the world's smallest double bed and ready to explode from frustration.

Surely her imagination wasn't good enough to have imagined that flirtation last night. Joe was the one who had brought up the subject of spooning, and when she'd decided she was so goddamned turned on that she didn't care any more whether it was a good idea or not, and all but wiggled her arse at him, he'd literally turned his back on her—the body-language equivalent of 'thanks, but no thanks'. Only less polite.

So when she'd woken first this morning, there was no way she was going to hang around for him to wake up and rehash the whole thing. One rejection was plenty, thanks. She'd known as soon as she told him about her infertility that she was taking herself well and truly off the market as far as he was concerned. It had been stupid to expect any other reaction to her advances than the one that she had got.

So she'd got up and found Joe's mum already in the kitchen, and before she quite knew what was happen-

ing there was a cup of strong tea in front of her and
the smell of bacon coming from the stove.

'Did you sleep well, then, love? Oh, I shouldn't
ask that really, should I? Not to a newly-wed. And
that bed in there's so small. Not even a proper double.
Hardly room to—'

'Shall I put the kettle on?'

Charlie breathed a deep sigh of relief—not the emotion she'd expected to feel when setting eyes on Joe
that morning. He leaned in the kitchen doorway, colour high on his cheeks as he crossed his arms and
gave his mum a look.

'No need, love.' His mum bustled round, pouring
another cup from the pot and setting it on the table
for Joe.

'I was just saying to Charlie—you are sure it's okay
for me to call you Charlie?' She didn't stop for an answer. 'I was just saying that the bed in your room.
It's hardly big enough for you on your own, never
mind for the two of you great tall things. We'll have
to do something about that. Maybe you should have
our room.'

Joe kissed his mum on the cheek and extracted the
tongs from her clasped fist.

'You're babbling, Mum. Sit down and drink your
tea.'

His mum sat and he shot a glance over her head to
Charlie, who smiled conspiratorially in return.

'You sure you don't want to come with us today,
Mum?' Joe asked as he served up the bacon sarnies.

'Me in all that mud? You must be mad, love.'

'Mud? It's twenty-five degrees outside. Not every
festival is Glastonbury in the rain, you know.'

'I've seen these things on the telly, love. Maybe if you were playing, but I'll give it a miss. You two love birds don't want me and your father there playing gooseberry anyway.'

Joe rolled his eyes as he picked up a sandwich, 'Mum, there'll be thousands of people there. It's not like we're expecting to be alone.'

'Don't be obtuse, Joe. You know full well it's not the same.'

'I feel awful shooting off like this,' Charlie said. They'd sat down to dinner barely an hour after they had arrived last night, and she'd been so beat after four courses and dessert wine that they'd retreated to bed long before midnight.

'Don't be daft, love. You young people are so busy, and Joe's already told me how hard you work.' Interesting…when had he told her that? 'It's been lovely that you made it up here with everything that you've both got going on. Don't go and spoil it by overstaying your welcome.'

Charlie smiled, surprised by how at home she felt with Joe's parents already. As if she really were becoming part of the family. Probably best that they were leaving this afternoon, then. Before this became another reminder of how hard it was becoming to keep reality and pretence straight in her head.

They climbed into Joe's car, chased by kisses and offers of baked goods for the journey. The festival was out in the countryside, about half an hour from his parents' house. Thank God it was no further, Charlie thought, twenty minutes of isolated confinement later. There was a limit to the tension that her body could take, and she was rapidly approaching it.

They were going to have to talk about what had happened last night. She'd hoped that maybe they could just ignore it—forget it had happened. And then his mum had been so funny with her babbling that she'd thought that they'd taken a shortcut and moved past it. But after breakfast they had been back in Joe's tiny bedroom, trying to pack their bags without touching. Moving around each other as if they were magnets with poles pointing towards one another. And she knew it would take next to nothing for those poles to flip and they would be back where they had been last night, drawn together, with only their self-control and better judgement fighting against the inevitability of the laws of nature.

She rested her chin on her hand; her elbow propped on the door as she gazed out of the window. They had barely spoken a word since they'd climbed into the car.

'Have you played here?' Charlie asked, needing the tension broken—before it broke them. The question counted as work. Talking about the band and work was safe. It was the only safe zone they had.

'Two years ago,' Joe replied, his eyes still locked on the road. They hadn't left it for a second since they'd left his parents' driveway. 'Were you here?' he asked.

'Yeah, with one of my artists. I didn't see you.'

'I wonder how many times that's happened,' he said, and for the first time he glanced over at her.

She furrowed her brow. 'That what's happened?'

'That our paths have crossed and we've not seen each other.' His eyes were back on the road now, but he looked different somehow, as if he was having to work harder to keep them there.

She tried to keep her voice casual, not wanting to

acknowledge the way the tension had just ratcheted up another notch. 'I don't know. Must be loads if you think about it.'

'I can't believe it,' he said.

She looked over at him again, to find him watching her. They'd pulled up at a junction, but his attention was all on her, rather than looking for a gap in the traffic crossing their path.

'Why?'

'Because...*this*. Because of the atmosphere in this car for the last twenty minutes. Because of how it felt in Vegas, knowing that you were watching me. I just can't imagine being in a room with you and not feeling that you were there.'

How *what* had felt in Vegas? She thought back to that moment when she was watching him from the side of the stage and their eyes had met. He had felt that too?

He reached for her hand. She considered for a split second whether she should pull away. It was what he'd done last night. She'd reached out to him, and he'd known it was too dangerous. A bad idea.

Could she be as strong as he had been?

His hand cupped her cheek, and she knew she could. She could be strong and resist, as he had. But maybe she could be a different kind of strong. Maybe looking at all the reasons this was a bad idea, all the reasons it was a terrifying choice, and *still* choosing it, maybe that was strong too.

She leaned forward across the centre console, sliding her hands into his hair and bringing their mouths together.

Her body sighed in relief and desire as his tongue

met hers, simultaneously relaxed and energised by this feeling of…perfection. This was it. This sense of fitting together.

A horn blared behind them and she sprang back, reeling from her realisation.

He grimaced as he slid the car into gear and pulled away, with just a slight lurch as the clutch found its biting point. This was what she'd been waiting for; and it was what she'd been dreading. She'd been running from it her whole adult life. She didn't want to be completed. She didn't want to belong with someone. Her one-off dates and casual boyfriends—she never had to tell them she was infertile. Never had to spell out the future that they would never have. Never had to explain that if she shacked up with someone long-term and the babies didn't come that they'd be hounded by the press and his virility would be called into question. Their bins would be searched and their doctors harassed. Her body had been public property since before she was born. Anyone who wanted to spend their life with her would be volunteering for the same deal—who in their right mind would do that?

Ten more minutes. She had to survive just ten more minutes in this space with a man she was finding it impossible to remember to resist. They showed their passes at the gate and, in silence, Joe directed the car through the gates and down a rucked track towards the VIP parking, waved along by marshals. When they arrived, Joe pulled on the handbrake and opened the door, while she gathered her things from the footwell. Her door opened, and Joe was there, holding out his hand like a cartoon prince.

'Very gallant,' she said lightly, knowing that her

confusion was causing a line to appear between her eyebrows.

He handed her down from the car, and as her feet reached the ground he pressed her back against the rear door, one of his knees nudging between hers. His hand caught at the ends of her hair and he pulled gently, bringing a gasp of pleasure and anticipation to her lips. She tilted her head to one side as she met his eyes, and saw passion and desire. Another inch closer and she was trapped. Car behind, hard body in front, and still that hand in her hair, pulling to one side now, exposing the pulse of her throat. She licked her lips in anticipation and closed her eyes as Joe moved closer. First cool lips descended and then a flicker of warm tongue in a spot that made her shudder. The butterfly caresses of his mouth traced up the side of her neck, then suddenly down to her shoulder, where her shirt had slipped, exposing her collarbone. The sharp clamp of his teeth on her sensitive skin made her gasp in shock. But the noise was lost as his lips were suddenly on her mouth, and his tongue was tangling with hers.

She wound her fingers in his hair, levering herself a little higher, desperate to bring their bodies in line. Cursing her decision to wear flat biker boots instead of her usual heels. Who cared about practicalities when there was a man like this to kiss?

Joe pressed into her with an urgency she'd not felt from him before. An urgency that made her wonder how spacious the back of his car was, and how much faith they wanted to put in the tinted windows.

It was as his lips left hers, to dip again to her neck, that she heard it.

Click.

Her eyes snapped open and she pushed at Joe's chest. She didn't have to look far over his shoulder to see the photographer. She took a second, breathing heavily and trying to remember that she was meant to be pleased about the press involvement in her life for once, before she spoke.

'You knew he was there?' she asked quietly, her lips touching Joe's ear. Her calves burned as she stretched up on tiptoes, but she wasn't ready to back down, back away, just yet.

'Spotted him as I got out of the car,' Joe whispered back.

Which explained the little display he'd just put on, then. Thank God she hadn't suggested taking the party back into the car.

'You okay?' he asked, and she forced a smile, pushing slightly on his chest and trying to regain her equilibrium. Desperate for a balance between trying to convince the photographer that that kiss had rocked her world, and not letting Joe see the truth of it.

'I'm fine.'

Their encounter with photographers at the airport seemed a long time ago and a long way away. She'd barely noticed over the past week that they hadn't been harassed by the paparazzi as much as she'd thought they might be—perhaps her mother had had a discreet hand in that. But there was no way that even her mother could keep them away here. The reality of the situation struck her—something she'd not counted on when she and Joe had been making plans for seeing family and work: they were going to be on display, all day. They couldn't afford to slip up. She closed her eyes and kissed Joe lightly on the mouth, telling herself it was just her way of warming up for the performance she knew that they had to nail.

'Want to go listen to some music?' she asked.

'No,' he said with a smile. 'I want to stay here and kiss you.'

She couldn't help grinning in return, not even trying to work out if it was for real or for show. Leaning back against this car in the sunshine, kissing a superhot guy—that sounded pretty good to her too. But the moment was gone, and she couldn't lose the photographer from the corner of her eye.

'You're so going to get me fired,' she said. 'I'm meant to be working.'

'Well, then, jump to it, slacker. I'm not going to be one of those husbands who expects you to stay home and play house. Get out there and earn your keep.' He took a step back from her, and she slid her hands behind her butt. She knew real life was waiting for them, but what was just a few more minutes?

'I'd make a lousy housewife.'

'Oh, I don't know,' he said with a laugh. 'Some people like the hovel look. I hear it's big this year.'

She poked him in the ribs and laughed back.

'I'm not that bad.'

'You're worse.' He turned and stood beside her, draping a casual arm around her shoulder and pressing a kiss to her temple.

It would be too easy to take this little scene at face value, she knew. A week ago she'd be giving herself a stern talking-to. That all this was for the benefit of the photographers and the eager public. But today... today the line was more blurred. Her first thought had been that Joe was just putting on a show, but they had been moving so much closer for the last few days that she knew that some part of it was real. Their performance, it didn't feel like some random invention—it was more... Maybe it was what their relationship might have been if their lives were simpler. If she weren't a princess with a wonky reproductive system. If he formed actual emotional relationships rather than using women to get what he needed. Would it work? she couldn't help but wonder. If they had been two ordinary people, with ordinary lives, would they have been happy together?

'Come on, then,' she said at last, pushing herself away from the car, trying to shake the thought from her mind. It didn't matter if it would work that way, because they weren't those people, and never could be. Joe moved with her, his arm still around her shoulders as they made their way into the festival.

As Joe had promised, they were in the VIP zone for no more than half an hour before she was dragging him through a dusty field of festivalgoers, littered with abandoned plastic cups. She refused to watch the band from the side of the stage—she wanted the full experience, to see what she would be working with if she ever got this band to agree to sign with her.

The Sunday afternoon vibe was chilled and relaxed, with families dancing to the music, kids on shoulders, or eating on picnic rugs on the ground. Groups of people sat on the floor, passing round cigarettes and bottles of drink.

The sun was hot on her back, and she was pleased she'd pulled on one of Joe's long-sleeved shirts with her denim shorts, protecting her shoulders from burning.

For a while they just wandered, soaking up the atmosphere of a group of people united by a passion for music. Joe's fingers were loosely wound between hers, keeping her anchored to him. To their story. The impression of that kiss was still on her lips, and had been refreshed every now and again with a brief re-enactment. They couldn't just keep an eye out for cameras and people watching. For the first time since they had arrived back in the UK, they were truly having to live out their fake marriage in full view of the public.

And the weirdest part…it wasn't weird at all. In fact, it felt completely natural to be walking round with her hand in his. The way he threw an arm over her shoulders if they stopped to talk to someone. For once, she decided she actually liked being in flat shoes. Liked that his extra height meant that she was tucked into his body when he pulled her to him. It felt good—warm, safe, protected. Everything she'd been telling herself she didn't want to be.

'Want to find something to eat?' Joe asked when the band they had been watching finished.

'Dirty burger?' she asked, with a quirk of her brow.

'Whatever turns you on.'

You know what turns me on. The response was right there on the tip of her tongue, but she held it back, not trusting where it might lead them.

'Come on,' she said, pulling him towards a van selling virtuous-looking flatbreads and falafel. 'These look amazing. I'm having a healthy lunch, then I'm going in search of cider.'

With lunches in hand, they picked their way across to another stage, where Casual Glory, the band Charlie wanted to see, were just warming up at the start of their set.

'I saw these guys in a pub last year,' she told Joe. 'I wanted to sign them then and there. But then all the suits got involved and… I don't know, maybe they got spooked but somehow it didn't come off. I don't want to let them out of my grasp again.'

'They're still not signed?' Joe asked.

She dropped to the floor and sat cross-legged, watching the band while she ate.

'Free spirits. Didn't like the corporate stuff. And I'm not sure what I do about that, to be honest, because the music business doesn't really get much more laid-back than with Avalon.'

'You think you can get them to change their minds?'

Charlie nodded. 'I'm going to. I'm just not sure how yet.'

'You're not going to marry him, right?'

She laughed under her breath.

'One husband's already too many, thanks.'

He wound an arm around her neck, pulling her close and planting a kiss on her shoulder.

'You're right: they're good,' Joe said after they finished another song. 'Loads of potential. You should bag them.'

'Yeah, well, try telling them that,' she joked.

'I will, if you want. Are we going to say hi when they're done?'

'That's the plan.'

She leaned against his shoulder, soaking up the sun warming the white cotton of her shirt. Her head fell to rest against Joe's and she shut her eyes so she could appreciate the music more.

'Tired?' Joe asked in her ear, and she 'mmm'ed in response. She couldn't remember the last time she'd had a properly restful night's sleep. Turned out being married was more likely to give you black bags than a newly-wed glow.

'Come here, then.'

Joe pushed her away for a moment, then slung his leg around until she was sitting between his thighs, her back pulled in against his front. She relaxed into him, shutting out all thoughts of whether this was a good idea or not. Just letting the music wash through her. Soak into her skin and her brain.

'Comfortable?' Joe whispered in her ear.

'Too comfortable.'

She felt more than heard him chuckle behind her as his arms tightened. A press of lips behind her ear. A kiss on the side of her neck. A tingle and a clench low in her abdomen: a silent request for more and a warning of danger ahead.

Instead of heeding it, she let her head fall to one side, just as she had done by his car. They were in public, she reasoned with herself. There was only so far this could go. It was all a part of their performance.

'How about now?' he asked, pulling her hair over to her other shoulder. 'Feeling sleepy still?'

God, he was driving her insane.

'Like I could drop off at any moment.'

He growled behind her and she smiled, revelling in the way she was learning to push the boundaries of his self-control. His hand in her hair was tough and uncompromising now, and she let out a gasp as he pulled her back slowly, steadily, never so hard that it hurt. Making her choose to come with him rather than forcing. She opened her mouth to him without question. The hand still round her waist flattened on her belly, pressing her closer still.

She let out a low sigh of desire and her arm lifted to wind round his neck, opening her body. Was Joe controlling her without her realising? She didn't remember meaning to do it. Then his hand dropped from her hair and cupped her jaw: the kiss gentler now, sweeter.

She opened her eyes and smiled back at him, and she knew her eyes must look glazed, dopey. 'All right, I'm not likely to sleep in the next year. Is that what you wanted?'

'I'll take it,' he said with a smug smile. She leaned back into him again, languor and desire fighting to control her limbs.

CHAPTER TEN

'I WISH WE didn't have to go back tonight,' Joe said, stretching out his legs and leaning back on his elbows. Maybe it was the sun making him lazy, making him feel that he never wanted to leave this place. Charlie moved so she was lying to one side of him, her head propped on her hand.

'I thought you'd be dying to get back in your studio,' she said. 'You seemed all…inspired and stuff yesterday.'

'I am. I do want to write.' He'd had ideas swirling round his brain for two days; when they'd been at his parents' house he'd been desperate for a bit of space and time to try and get them down on paper, or recorded on his phone. But since they had arrived at the festival, since that kiss, everything felt different. 'I can't remember the last time that I was relaxed like this. The last time I felt still. I like it.'

'You can be still in London,' Charlie said.

He shrugged—or as best he could with his body weight resting on his elbows. 'I don't know if I can. Or maybe it's that I know that I won't.'

She sat up and gave him a serious look. 'Not every day can be Sunday afternoon at a festival. Real life is still out there, you know.' Of course he knew, but somehow he was managing not to care.

'I do know. But it feels that it can't get us here.'

'What are you worried about "getting us"?' she asked.

Why did they have to think about that now? Why couldn't they just enjoy this? He wished he knew. He'd just told her he felt still—what he'd wanted to say was that he felt happy. Content. He'd wanted to say that he'd stopped trying to work out if what she was saying was loaded. A way to get something more than they'd agreed from their arrangement.

Here at the festival, life was simpler. He could kiss and touch her. Laugh with her. Treat her as the woman he was in love with. No holding back.

Was that really it? Was that what was making him feel so…serene? Because he didn't have to pretend not to love her?

His phone chirped and he fished it out of his pocket, grateful for the distraction from his own thoughts.

'Amazing, they're here. Some friends of mine have stopped by,' he told Charlie. 'Want to say hi after you've done your work stuff?'

'Sure, why not? Who are they?'

'Owen's band supported us at a couple of gigs a few years ago. We hung out a bit. His wife's lovely too. You'll like them.'

He stood and pulled her up as Casual Glory finished their final number. His arm fell round her shoulders in that way that felt so completely natural. Perhaps it was just their height, he thought. He'd told her that he'd liked that she was so tall, but her flat biker boots today meant that he was a few inches

taller than her. Or maybe it was something else—
something to do with escaping their real lives and real
pressures. They were meant to be putting on a show
to the public today—but in reality it had given them
permission to stop pretending for the first time since
they had woken up married.

They passed through security to the VIP area,
and Charlie headed straight for the lead singer of
Casual Glory and gave him a hug. Joe hung back a
little, watching her work, impressed. She didn't just
schmooze—though she did compliment them on
their awesome set. She also challenged them, asked
them about their goals and their hopes for the future.
Showed them subtly that she would be their ally if
they wanted to make that a reality. And she made sure
that each member of the band left with her business
card in their pocket and some serious thinking to do.

Charlie cut the conversation short before they out-
stayed their welcome, and they headed over towards
the bar. He surveyed the room once he had a jar of
craft cider in hand—it was full of people resting their
feet, snatching glasses of free champagne, and trying
to get a sneaky snap of the VVIP whose hen do was
in full drunken flow in the corner.

He tapped the side of his glass, wondering whether
he had missed his friend, and whether they should
commandeer one of the golf buggies to go in search
of him when he recognised Owen's shaggy, shoulder-
length hair and waved at him from across the crowd,
squeezing Charlie's hand at the same time. He wondered for a split second whether he had done the right
thing in looking Owen up, but it was too late to back

out now. Owen turned and saw him, waving from across the tent.

'Hey,' Joe called out, making a move towards his friend.

Charlie followed the direction of Joe's wave and saw Owen—she recognised him from a gig she'd been to last year. And then a blonde woman—polished and beautiful—stepped from behind him, a chubby baby settled on her hip. Charlie's stomach lurched and she felt bile rise in her throat. Joe should have warned her.

He was the one who had called her out on how uncomfortable she had been acting around her sister and her kids. He had to know just how hard this would be for her. Especially with the way that talking about everything had been tearing open old wounds recently.

She realised that she'd come to a halt, and only Joe's hold on her hand pulled her forwards.

'Owen, hey, man. Alice, you look gorgeous.' Joe shook his friend's hand and kissed Alice's cheek. 'Guys, this is Charlie.' He'd pulled her to him and wrapped his arm around her waist. He was putting her through this and he didn't even care—didn't even think to try and understand how much this was hurting her.

Alice leaned in and kissed her cheek and Owen shook her hand.

'Congratulations, you two!' Alice said with a friendly smile. 'I can't believe someone's tied this guy down. You deserve a medal, Charlie. I can't wait to hear all the details.'

Charlie tried to return her smile, but felt her facial muscles stiffen into a grimace.

'And who's this?' Joe asked, chucking the baby's cheek and being rewarded by a belly laugh. 'Looks like we should be the ones saying congrats.' Charlie sensed something slightly forced in his cheerful tone. What was he up to?

'This is Lucy,' Alice said, and shifted the baby to hold her out to Joe. 'Want to hold her?'

'Are you sure?' He took the baby awkwardly and held her up to his face, pulling funny faces. Joe with a baby. Charlie watched him closely, trying to work out what he was feeling. His smile was open and straight-forward, and she envied him for it. She wished she could enjoy the sweet, heavy weight of a baby in her arms without being haunted by the inevitable regret and sadness.

'That must have moved quickly, then,' Joe was say-ing. She struggled to follow the conversation—feeling as if she had missed some vital part. 'The last time I saw you, you were still mired in bureaucracy trying to bring this one home.'

'Our social worker was awesome,' Alice replied. She turned to Lucy with another megawatt smile. 'We've adopted Lucy,' she said.

And the bottom fell out of Charlie's stomach. She stumbled, and the only thing to grab hold of to stop her falling was Joe. Again, goddamn him.

Had he planned this? Manipulated her into meet-ing this gorgeous family, with their beautiful baby?

Of course he had—that was what she'd heard in his voice. He'd been planning this behind her back. So after everything he had said about her being enough for any man just as she was, and it didn't matter if she could have children or not, here was the proof that he felt otherwise. She'd always known that it was always going to be true in the end.

It was as if he'd not listened to a word she'd said since they'd met. As if he didn't know her.

'L-lovely to meet you,' Charlie managed to stammer, and then she turned and started walking. She didn't even care where she was going. She just had to get out of there. Away from Alice and her gorgeous baby. Away from Joe and his lies and manipulations.

She reached sunshine and fresh air but kept walking, wanting as much distance as she could get between her and Joe. She couldn't remember where the car was so she just walked out. Out as far as she could. Tears threatened at the edges of her eyeliner, but she knew that she must not let them fall. Even now, they had to make this deception work, or what had been the point of any of it? She spotted the VIP car park and headed towards Joe's car. She just wanted to not be here.

The keys. Damn it. Well, maybe there would be someone else leaving and she could hitch a ride—

'Charlie!'

She recognised Joe's voice, her body responded to it—to him—immediately, but she fought it and kept walking. He couldn't possibly have anything to say to her that she would want to hear.

'Charlie, stop. Please!'

Ahead of her, someone was staring at them. She wanted so much not to care. To be a nobody—unrecognisable in a crowd. Someone no one knew or cared about. But she stopped, because she wasn't that person. She could never be that person.

Joe caught up with her, rested his forearms on her

shoulders. God, if he asked her what was wrong, that was it. She was running and crying and she didn't care who saw.

'I'm sorry,' he said. 'I should have warned you that they have a baby.'

She shrugged his arms off her shoulders. He was trying, but he still didn't get it. 'I'm not angry about the baby, Joe. Babies don't make me mad. I'm angry because you tried to manipulate me.'

'Manipulate you? How?'

He'd raised his voice, but then looked around. Remembered where they were.

'Maybe we should talk about this in the car.'

She narrowed her eyes. Right—they needed to protect their secret. He climbed into the car and she sat on the passenger seat, looking straight out ahead, not able to face looking at him properly.

'I should have warned you about the baby,' he said again. 'But I thought I was doing something good. I thought seeing how happy they are to have her would help. That they're a family, even if not by conventional means.'

'So what are you telling me—you want to adopt a kid? Is that your next big idea? Your next publicity campaign? It doesn't matter that I'm damaged goods, because you can always stick a plaster on that?'

'Don't be ridiculous, Charlie. This isn't about me and you know it.'

'Oh, of course, because all this is just for show. It's all about your career.'

'Yours too,' he bit back. 'You make me out to be mercenary, but don't pretend that you're not using me every bit as much as I'm using you.'

He was using her.

Of course he was, she had known that from the start. But to hear him say it like that—no sugar coating—it winded her. And he thought that she was just as bad as him. That she had made a cold, calculated decision to use him. Well, she couldn't let him go on believing that. She wasn't that much of a bitch.

'My career? You know that that wasn't why I married you. Unlike you, I'm not that mercenary. I saw a headline in the news, that night. My parents trying to marry me off to one of those suitable husbands who'd be waiting for his heir and spare. I married you because my family were trying to force me into being the happy wife that I knew I never could be. When I have reminders of my infertility thrust in my face, Joe, I have been known to go a little crazy and act out. I could see the life I had built for myself slipping away and I was so heartbroken I couldn't think straight. That doesn't make us the same.'

CHAPTER ELEVEN

'You were still using me,' Joe said. Charlie rolled her eyes at him, but he was still reeling.

'Oh, because you're such a goddamn expert, are you?' she said. 'Is it all women that you know so well, or is it just me? Because I've been on your telly and in your newspapers my whole life you think you know what I'm feeling.'

'I never said I think I know you—but I think I know something about women. About relationships. I do have some experience of this.'

'Oh, so we're finally going to get to the bottom of this. Good. It was Arabella, I assume, who broke your heart.'

'Nobody said my heart was broken.'

'You scream it without saying a word, Joe. You with your trust issues and fear of commitment. You've already seen every article of my dirty laundry. Are you going to tell me what went on to make you such a cynical son of a b—? Or are we going to carry on trying to work out what's going on with us while having to avoid stepping on the elephant in the room?'

He slapped the steering wheel. Why was she so determined to make this about him—to make him the bad guy? He had been trying to help, and now she wanted to drag up his past as if that had anything to do with what they were arguing about. 'There is no elephant. Arabella and me—it wasn't a big deal. I wasn't heartbroken. If anything I'm grateful to her. She taught me a lot.'

'Like what?'

'Like how relationships actually work—and I don't mean the hearts and flowers rubbish. I'm talking about real adult relationships where both partners are upfront and honest about what they expect.'

'And let me guess, what Arabella expected wasn't just to enjoy your company. What else did she want?'

He tried to wave her off, but he knew that she wasn't going to let this drop. The fastest way out of this argument was just going to be to tell her the truth. Then she'd see that Arabella had nothing to do with any of this.

'She wanted to piss off her parents. She thought that taking me home to meet them would do that.'

Charlie raised her brows. 'And when did you find this out?'

'When we turned up at her house for the weekend. They were perfectly nice to me and Arabella was furious. I think that she thought that one whiff of my accent and they'd be threatening to disinherit her. She'd read too much D H Lawrence.'

'And before that… Were you in love with her?'

He shrugged, because what did it matter how he had felt when he was a naïve eighteen-year-old?

'Before that, I thought things were as simple as being in love with someone. I know better now.'

'That's a pretty cynical way to go through life.'

'Is it? Are you telling me that if you meet a guy you love you'll just marry him—no thinking about real life, your family, your career? Children?'

'I married you, didn't I?'

He didn't know what he could say to that. She had just told him that she hadn't been thinking straight. Surely she couldn't be saying that she loved him. But she didn't deny it either. He shook his head—he had to try and make Charlie understand how Arabella had helped him. That he was happy with his life as it was. Or he had been, until he had met her.

'All I know is that since Arabella, I've not been hurt,' he said. 'Someone tried. Pretended that she wanted me, when all she wanted was something she could sell to the papers. If I'd not learnt my lesson after Arabella, maybe that would have affected my heart too. But I'm a quick study.'

Charlie reached for his hand and absent-mindedly traced the lines of the bones beneath the skin. He tried not to notice, tried not to feel that caress in the pit of his stomach. She was still looking out of the window, and he was cowardly grateful that she wasn't making him do this eye to eye.

'And is that what you want from life?' she asked. 'From the women in your life—just to not get hurt? Or, one day, are you going to want more than that? Are you going to want to risk going all-in? Risk your heart, and see what you get back.'

He let his head fall back against the head rest, and let out a long, slow breath. 'I don't know, Charlie. What could be worth that?'

She turned to face him, and he knew that she was not going to put up with his evasion any more. That all pretence that they were not talking about them now was flying out of the window.

'Are you serious?' she said, her eyes blazing. 'Don't you think that this could be worth it? That *I* could be?'

Her expression was wide open—she was holding nothing back, now. No more secrets. Nowhere left to hide.

'This was meant to be all for show,' he said.

'And yet here we are. We both know we didn't go in to this for the right reasons, Joe. But the more time we spend together, the more I feel this…this pull between us that I've never felt before. And I don't know what to call it. I'm scared to call it love, but nothing else seems to fit.'

'But what do you *want*, Charlie?'

'For God's sake. Why do I have to want anything, Joe, other than you? Why can't you believe that that's enough? I want what we had last night, whispering and laughing in bed together. I want yesterday, at the piano, feeling like I can see into your soul when you play and sing just for me. I want this afternoon, sitting in the sun with my eyes closed and your arms around me, not able to imagine feeling more complete. But what about you? Do you want a string of girls who will give you what you ask for and nothing more, or do you want a relationship? A connection. Something *real*.'

He opened his mouth to speak, but she held up a hand to stop him. He wanted to tell her that of course he wanted all that, but how was he meant to know if that was what she really wanted too? That laying his heart out there in the open felt like asking to have someone come and smash it until there was nothing left.

'I don't want your knee-jerk reaction,' she told him. 'Whatever the answer is going to be, I need to know that you've thought about it. That you mean it.'

They sat in silence for a long minute.

'I think we both need some time,' he said eventually. 'And some space. I don't think you should come back to London,' Joe said. 'Not yet.'

Her face dropped instantly, and he knew that he had hurt her. He reached out to her and softened his expression. 'Go back to your mum. Tell her what you've told me, and make your peace with her. Make your peace with what your parents want for you, and decide, with all your cards on the table, whether it's what you want too. If it is, we'll find a way to get it for you. I'll disappear from your life if that's what you need from me.

'But if you don't...even if, with no secrets, you still want to be married to me? Come home to me, Charlie.'

CHAPTER TWELVE

CHARLIE SAT IN silence as the car sped along the roads that were so familiar to her from her childhood. She had spoken to her mother as soon as she had set off for the airport, and sensed that she wasn't entirely surprised that she was on her way back already.

She still hadn't decided what she wanted to say to her. How she would explain that she loved her parents, all her family, but that she didn't want the life that they had decided on for her.

Now the heat of the argument had faded, she could see that Joe hadn't been cruel to introduce her to his friends. The opposite, in fact. He'd shown her what she should have seen all along. Her ability to bear children or not had never been the problem—if she couldn't have kids naturally that was something that might be sad, and difficult for her and a husband to overcome. But it didn't mean that she could never have a family on her own, and it definitely wasn't a reason not to marry at all.

No, her reason for not marrying the men that her parents had introduced to her was much simpler—she didn't want them.

She didn't want the men, or the families, or the life that they represented.

She didn't want to give up her home in London, or her job, or the pride that she had built in herself and her abilities since she had left home.

She didn't want to go back to Afland just because of a promise she had made when she was eighteen and wanting to leave. Didn't want the life that she had made for herself to be over just because the date on the calendar ticked over and she was twenty-eight years old instead of twenty-seven.

Charlie bit at a nail as the car pulled through the gates of the palace and her hand barely moved from her mouth until she was in her mother's study, sitting on the other side of her expansive desk, feeling more like a job candidate than a daughter. And then she remembered that she was the one who had stalked in here and sat, leaving her mother standing on the other side of the desk, arms raised in greeting.

'So, was there something in particular you needed to talk about, sweetheart?' Adelaide asked, drawing her chair around the desk to sit beside her daughter.

Charlie felt her spine stiffen as she thought about all the things that she'd not said to her mother over the past ten years, not knowing where to start.

'I don't want to come back, Mother. After my birthday. I know I promised I would—'

'That was a long time ago,' her mother interrupted gently. 'I'd hoped that you would want to come back to live here, that your father and I might see a little more of you. But I'm not going to force you. I don't think I could if I wanted to. Now, are you going to tell me what this is really about? Is it Joe? Because we never really had a chance to talk properly before. I thought when you called after the wedding, maybe you had done something that you regretted, but then when you were here…honestly, darling, the atmosphere between you.'

Charlie couldn't help but smile when she thought of him.

'So I'm right,' her mother continued. 'You two are crazy about each other.'

'It's complicated,' Charlie said with a sigh.

'Well, I think it often is.' Her mother gave her an encouraging smile. 'Maybe if you tell me everything, it would help.'

'I wish it would, Mum. But the thing is…' She couldn't believe that she was about to volunteer the information that she'd held secret for so long, that she'd had nightmares about her mother finding out. What if she did react as she had in her dreams? Pushing her out of the family, banishing her from the island of Afland for ever? But wasn't that what Charlie had done to herself? She'd all but cut herself off from her family—her mother couldn't do any worse than that. She took a deep breath, squeezed her fingernails into her palms and spoke.

'The thing is, I might not be able to have children.' The words tumbled from her mouth in a hurry, and she kept her gaze locked on the surface of the desk, unable to meet her mother's eye.

Adelaide reached for her hand, and held it softly in her lap. 'I'm so sorry, darling. That must be terribly hard for you. And is having children important to Joe?'

'No.' She shook her head, and finally lifted her

gaze to meet her mum's eyes. The gentle kindness and love on her face made a sob rise in her throat, but she forced it down, wanting to finish what she'd started. Wanting, more than anything, her mum's advice. 'He says… It doesn't matter, does it? It's not about Joe. It's about me, it's about the fact that I'm never going to be who you want me to be.'

'I just want you to be *you*, darling. And more than that, I just want you to be happy.'

But that was crap, because she'd seen for herself what her mum wanted for her. A suitable husband, marriage, babies. 'Then what was all that with Philippe?' she asked, an edge to her voice. 'Why was he talking about engagements and moving to Afland with your blessing? Why did I have to read about it in the paper?'

'Honestly, Charlie, after all this time how can you believe anything that you read? Philippe came for dinner with his parents and he asked if you were still single. You know that he'd always had a soft spot for you. Then his father asked if you were planning on moving back to Afland. I don't know where he got the rest of it from. If I know his father as well as I think I do, the story probably came directly from him. I'm sorry that the press team weren't able to keep his mouth under control. I'm not going to lie and say that I haven't thought that you might be happier if you moved home and made a good match. It's kept your father and I happy for thirty-odd years, and your sister fairly blissful for the last seven. But we were never going to force you. Did you really think that we would?'

Yes, she had. She'd thought that there was only

one way that she could make her parents happy and proud of her, but she could see from her mum's face that she'd got it wrong.

'No, I don't think you'd force me, Mum.' She stayed silent for a moment. 'I'm sorry that I've not been home much.' Her mum wrapped an arm around her shoulders. 'But seeing Verity, and the children...'

'That must have been hard.'

'I just knew that that might never happen for me, and if it doesn't then where do I fit in this family?'

Adelaide squeezed her shoulders and reached for a tissue from the silver dispenser on her desk. 'You're my little girl, Charlie. That's where you fit. Where you'll always fit. But maybe things aren't as bad as they seem. Have you seen a doctor about it?'

'Not since I first found out. I didn't want to talk about it, didn't want the press getting hold of anything.'

'Well,' Adelaide said. 'How about I set up an appointment with my personal doctor, and you can have some tests? At least then you might know where you stand. If you knew the secrets that man had kept for me...well, let's just say I know that he can be discreet.'

'And if I definitely can't have children?' Charlie asked, a shake in her voice.

'Then it won't change the way I feel about you even a tiny bit, Charlie. Surely you know that. I just want you to be happy. Is Joe making you happy?'

'He's trying. I'm trying.'

'That's good. Keep trying, both of you.'

Charlie looked up and smiled at her mum, and could see from her expression that they weren't finished yet.

'What, Mum? I know there's something else you want to say.'

'I just… I'd like to see you at home more, darling. I know that you want to stay in London. I know how important your career is. But it doesn't have to be all or nothing. You could come back to visit more. We'd love to see you. And maybe you could do a few official engagements. I can't tell you how much I've missed you.'

Charlie plugged in her headphones as she climbed into the car and cued up the tracks that Joe had sent her. They had only been apart for a night—nothing in the grand scheme of things—but the already so familiar resonance and tone of his voice managed to relax her muscles in a way she didn't know was possible. She closed her eyes as the car crept along the London streets from the airport, drumming her fingers in time to the music in her ears, remembering the morning they'd been in the music room, sitting at the piano where she'd taken lessons as a girl, next to a man who made her skin sing.

Was it pathetic that she'd broken into a smile as soon as she'd seen his name on her phone?

She tapped at the screen to bring the message up again.

Call me when you get in.

Did he mean it? Or was it just a pleasantry? Like, *Call me when you get in, but obviously not if it's late, or inconvenient. Maybe just leave it till morning.*

Ugh. She was irritating herself, sounding like one

of those pink glitter princesses she'd tried all her life not to be.

She shot off a text, the traditional middle ground between calling and not calling, telling him she'd landed and was heading back to her place. It was too much to just turn up on his doorstep, especially when she wasn't even sure that he wanted her there.

The car twisted through the darkened streets of the city, over brightly lit dual carriageways, past the twisted metal of the helter-skelter sculpture in Stratford, and on towards her flat.

Her stomach sank at the thought of another night sleeping without Joe. She told herself that a month ago she'd been perfectly happy barely aware that he existed. But that had all changed the minute that she had set eyes on him, and they couldn't change that now. Somehow, she knew that without him her flat would feel empty, even though he'd never set foot there before.

As the car approached the stuccoed, pillared front of her apartment building, she spotted a dark shadow on the front steps and her stomach lurched. She glanced back through the windshield, checking that the police officers she knew should be on her tail were there, and breathed a sigh of relief when she saw one of the officers speaking into a radio.

Just as the driver asked her over the intercom whether she wanted him to drive on, the headlights illuminated the steps, throwing light onto Joe's face, and shadows into the space behind him. She let out the breath she had been holding, and told the driver that it was fine, he could stop. She took a moment before she opened the door to gather herself, prepare for what might come with Joe.

Had he come to tell her that he wanted her? That he wanted to make this a real marriage, or that he wanted out?

'Hi,' she said as she stepped out of the car and up the steps.

'Hey,' Joe replied, giving nothing away.

She grabbed her bag from the driver and stepped past Joe, unlocking the door and pushing it open.

She reached down to grab the mail and then dumped it on the hallway table, glancing round and trying to remember what state she'd left the place in. She didn't normally care about the condition of the flat, as long as it was warm and watertight. She had spent her whole childhood and adolescence looking forward to the freedom of space that was entirely her own. But there was something selfish and lonely about that, about the fact that she didn't have to consider a single person's feelings except her own. Maybe that was why she felt irrationally pleased that the worst of the mess had been bundled into bags and carted over to Joe's place. Her flat was usually her sanctuary but today it felt cold and unloved, and for a second she thought about the warm exposed brick and softly waxed wood of Joe's warehouse and felt a pull of something like homesickness.

She shook herself as she crossed to the windows and pulled back the curtains and blinds and opened a window. It was just feeling a bit neglected in here, because she hadn't been home for a few days, she reasoned. It was nothing a bit of fresh air and the warm light of a few lamps wouldn't fix.

'Want a drink?' she called out to Joe—anything

to stall actual, meaningful conversation. She grabbed them both a beer from the fridge and handed one to him.

'Nice place,' Joe said. Small talk. Good—she could handle small talk. She had plenty of formal training. Or maybe it had been bred into her. Either way, she grabbed his opening gambit and held onto it like a raft.

She chatted about the flat. How she'd chosen it for the big south-facing windows. The French doors out into the shared garden. The view of the park and lack of traffic noise from the front. She sounded like a desperate estate agent trying to close a sale.

Opening the French doors, she took her beer out to the patio, dropping onto one of the chairs and propping her knees against the edge of the little bistro table. The fairy lights her upstairs neighbour had threaded through the boughs of the trees twinkled at them, creating a scene she could have found in a fairy tale.

Shivering, she wished she'd grabbed her jacket, but she was too bone-tired to move.

'You're right, it's quiet out here,' Joe said, following her. 'Peaceful, and pretty. I can see why you like it so much.'

She looked up and met his eye, trying to judge if he was being sarcastic. But he looked genuine. He sat in the seat beside her, his thighs spread wide as he leaned back and let out a sigh.

'Long trip back,' he commented. 'For both of us.'

She 'hmm-ed' in agreement.

'Lots of time to think,' he added.

She looked up at him, wondering if this was it. When all their tiptoeing finally stopped and they decided if they wanted to run from the relationship they'd both been fighting from the first.

'Come to any conclusions?' she asked.

She wasn't sure she even wanted to know, because, whatever the answer, she knew that they still had a lot of work to do. He could declare his undying love for her this minute and that wouldn't remove a single one of the obstacles in their way. Still, even the thought of it made the hairs on her arms stand up.

'You're cold,' Joe said, stripping off his jacket and handing it to her. She draped it round her shoulders, refusing to acknowledge how delicious it felt to be wrapped in the warm, supple leather that smelt of him.

'I care about you, Charlie. I think you know that I do. But it's not as simple as that, is it?'

'I don't think that it ever is.'

'Honestly, after Arabella, and then the kiss and tell, when I'd picked myself up and convinced myself it hadn't been that bad, I thought I'd cracked it. That I'd finally figured out how these things work. And I've had no reason to doubt that I was right. What I was doing—it was working for me. Honestly, I've had no complaints.'

'So that's what—'

'Please, let me finish,' he said with a gentle smile. 'It was great, until I saw you watching me from the side of the stage in Las Vegas, and I felt something so overwhelming I still don't have the words to describe it. And I told myself that getting married was a great joke, or a killer career move or... I don't know. I told myself it was about anything except falling in love with you before I'd even said hello.'

Her heart pounded. She was desperate to say something, to ask if that was what he felt now—love. But he'd asked her for space to talk, and he deserved that.

'But I was kidding myself. I love you, Charlie. I think you knew that before I did.'

She let out the breath she had been holding, her thoughts whizzing by so fast it was impossible to concentrate on just one of them.

He sat watching her for a moment, and then grinned. 'That's it. I'm done,' he said. 'Twenty-four hours' thinking and that's all I've worked out. Say anything you like.

'Did you speak to your mum?' he asked eventually, his face falling when she couldn't think of what to say in response.

She nodded, still searching for the words. 'It was good,' she said eventually. 'I think… I think I got a lot of things wrong.'

'About me?'

She smiled, tempted to call him out on his self-centredness that only a rock star could get away with.

'About family, about children, about myself.' She looked up and met his eye. 'Yes, probably a few things wrong about you too.' She sighed, knowing that she was going to have to dig deeper than that. For so long, she'd kept as much as she could get away with to herself, but Joe deserved more than that from her.

'I'm not going back, to Afland. Well, not properly. I told my mum I'd take on some official duties, but my life will be here, Joe. I'm staying in London. And I hope to God that it's with you, because I've missed you like… I don't know. Like I suddenly lost my hearing and there was no music in the world.'

Now it was her turn to squirm, looking into her

man's eyes as she waited for him to reply. 'Is that what you want, Joe?'

'I want you, Charlie. Any way I can have you. Is that enough?'

She leaned forwards and pressed a hard kiss against his lips, gasping with pleasure as his hands wound around her waist under the warm leather of his jacket. 'It's enough,' she managed to whisper between kisses. 'We can make it enough—if we both want it.' His arms pulled tighter around her waist and she moved away from him for just a split second, and then she was sitting on top of him, her legs straddled around him and the chair. He leaned back, meeting her eyes as she settled on top of him. 'We're doing this?' he asked.

She answered him with a kiss.

EPILOGUE

'YOU KNOW, YOU HAVEN'T said it,' Joe said sleepily, brushing a strand of her hair back from her shoulder. He pulled the duvet up around them and Charlie in close, settling her in the crook of his arm as he laid his head on the pillow.

'Said what?'

Her eyes were shut, her body loose and languid, and her voice so sleepy she barely formed words.

'You know what.'

She opened her eyes and looked up at him, a teasing smile on her lips. 'I can't say it now that you've asked.'

Joe pressed a kiss into her hair. 'I don't need you to. But, you know, tomorrow, if you happened to feel the urge…'

'I predict lots of urges, tomorrow.' She smiled wickedly. 'It's a long, long list. But if that's the one that you want to put at the top…'

If he'd had any energy left, he would have rolled on top of her and taken care of a few of those urges right now. But instead he pinched her waist. 'Give me an hour's sleep and I'll put myself entirely in your hands.'

'Good. Exactly where I want you. Later,' she said,

with another kiss against his chest. 'I think there's something we need to talk about first.'

He sighed sleepily. 'I thought we were done talking.'

She shuffled away from him on the bed, pulling up the sheets to try and find some modesty.

'It's important, Joe,' she said, and he opened his eyes properly at the serious tone of her voice. 'There's a lot we didn't talk about. Children for one. It's not a fun conversation, but we have to have it. I'm going to see my mum's doctor, but there are no guarantees. What if it never happens for us?'

He rubbed his face and sat up. 'If it comes to that, Charlie, we'll deal with it. Together. There are other ways to have a family.'

'Is it what you want?' she asked, a wobble in her voice. 'Because I don't know if adoption is something that I could take on. With my family, the succession, it's complicated.'

He kissed her on the forehead, smoothing a hand down her spine. 'I know that. But no, it doesn't matter to me. You're what matters to me.'

'But I might never have a family, Joe. And there's no point taking this any further if that's not something that you can live with. If you're always going to want more.'

He stopped her with a kiss on the lips. 'The only thing I want in my future is you,' he said, between kisses. 'We're going to travel the world. We're going to make beautiful music. We're going to party until we can't take any more. If children come along, the more the merrier. But nothing, *nothing* is going to make me a happier man than knowing that you will come home with me every night, and wake up with me every morning.'

'I love you,' she whispered, and he smiled as he squeezed her tight and pressed a kiss against her hair. She ran her hands over his chest, and he stretched, bringing their bodies into contact from where she had propped herself on his chest right down to their toes.

'And I love you too. Now, are we making a start on that list of yours?'

* * * * *

AMBER AND THE ROGUE PRINCE

ALLY BLAKE

For all the women dreaming about
their next chapters.

And Bec, who leapt into hers with enthusiasm,
fortitude, grace, humour and style, taking her
first steps alongside me, and naming
Ned the dog along the way.

CHAPTER ONE

AMBER PLONKED HERSELF onto the rickety stairs out front of the shack hovering on the edge of Serenity Hill. Stretching her arms over her head, she blinked sleepily at the view.

A misty glow slithered over the acres of wild lavender carpeting the hillside. The first hint of morning sun peeked between the hilly mounds beyond, creating a starburst of gold on the horizon and making silhouettes of the willows meandering along the banks of Serenity Creek below.

"Could do with some rain," said Amber. "That said, can't we always?"

Ned stared fondly up at her from his mismatched eyes. She gave the mottled fur behind his good ear a thorough rub.

Then, nabbing her bright yellow gumboots, Amber tugged them on over faded pyjama bottoms. She rubbed a smudge of mud from one of the bees that Sunflower— who lived in the bright purple caravan up on the hill—had painted on them for her. Then she twirled her heavy hair into a low bun and ducked her head into her fencing-style veil. Last came elasticised gloves, then, finally ready, she pushed herself to her feet.

"You ready?"

Ned answered with a wag of his tail.

"Then let's do this."

But Amber only made it down one more step before

she spied Sunflower hustling down the hill behind the shack towards her.

With her fluffy strawberry-blonde hair and pixie face, her feet bare beneath her long paisley skirt, Sunflower looked as if she'd fallen to earth on a sunbeam. But like everyone in Serenity she'd come in search of sanctuary.

Amber pulled off her veil and tucked it under her arm before wiping the dislodged strands of hair from her eyes. Not used to seeing anyone else out and about this early, Amber called out, "Everything okay?"

Sunflower waved a hand while she caught her breath. "I have news."

"For you to be out from under your blanket this early it must be pretty good news."

The look Sunflower shot her was thick with meaning.

"Not so good, then."

Sunflower shielded her face against the rising sun and said, "I'm actually not sure. The news is they've opened up the Big House."

Amber glanced up the hill, even though Hinterland House—the big, deserted, Tuscan-style villa that everyone in the area simply referred to as the Big House—was perched too far over the other side to be seen.

"Grim mentioned seeing smoke coming from the chimney a couple of weeks back. But considering Grim lives in a cloud of smoke, I ignored it. Then Daphne claimed she saw sheets on the clothesline and I began to wonder. Last night, when he was taking one of his wanders, my Johnno saw a fancy black car barrelling up the drive and pulling into the garage." She paused for effect, then announced, "It seems the family is back."

"What family? The way the place was always kept so well-tended I'd figured it was a tax write-off for some overseas conglomerate."

"Oh, no," said Sunflower, her eyes now dancing. "It

belongs to the Van Halprins. A family as famous for their money and power as their terrible bad luck. As the story goes, they all died off, in one tragic manner after another, until only one remained—the youngest daughter, Anna, who was very beautiful. Twenty-one and all alone in that big house—the townspeople feared what might become of her. Then, in a fairy-tale ending, she married a prince from some far-off land and the place has been barren ever since."

"And now this fairy-tale princess is back?"

Sunflower shook her head, her eyes sparking. "The person my Johnno saw driving the car was a man. City haircut. Deadly handsome. They say it's *him*."

Amber knew she was meant to say, *Him who?* but her throat had gone dry. Her earlier frisson of concern now bore the hallmarks of fully fledged anxiety: sweaty palms; ringing in her ears; a strong desire to run inside and bar the door.

But the door to her shack was barely holding onto its hinges as it was, so what would be the point?

Oblivious, sweet Sunflower went on. "It *has* to be Anna's son! Anna's *royal* son. Prince Alessandro Giordano himself."

Not one to follow that kind of thing, Amber didn't know Prince Alessandro from Prince Charming.

Only, she had an awful feeling she did.

"Don't you see?" Sunflower went on. "As heir to the Van Halprin estate, Prince Alessandro owns Hinterland House, which means he also owns pretty much every bit of land you can see. From one side of the hill to the other, from the river to the township. Including the land you and I are standing on."

Amber found she had to swallow before asking, "Whoa. Back up a little. I assumed the commune owned this land. Or that the township simply let them stay." So deeply grateful had she been for a place to stay, she'd never thought to ask. "Are you saying that this *Prince* owns Serenity Hill?"

Sunflower nodded slowly. "And there are more rumours."

There were always rumours. Especially in a town this size. Having had parents whose chief personality trait was "being deeply involved", Amber had developed a sincere lack of interest in knowing other people's business.

Sunflower said, "Apparently a man fitting that description—tall, citified, handsome, *and* with an accent—has been seen meeting with the town council. And the only reason for an outsider to meet with the council is—"

"Town planning."

The wind had picked up, creating eerie paths through the field of lavender. And despite the sun lifting into the air, Amber shivered. She wriggled her toes in her gumboots in order to keep the blood flowing.

Unlike some of the old-timers living in tents, wigwams, caravans and Kombi vans up the hill, Amber was a relative newcomer to Serenity. But, while her history of the area was sketchy, her experience with the law was sharp and clear.

"The commune has been occupying this land for years. Decades, right? Long enough to build structures. To hook in plumbing. Electricity. To have signs pointing the way. It's even noted as a point of interest on the tourist map. Surely that gives us rights."

Sunflower blinked. "Rights?"

Before Amber could take the thought further, something banged inside her shack. Both women turned to see what it was. Amber took a subtle step back up onto the porch.

"Probably Ned demanding breakfast."

Sunflower backed away. "Of course. I'm off to spread the news to the rest of the morning folk. See what else we can unearth. Feel free to fill everyone in yourself. Fire-pit meeting tonight. At sunset."

Another bang came from inside Amber's shack. She took another step nearer her front door. Said, "You bet. See you then. I'd better check on Ned."

Of course, at that moment Ned came running out of the fields below, purple flowers caught in his fur.

Amber madly ushered Ned inside the shack, then yanked the door shut behind her before leaning against it, holding the doorknob tight.

In the quiet her heart thumped against her ribs.

All she had to do was lean forward to see past the cupboard-cum-kitchen wall and into her small bedroom. To spot the crumpled sheets. The colourful crocheted blanket kicked into a pile on the floor.

And the masculine shape of the stranger in her bed.

A chop of sun-kissed hair slid over one eye. Broad shoulders lifted and fell as he breathed. The profile cast against her pillow was achingly handsome. Even now. Even with the indignation building inside of her.

To think, she'd only slipped out from under the warm, heavy weight of his arm ten minutes before, smiling at what a deep sleeper he was. And the reason why.

He'd said his name was Hugo. And she'd believed him.

That particular something in his eyes—directness, authority, unflappability—had allowed her the rare luxury of taking everything he'd said at face value. No doubt the foreign accent had helped too. Not only was it devastatingly sexy, but it also meant he was a tourist, just passing through. There was no point worrying too much about details when their dalliance was only ever going to be short-term.

And yet, it sounded like the man she'd just indulged in a clandestine three-week affair with was none other than

Prince Alessandro Giordano—and he was also known as the owner of the land on which she and her friends lived illegally!

Three weeks earlier...

Amber breathed in the scent of lavender as she looked out over Serenity Hill.

There had been a chill in the air that morning. Like the blast of an open fridge door on a hot summer's day.

It was the sign she had been waiting for. Time to harvest her bumper honey crop for the year. Collect at the right time and the honey would be ripe, sweet, in its prime. Leave it much longer and the colony would start eating the wares or moving it lower into the hive, making it near impossible to collect.

By late afternoon there was no need for the smoker. Warmth had settled over the valley and crept up onto the hills, meaning the honey would be warm, running easily, and the bees would be calm.

Dolled up in her veil, overalls and gloves, gumboots slapping against the stairs, she realised Ned was not at her side. No point whistling for him—he was nearly deaf.

She tipped up onto her toes to see if she could spy his fluffy tail cutting through the field. No luck. Maybe he'd headed up the hill to visit the others. But that wasn't like him. They knew better than to feed him scraps. Amber had made it clear that he was her responsibility, nobody else's. That in taking him on she wouldn't put undue pressure on the commune's resources.

About to give up and head off alone, she saw him by the pair of trees down the hill, watching the hammock slung between them with great interest.

As Amber neared she realised why.

A stranger in fact was lying therein. Asleep.

Not just a stranger…a man. A *long* man. Longer than the hammock, his big feet poking out of the end. His T-shirt had twisted to cling to a sculpted chest. The bottom edge lifted to reveal a tanned stomach, and a dark arrow of hair leading to…jeans that left little to the imagination.

Even in sleep he was riveting. Deep-set eyes beneath dashing, slashing brows, and overlong hair that fell across a brow furrowed as if he was dreaming important dreams. The rest of his face was rough-hewn, but handsome with it—a stubble-shadowed jaw and cheeks that appeared carved from rock. A veritable modern-day Viking.

Not from around here, or she'd have noticed. A tourist, then. Not the seasonal fruit-picking kind. Or the type who came to Serenity looking for enlightenment. Or absolution. His clothes were too nice. His aura too crisp. But people didn't just happen to pass through Serenity. They came with a purpose. So what was his?

Her gaze running over every inch of him as if she was committing him to memory, Amber realised with excruciating discomfort just how long she'd been living in this patch of pretty wilderness dotted with leisurely artisans and gentle hippies, none of whom had made her nerves twang. Not like this.

She swallowed the thirst pooling in her cheeks and reached out for Ned.

Ned looked at her with his contented face.

"What are you grinning at?"

Forgetting the fact that in all likelihood the stranger was not as deaf as Ned, Amber hadn't thought to lower her voice.

The stranger sprang to sitting as if he were springloaded. His feet hit the ground, his hands gripping the edges of the hammock, the muscles of his arms bunching as the hammock threatened to swing out from under him.

He was even bigger sitting up. Well over six feet. Strong with it. Yet Amber felt compelled to stay. To watch. To wait.

A few beats later, the stranger shook his hair from his eyes before palming the heels of his hands deep into the sockets. With a heavy breath he dropped his hands, opened his eyes, took one look at Amber and leapt out of the hammock so fast he nearly tripped over his own feet.

A string of words poured from his mouth. Italian? French? Who cared? It was the sexiest sound Amber had ever heard. Raw and deep, it scraped against her insides like a long, slow, rough-tongued lick.

Ned loved it too, what little he could hear of it. He bounded to his feet and ran around in a circle, barking at the sky.

The stranger looked over his shoulder, then back at Amber. He looked down at Ned, then back at her again. This time his gaze caught. And stayed. A beat slunk by in which deep breaths were hard to come by.

Then, in lightly accented English, "Please tell me you come in peace."

She reached up and slowly pulled her bee-keeping hat and veil from her head. As usual, the mesh caught on her hair, pulling long blonde strands free of her bun until it fell over her face in a wispy curtain. She tried wiping them away but the heavy glove made it next to impossible.

In the end, she threw her veil to the ground, slid off both gloves and threw them down too. Feeling overheated, she unzipped her overalls, pulling them down to her hips, the arms flapping about her thighs. She fixed her tank top, pushed her hair back off her face, and—hands on hips— stared the stranger down.

The effect somewhat lessened when Ned saw his chance and went for her gloves. He managed to get both, but dropped one about a metre away as he took off into the lavender with the score in his delighted teeth.

Not that the stranger seemed to notice. His eyes never left hers. In fact, they had warmed, distinctly, the edge of a very fine mouth tilting at one side as he took her in.

Flustered, Amber pressed her shoulders back, angled her chin at him and said, "I might ask the same of you."

"Me?" He stretched his arms overhead, once again revealing his flat, tanned belly, and Amber gritted her teeth as she looked determinedly anywhere else. "I am all about the peace."

"Well, next time keep your peace far from my hammock. *Capiche?*"

"If I said I really needed a nap at the exact moment I came upon it, would that help?" One side of his mouth kicked up, and her tummy tumbled over on itself in response.

"What do you think?" she deadpanned.

"I think perhaps not," he mumbled, running a hand through his hair. It was a little rumpled from sleep on one side. He wore it well.

He took a step her way, and Amber took an equal step back, which was ridiculous. If she screamed, a dozen hippies would rush down the hill to check on her. Well, maybe not rush. Amble with intent.

She pressed her gumboots into the ground. It wasn't concern for her safety that had her on edge. It was concern for her hazy judgement.

He stepped sideways, picked up the glove Ned had dropped and ran his thumb over the honeycomb stitching. "How about if I said I tripped and fell into the hammock, knocking myself out?"

"I'd think you were an idiot."

A smile tugging at the corner of that mouth, he looked out over the lavender, all the while taking a step closer to her. "Then here's the unvarnished truth: a wicked witch lured me here with a peach. I took one bite and fell into a deep sleep."

As punctuation, he held out her glove. Naturally, she reached out to take it. Only he did not let go, capturing her gaze right along with it.

His eyes were a deep, intelligent hazel, his mouth on the constant verge of a smile. The fact that his nose appeared to have been broken at some time only added to his stunning good looks.

"It was an apple," said Amber, her voice breaking on the last syllable.

"Hmm?" he said, gently letting the glove go.

"Sleeping Beauty was felled by an apple."

Again with the devastating half-smile. "Wasn't that Eve with the apple? Tempting poor Adam."

"Forbidden fruit. No mention of an apple, specifically."

"Right. I stand corrected."

At some point in the past few minutes, the sun had begun to set, stretching shadows over the stranger's arresting face.

But it was the words that had her transfixed. The locals were so earnest she couldn't remember the last time she'd indulged in spicy banter. It felt good. Really good. Like slipping into a freshly made bed after a long day on her feet.

"Who are you?" she asked, the desire to know far too obvious in her tone.

He held out a hand. "Hugo. And you are?"

Feeling as if she was about to step off a cliff, she took his hand. His fingers were long and strong. His grip dry and warm. The tingle that zapped up her arm had her shaking once and letting go.

"Amber."

"It's a very great pleasure to meet you, Amber."

"I'll bet."

At that he laughed.

The sound tumbling about inside her belly made her feel empty. Hungry. She breathed through it. "Wicked witch or no, this is private property, so you'd best get moving on. It doesn't get fully dark for another hour. If you walk with pace you'll make it to the village in time. There you'll find somewhere else to sleep."

The man slid his hands into his pockets and rocked back on his heels, going nowhere.

Amber crossed her arms and shook her head at the guy. But he only smiled back, the directness in his eyes telling her she wasn't the only one having an "interested at first sight" moment. She rolled her eyes, turned on her heel and beckoned to him over her shoulder.

"Come on, then, Hugo. This way."

CHAPTER TWO

HUGO TWISTED AND stretched, enjoying the creaks and cracks of muscles well-used.

Still half-asleep, he couldn't be sure if the images skirting the edges of his brain were real, or the remnants of a very good dream. Then slowly, like drops of mercury melting together, he recalled slippery limbs sliding over each other. Warmth easing towards heat. Sighs, laughter, a gasp.

No dream. Just Amber.

A bump to the bed echoed through him, as if it wasn't the first.

He dragged his eyes open, battling the sharp morning sunshine, to find Amber no longer tucked into his side. Instead, she stood by the other side of her bed, glaring at him.

And he found himself riding a wave of déjà-vu.

The first time he'd laid eyes on her she'd worn the white veiled hat and the long, chunky gloves, the bulky overalls and those wild yellow boots. She'd looked like something from a nineteen-fifties space comic. Then she'd stripped down in front of him, all sun-browned shoulders, wildly tangled lashes over whisky-brown bedroom eyes, full lips, her long hair a halo of honeyed gold falling halfway down her back.

The difference this time: her lips were pursed. Her hands white-knuckled on her hips. And her narrowed eyes shot daggers his way.

That didn't stop him from weighing up the likelihood of dragging her back to bed. He deemed the chances slim.

Brought up never to readily surrender the advantage of position, Hugo sat up, the sheet dragging with him. His feet curled as they hit the rough wooden floor. Then he pulled himself to standing.

Amber's gaze flickered to his bare chest and she sucked in a sharp breath. The chances looked slightly more promising.

But then her arm lifted, one pointed finger aimed towards her front door, and she said, "Get out."

"Excuse me?"

"I said, get out. Do you not understand what that means? Were you raised by wolves?"

"Nannies. Mostly."

"Of course you were. Get out of my bed. Get out of my shack. Now."

Hugo ran both hands over his face, hard and fast. Better to be fully awake for this. "Start at the beginning. You're not making any sense."

"Then look at my face. Look deep into my eyes so that you see I am serious. I want you to get out."

Well, this was new. Her voice rose with each word, rare emotion tinging her words. She was genuinely upset.

"I will go. Of course. If that's what you want. Look, I'm already out of your bed." The sheet at his hips slipped as he reached up to scratch his chest.

Her tongue darted out to wet her lips, which alleviated his concern, at least a little.

"In the spirit of fair play, I deserve to know why. What has changed in the world since you fell asleep while trying to convince me that honey was better than peanut butter?"

Her hand dropped, just a fraction. Then she regrouped, pointing her finger towards the door with renewed conviction. "Nothing has changed. Not a single thing. Apart from the fact that I now know who you really are."

Time stood still for the merest fraction of a second, but when it resumed, everything seemed to sit a little off from where it had before.

He nodded, dropped the sheet back onto the bed and ambled over to the metal chair in the corner to gather his clothes. His underwear was nowhere to be seen, and, not about to go searching, he went commando, pulling on his jeans, taking care with the fly.

He'd known their liaison would end. They both had. That had been the underlying beauty of it.

In the first few days it had been diverting, watching things unfold from a safe mental distance. Distance was his usual state of being and Amber had seemed glad of it. The guiltless pleasure, the ease of transaction, the lack of desire on both sides to pry deeper than what the other might like for lunch had led to a beautifully contained affair.

Somehow, in all the hazy sunshine, with the cicadas a constant background hum, the clear edges of their association had begun to blur…until he'd found reasons to come to her earlier, to stay longer. They'd fallen into a rhythm of days lit bright and nights lost to exquisite, immoderate pleasure and murmured nothings in the dark.

As he pushed one arm through his shirt, then the other, he no longer felt distant. The dissatisfaction he felt was real.

But only a fool would have expected the halcyon days to remain that way—like a bug trapped in amber. So to speak. And Hugo was no fool.

"Is that it?" Amber's words hit his back like bullets. "You don't have anything to say for yourself?"

He patted his jeans pockets in search of his wallet, phone, keys—then remembered he didn't carry any. Not here. So he snapped the top button before looking up at her. "What would you like me to say, Amber?"

"I don't know, that I'm acting crazy? That I've been duped—by someone other than you, I mean. That it's not true."

She looked so incorruptible, like a force of nature. But something he'd learned in his month in this part of the world—nobody came to Serenity without a good reason. Or a bad one.

He opened his mouth to call her on it, but he stopped himself in time.

He'd never known someone to wear their absoluteness like a badge of honour the way she did. The moment she'd decided to let him into her house she'd decided to let him into her bed. No coquettish equivocation. Only firm decision.

This was the first time he'd seen it waver. Enough for him to take heed. To hold out his hands in conciliation. "I never lied to you, Amber. I am Hugo to my friends, my closest family."

"To everyone else?"

"I am Prince Alessandro Hugo Giordano, sixth in line to the principality of Vallemont."

The quiet that followed his statement wasn't new. The rare times Hugo found himself in a conversation with someone who wasn't aware of who he was, what he was worth, and who his relatives were, it was clear when the penny dropped.

Though this might have been the first time he was half-dressed when that realisation occurred, he thought ruefully.

A hippy beekeeper on the Central Coast of Australia had not been in the plan, meaning it was taking him a little longer to decide upon the appropriate protocol with which to navigate this moment.

Meanwhile, Amber's nostrils flared, fury dancing behind her bedroom eyes. He imagined she was finding it hard not to climb over the bed and tackle him. As unmoved by convention as she was, she could do it too.

For a man whose entire life had been ruled by ritual, no wonder she'd been impossible to resist.

"Wait," he said. "Fifth. I'm fifth in line. My uncle's recently abdicated all rights and moved to California to produce movies. Not that it matters. I am a prince in name only. I will never rule."

She blinked and it was enough to snap her from her red haze. "I don't give a flying hoot if you are set to be Master of the Universe. Don't even think about turning us out on our ears."

"Excuse me?"

"These people are special. The community needs this place. The commune is Serenity's heart. If you mess with that you will kill it dead."

That was what had her so het up? Not *who* he was, but the plans he had for this land?

What the hell had she found out? And how? This wasn't his first rodeo. He'd been discreet. Painstakingly so. Who had talked?

He did up a couple of quick buttons on his shirt before re-rolling the sleeves to his elbows. Then he moved slowly around the bed, hands out, palms up.

"Amber, until this point in time, we have been having a nice time together. I'd go so far as to say very nice. With that in mind, I suggest we sit down, have a cup of coffee and discuss any concerns you might have."

He could still fix this.

"I don't want to discuss anything with you. I just want you to tell me, right here, right now, if the rumours are true."

"Which rumours might they be, exactly?"

"That you have been meeting with the local town council. Discussing plans…development plans that may or may not put the commune in danger."

"Would that be such a bad thing?"

Emotion flickered behind her eyes. Deep, frantic, fierce. "Yes," she managed. "It would be a terrible thing."

"Look at this place, Amber. It's falling down around your ears."

"Not every home has to be a castle."

Touché. "And yet if you have the chance to sleep somewhere that doesn't whistle, drip, or threaten to fall down the hill every time you step onto the porch, it's worth considering."

"My sleeping arrangements are none of your business."

"They became my business when I began sleeping here too."

"Lucky for you that is not a problem you'll have to face again."

Hugo breathed out hard, while emotion darted and flashed behind her big brown eyes. With the tension sparking in the air between them, it was all he could do to keep from going to her and letting the slow burn of her fill the empty places inside.

"Tell me, right now, if we have made incorrect assumptions. Are you planning on developing the land? Should we be concerned?"

A muscle ticked beneath his eye. And she took it for the admission it was.

Amber slumped onto the corner of the bed, her face falling into her hands. "This can't be happening."

"I hope you understand that until anything is concrete I can't discuss the details."

She looked up at him, beseeching. "Understand? I don't understand any of this. Like why, if you are so offended by my home, you kept coming back. Was I reconnaissance? Were you hoping to create an ally in your devious plans?"

"Of course not, Amber." Hugo's stomach dropped and he came around the bed, crouching before her. "Amber, you know why I came back. And back. And back. For the same reason you took me in."

He lifted a hand and closed it around hers. Her soft brown eyes begged him to stop. Heat sat high and pink on her cheeks. Her wild waves of hair caught on a breeze coming through one of the many cracks in the woebegone shack in which she lived.

Then her fingers softened as she curled them into his.

A moment later, she whipped her hand away and gave him a shove that had him rocking onto his backside with a thump that shook the foundations, raining dust over his head as she scrambled over him and into clear space.

As he cleared the dust from his hair, his eyes, Hugo wondered how his life had come to this.

The downward spiral had begun several months earlier when he'd agreed to his uncle's sovereign command to enter into a marriage of convenience. His former fiancée—and long-time best friend—Sadie, had come to her senses and fled before they'd said *I do*, bringing about a PR nightmare for the royal family…and freedom for Hugo. The fact that he would likely have gone through with it had been a wake-up call. What had he been thinking? Where was his moral compass? Not that that should be much of a shock—he was his father's son after all.

Afterwards he'd needed to get away. Clear his head. Recalibrate. He'd never have imagined that would lead him away from a life of luxury to camping out in a small, lumpy bed in a country town in the middle of nowhere, Australia, tangled up with a woman he barely knew.

He'd not hidden his position on purpose, she'd simply never asked. Their affair had been lived in the moment, fulfilling basic needs of hunger and sleep and sex while talking about everything from *Game of Thrones* to Eastern philosophy…but nothing truly personal. His family had not come up. Nor, for that matter, had hers. He'd been so grateful to avoid talking about his own that he had given no thought as to why she might also be glad of it. Perhaps he was not the only one for whom that question opened Pandora's box. Either way, after a while, the privacy had felt like a true luxury.

"I need you to leave, Hugo," said Amber, yanking him back to the present, only this time she added, "Please."

It was enough for Hugo to push to standing. He looked around the small, dilapidated room, but he'd left nothing behind bar the impression of his head on the pillow. It didn't seem like enough.

Too late to rectify that now, he turned to walk out.

"Wait," she called, grabbing him by the arm. Before he even had the chance to feel relief she pressed past him and headed out onto her wonky porch, causing the area around her shack to tremble in response.

Ned nuzzled against his hand. And Hugo lost his fingers in the dog's soft fur, taking a moment to work out a burr.

"All clear," Amber called.

"Wouldn't want your friends to know you've been harbouring the enemy."

She glanced back at him, the morning sun turning her hair to gold, her eyes to fire. When she saw Ned at his side her mouth pursed. "Away," she called. But Ned didn't move, whether because of his deafness or his obstinacy. She clicked her fingers and with a *harumph* the dog jogged to her side.

He joined them on the porch. The old wood creaked and groaned. A handmade wooden wind chime pealed prettily in the morning breeze.

"Is that why you came to Serenity?"

Now, there was a question. One she might have thought to ask at any point during the last few weeks if she'd had a care to know anything at all about the man she'd been sleeping with. "You really want to know what I came to Serenity hoping to find?"

She only nodded mutely.

"Absolution. How about you?"

She snapped her mouth shut tight.

He raised an eyebrow. *Now, what do you have to say about that?*

Nothing, it seemed. He'd finally managed to render Amber speechless.

With that, Hugo left her there in her bright yellow gumboots, her tank top clinging to her lovely body, her hair a wild, sexy mess. He jogged down the steps and headed down the hill, past the hammock, through the field of lavender to the small dead-end dirt road on which he'd parked his car.

The urge to look back was acute but he kept his cool. Because he had the feeling that it wouldn't be the last he saw of Amber.

She might be done with him, but he wasn't done with Serenity. For he did indeed have plans for his mother's ancestral home—plans which had him excited for the first time since the debacle of the wedding that never was. He might even go so far as to say they excited him more than any other development he had ever actualised.

For Hugo was renowned for taking underused or overlooked tracts of land that others would deem too remote or too challenging, and turning them into stunning holiday playgrounds for diplomats, royalty, the rich and famous, and families alike. His series of Vallemontian resorts—including a palatial masterpiece tucked into the side of Mont Enchante and an award-winning titan overlooking Lake Glace—had been a revelation for the local economy, making him invaluable to his uncle in terms of commerce if not in terms of the line of succession.

But this one, this place...it would be all his.

When he reached the bottom of the lavender field he did look back, Amber's shack and the rest of the commune relegated to glimpses of purple and red and orange obscured by copses of gum trees.

He'd keep the natural landscape as much as possible, but the caravans, tents and shanties would of course have to go to make way for the bungalows, tennis courts, lagoon-style pool and a peach grove where Amber's shack now wobbled.

Hugo wasn't some monstrous land baron. With the council's help, he would assist them in their relocation. Help them find safer places to live.

And he would create something beautiful, something lasting, something personal to break the cycle of tragedy in his mother's family.

He would make his very personal mark on the world without trading on his family name, a constant reminder of the top job for which he and his heirs would only ever be back-ups.

Amber would just have to lump it.

Serenity's Town Hall was packed to the rafters, with people lining the walls and spilling out through the open doors. It was late enough that young ones would normally be home in bed, but nobody was missing this meeting, so they sat in messy rows on the floor at the front, making occasional mad dashes across the stage, followed by their harassed parents.

There was only one reason for the big turnout: the news had spread. Nothing this momentous had happened in Serenity since Anna had been swept away to an exotic foreign land.

Amber slumped on her bench in the third row, her legs jiggling, her thumbs dancing over her fingertips. There was a good portion of the commune lined up beside her, including Sunflower, who was humming happily despite the cacophony of white noise, and Johnno, who was staring out into space.

Only, Amber wasn't here in the hope of spotting the exotic stranger. She'd seen enough of him already, from the scar above his right eyebrow to the birthmark on the base of his left big toe—and everything in between. She shifted on her seat and cleared her throat.

She was here in case the Hinterland House plans—whatever they might be—were on the agenda in the hope she could see with her own eyes as someone shouted it down. Then Hugo would leave and things could go back to normal. Or as normal as things ever got in Serenity.

Someone, but not her.

It hadn't passed her by that her parents would have loved this kind of David and Goliath fight—though nobody would have mistaken them for David in their Gucci suits and Mercedes four-wheel drives. It made them great lawyers, but terrible parents.

How could they be expected to nurse a "difficult" baby when there was so much injustice to stamp down? Enough that Australia's most infamous human rights lawyers put the care of their only child into the hands of daycare and night nannies from six weeks of age. Their work was far too important for them to abide the distraction.

The smack of a gavel split the silence and Amber flinched, reminded of the number of courtrooms she'd been in as a child. Well, she didn't have the mental space to think about her parents today. Or ever, if at all possible. She sat taller, stopped her nervous fidgets and waited.

"Squeeze up," called a voice as someone managed to squash into the end of Amber's row, the rickety wooden bench wobbling as the crowd sardined. When she looked back to the stage, Councillor Paulina Pinkerton—the leader of the seven-member local council—and her cohorts trailed onto the stage then took their seats.

The gavel struck a second time. Amber flinched again. It was a conditioned response, like Pavlov's ruddy dog. The twitters settled to a hush, chairs scratched against the wooden floor, a teenaged boy laughed. Somebody coughed. A baby started to fret. And the town of Serenity held its breath.

"Nice to see so many of you here today. I might choose to think it's because you've heard around the traps how darned interesting our meetings are, but I fear there is some issue that has you all aflutter. So let's get through the necessaries."

The councilwoman swept through the minutes and old business with alacrity. Then she opened the floor.

"Any new business?"

The hum started up again. Whispers, murmurs, the shuffle of bottoms turning on seats. But nobody said a word.

"Fine. Next meeting will be...next Tuesday at— Ms Hartley? Did you have something to add?"

Amber blinked to hear her name being called from the councillors' table, only to realise she was on her feet. Did she have something to add? No! Legally emancipated from her indifferent parents at sixteen in a legal battle that had become a national story in a slow news week, she'd spent her life living like dandelion fluff, flitting from place to place, *not* getting involved.

Until Serenity. Sunflower had taken one look at her empty backpack, her bedraggled state and offered the shack for a night, then another, and somehow she'd found herself stuck in this sweet place, with these kind people, none of whom had a clue what was about to befall them.

This place…it was her sanctuary. And she'd harboured the enemy—however unwittingly. She owed it to them to do whatever it took to protect them.

Damn him. Damn Hugo Prince Whatever-His-Name-Was and his whole crazy family for making her do this.

Amber scooted past the knees blocking her way down the bench. Once she had reached the small rostrum—a literal soapbox attached to a stand fashioned out of a fallen tree, which had been a gift to the town from Johnno, who was a pretty brilliant artist when he was in the right head-space—Amber squared her shoulders, looked each councilman and councilwoman in the eye and prayed her parents would never hear word of what she was about to do.

"Ms Hartley." Councillor Pinkerton gave Amber an encouraging smile. "The floor is yours."

"Thank you. I'll get right to it. I have come to understand that the owners of Hinterland House are back and I believe that they have plans to develop the land. Firstly, I'd like to know if the latter is true, and, if so, I put forward a motion to stop it."

Once she had started, the words poured out of her like water from a busted pipe. Energy surged through the crowd behind her like a snake. It was electric. And she hated it. Because the thrill of the fight was in her veins after all.

"Much of Serenity belongs to the Van Halprins, Ms Hartley, and, apart from the segments bequeathed to the township, they are within their rights to develop that land."

"Into what?"

The councillor paused, clearly thinking through how much she was legally allowed to say, and legally allowed to hold back. "The plans as they are will be up for local consideration soon enough. The Prince plans to build a resort."

Whispers broke out all over the room.

Amber breathed out hard. Sunflower's rumours were one thing, Hugo's indefinite admissions another. But hav-

ing Councillor Pinkerton admit to as much had Amber
feeling sick to the stomach. In fact, she had to breathe for
a few seconds in order to keep her stomach from turning
over completely.

She glanced over her shoulder and saw Johnno grinning
serenely back at her; found Sunflower watching her like a
proud sister. Her gaze landed on another dozen members
of their collective community—all of whom had come to
Serenity in search of acceptance and kindness and peace.

Where would people like them, people like her, go if
they had to move on?

She turned back to the front, her heart pumping so hard
it seemed to be trying to escape her chest. The room was
so still now, even the fretting baby had quieted, meaning
her voice made it all the way to the rear of the room and
out into the halls, hitting every ear as she said, "I ask that
Council accept the inclusive community living on Serenity Hill has been in residence long enough to legally remain. I cry adverse possession."

The murmurs began in earnest. Most asking what the
heck adverse possession was.

"For those who do not know the legalese," said Councillor Pinkerton into her microphone, "Ms Hartley is claiming squatter's rights."

At that, the town hall exploded as a hundred conversations began at once. Cheers came from some corners, jeers
from others. The fretting baby began to cry in earnest.

The gavel smacked against the wooden table, quieting
the crowd somewhat. And this time it rang through Amber
like an old bell. Sweet and familiar and pure.

"Thank you, Ms Hartley. Your position has been noted.
Does anyone else have anything to say on the matter?"

Amber glanced over her shoulder to find movement at
the back of the hall.

A man had stepped into the aisle, a man with overlong

hair swept away from his striking face and dark hazel eyes that locked onto Amber. She didn't realise her lungs had stopped functioning until her chest began to ache.

Hugo. But not the Hugo she knew. Not the man in the worn jeans and button-downs who was happy rolling on the ground with Ned, watching her collect honey, or sitting on her stairs staring towards the horizon chewing on a blade of grass.

This was Hugo the Prince. His stark jaw was clean-shaven and he looked dashing in a slick three-piece suit with such bearing, composure and self-assurance he was barely human. Behind him stood a big, hulking bald man in black, watching over him like a hawk.

She hoped no one noticed how hard she clenched her fists.

"Your Highness, good evening, sir," said Councillor Pinkerton, the friendly note of her voice making it clear it was not the first time she'd set eyes on the man.

Hugo's deep voice rang out across the room. "If I may?"

Councillor Pinkerton waved a hurry-up hand. "Up you come, then. State your name for the record. And your purpose."

While Amber had had to climb over a tangle of legs to get to the lectern, the crowd parted for Hugo like the Red Sea.

He slowed as he neared, his head cocking ever so slightly in a private hello.

Amber hated the way her cheeks warmed at the sight of him, her heart thumping against her ribs as if giving the death throes of remembered desire. Nevertheless, she held her ground, waiting until the last moment to give up her position. Then, with an exaggerated bow from the waist, she swooshed out an arm, giving him the floor as she backed away.

Laughter coursed through the crowd.

Hugo's smile eased back, just a fraction. Enough for Amber to know she'd scored a hit.

All's fair, she thought, in love and war. And this was war.

"Councillor Pinkerton," he said, "Council members, good people of Serenity. I thank you for this opportunity to introduce myself to this community."

His hand went to his heart on the last few words, and Amber rolled her eyes.

But the crowd? They were hooked. Straining forward so as not to miss a word spoken in that deep, hypnotic, lilting voice. And he was ramping up the accent. Big time. Playing the dashing foreigner card for all it was worth.

"It has taken me far too long to return to the home of my mother's family, but in the days I have spent wandering the hills and vales your home has come to hold a special place in my heart. And I cannot wait to tell my friends and family about this gem of a place. To invite them here to meet all of you good people. To give the world a taste of Serenity."

Amber rolled her eyes again. But when she looked out over the crowd she saw even members of the commune listening with interest. Including Sunflower, who looked entranced. And then came a smattering of delighted applause.

Enough. Amber marched back up to the rostrum and gave Hugo a shove with her hip, ignoring the wave of heat that rocked through her at his touch. She grabbed the microphone so roughly that the feedback quieted the room.

"Really?" she said, her voice echoing darkly around the room. "*A taste of Serenity...?* It's like a cheesy brochure."

Hugo laughed. And she knew she had surprised him. He licked his lips, swallowing it back, but the light of it lingered in his eyes.

"He," said Amber, pointing an accusing finger towards

the Prince, "is *not* one of us. His words might be pretty but his plans are not. And I can't stand to—"

Something lodged in her throat then. Something that felt a lot like a swell of deep emotion, the kind that preceded tears.

Come on! She wasn't a crier! She breathed out hard. And managed to keep her cool.

"It would be a grave injustice to see Serenity lost under the overwhelming influx of tourism that would come by way of a resort. I hope, I *believe*, that you are with me on this point: Serenity's future must be allowed to evolve as it always has—organically."

If Hugo's words had been met with happy claps, Amber's were met with a standing ovation, and a cheer that all but lifted the roof off the place.

The gavel banged several times before Councillor Pinkerton regained control. "Assuming that's all the new business, we will keep further discussion to next week's town meeting. Date and time as mentioned earlier. Meeting adjourned."

With that, Councillor Pinkerton and the others made their way back behind their private closed door, leaving the people of Serenity to ease off their numb backsides, stretch their arms and talk excitedly amongst themselves.

Hugo stepped in and took Amber's elbow. Gently. Respectfully. But that didn't stop the sparks of heat from travelling up her arm and making a mess of her synapses as he tilted his head to murmur near her ear.

"You can't possibly believe I want Serenity to suffer."

"You have no idea what I believe. You don't know me at all."

His eyes didn't move but she imagined them sliding up and down her body as a slow smile tugged at the corners of his mouth. "You have a short memory, Ms Hartley. Or perhaps selective would be a better description."

"You want words? I can think of so many words to describe you right now, *Your Highness*. We could go on like this *all night long*."

Hugo's eyes darkened. And yep, she'd heard it too. Dragon fire gathered behind Amber's teeth as conflict and desire swirled through her like a maelstrom. But behind it all, the need to protect her town, her people, herself.

"Game on," said Hugo as he was swallowed by the crowd.

Bring it on, Amber thought as she crossed her arms and backed away. Bring. It. On.

CHAPTER THREE

HUGO TUGGED HIS cap lower over his eyes and hunched into his shoulders as he made his way up a gravel path winding through the quaint market town of Serenity. The kind of place where business hours varied daily and where as many animals sat behind counters as people.

Prospero—the bodyguard Hugo's uncle had insisted upon—was not happy about it. He did not like being in the open. Or moving slowly. Or places with tall buildings. Or cars with open windows. He particularly didn't like the fact that Hugo had ditched him in Vallemont a couple of months before and had only just made contact again, requesting his presence, now that he had been outed.

But for all the big guy's efforts at keeping Hugo safe, Hugo blamed him for the sideways glances and double-takes. The size of a telephone box, dressed in head-to-toe black, a clean-shaven head and *Men in Black* sunglasses, he looked like a soccer hooligan on steroids.

Otherwise there was no way the locals would make the connection between the guy in the ripped jeans, Yankees cap and skateboard shoes and the Prince in the three-piece suit from the meeting the night before.

Though it wouldn't take long for that to change. There was no doubt the story of Hugo's public life was being shared and spread.

A prince, fifth in line to the throne of the principality of Vallemont. An Australian mother, a father who had died when his son was fifteen, having infamously run his car off a cliff with his young mistress at the wheel. Now he was the black sheep: independently wealthy and single.

The official palace statement was that Hugo was back at work, but after the wedding debacle he'd needed to escape. Eventually he'd found himself in Serenity. Where his mother had been born.

Days had dissolved into nights, a blur of time and quiet and nothingness; of exploring the empty, echoing house which seemed uninspired by his presence as if he too were a ghost.

Until he'd walked over the other side of the hill and found a hammock strung between two trees in the shade. He'd sat down, kicked off his shoes and fallen asleep.

Upon waking, he'd looked into a pair of whisky-brown eyes. And seen colour for the first time in as long as he could rightly remember.

"Alessandro!"

Hugo followed his name to find Councillor Pinkerton sitting at a colourful wrought-iron table inside a place calling itself "Tansy's Tea Room", which looked like a middle-eastern opium den.

She waved him in and, since he needed her support to be granted planning permission for his resort, he entered, leaving Prospero at the door with a, "Stay. Good boy."

"Sit," said the councillor. "Have some tea. You look tired. A man as rich and good-looking as you should never look tired. It gives the rest of us nothing to aspire to." She clicked her fingers, called out, "A top-up on my 'Just Do It', and a 'Resurrection' for my friend, please."

"Should I be afraid?" he asked.

"It's just tea. Mostly chamomile. I'm on your side."

"Glad to hear it."

"Don't get me wrong, I'm on Ms Hartley's side too."

"I see."

"Do you?"

"You want what is best for Serenity."

"I do."

"Councillor?"

"Paulina, please."

"Paulina. Before the town meeting last night, your council had seemed extremely positive about my proposal."

"They were."

"And now? Is a green light still assured, or are we now leaning towards…khaki?"

The councillor smiled. "I can see that the resort would be good for us. An influx of tourists means an influx of the kind of money which cannot be sneezed at for a town of our size. But Ms Hartley had a point. The beauty of Serenity is its way of living. The openness, the quiet, the kindness and, most of all, the community. We are self-sufficient in the most important ways, in a great part thanks to the commune."

"I would have thought the presence of a commune has negative connotations in this day and age."

"Which is why we call it an 'Inclusive Community' on the brochures."

Two pots of tea landed on their table, slopping towards the rims as the unsteady table rocked.

Paulina poured. "So how is your mother?"

Hugo stilled at the unexpected turn of conversation. "My mother?"

"Anna. Yes. I knew her, you know. Before." She waggled her fingers as if about to go back in time. "We were good mates, in fact. Went through school together, met boys together. So how is she?"

Hugo went to say *Fine*, but something about this woman, her bluntness, the intelligence in her eyes, the

fact she'd known Hugo's mother in the before, had him
saying, "I think she's lonely."

"Hmm. She is remarried, no?"

"Yes."

"To a French businessman, I hear?"

"An importer, yes. He travels a great deal."

"Ah." The councillor nodded again. "Handsome though,
I expect. Your father was a very handsome man. I might
even go so far as to say, devastatingly so. Add the Giordano charm and..." Paulina pursed her lips and blew out
a long, slow stream of air.

"So I have heard."

Paulina's eyes hardened. Then she slapped herself on
the hand. "Sorry. Insensitive."

Hugo waved a hand, releasing her of any apology.

His father *had* been charming, famously so. His mother
was only one of the women who'd loved him for it. The
mistress who'd been driving the car that had killed him
was another.

"I was there the day they met. Your mother and father.
Would you care to hear the tale?"

Since Hinterland House, with its air of quiet slumber,
had not yet given up any secrets, he found he cared a
great deal.

"Your father was ostensibly in Australia to see the reef
and the rock and forge relationships on behalf of his little-
known country—but mostly to watch sports and try his
fair share of our local beers. He came to our small corner
to pick peaches. Your mother and I were working at the
orchard that summer, handing out lemonade to the tourists. I remember so many long-limbed Germans, sweet-
talking French, Americans full of bravado. And there was
your father—the brooding Prince.

"A good girl, your mother. Seriously shy, she ignored
his flirtation, which was a good part of why he kept it up.

He could have offered diamonds, played up his natural charisma, but he was cleverer than that. He brought her hand-picked wild flowers, notes scratched into sheaves of paper bark, the very best peach he picked every day. It took three days. When she fell, she fell hard. And I was glad to see his adoration didn't diminish for having her. They were so very much in love.

"He left for Sydney a week later. A week after that he came back for her with a ring and a proposal. And I never saw her again."

Paulina smiled. "I was sorry to hear of his passing, not only for your mother's sake. How old were you?"

"Fifteen," Hugo said without having to think about it. His headmaster had been the one to inform him, having been instructed by his uncle to wait until after the funeral. A decision had been made not to send Hugo home to keep him away from the scandal.

"Ah. A trying period in the life of a boy, at the best of times."

Hugo merely nodded.

"Ah," said the councillor, looking over Hugo's shoulder, a smile creasing the edges of her eyes as someone approached their table.

Hugo knew who it was before a word was said. The wild energy snapping at the air behind him disturbed the hairs on the back of his neck.

He let his voice travel as he said, "Now, Paulina, about that woman who stood up in front of the council last night—shall I buy the bag of lime and shovel or simply pay you back?"

The councillor's eyes widened in surprise before a smile creased her face. "Good morning, Ms Hartley."

A beat, then, "Good morning, Councillor Pinkerton."

"Paulina, please."

Hugo pressed back his chair and stood. Amber wore a

short summer dress that hung from her tanned shoulders by thin ribbons tied at her shoulders. A battered pork-pie hat sat atop her head, leaving her long honey-blonde hair to hang in waves over one shoulder.

But it was the eyes that got him every time. They were devastating. Fierce, wanton bedroom eyes that could lay civilisations to waste.

"Well, if it isn't my worthy adversary," he said.

Amber tilted her chin and looked only at Hugo's companion. "I'm so glad to have run into you, Paulina. I was hoping to have a word."

"Any time. Won't you join us?"

Amber's chin lifted. "Considering the subject, I don't think that's wise."

"I think quite the opposite. Did the two of you manage to meet properly last night?"

Hugo looked to Amber with a smile, allowing her to respond.

She gaped like a fish out of water before saying, slowly, "We did not meet last night."

"Then allow me. Amber, this is Prince Alessandro Giordano of Vallemont. Prince Alessandro, this is our supplier of all things sweet and honeyed, Amber Hartley."

"A pleasure to meet you." Hugo held out a hand. Amber's face was a concerto of emotion as she fought against the need to play nice, at least in front of others, so she didn't look like an ass.

Finally, Amber's eyes turned his way. "Prince *Alessandro*, was it?"

He nodded. "My friends call me Hugo."

"How nice for them." Then she took his hand, grabbed a hunk of skirt and curtseyed. Deeply. "Your Highness."

Until that moment Hugo hadn't realised a curtsey could be ironic. Laughter knocked against his windpipe, desperate to escape. Only years of maintaining a neutral countenance in affairs of state made it possible to swallow it down.

"Amber, sit," said Paulina. "I insist. Talk to the man. Work out your grievances. At least attempt to come up with a workable plan, for your sake and for the sake of the town. If you can't, well, you can tick 'having tea with a prince' off your bucket list."

Councillor Pinkerton pushed back her chair and stood. Hugo reached for his wallet.

"No," said the older woman. "My treat. Wouldn't want anyone thinking you'd bribed me with a pot of tea, now, would we?"

Then she held out her hand, offering the seat to Amber.

"No," said Amber, waving both hands to make it clear she meant it. "Thank you. But I couldn't."

"Your loss," said the councillor. Then, at the door she called, "She's got mettle, this one. Might take more than a peach."

Hugo's laugh left his throat before he even felt it coming. Then he ran a hand up the back of his neck, settling the hairs that were still on edge.

Amber continued to glare.

"Please join me. At the very least so that I don't have to stand here all day."

"You'd like that, wouldn't you, *Prince Alessandro*? Get some paparazzi shots of us hanging together so as to muddy the waters regarding my side of the case."

"It's Hugo. Paparazzi a fixture here in downtown Serenity?"

"Well, no. But now word is out that you are here I'm sure it won't be long."

Hugo was sure of it too, meaning his blissful few weeks of anonymity truly were over. And the time to get the plans put to bed was ticking down.

"I'm going to sit," he said. "The chair is yours if you want it."

Amber glanced around, found the table beside his was empty, and sat there instead. With her back to him.

She turned her head ever so slightly. "This isn't the first time for you, is it?"

"Hmm? I didn't catch that with you sitting all the way over there." First time for what? he wondered. Drinking tea that smelled like feet? Or locking horns with a stubborn woman he couldn't get out of his head? "First time for what?"

"Tearing the heart and soul out of a town and turning it into some fancy, homogenised getaway for the idle rich."

"Ah. I probably won't use that as the tagline of any future advertising, but yes, I have experience in this area. This will be my...seventh such resort." A beat, then, "Have you been Googling me, Amber?"

Her shoulders rolled. "It was a stab in the dark. The only semi-decent Wi-Fi around here is at Herb's Shiatsu Parlour. You can go grey waiting for a picture to load."

"But at least you'd feel relaxed while doing so."

Her mouth twitched before she turned her back on him again. He spotted the edge of the dandelion tattoo that curled delicately over her shoulder blade. He remembered the slight rise of it as he'd run a thumb over the area once. The way her muscles reacted, contracting under his touch.

"I've come up against people like you before," she said, "privileged, successful, glowing with an aura that says *don't worry, I've done this before, you're in good hands.* But just because you think you're in the right, doesn't mean that you are."

"I could say the same for you."

"I live in a shack, Your Highness. I collect and sell honey for a living. You and are I are not on the same playing field. But the biggest difference is that, while you think you are in the right, I know I am."

Hugo could have argued relativism till the cows came home. In fact, if they'd been rugged up in her bed, limbs curled around one another, it might even have been fun.

"What were you telling Councillor Pinkerton about me?" Amber asked, and Hugo gave up pretending he could focus on anything else while she was near.

He pushed his tea aside and turned back to face her. "Until the moment you arrived your name did not come up."

"I find that hard to believe."

"Are you a subject of much chatter around these parts?"

A pause. "No. Maybe. At one time. I was a newcomer too once."

"The councillor and I weren't talking about my plans at all. It turns out she knew my mother. And my father."

Talk of family? Talk of something personal? He half expected Amber to leap over the table and bolt. But her head turned a little further, giving Hugo a view of her profile. Full lips, neat nose, and a fine jaw disappearing into swathes of golden hair. When she lowered her eyes he was hit with the memory of her sleeping; hands curled under her ear, lips softly parted, lashes creating smudges of shadow against her cheeks.

She asked, "Was that a surprise?"

"It was. A good one, though."

She turned a fraction more on her chair, until her eyes found his. Big, brazen pools of whisky that he knew, from experience, darkened with desire and brightened when she laughed. "Prince Alessandro—"

"Don't do that." Hugo's voice dropped so that only she could hear. "Amber, I am still the same man you found sleeping in your hammock and took into your home. Into your bed. I am still Hugo."

Amber's throat worked as she swallowed. "Ah. But that's the name your friends call you. And I am not your friend."

"You could be." Hugo called upon years of royal conditioning to keep his messier emotions at bay, to keep himself apart. He leant towards her, close enough to see the creases now furrowing her brow, the single freckle on her neck, the way her lashes tangled as they curled. "I'd like it very much if you were."

Her chest rose and fell as her eyes darted between his. She licked her lips then glanced away. "You have history here, I understand that. But you're not the only one. Think on that as you sit in your big house, poring over your Machiavellian scheme to destroy this community."

"You paint quite the picture. You must have spent a great deal of time imagining what I've been up to since you threw me out."

Pink raced up her cheeks as her jaw clenched. "I can assure you, *Prince Alessandro*, the amount of time I have spent wondering about you is entirely proportional to my desire to figure out how to make you walk away for good."

"Hmm," he said, not believing it for a second. The deep breaths, the darkness in her eyes—she was still as aware of him as he was of her. As much as she might want to switch off the fascination they had in one another, it was still alive and well.

"Amber?"

Amber blinked several times before they both turned towards a man with raging red hair gelled into painful-looking spikes. "Tansy. Hi. Sorry, I'm taking up a table. I..."

Amber stopped when she realised that was clearly not Tansy's concern. For Tansy was staring at Hugo as if he were an alien who'd landed a spaceship inside his shop. And behind him Tansy had amassed a small crowd, a veritable sea of tie-dye and hemp.

"Is this…?" said Tansy. "Is he…?"

"Why, yes," said Amber, her voice nice and loud. "Tansy, this is Prince Alessandro Giordano, the man who is planning on stripping our hill bare."

Tansy shoved a hand between them. "So pleased to meet you, Your Highness."

"Hugo, please. My friends call me Hugo."

When the shake was done, Tansy's heavily tattooed hands fluttered to his heart. "A prince. In my tea room. I honestly don't know what to say."

"How about *Get out*?" said Amber as she hopped out of the seat and melted into the crowd. "How about *Leave our village be*? How about *We don't want your type here*?"

Hugo saw Prospero begin to head inside, clearly not liking the growing crowd. Hugo stayed him with a shake of the head.

"Will you be King?" asked a woman twirling her hair and looking at him as if he were a hot lunch.

Hugo searched the crowd until he saw Amber's profile. She was whispering to someone in the back, no doubt working them to her favour.

"No," said Hugo. "Vallemont is a principality, not a kingdom. It is protected and overseen by a royal family, the head of which is my uncle, the Sovereign Prince. There are several people between me and the crown."

A ripple of disappointment swept through the small crowd.

Hugo bit back a laugh. He heard that. But since his chance at a possible shot at the crown had been ripped away from him at the age of fifteen, he'd had to find other uses for himself. Building resorts gave his life meaning.

"Now, who here loves a lagoon? Tennis courts? Who thinks this town could do with a yoga studio?"

He no longer kept looking for Amber, but he could feel her glaring at him just fine.

* * *

Dying sunlight poured tracks of gold over the stone floor of the tiny little shopfront in Serenity she had inherited along with the beehives when she'd first arrived in town.

Honey-Honey was a teeny-tiny mud hut with a desk, an old-fashioned cash register that binged winningly as it opened, and a small back room behind a curtain. The shop floor boasted a handful of shelves filled to the brim with pots of honey and beeswaxy goodness. And Ned, who was curled up on his soft doggy bed in the sunniest corner, his face twitching as he dreamed of chasing dandelion fluff and finding an endless supply of used socks.

Amber's ancient broom tossed dust motes into the light as she swept the stone floor, preparing to close up shop for the day, when she looked up and saw a man in black as big as a house, the man she'd seen hovering around Hugo at the town meeting and again at Tansy's.

"Amber."

So busy gaping, Amber hadn't seen Hugo lurking behind him until it was too late.

Ned on the other hand was all over him— bouncing about on his back feet, nose nuzzling Hugo's hand, tail wagging as if he was in utter bliss. The big man with Hugo looked ready to take down the dog at the first sign of teeth.

"Ned, heel." She clicked her fingers, knowing he'd feel the vibration if he didn't hear her words, and Ned gave her a side eye before ambling to her feet and plopping to his haunches with a snort. His version of a doggy eye-roll. "We're closed."

"This is the honey we collected?"

She winced at the use of "we". "Some. Several local apiaries sell their wares in this space. Different bees, different flora, make for different tastes, different texture, different healing properties." Amber tugged the strap of her bag over her head until it angled across her body. Not as if it was some kind of shield. Righteousness was all the armour she needed. "What are you doing here? I said all I needed to say at the tea room."

"I didn't. Are those live bees in the wall?"

He peered through the dark hexagonal observation pane where a small hive of bees buzzed and worked. Huffing out a breath, Amber turned on the nearest lamp, creating a pool of gold on the floor and showcasing the sweet little hive in her wall.

Hugo pressed a finger towards the glass but didn't touch. The one person she'd ever seen think before leaving a fingerprint she'd have to clean.

Humming contentedly, he moved around the space, picking up tubs of wax, reading over the names of the several flavours of honey. "Amber, this is charming. Why didn't you tell me about this place when we were…?" Hugo waved a hand to intimate the rest.

"Hooking up?" she finished helpfully.

The man in black squeaked, then covered it with a manly cough.

Hugo turned, ignoring his big friend, his eyes only for Amber. "Is that what we were doing?"

"Sure. Why? What else would you call it?"

Amber tucked her hair behind her ear and feigned non-chalance, even while her knees started to tingle at the way he was looking at her. But he didn't offer an alternative. He did rub at his hand, no doubt aching from having shaken the hand of every person in town since his "disguise" had been blown. Traitors. Fawning over the enemy just because of an accident of birth. And charm. And those magnetic good looks.

She pressed her palm to her belly and rolled her shoulders.

The townsfolk might all be blinded by the trappings but

not her. She could take him down all on her own. They'd thank her for it later.

He rubbed at his hand again, wincing this time.

"Oh, for Pete's sake." Amber turned on her heel and went to the freezer behind the curtain in the back, grabbed a bucket and filled it with ice. She plonked the bucket onto her counter and clicked her fingers at Hugo.

He came as asked.

"Good boy."

A solitary eyebrow shot north. Amber tried her dandiest to remember that she didn't find the move seriously sexy. Not any more.

When Amber looked back at Hugo it was to find his gaze had dropped to her smile, where it stayed for a beat or two. Her lips tingled under the attention, remembering how that look usually ended. Heat trickled through her veins and she began to itch all over, her body wanting what it could no longer have.

"Give me your hand," she demanded, all business.

He looked at his hand, surprised to find he'd been rubbing it. Then he looked at the bucket of ice. "I don't think so."

"Don't be such a baby."

The big guy made another strangled noise in the doorway, though this one sounded more like a laugh.

"Have you never had this done before?"

"I'm usually better protected."

The laughter from the doorway came to an abrupt halt.

Amber took her chance, grabbed Hugo's hand, and before the warmth of his skin, the familiarity of his touch, overcame her she shoved it into the ice.

Hugo let forth a string of expletives, in multiple languages no less. Amber enjoyed every one. Hugo shifted from foot to foot and cleared his throat.

"You okay there, buddy?"

"Peachy," he muttered.

And she shoved his hand just a little deeper. "So who's the elephant in the room?"

"Hmm?"

"The giant who is trying very, very hard not to tackle me right now."

"That would be Prospero. My bodyguard."

"Why the heck do you need a bodyguard?"

Hugo raised the single eyebrow.

She raised one right back. "Seriously. If you were a president or a drug lord or something, sure. Are you afraid the townspeople will throw mantras at you? Or is this because of *me*? Wow. Does he have a dossier on me? What's my code name?"

Hugo's brow furrowed, reminding her of the Furrows of Important Dreams on the day they had first met. That gravity that had drawn her to him in the first place. It was almost enough for her to let it go. Almost.

"Why do you need a bodyguard? I really want to know."

"Last year my uncle and his family were having a picnic by a local waterfall when a band of masked men attacked. Whether to kidnap, scare or worse, it was never clear. The small security detail managed to fend them off but the perpetrators got away. The royal family upped security across the board. Prospero has been my devoted body man ever since. Though I believe he feels as if he must have done something terrible in a former life to end up on my detail. Right, big guy?"

Aw, crud. "Was anyone hurt?"

"Not physically, no. But my uncle has been hyper-vigilant ever since, making demands on the family no one in power should ever make."

Amber had a thought. "Is he the one making you turn Serenity into a resort?"

Hugo smiled. "No. In fact, when he finds out he will not be pleased."

"Why?"

"Because every decision he makes is for the good of Vallemont. This decision is for the good of me."

"No kidding."

It was hard to get her head around. For Amber had known him before he was royal. Or at least before she'd *known* he was royal. The point was she'd known him when he was *Hugo*. A man of unremitting curiosity, acerbic wit and nothing but time. An avid listener with an easy smile. Smart as anyone she'd ever met, including her parents, who were called on to untangle the trickiest international laws on a daily basis. But, basically, a dissolute gadabout.

Yet he was a successful businessman in his own right. He accepted a bodyguard because he was deemed important to the crown and yet was content to stand up to his uncle if he believed it was the right thing to do.

While her brain understood the duality, a small part of her was still clinging on to the man who'd cleaned out her gutters when he'd seen grey clouds on the horizon; who'd rubbed her feet without being asked as they'd snuggled on her ancient couch.

She'd kicked that man out of her bed.

And created an adversary.

No. He'd done that. He wanted to build this resort of his for his own ends. She was merely standing up for what she believed was right.

Hugo made to lift his hand from the ice and she grabbed it. "Stop moving." She wasn't done with him just yet. "So this bodyguard of yours. Where was he when we were...?"

She flapped a hand.

"I was playing hooky."

"From?"

"Real life."

"Seriously?"

"You keep questioning the veracity of my answers. I have no reason to lie to you, Amber. I never have. All you ever had to do was ask."

She shook her head, but didn't have a comeback. It wasn't the first time she'd been accused of avoiding intimacy, but it was the first time she stuck around to continue talking to the person who'd made the accusation.

She told herself it was a learning opportunity. How not to get fooled next time. Next time what? Next time she found a hot man in her hammock and dragged him back to her cave to have her way with him for a few weeks?

Cheeks heating, she gritted her teeth. "From the little I know of Vallemont, it sounds like one of the prettiest spots in Europe. All craggy mountains and verdant valleys? Am I right?"

Hugo nodded.

"So, as far as real life goes, being a prince of such a realm must have been terrible. And being rich and handsome and royal surely feels all the same after a while."

His smile turned to laughter—rough and soft, so that she felt it right deep down inside.

"Alas, now real life has found you again," she said, "you have to go back to princeing. Is that the right verb?"

"You done?"

"For now."

"Good. Because it's my turn. Are you ready to tell me how you ended up here yet?"

Amber flinched. And said nothing.

"Nothing? Really? I showed you mine, now you show me yours. Quid pro quo. Or else I'm no longer the bad guy for not sharing my life story."

Dammit. He had her there.

"So what were you running away from?"

"Who said I was running away?"

"Those of us who are not where we started are all running from something. Responsibility. Danger. Boredom. So which was it?"

"I didn't run," she said, the words feeling as though they were being pulled from her throat with pliers. "I had an honest-to-goodness chance at a fresh start so I took it. I wasn't running, I was exploring."

"To what end?"

"It didn't even matter. It was all new for me out there. And all mine."

She knew she wasn't making sense to anyone but herself, but Hugo didn't press. He had a way of knowing just how far to push before giving her breathing space. She'd never met anyone who could read her the way he did.

Feeling as if a spotlight was shining on her, about to give her deepest insecurities and darkest fears away, she glanced over Hugo's shoulder to the shadow in the doorway. "So how did he summon you, Prospero? Did he send up a bat signal? Or would that be a crown signal? One in the shape of a ceremonial sword, perhaps?"

"He used a telephone signal, ma'am."

"How modern. I hadn't realised he even had a phone. Or a title, for that matter."

Hugo laughed deep in his throat, only just loud enough for her to catch it. The way it was when they'd lain in bed at night. The way it was when he'd swept her hair from the back of her neck to find that kiss spot that brought her out in goosebumps, before murmuring all the things he planned to do to her the next moment he could get her naked.

In the quiet that followed, Amber held her breath, hoping Hugo had no clue where her thoughts had gone. His charm was dangerous. His likeability her liability. His power, his political and personal influence, a real, living thing.

People like Hugo, like her own parents, were used to getting their way.

Not this time.

Not on her watch.

"And what exactly did our friend *the Prince* tell you about where he had been, Prospero? And what he had been up to?"

Prospero shot a slightly panicked look to his boss. "His Highness does not kiss and tell."

Amber burst out laughing. "Meaning he did exactly that. I never mentioned kisses, and nobody else in town knew about any kisses, so that leaves him." Amber waggled a hand Hugo's way.

Hugo caught her gaze, held it. "You really didn't tell anyone about what had kept you so busy the last few weeks? Not a girlfriend? A shaman? A friendly possum?"

Amber folded her arms loosely across her chest and slowly shook her head.

"More's the pity. My reputation could do with some bolstering in this town."

She laughed again. "Not going to happen."

"Really? You haven't been fighting the desperate urge to drop into casual conversation that I am a man of experience."

"No."

"And taste." His gaze dropped to her mouth before lifting back to her eyes. His expression darkening, all touches of humour now gone. "And unparalleled skill?"

"Hugo."

He paused. A slow, warm smile spreading across his face and making her knees shiver. Because—dammit!—she'd called him Hugo. She'd been so determined to stick with *Your Highness*.

"Amber," he lobbied, with grave deliberation.

His deep voice, the crinkle around his eyes, did things

to her basic structure. Turning her bones to liquid. Quieting her worries. Until she felt as if she was floating just a little above the ground.

She cleared her throat. "How's your hand?"

"Numb."

Rolling her eyes, Amber dragged his hand from the ice, feeling a little bit better when he winced. "And now?"

Hugo wriggled his fingers, twisted his hand and grinned at her.

She grabbed a tea towel and threw it at him. "Try not to drip. I've just swept. Now, while this has been a delight, you really must leave. It's time Ned and I got home."

Hugo wiped his hand. And nodded. "Fine. But first, the reason I came by. I brought you this." He held out his hand and Prospero handed over a rolled-up sheaf of papers held together with a pink and gold ribbon.

Amber looked at it warily. "What is it?"

"Take it home. Look it over. We can talk about it tomorrow. Once you've had time to think."

"I've thought. I don't want to talk to you tomorrow. Unless it's to hear you say you were mistaken and you're sorry for causing our quiet little community such distress. And that you are leaving and never coming back."

Hugo's eyes darkened. And he took a step closer. Or maybe he didn't. Maybe he just looked at her in that intense, indulgent way she found so overwhelming. As if she'd been tumbled by a rogue wave, not sure if she'd find her feet ever again.

"Fine," she said, whipping out a hand to take the sheaf of paper. Taking care not to let her fingers touch his. Those fingers had a way of stripping her defences and right now those defences were all she had.

When Hugo stepped back she felt that too. As though someone had pulled a blanket from her shoulders, and a stone from her chest.

He turned to leave before looking back. "Amber."

Swallowing his name, she simply waited.

"Is fighting this what the town needs? Is it even what they want?"

Amber reeled. "Of course it is."

"They seemed pretty happy about the idea at the meeting."

"They were happy a real live prince was in their midst. And you knew they would be. Why else did you shave? And wear that slick suit? And give them your smile?"

"My smile?"

"You know the one. All teeth and charm and eye crinkles. You are well aware that it makes knees go wobbly from a thousand paces."

Amber found herself glad the light was low, otherwise the look in his eyes might have melted her on the spot.

"I know perfectly well how stubborn you are, Amber. And how much you care. Take care you don't lose yourself inside a blind crusade."

Amber flinched. Hugo could not have picked better words with which to cut her. Deep. The number of times she'd accused her parents of getting caught up in doing right, in fighting for the little people, in pursuing justice at all costs, without really stopping to imagine the consequences...

She stamped her foot so that Ned would come to her side and lost her hand in the familiar softness of his fur. "I know what I'm doing."

"Okay, then." He reached a hand to the doorjamb, breathed, and turned back to her one last time. "You were quite the sight up there at the town meeting. Banging on the lectern. Riling the masses. I was waiting for you to climb the thing and punch your hand in the air. If you had I am absolutely certain the council would have agreed to anything. Including running me out of town with flaming pitchforks."

Amber breathed. Or at least she tried. Her throat threatened to close down. She wasn't good at taking compliments, never having had reason to learn when she was a kid.

With that he tapped his knuckles on the counter, gave Prospero a look and left.

Leaving Amber all alone with her weak knees, her deaf dog and the insatiable hunger that was gnawing at her insides.

Though it wasn't for food. Not even a bit.

CHAPTER FOUR

"IS THAT A HELIPAD?" Johnno's voice hummed at the corner of Amber's brain as she sat back in one of Sunflower's straw-filled beanbags and rubbed at her temples, breathing in the scent of Sunflower's stew warming over the brazier near her feet.

"And stables. Look!" That was Sunflower, resident animal whisperer, her fey voice tinged with excitement.

But Amber didn't want to look. She wanted to figure out what it meant that Hugo had given her the architectural plans in the first place. Plans so detailed they had clearly been worked on for some time.

"Does he think I'll go all gooey at the fact he has given away a big chunk of advantage? Does he think I'm that easy?"

"Honey," said Sunflower. "Who are you talking about?"

She flung her arm away from her eyes and said, "Hugo!"

At the concerned faces of her friends, her comrades, these sweet, trusting souls, she remembered everyone else knew him as Prince Alessandro Giordano of Vallemont. "The Prince. The Prince gave them to me."

"Oh, my."

Amber sat forward as best she could in the lumpy homemade beanbag. Firelight sent long, scary shadows over Sunflower's brightly painted caravan beyond. "You all agree, right? That we need to fight this? I'm not on some kind of blind crusade."

"Oh, yes." Sunflower swayed side to side to the music in her head.

"Johnno?"

"Hmm? Sure thing. I only wish he was dastardly. It'd be easier to dislike the guy."

Sunflower leaned down to give her man a hug. Then shoved a bowl of stew under Amber's nose. "You look pale. Eat."

Knowing better than to argue, Amber ate, spooning mouthfuls of unexpected vegetables and some kind of gamey meat into her mouth.

While Sunflower said, "Everyone does seem to be stuck on how charming he is. And how handsome. Do you think he's handsome?"

Johnno nodded.

Amber loved these people with every recess of her stone-cold heart, but at times she wished they were a bit more commercially switched on.

"Don't you think he's handsome, Amber?" Sunflower asked.

She put the half-eaten stew on the ground. "Sure. I guess." *Handsome didn't even come close.* "But what that has to do with any of this, I have no idea."

"Don't you?"

Something in Sunflower's voice made Amber wonder exactly how much she had been paying attention. Was it possible she'd known Hugo was in Amber's bed the morning she'd come by? That Ned hadn't been the one making the banging noises?

If any of them knew she'd been the one feeding him and watering him while he made his devious plans she was sure they'd never look at her the same way again.

Then Sunflower grabbed a set of bowls to hold the corners of the plans down. "I just don't see it. Far too clean-cut for my taste. Not like my darling scruffy Johnno. Though it is hard to believe he was left at the altar."

"He was what, now?" said Amber.

"Left at the altar by a runaway bride."

Amber looked from one friend to the next to find them nodding along. "How did you even know about this?"

Johnno stuck a stick in the fire and sparks shot up into the sky. "Everyone knows."

Amber let out a breathy, "Jeez…"

Playing hooky from real life, my ass.

"So this was recent?"

"Oh, yes."

When he'd opened his eyes and looked into hers that very first day, she'd had to brace herself so as not to fall right into his gaze. For she'd felt his pain in that unguarded moment as if it had been her own.

Like a standing redwood suffering the notches of an axe. Not broken so much as wounded. Needing somewhere safe to hole up. To heal. It had been half the reason she'd thrown caution to the wind and invited him into her home.

Had she been a transition fling? Why the heck did it matter?

Because you're envious of some other woman who turfed him out, when you should be high-fiving her. Starting an exclusive club—women who've turned away the estimable right-royal Hugo.

Sunflower went on, oblivious, "As the story went, he handled it like a true gentleman, not saying a bad word about the girl. A few days later they did a television interview together. It was honest, forgiving. Turns out they're old friends and they both wished the very best to one another for the future."

Sadie. The fact that this mystery woman had a name felt like a dagger to Amber's stomach. Which was ridiculous.

Amber had no hold over Hugo. And he none over her. Her stomach would simply have to catch up.

"He might be the big bad wolf, but boy, does he make it look appealing."

Amber dropped her head into her hands and let out a sorry sob.

"Hey," said Johnno, back with them. "Doesn't this design remind you of a honeycomb shape?"

Of course she had noticed.

"Oh, my," Sunflower breathed, glancing at Amber. "How about that?"

"And did you also see where the buildings are situated? Right here, on this exact spot." The colourful caravans, shanties, tents, tree houses and demountables obliterated by the stroke of a pen. As if they'd never been.

Just about the only section of the hill which had been preserved were the two trees to which her hammock was hitched.

Rubbing the heels of her palms deep into her eyes, she tried to hold back the memory, but it came anyway.

It had been late afternoon. The air had been filled with pollen and that strange heaviness that heralded a storm.

She'd snapped off a chunk of honeycomb and given it to him. He'd carried it back through the forest to the shack, holding it up to the sun, rubbing it between his fingers, licking the thing till she'd tripped over her own feet.

Somehow they'd ended up at the hammock, then in the hammock. Together. It had been one of the most perfect moments of her entire life.

And then it hit her. *That* was why he'd given her the plans.

He knew she'd see that he'd saved those trees. *That manipulative bastard.*

She was furious she hadn't seen it straight away. She'd been raised by master manipulators after all.

Her parents, Bruce and Candace Grantley—OBEs—
had been "influencers" before the term was popular. On
the surface that seemed like a compliment. A sign of respect. But really it meant they knew how to sway, ca-
jole, manoeuvre, distract, use bias to engineer outcomes
to their liking.

Embroiled in an international child labour case, they'd
begun bringing Amber along to newspaper photo shoots,
on television interviews, using her as an example of a child
of privilege. A counterpoint to the children they were representing in some far-off country. But only after taking her
braces off five months early. She'd overheard her mother
telling her father a bright white smile would "play better".

Now, at twenty-seven, she had bottom teeth that over-
lapped. Just a little. Just enough to remind her the lengths
her parents had gone to in order to get their way.

"True gentleman my ass," Amber muttered, sweeping
the plans up into her arms, shoving them under her arm
and taking off up the hill.

Hugo sat on the large portico at the rear of Hinterland
House, watching the dragonflies dance over the surface
of the moonlit fountain beyond.

His phone buzzed. A quick check showed him it was
from his aunt Marguerite.

He ignored it.

He'd been getting messages from the palace—mostly
from his aunt—since he'd first taken off. He'd made it
clear he had no intention of telling them where he was
until he was ready.

He was a grown man. And not near enough to the throne
for his whereabouts to matter to anyone but his mother.
He was in one piece, he was keeping his head down, and
after recent events he needed some time. And he would
very much appreciate it if they'd leave him the hell alone.

When the phone buzzed again, he switched it off.

Prospero came outside with a green metal coil and a box of matches. He lit the end until a whirl of sweet-smelling smoke curled into the air.

"What is that?" Hugo asked.

"They call it a mozzie coil. One of the women in town gave it to me earlier when she saw my bites." Prospero tugged a black sleeve up to his elbow, revealing a handful of red welts.

"Do you need those seen to?"

The big man shook his head. "Just mosquitos. Saliva takes out the itch."

"Did the woman in town help you with that too?"

Even in the growing darkness Hugo saw the red creeping up the big man's throat.

He'd been in town a few days now. It would be worth getting his take on the situation. "So, Prospero, you have been paying attention." One could only hope. "What do you think of my plans?"

Prospero did his soldier poster move, looking out into the middle distance. "I couldn't say, Your Highness."

"You couldn't or you won't?"

"Yes, sir."

Smarter than he looked. "And what do you think of my opposition?"

"Sir?"

"Need I be worried about Amber Hartley?"

Prospero stilled. "In what way? Do you think she is dangerous? Has she threatened you again?"

"I don't think she is about to jump out of the bushes and attack me, if that's what you're worried about."

Prospero's face worked before he came to a decision. "You joke. I understand that. But you must know, Your Highness, that the possibility of someone jumping out of the bushes and attacking you is why I am here."

Hugo winced. Right. Bad choice of words.

As he had intimated to Amber, not that long ago his uncle, aunt and their multiple sets of twins had been near-victims of a targeted attack while on a family picnic within the palace grounds.

Hugo sat forward. "I am not blasé, Prospero. I promise. I have every intention of living a long and healthy life. If you feel that I am placed in any real danger, I will heed your concerns. Now, please tell me you understand I was joking. That Amber is not a physical threat."

A muscle twitched under Prospero's eye. "My observations suggest you do not see straight when it comes to Ms Hartley. You are not careful when you are with her."

Hugo blinked. "I believe you are right."

For Amber Hartley had been a safe haven when his life was in upheaval. A slip from reality when reality chased hot on his heels. No expectations, no burden, no demands. He could not have been more grateful that he had met her when he had. And that kind of thing left a mark.

Which didn't even begin to cover the way his blood still heated at the sight of her. How precisely he could remember the scent of her hair. The taste of her skin. How deeply satisfied he felt when he made her smile. Even fighting with her was the most fun he remembered having in years. *Years.*

Yes, Amber Hartley had left a mark on him. A brand.

But he would not change his mind about the resort because of it. No matter how much he wished he'd had one more week in her bed.

While his father had been Sovereign Prince, Hugo had been the next successor. But when his father died he'd been too young to take the throne and his uncle had acceded instead, shunting him to sixth in line as his uncle's children now took precedence. It had forced Hugo to reimagine his life. It had taken time. He'd been angry for a while, had acted up, thrown money around. Until one of his wild investments had paid off. And just like that he'd found purpose. His resorts had seen stupendous success, channelling millions into the Vallemont economy and projecting the small, quiet principality into the international consciousness.

Families in Vallemont had safer jobs and better incomes, in thriving townships because of him. It was no crown, but it was a fine legacy, something of which he was immensely proud.

One he planned to keep refining, perfecting, until he made a true name for himself, by himself. Until the loss of the crown no longer mattered at all.

"Fear not the beautiful blonde in our midst, my intrepid friend. Once the resort plans are through council, my work here will be done and the project team will take over from there. We will head home."

Prospero wasn't the sharpest tool in the shed. Slipping away from him in Vallemont had been far too easy. But, as Hugo was beginning to find, he was a genuinely nice fellow.

"Do you feel as if you are being punished for something, having ended up with me, Prospero?"

Prospero swallowed and said, "I won't leave you. Not again."

"No. Of course. I totally understand. I just thought it would be a good opportunity to case the place. Perhaps see if any...women have an insight into the seedy underbelly of the town once the sun goes down."

Prospero looked to the door, then to Hugo, then to the door. "You keep your phone near by and you answer if I call."

"Yes, sir!"

"I see how you ignore the phone when the palace calls. Promise me."

Right. "Promise. Cross my heart. Hope to die."

His face looked pained at the thought. Big guy needed to lighten up.

"Lock all the doors. I will be back in an hour."

"Why don't you make it two?"

Hugo sat and listened to the rustle of wind in the trees, breathed in the sweet scent of gum trees and red dirt and wondered how he'd gone thirty-some years without feeding the Australian half of his soul.

The patter of feet on stone caught Hugo's attention moments before Ned bounded up onto the patio.

"Hey, Ned," Hugo said, leaning forward and opening his arms to the dog who came in for a cuddle.

Meaning his owner wouldn't be far behind.

Like a ghost she emerged from the shadows, skin glowing in the moonlight, hair floating behind her. A sylph, ethereal, so beautiful, Hugo's heart stuttered.

"Down, boy," Hugo murmured, pulling himself to standing.

While Ned, lovely, near-deaf Ned, who could pick up on human emotion from a mile away, dropped to his haunches in response.

"Okay," Hugo said, releasing him, after which the dog happily trotted off inside the house, then, "Well, if it isn't Amber Hartley, local beekeeper, representative of the little people, and excellent cooker of pancakes."

She baulked at the reference to the one time she'd cooked him breakfast before their cocoon had imploded. But then she collected herself and jogged up the back stairs and slammed a bunch of scrunched-up paper on the table beside him.

"Would that be the plans I gave to you earlier, rolled up all neat and tidy?"

"Sorry," she said, clearly not sorry at all. "I hope you have spares."

Hugo poked a thumb over his shoulder and Amber followed with her gaze. Her eyes widened when she saw the state-of-the-art computer system he'd set up on the Queen Anne dining table, the plans open right now on one of the three forty-inch monitors.

"I can't believe your gall!"

"Which gall?"

"Tennis courts. Seriously? And a spa? As for us, you levelled our part of the hill. As if we never existed."

"You didn't like it, then?"

"Like it? It made me feel physically ill!" She even looked a little grey, but it could have been the moonlight.

"And your friends? I'm assuming you shared the plans with them."

She snorted. "Johnno now wants his own helipad."

Interesting. "So what didn't *you* like about it? Be specific."

"Apart from the fact you plan to wipe out the commune in one fell swoop?"

"*Move* the commune."

"Excuse me?"

"There is a tract of land on the other side of town I had the planners put aside with space to build a number of cottages. More than enough to relocate everyone."

She blinked. "Those were meant for the commune? With the vegetable gardens? And neat little paths? The window sills filled with lavender?"

"Yes." Hugo realised he'd crossed his arms.

"Have you actually visited the hill? Apart from my place, of course."

The two of them locked eyes a moment, a spark zapping between them as they both remembered. Amber looked away first, tucking her hair behind her ear before frowning at the floor.

"Willow's caravan broke down on the hill twenty-five

years ago. Tomas, her ex-husband, came down from Sydney to help her fix it and has lived in his tent next door ever since. Dozens of others have come and gone since. Sunflower and Johnno arrived a couple of years before I did. They'd been struggling to have kids for years, and coming here, to a place that was quiet and clean, helped them lick their wounds, to start afresh. Johnno lives in a tree house outside Sunflower's van. It could never be replicated. This community has been here long enough that nature has grown up around it. Grass and flowers and trees and shrubs connecting their homes to the earth. And you want to move them into matching cabins?"

"I'd be amenable to hearing input from the commune about the exact designs."

Amber ran a hand over her forehead, clearly not fine with it. And he knew that if he offered to move them an inch to the left but keep everything the same she'd still fight him.

"I don't have to make any concessions, Amber. The land is mine."

"I'm well aware—"

Hugo leaned forward. "I had my lawyers look into it. And by lawyers I mean the Sydney branch of the top firm in New York, so they are au fait with local law. Squatters' rights don't apply in your case."

She took so much time to speak he wondered how long she could hold her breath. "Why not?"

"I'm more than happy to give you a copy of their findings. It goes for over a hundred pages."

She held out a hand.

He coughed out a laugh. "I don't have one on me, but I promise I will get it to you."

Hugo pictured the plans for the estate. The vineyard that would sit so prettily on his side of the hill, the beautifully crafted structures taking advantage of the views on her side. The way his family's land, his mother's land, could be of use…his mother who had not felt much at all since his father's death, merely going through the motions of living her life. The way he could create something beautiful, functional, recreational and successful on his own. For her. And for himself. Without palace backing, palace oversight, or palace fingers delving into his financial pockets. He needed to do this. To create a legacy that was his alone.

With a growl, Amber plopped down in the cane chair beside his; legs stretched out in front of her, one arm bent behind her head, the other lying gently across her belly.

"That's it? You've given up? If I'd known it would be that easy I'd have got my lawyers onto you sooner."

"I come from a long line of lawyers; they do not scare me." She smiled from beneath the mask of her arm. "I'm just suddenly feeling very, very tired. Can we call a truce? For five minutes."

"Let's make it ten."

She held out her hand and he shook it. Holding on longer than necessary. Then again, she didn't let go either.

Finally, their hands parted, fingers sliding past one another, leaving tingles in their wake. And her hand once more moved to rest across her belly.

Watching her lie there, a picture of long-limbed, brown-skinned, earthy grace, he was well aware that there was something to be said for simply wanting *her*. She stirred and he dragged his hungry gaze away.

"Can you smell that?" she asked.

Hugo sniffed. "Cut grass? Night air?"

"Exactly. I don't know what it's like where you're from, but the cities I've lived in don't smell like this."

"No, they do not."

A pause, then, "What is it really like? Where you're from?"

"We have grass in Vallemont, like here. Night skies, like here."

"Fine...but—"

"Fine. It's...glorious! Tucked into a valley, surrounded by stunning mountains. Lakes like glass. Towns out of a Christmas card. With smart, sophisticated, friendly people. Last year we were also voted as having the cutest sheep on the planet."

"Sheep."

"Fluffy, white, say 'Baa' a lot."

The woman knew how to deadpan. "If it's so perfect over there, why did you really come here? And none of that 'playing hooky from real life' bull. Give me the unvarnished truth."

"So bolshie this evening." Her face was blank, but something—in her voice, in the shift of her body—alerted him. The town had been talking and she'd been listening. "You've visited Herb's Internet Café and Shiatsu Parlour, haven't you?"

She rolled her eyes. "I haven't Googled you! Why would I need to when you are right here?"

"Because you don't like asking hard questions when it might mean having to answer some of your own."

She growled again, this time shaking fists at the sky. "I thought princes were meant to be diplomatic."

"I thought hippies were meant to be mellow."

The growl turned to laughter. "You are infuriating, did you know that?"

"I've always thought myself rather charming."

"I'll bet." Her fists dropped, softening before her hands landed on her belly yet again. "The people in this place... For all its inherent loveliness, it's a small town. News travels fast and twists and turns as it goes. Whatever I might have heard, I'd prefer finding out the truth from the horse's mouth."

"Neigh."

She laughed again, then frowned at him as if she was struggling to figure him out. "Tell me about your wedding."

This time he had seen it coming. "You mean my non-wedding."

"If you like."

He sat forward, looked out into the dark night, and chose his words with care because this one wasn't all on him. "After the attack on my uncle he saw need to put his house in order, and so he offered me a deal. Marry or else."

"Or else what?"

"Being that she was born here, my mother is not of royal blood. After my father died, her link to the royal household diminished. Once I turn thirty-three, it diminishes further. If I am not married by that date my place in the line of succession will be forfeited and my royal rights depreciated, making my mother's rights non-existent. With no prince as her husband, no prince as a son, her title would no longer have meaning. The palace—her home for the past thirty years—would no longer be available to her."

"You can't mean that he intended to kick her out?"

Hugo could feel Amber's sense of righteousness kick in. It flowed from her pores like the electricity that rumbled through the air around here right before a storm. He fed off it, releasing his own indignation, which he had kept held down deep inside all this time.

"Most unfair but there you have it."

"That's scandalous. It's...it's blackmail."

"Pretty much."

She shook her head; livid, riled, she could have been a Valkyrie. "I thought my parents were master manipulators, but your uncle takes the crown."

"Literally."

She looked to him then, a moment passing before she

caught up. A smile passing over her bright eyes. "But you didn't marry."

"No, I did not."

"So, the girl. The woman. Your…" She flapped a hand at him, the way she did when she hit a thought she found too uncomfortable to voice. The fact that his ex-fiancée fell into that pile was interesting, to say the least.

"Sadie," Hugo said, "my intended, grew up in the palace, the daughter of a maid, and has been my best friend since as far back as I can remember. When I told her of my predicament she agreed to marry me out of the goodness of her heart, not for any romantic reason at all. But at the last she decided blackmail wasn't the best way to start a marriage. So she jumped out of a window at the palace and ran for the hills. On the way, a friend of mine—Will Darcy—found her on the side of the road, rescued her, whisked her away to safety, and the two of them fell madly in love."

"Oh. Wow. That news did *not* make it to Serenity."

"Small mercies."

"Were you—*are* you—okay with that?"

"Will and Sadie? I am immensely grateful they found one another. It let me off the hook big time."

He smiled, but she simply waited for him to stop joking and answer the question she'd asked.

"They are both wonderful people whom I care for very much. And I am truly happy for them both. Does that make me sound warm and generous, or a monster for not being broken-hearted?" It was a question he had asked of himself more than once in the weeks since it had all gone down.

She thought about it. "It sounds like not marrying her was the right decision. Happy ending."

Right. Okay, then. A weight he didn't even know he'd still been carrying lifted away from his shoulders.

"And what happened with your mother?" she asked.

"What with the PR disaster brought upon us by my run-away bride, Sadie and I managed to make a deal with my uncle that suited us all better. She promised not to marry me or anyone in my family and he would agree to leave our mothers alone and never to meddle in our love lives again."

A light lit Amber's eyes. "Sounds like a good deal."

"Sadie is a much better negotiator than I will ever be."

"I like the sound of her."

"I believe she'd like the sound of you too."

Hugo hadn't felt the words coming, but as soon as they were said he knew them to be true. Sadie would take one look at Amber and see a kindred spirit for sure. Something unlocked inside him at the thought.

"So you don't have to marry any more?" Amber asked, her voice now more careful.

"I do not." And then he understood the reason for her care and he felt another door open inside. If he didn't curb the unlocking soon he'd have nowhere left to hide. "I did not latch on to you hoping you might be my next victim, Amber. What happened between us…"

"Yes. Okay. No need to go there."

In the moonlight, this beautiful woman made of fight and fire lying within reach, he wasn't so sure any more.

But Amber went on. "And your mother is now safe. I'm glad for her. It must have been frightening, the prospect of being kicked out of her home for no reason other than the whim of one man."

Hugo went to nod…but caught himself in time. Clever girl. While he'd been trying to figure out ways of getting her to trust him again, she'd just tied him neatly in a big fat knot.

"Ironic, don't you think?" she went on. "That fear for the loss of home sent you rushing to marriage. Yet that is what you plan to inflict on all of us. On me."

His smile was without humour. "Ah, but I did not fear

the loss of my home for myself. My connection to the palace is tenuous. I could happily live anywhere. A four-poster bed in Paris. A tent in the Sahara. A hammock slung between two gum trees. As, I believe, would you."

He'd said it in jest. But beneath it, like a silver thread in a sea of black, it twisted through the night connecting them. Like a language only they knew. Secret stories, stolen moments that belonged only to them.

"So there's really no chance you might one day rule?"

"The succession plan is ancient and twisted. And if you ask Reynaldo, the current uncle in charge, he is going to live for ever." He sat forward on the chair, leaning towards her, now determined to find another way in. "It's just a title, Amber. A side note in my bio that refers to the family into which I was born. Just as you are a Hartley, I am a Giordano."

"Ah, but I was not born a Hartley."

Just when he began to feel comfortable, she knocked him sideways. Yet again. "You weren't?"

"I was born Amanda Grantley. But after I legally divorced my parents when I was sixteen I also changed my name."

"Excuse me, you divorced your parents?" His mind shot back to the rare times he'd been able to get anything out of her about them and all he came up with was lawyers and master manipulators.

"Separated. Emancipated. No longer governed by. Anyway, I picked a name near enough to instinctively respond in answer to it, but still wholly my own. Now it feels like Amanda was a poor, sad little girl I once knew."

Sixteen? Hugo had been in boarding school in Scotland at sixteen. His father had been gone a year, his connection to the palace now tenuous, his biggest concern how to sneak beer into the dorms. He'd barely been able to make a decision about which socks went with which pants at sixteen. Or what to do about his first crush, his oldest friend Will's sister, Clair. While Amber...

"You were declared an adult by the state. At sixteen."

She nodded. "For all intents and purposes. I was precocious. I had to be. My parents are in demand in the human rights field, and their work keeps them occupied. I was pretty much raised by nannies. When they opened their eyes one day and decided that they quite liked the young woman I had become I was suddenly of interest to them. When they began to bring me out at parties, showing off their daughter like I was one of their Picassos, I took them to court, proved my maturity, and their lack of parental care, and won."

"Hell, Amber."

"I've shocked you a little, haven't I?"

"I'll say."

"Good. I feel ever so slightly like I've just clawed back some ground."

Keep clawing, he thought. Maybe there was a chance they could meet back in the middle once more.

"How long has it been since you saw your parents?"

"I told you, not since I was sixteen. No, I lie. I was working in a bar in Sydney once when they came on the TV. Looking all sanctimonious as they talked about the children they had helped all over the world. I packed up and left. Not long after that I found my way here."

"So we both had a pretty regular upbringing, then?"

"Sure. Only yours had more tiaras." A smile hooked at the corner of Amber's mouth. A razor-sharp sense of humour, and just a little vicious...the way he liked it.

There was something still going on here, between them. Something rich and deep and untapped. If only he knew how to make her see.

She got in first. "One more question, then I will let this be."

"Ask away." The fact that they were talking, really talking, had him feeling better than he had in days.

"Do you wish you could one day be in charge?"

And just like that she cut right to the heart of things. "Once upon a time. But now? I am content with my contribution."

"Which is?"

He pulled himself to sitting, putting his feet to the ground. "I find tracts of royal land near towns that are enduring hardship because their industries—milling, mining, transport—have dried up. Families are struggling to support themselves without welfare. And I build—"

"Resorts. Of course you do." Amber hauled herself upright, her feet hitting the ground as well. Her face sank into her hands.

"I give families jobs; first in construction, then in services. My developments give struggling communities a future."

"Admirable."

"Thank you. I want to turn my mother's home into something workable, useful, beautiful too. To allow it to thrive I will put money into town infrastructure. Shopfronts such as yours can expand. Sunflower and Johnno will have access to top-notch medical attention. It will bring this place alive, giving back to the community that looked after it while my family was gone. It was you who gave me the idea, Amber. You woke me up."

They locked eyes in those few moments, connecting them in ways Hugo wasn't equipped to name.

The last time he'd felt anything close to this he'd been a young man. He'd not long lost his father. Barely able to control his thoughts, much less his hormones, he'd met Clair—Will's twin sister. They'd shared an unexpected summer in Vallemont while Will was stuck at home in London with a broken leg. He'd barely begun to know her before she'd fallen ill. And succumbed. On top of the loss of his father, the tragedy of losing Clair had emptied him.

For a long time, Clair had been his *what if?*. A valid reason not to get too close.

Until Amber.

Now he knew his attraction to Clair had been forged from limited supervision and adolescence, the memories drenched in the golden glow of youth.

With Amber he was a grown-up.

Those weeks in her shack—the long, lazy days, the soft, warm nights, the talk of nothing, the luxurious quiet—had put him back together in places he'd not even known he was still broken.

Now the world shrank around them. All he could see was Amber; fierce, tough and confused. About him. It was a start, he thought, a way back.

But then she pulled herself to her feet. "Truce over," she said. "Our ten minutes is up."

On his feet now too, Hugo said, "Amber, come on."

She held out a hand, as imperious as any princess he had ever known.

But he took a step towards her. Then another.

She looked spooked. "How dare you suggest the resort idea was my fault?"

"It was absolutely your fault." His next step brought them toe-to-toe. He hadn't been this close to her in days. The scent of her skin, the power in those eyes—he felt drunk on her nearness.

His voice was rough as he said, "Amber."

He didn't even realise his hand was on her cheek until she leant into it. The feel of her skin after missing it, missing her, for the past few days was like an elixir. His blood, sluggish before then, began to pump in earnest.

Amber pulled away, turning, holding both arms across her belly. "I don't feel good."

"Neither of us feels any good. The way things ended… it feels unfinished. We feel unfinished." His mouth suddenly dry, he pushed past it, knowing he'd never forgive himself if he didn't try. "I never had any expectation of our time together. I still don't. But I miss you, Amber. I miss waking up to find you've stolen all the pillows. I miss watching you dress in your spacesuit. I miss watching you get out of your spacesuit. I miss listening to your voice as you tell stories in the darkness."

Amber shook her head hard. "No, I mean I really don't feel good."

She pushed away from him then, ran to the nearest flowerpot and threw up into a rose bush.

CHAPTER FIVE

AMBER LEANT AGAINST the open door of her bathroom, relishing the feel of the cool wood against her cheek. Whatever had been in Sunflower's stew the night before had not agreed with her. And had continued not agreeing for many, many hours.

In fact, it had been a rough night all round.

After embarrassing herself in the flowerpot, Hugo had insisted on taking her home. But she'd been adamant, telling him she was not about to fall for his plan to muddy her case by being seen coming out of her place in the dark of night.

But the truth was she was mortified beyond belief. The thought of him being nice to her, looking after her, was too much.

She'd gone over there to put her foot down, to insist he make changes, or give up the idea wholesale. Instead she'd come over faint and had to lie down.

And in the quiet that followed, it had felt far too much like before—when talk had been easy, when they'd been... *together*. And then there had been a moment—if a long-drawn-out stretch of breathlessness and anticipation could ever be deemed a mere moment—when the space between them had contracted as if it was being sucked into a black hole.

Throwing up in the bushes had merely been the cherry on the cake.

When Prospero had arrived and Hugo had asked him to escort her in his stead, she'd wept with relief. Literally. And she wasn't a weeper. Just another level of mortification to add to the rest.

But Hugo had taken it in his stride. He'd been kind, protective and supportive. *A true gentleman.*

Her stomach roiled. She closed her eyes, placed a quieting hand on her abdomen and breathed. Maybe it wasn't food poisoning. Perhaps it was a stomach bug. Or—

Amber's eyes flew open and she stared into the middle distance, calculating madly in her head.

No. It couldn't be that.

She crawled back to bed and grabbed her phone, checking the app where she kept track of her periods, before sliding to her backside, extremities numb, sweat prickling all over her skin.

She was a little irregular, could be a few days out, here and there. But even she couldn't justify the great red "negative twelve" glaring back at her, meaning her period was nearly two weeks late.

An hour later, Amber sat on the corner of her bed, with Sunflower holding her hand, the two of them staring at the small white plastic doo-hickey resting on Amber's bathroom sink.

"I'm so sorry," Amber said for the thousandth time.

Sunflower squeezed her hand harder. "Shut up, okay? I'm glad you came to me. I'm happy to be here for this, as I know how terrifying this moment can feel."

Everyone knew. Sunflower and Johnno had been trying to have a baby for years. It was how they'd ended up in Serenity—in the hope a holistic life would make all the difference. Which was why Amber had called, begging one of the dozen pregnancy kits she kept on hand, just in case.

"But if it's good news for me it will only hurt you. Don't pretend. I know how much you want this."

Sunflower turned to her with a smile. "The fact that you'd consider it good news is good enough for me."

Good news.

Amber wondered if she'd used those words simply out of kindness for her friend. It couldn't possibly be how she really felt.

She was a nomad. An anonymous traveller, following her nose. Or she had been until she'd landed here.

Now she had a roof over her head. But Hugo was right—there was a bucket to catch the drip in the roof; air whistled through the walls; a very good blanket and Johnno's potent moonshine had kept her warm through winter.

A person could survive that way. But a baby?

She squeezed her eyes shut and for the hundredth time in half the amount of minutes tried to figure how it might have happened.

She wasn't on the pill—it always made her feel nauseous. But as fast as things had heated up, not once had she or Hugo forgotten to be careful. Meaning that if two little blue lines appeared on that stick, their protection had failed.

But good news?

Sunflower gripped her hand harder. "I'm going to ask, and you can tell me to shut it, but do you know who the…"

Amber nodded.

"Super. And, again, tell me if I'm overstepping, but if I were to hazard a guess, might he be a certain newcomer in our midst?"

Amber's gaze shot to Sunflower to find her sweet face warm and open.

"The sexual tension between the two of you is palpable.

The entire town saw it at that meeting. Electric! And, I'm happy to say, contagious. The entire commune is going through a red phase. Johnno and I have been at it like rabbits. While Willow and Tomas are back on for the first time in years, much to Tomas's delight. And—"

Amber held up a hand. "It's okay. I don't need the full run-down. Truly."

Sunflower laughed her fey laugh. "Okay. I just find visualisation helps. You know who the father is, and you clearly have a spark. You think a baby would be good news. All signs point to positive to me." She gave Amber a quick hug, leaning her head on Amber's shoulder. "Come on, baby," she whispered. "You can do this."

Amber looked at the ceiling in an effort to hold back tears as she tried to sort through the mess to see how she truly felt about this.

She had been conceived on purpose and her parents had failed miserably. If she was pregnant, it was very much an accident but that would not have to colour the child's life in any negative way. It would be all about the choices she made next.

Her hands were slippery with sweat, and they shook as she reached out for the indicator.

Time slowed. Her hearing turned to fuzz as blood rushed through her head. She lifted the white stick, turned it around and…

Her brain filled with so many thoughts she couldn't pin them down.

"Amber?" Sunflower called out.

"Hmm?"

"What news?"

Sunflower stood and came to her, looking down at the stick, breathing out a long sigh.

A knock banged so hard at the front door the entire

place vibrated, dust falling from a light fitting. And they both coughed and brushed dust from their eyes.

"What am I doing in this place? It's a death trap," Amber said, her throat tight.

Sunflower winced. "I did wonder if you'd ever notice."

"The railing wobbles. The front step is on the verge of snapping in two."

Another knock came and with a snap the door swung open by itself, as it tended to do.

And there stood Hugo, backlit, hand raised to knock, hair tumbling over his forehead in that way that made Amber feel all warm and fuzzy.

"Sorry about the door. I'll fix it, of course. I brought the papers from my lawyers that I promised. And I wanted to see if you were feeling..."

Even with his face in darkness she saw the moment his eyes saw the stick she was holding in her hand.

Sunflower placed a hand on Amber's shoulder. "I'll leave you be, honey. You two have a lot to talk about." She leant in and whispered, "Take it easy on the guy. A man with eyes that dreamy can't be all bad. Hey, Hugo."

Hugo nodded as Sunflower wafted past. He even found a smile. "Sunflower. Lovely to see you."

Sunflower put a hand to her heart and gave Amber a last look.

Then it was just the two of them, together in her shack for the first time since she'd kicked him out.

Well, the three of them. Amber, Hugo and The Stick.

He took a step inside, filling the space with his calm, his strength, the scent of him, so familiar, so delicious. "Is that what I think it is?"

She nodded.

"Are you pregnant?"

She held up the stick in answer.

He tore his gaze away from her to glance at it. "One

blue line. No, two. There's a second faint one, right? I don't know what that means. Yes? No? Boy? Twins?"

Despite the tension gripping her every cell, Amber somehow managed to laugh. "Yes, Hugo. It means yes."

He breathed out hard through his nose, and before he had the chance to say anything nausea rose thick and fast in her throat and she spun on her heel and ran to the bathroom, this time taking an extra second to shut the door.

Nothing came up as she had nothing left. Her stomach ached from her spasming muscles. Sweat streaked her hair.

She slowly sat on the floor, shaking, in shock, her future a blur.

"Amber? May I please come in?"

She closed her eyes. "I'd rather you didn't."

She listened hard for footsteps but heard none.

"Can I get you anything?" he asked, in that voice of his. Velvet, deep, sure. "Food? Water? A doctor?" A beat, then, "Prospero tells me he helped deliver one of his nephews."

Again she laughed, only this time tears fell freely down her face. "Tell Prospero I won't be in need of his services for a good few months."

A few months and there would be someone in her life *looking* to her for support, food, shelter. And love. Change was coming at her whether she was ready for it or not.

"Amber?" His voice was so close she imagined him sitting on the other side of the door, his head leaning back just as hers was. "May I ask…your intentions?"

Amber closed her eyes. For all the wild and crazy going on in her head right now, she hadn't stopped to think about how he must be feeling. Shocked, sure, but in limbo too, not knowing what she planned to do with this news.

"I'm keeping this baby, Hugo."

She heard the outshot of breath even through the old door. "That's good news."

Good news. Those funny two words again.

"Do you mean that?"

"I believe my brain has gone to its most primal basic state, and I do not have the wherewithal to say anything but the absolute truth."

"Mmm. I hear that."

A few breaths went by and her tummy seemed to settle. Her nerves too. As if not having to go through this momentous thing alone was a relief.

"Hugo?"

"Yes, Amber?"

"I didn't plan for this."

"I know, *miele*. Neither did I."

A beat, then, "I'm sorry."

"Don't be. Don't ever think you have to be…"

She'd heard the emotion rising in his voice before he'd cut himself off. She swallowed, cringing at the awful taste in her mouth.

Hugo said, "I wish… I wish I knew what to say. To do."

"I don't expect anything of you, Hugo." Ugh. That sounded like a line from a bad teen angst movie.

Then Hugo said something she was sure would haunt her for the rest of her days. "That's always been our problem, Amber, you never have."

Amber's hand went to her belly, only this time not to curb the pain therein. For the pain she felt was higher, deep behind her ribs. "I need some time. To get my head around this. To clean my teeth. To sleep. To recuperate."

It was a good while before he said, "Okay."

She heard him shift from the floor, heard his footsteps echo on her rickety floor. Heard him fiddle with the door until it was properly shut.

Then there was nothing but the sound of her breaths. And the knowledge that, no matter what, she would never be alone again.

* * *

Hugo lay on the couch in the library, arm slung over his eyes to block out the sun streaming through the huge windows. His gaze glanced over the paintings on the walls—gum trees and billabongs, red dirt and bushrangers. Alien scenes to anyone who'd never seen Australia.

Summer was in its final throes, bringing with it dry winds and temperatures in the high thirties. Prospero was wilting.

What he wouldn't give to be sprawled out in Amber's hammock.

Amber.

Who was pregnant.

With his baby. At least, he assumed it was his. He hadn't asked.

Of course it's yours. This is Amber we're talking about.

He hadn't said much at all, in fact, his subconscious having switched to basic survival mode. All those years of rigid princely training had come to the fore, forcing any feelings about the news into a watertight box while the diplomat took over.

Yes, Amber. Of course, Amber. Whatever you need, Amber.

When she'd asked him to go, he'd gone. Even though he was pretty sure Amber Hartley had no damn clue what she needed.

As for what he needed… For a man who could schmooze in several languages, negotiate multi-million-dollar developments, he was damn useless at intimate relationships.

His first crush, the lovely Clair, had died tragically not long after they'd met and he'd had no idea how to process that. Thus losing his best school friend—Clair's brother, Will—because he'd been too thoroughly schooled in not showing weakness.

As for Sadie… After his uncle had made it clear he

would marry or face the consequences, he'd truly thought marrying his great mate Sadie was a good plan. It would give her and her mother security. Never occurring to him that she might not be so emotionally detached as he, and actually hope to one day marry for love.

Thank the gods she had panicked.

And then had come Amber.

A different kettle of fish from any woman he'd ever dated. Any person he'd ever known.

Sadie had known him her entire life and hadn't realised that beneath his outward confidence, the practised ease, was an emotional wasteland.

Amber had seen right through him from the moment they met. Damaged, deliberately isolated, detached. And still she'd taken him in. Until over the weeks, with her, those darker parts of himself had begun to fade, to seem less irreversible, to heal.

And now he was about to become a father. He had no choice but to leap into the unknown.

Hugo pressed himself to sitting, all the better to think. And breathe.

Thankfully he had time. Months, in fact. Could his plan to leave Serenity be put on hold? He had excellent teams in Vallemont who could manage the Dwell Forest resort that was meant to break ground in the autumn. Maybe.

But that was logistics.

This was far bigger than dates and times on a calendar. He was going to be a father.

A father. Considering the lacklustre examples he'd had in his life, he found himself struggling to know what that really meant.

He loved his younger cousins. He'd taught Kit how to catch a ball, and Kane how to ski. He'd frightened off any number of the older twins' suitors, but he was smart enough to know that being an uncle was wildly different from being a father.

The big question hovering on the edge of his mind since he'd seen those two faint blue lines was what if he, like every other man in the Giordano family, found a way to screw it up?

But this wasn't theoretical. Soon, if everything went as it ought, there would be a baby. A child. He would be that boy or girl's father. And Amber would be its mother.

Somehow, amidst the dark quagmire of disquiet roiling inside of him, that was the one shining light. He might not have a clue what kind of father he would make, but Amber as a mother…?

He'd watched her tend her bees with careful fingers and a calm voice. He'd seen her interact with the townspeople over the last few days—never too busy to stop and listen; to offer advice; to lend a hand; to have a laugh. She drew people to her like a flame.

He'd also watched her stand up to a town council, and a *prince*, in order to protect people she cared about.

She was considerate, serious, presumptuous and fierce.

Hugo could not think of a single person he had ever met who was more qualified for the role of mother.

With it came some other feeling—intangible, slippery, warm. But he couldn't hold on to it long enough to know its name.

Feeling as if he was on the edge of some realisation that would glue it all together, Hugo started when Prospero cleared his throat.

"We have visitors." Prospero's voice had bite to it, as if he were a Doberman who smelled trouble.

Hugo moved to the window, shifting the heavy brocade curtains aside to find a nondescript black town car had pulled up in his front drive.

A pair of men in dark suits hopped out. Something in

the way they moved, slow, careful, on high alert, had Hugo shifting closer to the wall. "The men who attempted the attack on my uncle at the picnic—?"

"Were not dressed in suits, Your Highness."

And paparazzi never drove such clean cars.

One of the men went to the back door of the car and pulled it open. A black high heel with a red sole hit the cobblestones, followed by another. Then, out stepped Hugo's aunt, Marguerite—the wife of Sovereign Prince Reynaldo.

Hugo yanked the curtains closed and snapped out of his daydreams. This was no time for exploring his tender side. He had to have his game face on in order to deal with his aunt.

Hugo was out of the door and down the front steps before the car door shut. "Aunt Marguerite."

Adjusting her face away from the snarky bite of the shimmering summer sun, she offered her cheek for a kiss.

"To what do I owe the pleasure?" Hugo asked, taking in the sombre bodyguards. Four in total…meaning the unrest back home was not over and done with.

"To the fact you seem to have forgotten how to answer your phone."

Others might falter at his aunt's impressively imperious tone, but she'd chased him and his cousins around the backyard with a hose when they were young enough not to be able to outrun her. "I told you I was safe, which Prospero no doubt reiterated in clandestine missives sent back to the palace."

Marguerite looked at him then, really looked at him. As if trying to see him as something other than the half-naked little boy running from the hose water.

Crickets chirped in the dry grass near by.

"Anyway, welcome to Hinterland House." With its Italianate yellow stucco, towering conifers, lead-light windows and neat shrubbery, it could have been transplanted whole from Tuscany.

Marguerite flicked a speck of red Australian dirt from her white skirt. "Yes. I have been here before."

The shocks kept on coming. "When?"

"Reynaldo and I holidayed here with your father—secretly, mind you, as we were not yet married—when he dragged us to this place, claiming a hankering for peaches. Ironic, that."

Hugo kept whatever retort he might have made to himself. He didn't remember his father well enough to defend him, even if his actions had been defensible. Which they hadn't. Would his child judge his choices as harshly one day?

Hugo put the thought aside. For now. Marguerite was a consummate royal—she could sniff out weakness at a hundred paces.

"It's smaller than I remember," said Marguerite.

"You are such a snob."

"Yes, I am. Now, are you going to invite me in or am I to melt into a puddle in this infernal heat?"

Hugo led his aunt into the house. One of her bodyguards stayed by the car, another at the door, one proceeded to case the house and the other camped out in a spot mirroring Prospero, who hadn't moved from his position by the front door.

"Drink?" Hugo offered. "Something to eat?"

Marguerite had barely removed a glove when she said, "Hugo, this is not a social visit. I am here with news. Three days ago, your uncle died."

Hugo's brain froze. One shock too many. "Which uncle?"

She shot him a look, one that asked that he please keep up. "The Prince. Reynaldo. My husband. The Sovereign Prince of Vallemont."

Only then did he see her hands were shaking, how drawn she looked, the tightness around her eyes. "Marguerite—"

When she saw him coming in for a hug she stopped with a hand. "We have no time for that. It has been three days. There is much to be done."

"Three days?" While he'd been busy at town hall meetings, having cups of strange tea and trying to keep his hands off the local honey-seller, his uncle had gone. What the hell was wrong with his family? The way he'd learned of his own father's demise was staggering in its similarity, tearing open old wounds until anger spilled through him like poison.

"How did I not hear of this? And don't tell me it was because I wouldn't answer my phone. You could have left a message. Email. Overnight mail. You've clearly been in touch with Prospero. What's wrong with you?"

If Marguerite heard the anger in his voice she did not show it. "We could not release the news without letting the people know who their next ruler will be. Officially, he is in bed with the flu, while he is actually in a freezer in the local morgue." She coughed at the end, a gloved fist pressing against her mouth.

Hugo's heart felt as though it had been squeezed.

Everyone in the palace knew that she and Reynaldo had been married in name only for years. They kept separate apartments in the palace—but that was perfectly normal in the royal household. They also kept separate calendars and engagements—again normal. The fact that she openly detested the man hadn't helped Hugo's views on married life over the years.

Bluebirds and love hearts might not be the theme of their relationship, but they'd had a family. Shared a life. Whoever had led her to believe she had to be stoic at a time like this deserved to be shot.

Whether she wanted him to or not, he moved in and wrapped his arms around her, breathing deeply, encouraging her to do the same. Until her short, raspy breaths matched his and her trembling abated. "Tell me what happened."

"It was awful," she allowed. "Too awful."

"What happened? And the twins? Are they okay?"

"His heart gave way."

"His heart?"

Reynaldo had been a big man with a beard like a Viking's. He'd seemed indestructible. As if he could protect Vallemont by sheer force of will alone. Yet the last time Hugo had seen his uncle he'd been ashen, Hugo's non-wedding having taken its toll. He swore under his breath.

"Do not blame your absence. It was a weak constitution and a lifestyle of excess. The belief he could do it all on his own. He was a Giordano after all." Marguerite smiled with her eyes. "The men in your family have not proven themselves equipped for longevity, delegation or fidelity."

Hugo's eyebrow twitched. The fact he'd just been navel-gazing about this exact concern hit home hard.

"Except for you, of course," said Marguerite, looking at him strangely. "Unless that's why your little friend left you at the altar?"

Hugo stiffened. "It is not."

"No. I wouldn't think so. If our country has any hope of producing a truly admirable Giordano it is you."

Something in Marguerite's tone was beginning to rub against the grain. Hugo ran a hand up the back of his neck and stepped away.

"What did you mean by 'letting the people know who their next ruler will be'?" The members of the royal household were versed in the twisted intricacies of royal succession before they could walk. With Reynaldo and Marguerite's twin boys too young to rule, it fell to Reynaldo's younger brother, Prince Ralph. "Uncle Ralph is married. Of age. And more than capable."

But Marguerite shook her head.

"It has come to our attention that he is not actually married to your aunt, Esmeralda, as she never divorced her first husband. As it turns out, Reynaldo discovered the truth of it a few months ago. Assuming he would live to see his own son grow up and take the throne, he kept it to himself. Yet—"

"The marriage requirement is invalidated." Hugo swore beneath his breath. "So that also means that Jacob—"

"Is a bastard."

Hugo gave his aunt a deadpan stare, but she didn't flinch. "I would not have put it that way. But yes." Meaning the succession of Hugo's other of-age cousin had been nullified in one clerical swipe.

Hugo moved slowly to a window, his gaze unseeing as he looked out on the happy blue sky over Serenity. His voice sounded as though it came to him from another room as he said, "So, unless I am mistaken, you are here to inform me that I am to inherit the throne of Vallemont."

"You sound honestly surprised. Did you not have an inkling? Did you not wonder why your uncle encouraged you to marry our dear Sadie? He wanted you to be ready for this."

Hugo turned on his aunt. "He did not merely *encourage* me to marry Sadie. He blackmailed me into it."

Marguerite's gaze was calm, measured. She came to him, put a cool hand over his. "Watching your father self-destruct pained him. Watching you turn rogue and wander further from the family broke his heart."

"That does not excuse his actions. He threatened Sadie's mother's job. Threatened to throw my mother out of the country."

"This is not about him," said Marguerite, politically savvy to the last. "Not any more."

Hugo ran a hand down his face, scraping against the stubble that had grown back. "And if I refuse?"

"Cousin Constantine."

Hugo's hand dropped. "You are kidding."

Marguerite shook her head. "He's next after you."

"He's eighty-three. And a clown. Literally. I remember him performing at my eighth birthday party. He scared the living daylights out of me."

Marguerite's shrug was as elegant as it was possible for a shrug to be. "Your country is rudderless. And I for one can think of no one better than you to steer the ship."

When Hugo realised he was holding his breath he let it go.

His entire childhood he had been prepared for this moment. When his father had died, the opportunity to put his knowledge, his education, his ideas to use had been snatched from his grasp, sending him spinning out into the world, a royal rebel whose success had been both a revelation and a thorn in his uncle's side.

With his next breath he felt the last vestiges of that rebellion dissolve away.

"I will have my lawyers double-check everything you have told me."

"I'd be disappointed if you didn't."

"And if this turns out to be fact, it will not be announced until I have spoken personally with Kit."

Marguerite raised a single thin eyebrow. "My son is twelve, and mourning the loss of his father."

"That is not all he will mourn. Reynaldo's first-born son was brought up believing that one day he would rule. He has not only lost his father, but also the only version of a future he has ever considered. No one understands the pain of *that* loss more than me."

Marguerite nodded.

"What else needs to be done?" Hugo asked.

"You must return home immediately. The sooner the funeral, the better for the children and stability."

"Agreed. But I would have to return immediately afterwards. I have loose ends that need tying up."

Marguerite made to insist before changing tack. "What could possibly bring you back here?"

Plenty, he realised. In a short space of time he had made real connections, his Australian roots digging in fast. Then there was the resort. And there was Amber. Amber, who was pregnant with his child.

Hugo closed his eyes against what felt very much like a wave of despair. His hope of sticking around, of shifting things in his life to accommodate months of getting to know her, to see if their connection was worth exploring above and beyond the fact they would have a child together, had just been unduly snatched away.

It was time for him to go home.

Marguerite went on, "After which you must marry some lucky girl, and fast. I will write up a list of suitable young women. The coronation will occur right after."

With that, she curtseyed. His venerable aunt, a fierce, battle-hardened woman, bowed before him, and said, "Your Highness."

Hugo rolled his eyes. "Stand up, woman."

She glanced up at him. "Is that a yes?"

He took a deep breath, giving himself one last moment to be sure. But his answer had been written on his heart the moment things had become clear.

"Yes," he said, his shoulder blades snapping together. "My answer is yes. Now, come with me while I find you a drink. And a room. In that order."

"Bless you, dear boy." Marguerite slowly untwisted from her curtsey and slid him an unexpectedly watery smile. "I knew you would turn out to be the very best of them."

"We shall see."

When his aunt was settled—prostrate on a spare bed, snoring quietly, a carved wooden fan pushing the hot air around the room—Hugo headed back to the library to find Prospero still hadn't moved.

Though move he did when he spotted Hugo, bowing deeply, with a deep, proud, "Your Highness."

"Don't feel so punished now, do you, big guy?"

Prospero looked up, his smile wide and full of straight white teeth Hugo had never seen before.

"I need you to do something for me."

"Anything, Your Highness."

Hugo wanted to command the big guy to call him Hugo, but considering the change of circumstances it might give him an aneurism. So he went with, "Stay with my aunt. Let me know the moment she wakes up. There is something I must do alone."

CHAPTER SIX

WHEN AMBER WASN'T to be found in her shack, Hugo went to look for her in the next logical place. Through the cool shade of the patchy trees to the north-east of the shack and then the darker depths of Serenity Forest.

This was where he'd imagined a string of secluded bungalows. Blond wood cladding, slate-grey roofs, muted colours to blend in with as much of the forest as they could save.

When the idea had first come to him, he'd called his uber-designer in Bern. Her response had been "nudes, taupes and creams" with "splashes of mossy green" to "effect an aura of calm, of solace, of rest". The woman could read minds. His dream had been to share the healing magic of this land with as many people as possible. And people would come. People needed a place like Serenity.

Stepping carefully now over fallen logs and random rocks, Hugo came upon her in a small glade.

Long shadows cast by saplings dappled in afternoon light cut across Amber's face, her loose white button-up shirt, her short denim cut-offs. Wild flowers brushed against her bare ankles. Her strangely beautiful dog sat lovingly at her feet.

Hugo kept to the shadows for a moment and took it all in. No wonder his embitterment had crumbled in this place. A person could only take so much light, and life, and exquisite beauty before he had to open up and let it in.

Amber stood by a hive he hadn't seen before. Where the others had been painted every colour under the sun, decorated with smiley faces, cartoony red mushrooms and star fields by Amber's friend Sunflower, this one was clean, white, new.

Bending over, peering into a hole at the front before moving to the back of the hive where she proceeded to attach a hunk of Styrofoam, Amber was tearing strips of tape from the roll with her teeth.

For all the time he'd spent with her—first in the quiet of the cabin and then the white noise of the public arena— the woman was still an enigma. She looked like a French film star. Spoke like a corporate lawyer. Pretended to be a flower child. And acted as though nothing and no one could ever hurt her.

But he'd hurt her. Having picked their relationship apart in his head over the past several hours, he knew that now.

He'd believed her when she'd acted as if her anger towards him was because of the resort, probably because it let him off the hook. But it had been more than that. Deeper. She'd been hurt because she cared. For him. He wasn't the only one whose life had been altered by their time together.

At least, that was what he was counting on. Because if he was wrong, if he was mistaken about her feelings for him, his plan would be defunct.

He ran a hand over his face. The fact that he'd had to choreograph a "plan" at all was less than ideal. If he had the luxury of time, things might be different. Hell, they'd *have* to be different. But none of this was normal. It hadn't been from the very start.

But the bigger truth was that there were bigger things at play now than her feelings. Or, for that matter, his.

A twig snapped, and then Amber bounced about, holding a bare foot.

Which was when Hugo realised something was very wrong.

Amber was tending her bees—meaning she ought to be covered head-to-toe in gloves, veil, overalls and those bright yellow gumboots.

Fear speared his guts like an arrow, panic swelling from the wound. And he was running before he even felt his feet move.

"Amber!" he called, rushing towards her, darting around saplings, waving his arms as if he might be able to distract the swarm before they touched her.

She quickly looked over her shoulder as if a bear might be behind her.

Then she turned to him, shoved her hands on her hips and shouted, "What the hell are you doing?"

"Saving you, you great fool!" Then he swept her into his arms and carried her away, bracing himself for the stings that would pierce his clothes any second. Not caring, as his caveman instincts had kicked in. *Protect woman. Protect child.*

"Let me down!" she said, wriggling like a fish on a boat deck.

"Not going to happen," he gritted out as he avoided getting smacked. And kicked. Bee stings had nothing on her. She was slippery too, sunscreen and sweat making her skin slick.

Hugo gritted his teeth and carried her until she was far enough away that he could be sure she was safe.

The second he stopped she wriggled free and pushed him away. She swept her hair from her face and stared him down. "Are you insane? Has the heat gone to your head?"

"I might ask the same of you." He waved an arm down her body, his gaze catching on the open neck of her shirt and the glimpse of a pink lace bra beneath. He knew that bra. He'd removed it with his teeth. And in the quick glance he saw that he'd left a tear.

Hot, mentally exhausted and turned on, Hugo's voice was a rumble as he said, "Where the hell is your gear, Amber? Are you trying to hurt yourself? And what about the…?"

The baby. He'd yet to say the word out loud. Even thinking it brought up more emotions than he could pin down.

Amber's eyes flickered at the missing word, but she didn't jump in to finish his sentence this time. Instead, she licked her lips, and said, "These are native Australian stingless bees, you idiot. Emphasis on the *stingless.*"

"How can you be sure?" he asked. He felt like an idiot as soon as he asked. And yet, if pressed, he knew he'd have asked the same again. His need to protect her outweighed not looking like a fool by a long shot.

And he saw the moment she realised it too.

It was a rare sight, seeing her eyes soften that way. Her already pink cheeks darkening in abashment. He drank it in. Drank her in. She had feelings for him, all right. What he hadn't counted on was his crumbling control over his feelings for her.

"Come on," she said, taking a step towards the hive. Then, rolling her eyes, she grabbed him by the hand and dragged him through the forest.

Ned leapt between them, happy the gang was back together, while Hugo's synapses fired and misfired by turns at how good, how right, it felt to have Amber's hand in his. How much he hoped she wouldn't fly off the handle; that she'd listen to what he'd come there to say.

He curled his fingers tighter around hers. She looked back.

But then she very deliberately let go, her hands tucking together. "Hugo."

"Yes, Amber."

"I'd like you to meet my newest hive. I've been saving up for these guys for months. They're not cheap. But they are so very worth it."

"And stingless?"

"Stingless."

He watched the hive but saw nothing except a small area of tacky black near the opening. But as they stood in the quiet glade he heard the hum. The gentle buzz. And then…there. One. And another.

"They're smaller than the stingy bees so they produce less honey. But what they do produce is delicious with lots of healing properties. But the best bit is that they are amazing pollinators. These little sweeties might just save the world."

Hugo planned to step in and save his country. Amber wanted to save the world.

Then her hand went to her belly and Hugo's world shrank to about two square metres.

"Are you okay?" Hugo asked, stepping in. "Was that pain? Or a…kick?" Hell, he had no clue.

By the flat stare she shot him, she clearly did. "I'm a month along, Hugo. There will be no kicking for some time."

"Then why did you wince?"

"I've been throwing up most of the day. It's left me a little tender, that's all."

"Right," said Hugo.

And Amber gave him a look. A look that connected them. It was the first time they'd spoken with any sense about the fact that they were going to have a child together.

"It may be obvious," said Hugo, "but I've never been in this…situation before."

Her eyebrows shot towards her hairline. "Me neither, thank you very much."

Going on instinct, he took a risk, asking, "Does this all feel as strange to you as it does to me?"

"If you mean you feel like you're living outside of your body and yet are truly aware that you are a living, breathing, cell-duplicating body for the first time in your life, then yes."

"Exactly like that."

In the shade of the hot summer's day, the both of them wildly out of their comfort zones, they burst into laughter.

This woman, he thought. His deep subconscious adding, *Do not let her slip away or I will never forgive you.*

There was a moment when he thought about revealing himself to her, telling her how much he wished they could go back to the ease, the simplicity, the warmth before real life had intervened with such alacrity.

But it was a risk he wasn't willing to take.

He was about to become the sovereign ruler of a country. Every decision he made from here on in would affect the lives of tens of thousands of people.

His only choice in the matter was to leave emotion out of it; to make her an offer she couldn't refuse.

"Amber," he said.

As she heard the serious note in his voice, her laughter dried up. "Yes, Hugo."

"I'm going to say some things now and, before you leap in with thoughts and questions and concerns, I'd like you to let me finish."

She opened her mouth to retort, but he held up a finger. An inch from her mouth. The warmth of her breath rushed over his skin. But he would not be distracted.

"And, once I'm done, I would like to hear your thoughts, questions and concerns. Every single one."

The sass slipped a little then. As if she wasn't used to being offered the floor. As if she was used to having to fight for it. It was enough for her to acquiesce.

Hugo filled Amber in on the turn of events. And then, "A week ago I was fifth in line to the throne. In a few days I will return home to be crowned the Sovereign Prince of Vallemont."

Amber's hand slipped from her hip to her belly. As well it might. For the second in line to the throne might well be growing inside of her.

To that, Hugo added, "There are certain stipulations that must first be met. I must be of age. Which I am. I must be male—"

She opened her mouth. He held up the finger again. Her eyes crossed as she stared at it, then she closed her mouth.

"—a stipulation which I would hope to change when the job is mine. And I must be married."

At that she stilled. Only her honey-blonde waves shifted in the hot, dry breeze.

"Your turn," he said.

"You're not married, right?" she blurted.

"No."

She breathed out, muttering, "That would have been the real cherry on the cake."

He opened his mouth.

She held up a finger. "My turn."

He closed his mouth.

"There's a strong chance I'm wrong, but I have a feeling that I know where you are going with this. And I think you should stop now. Before either of us says something we can't take back."

"Marry me."

"Hugo!" Amber paced away a few steps before pacing back again. Ned followed, panting, happily thinking it was a game. "I just said—"

"I don't want to take it back." He stepped in close, took her by the hand—both hands—holding her gaze with everything he had. "Amber, you are pregnant with my child. I will not be an absentee father like mine was to me."

He saw a flicker then. Of understanding. Of empathy.

"I must go home. It's not a choice, it's necessary to the future of my country. To the people of my country. There is only the slightest tinge of arrogance in my stating that I am the best chance they have for a bright, prosperous, safe future. Having you near me, *with* me, when our child is born, is of the utmost importance to me."

He then saw the moment she shut that empathy down. Her head shook side to side. "I can't. Hugo, it's a ridiculous notion. We barely know one another."

"Not true. I know that your parents did not appreciate you. I know that you are fearless, and kind. I know that you doubt yourself at times. And that everyone who knows you respects and admires you."

He hung every hope on the fact that she didn't blink.

"These past few days have been a challenge, but the time we spent together in your shack, talking rubbish, making one another laugh, making love, proves that if we choose to we can get along just fine."

She swallowed, her gaze dropping to his mouth, and he wondered if her vision of "getting along" matched his.

"That does not mean I am under any illusion that our relationship will ever be that way again." Only then did he realise how much he wanted it to. But no, now was not the time to speculate. "You would be made comfortable. You would have your own apartment within the palace. You would have complete freedom to do as you please. You could rule at my side or in name only. You could champion any cause that speaks to you, with the backing of a royal name, royal funds, royal gravitas. And our child will have a family. A mother and a father."

"Hugo," she said, her voice a whisper, and he knew he was giving her more than he'd intended. But the words were coming from some place real. And raw. And open. And, while fighting with her had been fun, this felt far better.

But he knew it would be short-lived. For he hadn't played his trump card yet.

He reached up and tucked a swathe of hair behind her ear, relishing the feel of her, the warmth of her, for it might well be the last time she let him this close ever again.

"One more thing."

Gripped now, discombobulated by the ridiculous drama of it all, her voice was barely a whisper as she said, "What on earth else could there be?"

He looked into her eyes, remembering what it felt like to fall into the bright whisky depths as she fell apart in his arms, and said, "If you agree to come with me, marry me, be my Princess, and raise our child in the Palace of Vallemont, I will give up the plans to turn Hinterland House into a resort."

And like that the brightness went away as her eyes narrowed. A crease appeared above her nose. And she let go of his hand.

"Hinterland House has been in my mother's family for generations, so I will save it for my children, our children, as well as five acres to the west. But I will gift the rest of the land to the town of Serenity. Including the lavender fields, the forest...and I will sign over your hill to the commune."

Amber swallowed hard, even as a tear ran slowly down her cheek. She quickly swiped it away.

He wished he could take her in his arms, run a hand down her back, over her hair. Kiss away those tears. Kiss her until she sighed. Until they both forgot what the hell they were even talking about.

He'd had no idea how hard this would be. How physically brutal. It actually hurt. Deep inside his chest. But with the future of his beloved country at stake and a child on the way, he did not see that he could have gone about it any other way.

"I don't expect you to make a decision right now. But time is pressing. I am heading home immediately for my uncle's funeral. I will be back in time for the town meeting. I will need to know your decision by then."

A shiver rocked her body and she seemed to snap back to her old self, her eyes flashing, her fists curling into hard balls. It was far easier to handle than the tears.

"My decision?" she hissed. "Let me get this straight. If I agree to marry you…" she stopped to swallow the words "…and move to the other side of the world, raise the baby I only found out I was having today, in a palace, then you will not tear down my friends' homes. But if I say no then you will go ahead with the plan to build your resort. Just because you can."

"Yes."

She breathed out through a hole between her lips. Her eyes were bright, her face was pale and she was glorious. This woman to whom he had just proposed. Who, no matter what happened from here, would never fully trust him for the rest of her life. Hugo soaked in the sight of her like a man on his way to prison.

"I knew you were a bender of the truth. I knew you kept things close to your chest. Until this moment I had no idea you were an asshole."

Hugo kept his cool by reminding himself his family had not prospered for as long as they had by being the nice guys. "I'd rather think of my offer as knockout negotiation."

"I bet you would. This isn't normal, Hugo. You do realise that?"

He ran a hand through his hair, his cool hitting breaking point. "We have never been normal, Amber, not from the moment we met. We ended up in bed before we even knew one another's names. Time lost all meaning as we lost ourselves in one another. I had no idea what day it was, what date, whether it was morning or afternoon. It didn't matter. I can't presume to know what it meant to you, Amber, but for me those weeks..."

Too much. The moment he caught her eye again, he knew he'd said too much.

But then Amber breathed, the air shaking through her like an earthquake. And he knew it had been as transformative for her as it had been for him.

And he knew, in that moment, how to get the answer he wanted.

He had one chance to get this right. It was off plan, and risky as all hell, but he went for it.

Reaching out to her, Hugo took her hand and gently pulled her into his arms, an inch at a time. Her hands moved to rest against his chest but she didn't push him away. She was listening now.

"Amber, every person I have ever met has seen me as a prince first and Hugo second. But for those weeks, with you, I was simply a man. You were short with me if I was presumptuous. You were cool with me if I made you angry. You didn't laugh if my jokes weren't funny. You berated me if I made you wait. And I wouldn't give up a second of it."

He dropped his hand to her side then, his thumb resting against her belly. Beneath that warm skin his child was growing, a child created during one of those meandering days—or one of those decadent nights.

"Not a single one."

He'd meant to leave it there, but having her in his arms again, swamped in memories of their time together, he found he couldn't let her go. He pulled her closer still and she let him. Then, before he could stop himself, he leaned down and he kissed her.

In the back of his mind he imagined the moment as a place-holder, a precursor to the official sealing of a deal.

But muscle memory took over and soon his hands were in her hair; hers gripping his shirt for dear life. And the kiss took on its own life, pulling him under. Deep. His heart thundered hard enough to burst.

His senses reeled. Shadow and light played on the backs of his eyelids. The taste of her was sweet and fresh and familiar. Her softness gave under his touch.

Heaven and hell. Wanting her, while knowing that if he had her it would be due to a devil's bargain.

As if remembering the same, she broke the kiss. Sighing as her lips left his.

Their foreheads touched for just a moment, before Hugo lifted his head and found her eyes. Whisky-brown. Flecked with sunshine and gold. And trouble.

"Think about it," he said, his voice rough. "Whatever you decide I will accept your answer unequivocally. The next town meeting. Let me know your answer by then."

And then he let her go, aching at the way she had to catch herself, as if her knees had gone soft.

Then he turned and walked back through the forest, seeing nothing. It was a miracle he didn't walk into a tree.

The sweet warmth of her body was imprinted on his. The honeyed taste of her lips still flowing like hot treacle inside him.

His head hurt at what he had just done. His gut burned. Even his bones throbbed.

Was this how Reynaldo had felt when he "encouraged" him to marry Sadie, blanketed by his sureness that it was the right thing to do?

Was this what it meant to rule?

If so, Hugo knew he shouldn't be so concerned about getting through with his heart intact. He'd be lucky to get by without destroying his soul.

* * *

Three days later Amber stood at the podium in front of the town council.

She'd sucked on a lemon just before coming out, so the nausea was at about a four rather than its usual nine or nine and a half. The lights glaring down on her made her head hurt.

Though perhaps that might have had more to do with the fact that her time was up. She had a decision to make that would change her life, and the lives of the townspeople, no matter which way she went.

She glanced over her shoulder at her cheer squad. Sunflower waved and Johnno gave her a thumbs up. Looking at them, she wondered if she ought to have confided in them. Asked their opinion. But she was so used to relying on no one but herself, she'd had no clue where to start.

Raising a child here with these good people would be magical. But if she stayed, the commune would no longer exist, not in the form it kept now, so that made the option redundant.

Also, and this was the thing that had kept her awake at night, no matter how she had come to care for them, they weren't her family. People came, and people went. The ebb and flow of the commune's population was what kept it so vibrant.

On the other hand—there was Hugo. And grrrr, she was so mad at him right now! Madder than she'd ever been at anyone in her entire life—her parents included, which she hadn't thought possible.

Meaning she'd had no choice but to think about why that was.

Sure, his marriage proposal had amounted to extortion. But he hadn't *had* to offer to give up the resort. For all the sangfroid he'd shown making his proposition, she understood he was offering a sacrifice to balance her own.

It was the sentiment that confounded her. He'd said that being near his child was of the utmost importance, and that he would never be an absentee father. As if he knew exactly how to rip right to the heart of her. Unless, of course, he'd been telling the truth.

Then there was the kiss. It had come from nowhere. Yet at the same time it had been brewing for days.

For a little over three weeks she had experienced the closest thing to comfort she had ever known; waking with Hugo's arm draped over her, protective and warm; falling asleep with him caressing her hair; listening to the deep hum of his voice as he'd chatted to Ned.

She let her gaze drift to the far corner of the room, where Hugo stood with Prospero a hulking shadow at his back. They were mobbed, the centre of a dozen conversations. And yet Amber could feel Hugo's attention attuned to her.

Her tummy fluttered at the sight of him. Nausea. That was what that feeling was.

And anger. Because she was mad at him still. Deeply, hotly mad.

The gavel struck and Amber looked to the front table. Her heart hammered against her ribs. Her vision began to blur.

Before Councillor Pinkerton could call the meeting back to order, Amber held up a finger. "May I beg a minute?"

The councillor looked towards Hugo's corner. "We can spare two."

On unsteady feet Amber turned and walked towards the side glass doors. She waggled a finger at Hugo, motioning for him to follow her.

Outside she paced, the long skirt of her loose dress catching around her ankles every time she turned.

Hugo slid through the door, looking ridiculously handsome with his sexy stubble and his hair falling across one eye. In jeans and a jacket this time, he reminded her far more of the man she'd known than the man he'd turned out to be.

He looked tired, no doubt thanks to flying to the other side of the world and back in the past few days. Burying his uncle. All the while not knowing what her answer might be.

Or maybe it had never really been under contention. Maybe it had always been about giving her time to pretend she had a choice.

"Ned," she croaked. And tried again. "What about Ned?"

"What about Ned?" he said, the first time she'd heard his voice in days.

"He's not mine. Not officially. He was a stray. And he sort of…got attached to me."

"I know the type."

She shot him a look, felt the heat of his gaze slice through her like a knife through butter. "I should leave him behind. This place is all he knows. And what with his hearing…" She flapped her hands, which were suddenly going numb. Her toes were too. She closed her eyes and wriggled her toes.

She felt Hugo take her by the elbows. "Breathe, *miele*. Just breathe. I simply assumed he'd be coming with us. That is what you want, isn't it?"

Amber swallowed. "But what about Customs? Don't you need a vet check? Or immunisation records? Proof he's not going to infect your entire country with some weird Australian disease?"

Every word became harder to come by. She glared at Hugo and felt a little better. Though her righteousness would feel better still if he acted more like an ogre while holding her to ransom. If he'd blackmailed her for profit, not for good. If his super-prince sperm hadn't managed to break through every protection she'd put in place.

"I vouch for him," he said, with a very European scowl. "What is the point of being Sovereign Prince if one cannot take advantage every now and then?"

"Do you mean that?"

"Of course. I plan on taking advantage wherever and whenever I can."

"No, I…" A beat, an unexpected smile, then she said, "You're kidding."

"Much of the time. I have spoken to the relevant authorities already, as I am also thorough."

Amber's thought went to her belly. Didn't she know it?

"Are you ready to go inside? If not I can take your place. I can give the council the news, whatever it may be."

Amber shook her head. "I started this. I'll finish it." But she didn't move.

She looked up, made sure he was looking at her, really paying attention, when she said, "I don't want my baby to be raised by nannies. Or governesses. Or to go to boarding school. Or to sleep in another wing of the palace. I want him or her sleeping with me, if that's what works. I want to carry her and cuddle her and take her everywhere I go. And if anyone—anyone—suggests otherwise, I reserve the right to tell them to back the hell off. No committee. No PR agency. Every decision, whether it is the kind of foods she will eat, or the friends she has, will be up to us, and us only."

She'd been entirely ready to say "me" and "I". But as she looked into Hugo's solemn eyes it had come out "we". For they would be in this together. For real.

She expected him to make some kind of quip to lighten the mood, but he placed a hand on her cheek, looked deep into her eyes and said, "What level of hell did your parents put you through, *miele*?"

She flinched. "I don't know what you—"

"Amber."

She swallowed. "Enough."

He said, "If that is what you wish then that is the way it will be. You have my word."

She nodded. Then, without another word, she went back inside and gave the council the news.

The resort was no longer in play. The commune was saved.

And she was leaving town.

CHAPTER SEVEN

IT HAD ALL happened so fast.

Amber's pregnancy.

His uncle's death.

The trip home for the funeral. The hand-picked interviews announcing his upcoming succession. The chance to fulfil the destiny he had grown up believing would be his.

A very fast visit to see Sadie and her new fiancé, his old friend Will, who had brought him back to earth.

And then back to small-town Australia to get his bride. And to officially remove his resort plans from council consideration.

Used to working by the seat of his pants, he'd taken each revelation and rolled with it.

Only now, in the dark quiet of the private plane, the ocean sliding beneath them with a half-finished glass of Scotch in his hand, did Hugo have the chance to unpack the enormity of what had happened.

He *had* the chance, but he chose not to take it. Instead he twisted his Scotch back and forth, hypnotised by the play of light in the golden liquid.

Sovereign Prince. Father. Husband.

Husband. Father. Sovereign Prince.

Closing his eyes, he lifted the drink and downed it in one go. Wincing as the heat burned the back of his throat.

"Hey."

Hugo looked up, saw Amber leaning in the doorway. Her hair was up in a messy bun and the colourful crocheted blanket she'd used to have on the end of her bed was wrapped about her shoulders. Her eyes were puffy from sleep.

"Are you drunk?" she asked.

"Not yet."

"Is this something I need to worry about?"

Hugo laughed, running a hand up the back of his neck. "Not at all. I was raising a quiet glass to my uncle."

"It looked like you were drowning your sorrows."

"Same thing, I would think."

"Mmm."

Hugo shook off the funk, quickly moving the paperwork he had piled up on the chair opposite his. "Sorry, come in. Sit."

"What's all that?"

He readied himself to brush it off as "nothing", before remembering Marguerite's assertion that the men in his family had not proven themselves equipped for longevity, delegation or fidelity. He had no problem with the third, and the first was out of his hands. But the ability to see and use the resources at his disposal? That was his bag.

Amber was an outstanding natural resource. It would behove him to start as he meant to go on.

"Details of coronation plans," he said, pointing to the document printed on Marguerite's letterhead. "Articles of law currently before parliament. The notebooks are Reynaldo's private records. If there's anything you're keen to have a look through, feel free."

She blinked at him and shook her head. But after a beat she moved to sit in the chair across from his.

"Everything okay?" he asked. "Do you need food? There are more blankets…somewhere. The staff are all over that. Shall I call someone?"

She laughed softly, then pressed a fist over a yawn. "I'm fine. Just…antsy, I guess." She curled her feet beneath her. "You looked to be in deep thought just now. Took me a couple of tries to get your attention."

"I have things on my mind."

"You and me both." A beat, then, "Anything you'd like to talk about?"

"With you?"

"No, with the seatbelts. Yes, with me!"

"You must understand my shock. You've shown an aversion to talking about anything more personal than the weather up until now."

She quelled him with a look. "I'm exhausted. It's messing with my equilibrium. I probably won't even remember this conversation in the morning." She sank down deeper into the chair and let her eyes drift closed. "But sit there and stew. See if I care."

Hugo shifted in his seat, leaning an elbow against the arm rest, balancing his chin in his fingers of one hand. Was she serious? Or pulling his leg? Only one way to find out.

"I was thinking about my aunt and uncle. About what it was like for them when they first found themselves in our position."

Her eyes fluttered open.

"Unlike our exuberant expectation, Reynaldo and Marguerite started their family late. After trying for some time they fell pregnant to much rejoicing all over the land. Then they had twin girls."

"Alas."

"Reynaldo's thoughts exactly. Three years later? Another set of twin girls."

Amber's eyes sparked. "I'm starting to like this story. Still no heir for poor blackmaily Reynaldo. Go on."

"He was beginning to feel punished."

"And why wouldn't he?"

"Our succession laws are ancient and complex, and certainly different from other Royal houses of Europe. Like a house given extensions in different architectural styles over centuries until it no longer makes sense as a building. But there it is, filled with people."

Amber snuggled a little deeper into the chair and leant her head against the leather seat, her eyes sleepy but engaged. And so he went on.

"Growing up, my father was second in line. Charismatic, roguish, larger than life."

"Sounds familiar."

"Ah. But my father's behaviour declined, making it abundantly clear that he wasn't interested in the role of Sovereign and could not care less about playing the part of dutiful public servant. Meaning that, unless Reynaldo had a boy, I was next in line to the throne."

Amber watched him carefully now. Taking in every word. "And then?"

"My father died. I can't even remember much of that time. Flashes of pain. And anger. Mostly anger. For it was a one-two punch. Not only had he left my mother and me for ever, but also with his death I lost my place in the line, relegated down back behind my uncle and his sons. Reynaldo insisted I could still be of use. But I wasn't interested. I gave up on the family and put my energies into other pursuits. And succeeded.

"Reynaldo was not happy. He made life as difficult as possible for my mother as punishment. I never forgave him for that. And he never forgave me for walking away."

"My, what a twisty family you have."

"You have no idea."

"Apple doesn't fall far from the tree though, does it?"

Hugo looked up, his whole body tight. "Excuse me?"

But she didn't back down. The look in her eye was

sharp. And unforgiving. "Don't you see that you pretty much used the exact same move to get me on this plane?"

"That's not what I—"

"*Marry me or else I'll tear down your home*? What would you call it?"

Hugo ran a hand over his face.

"Relax. It's done now. I'm too tired to go another round tonight. So I'm giving you a free pass. A one-time deal. And only because I can't see how any normal person could take the amount of stuff that has been thrown at you in the past few days and glide through with ease and grace. It's a lot."

Sovereign Prince. Father. Husband.

Hugo blinked. "It is rather. And I fear there's more to come. I did some press when I came home earlier in the week but I didn't stay long enough to see how it played out. After the wedding that never happened, and my recent extended absence, I'm not sure how the people will take to a 'rebel prince' as their sovereign."

"What do you imagine they'll do? Protest? Picket? Riot?"

He turned to her with a gentle smile. "You'll find we are a seriously civilised nation. Protests would likely be more in the order of satire. Snarky journalism. A lower than usual crowd at the coronation."

"Wow. Harsh. Brace yourself."

"Quite. It's not violence I'm concerned about. It's ambivalence. We are a proud country and rightly so. It would…sadden me to know I'd had a hand in depleting that civic spirit."

"But that's not the only reason." Her feet dropped to the floor and she leant forward, elbows on thighs, hands falling gracefully over her knees. "You present as if you don't care about all that much—with your slow walk, easy smile, and always with the wry humour. But when you talk about Vallemont you become a different man. This place is truly important to you, isn't it?"

He breathed out hard. "It's who I am."

"And you want to do a good job and look after your people fairly, equitably."

"Yes."

"Then you will."

"You can't possibly know that for sure."

She looked him dead in the eye then. And said, "I've seen you at your worst now, Hugo. And I've seen you when you're on song. You can do this thing blindfolded and with one hand tied behind your back. And if I can get past my stubbornness to admit I think you won't suck, then it must be true."

He thought he'd believed it too, but hearing her say it with such conviction, for the first time it felt real. Doable. As if the challenge wasn't overwhelming, but his for the taking.

A smile started down deep before tugging at his mouth. "Will you write my coronation speech? Truly. That was beautiful."

"You bet." She nodded. "And you can do something for me in return. Don't you dare pull any more of that Reynaldo-style rubbish on me ever again, or I'll take it all back. Every word."

"I won't."

"Say it."

"I promise."

"Okay, then." She yawned. "What time is it?"

"Where?"

"Good point."

She pressed to her feet and padded back through the doorway, shooting him one last pink-cheeked smile before she was gone.

"Hot damn," Hugo said, feeling as if he'd been let off

the hook and given the greatest gift of his lifetime all in one go.

He sat back in his seat and looked out of the window, at the blanket of stars covering the dark night sky, finally ready to take on whatever came his way.

They flew into Vallemont under shadow of night.

After more than twenty-four hours in the air, constant nausea, close proximity to a man who made her twitch and itch, as well as having to deal with the enormity of what awaited her at the other end, Amber was ready to claw her way out of the plane.

Instead, she allowed the flight attendant to heave open the plane door. Then shivered at the icy air that slithered into the breach, up her legs and into her very bones.

The private airfield was quiet bar the driver of a serious-looking town car with blacked-out windows; engine humming, its exhaust fumes created clouds in the cold air.

Hugo pressed a gentling hand to the small of her back and her skin tingled in response. Not his fault. That kind of thing was bound to happen when she'd agreed to marry a wildly handsome, deeply sexy, powerful man who had swept her off her feet to rescue her from a swarm of stingless bees. *Marriage.* That felt even more strange to her than the fact she would live in a palace and become a princess.

"Everything okay, *miele*?" he asked.

Amber swallowed. The endearment he'd started using screwed with her feelings. But if she called him on it he'd know she *had* feelings. It was a Catch-22.

"Amber, look at me."

She did.

"I meant it when I said you can change your mind at any point. I've been jilted at the altar once already, remember, so if it happens again I'll take it in my stride." He smiled then, as if he did mean it. But she had seen the strain around his eyes. The Furrows of Important Dreams had become permanent the past few days.

Handsome, sexy, powerful and selfless. The guy genuinely wanted to be a good servant to his public. She was in big trouble.

But resist she would. To surround her baby with family it would be worth it.

She shook her head. "I'm fine. Just tired."

"Of course. Let's get you to bed."

Amber closed her eyes for a moment, trapping behind them the plethora of images his words brought forth.

Think of the baby. This is all for her. Or him. Or them. Twins were in the family after all. What have you let yourself in for?

Hugo led her down the stairs and towards the car.

Once the bags were squeezed into the boot, Prospero sat up front with the driver and began speaking animated Italian, leaving Hugo and Amber in the back.

Leaving behind the last throes of Australian summer, they'd hit the end of Vallemontian winter. Through the window, neatly tapered evergreens lined the roadside, mist reflected off glassy lakes, and, framing it all, craggy, snow-dusted mountains created an eerie, otherworldly feel to the place.

"Is that a village up ahead?"

"Not quite yet." Hugo glanced out of the window to check out the lights she'd seen. "It shouldn't be. Not yet."

But then the lights brightened, and she realised they were coming from the side of the road. First sporadically and then in clumps. "Hugo?"

"I see it." He pressed a button in a panel in the back of the limo. "Prospero?"

"Yes, Your Highness."

"The lights?"

"We were given forewarning, Your Highness, hence the armoured car."

Armoured? She reached her hand along the seat until it found Hugo's. He curled it into his warm grip in an instant.

"Should I be worried?"

Hugo opened his mouth to answer but Prospero got there first. "It's the people. They are lining the street, carrying lanterns which they have been making in all the local schools for days. They've come out to welcome you home."

"But it's three in the morning," Hugo said under his breath, as the groups on the side of the road got deeper and deeper the closer they got to a village. Streamers began to float over the car, sliding off the windows. And it had begun to rain what looked like rose petals.

Hugo rolled down the window, against Prospero's protests, and the noise of the crowd intensified tenfold. When he waved, the faces swimming through the darkness beamed and cheered and sang.

Amber laughed, the sound catching on the chilly air pouring into the car and floating away. "And you were worried they might pillage."

Hugo looked at her, surprise and delight etched into his handsome face. He brought her hand to his mouth and kissed it. Hard. Several times. Until she couldn't stop herself from beaming. As for the first time since this whole debacle had begun she realised it might actually be rather amazing.

"Amber?"

"Mmm?" Amber opened her eyes to find she'd fallen asleep. Her head rested on Hugo's shoulder. His arm was around her; his fingers smoothing her hair, distractedly, as if he'd been doing so for some time.

She gently disentangled herself from his arms, and surreptitiously scrubbed her fingers through her hair to get rid of the feel of him. Or maybe not so surreptitiously, as he laughed. His eyes were dark and loaded with under-standing.

She looked away to find they'd pulled up outside a crumbling old building dripping with bougainvillea. Moonlight shone against an exoskeleton of scaffolding that seemed to be holding it together.

"Wow," she said. "I didn't imagine the palace to be so…quaint."

"We're not at the palace."

"We're not?"

Hugo grinned. He actually grinned. It reminded her of how he was before.

Careful, commanded the voice in her head. He might be a fixture in her life, which meant amity was more sen-sible than animosity, but this was an arrangement, not a relationship.

"This used to be a hotel called La Tulipe, but is now the headquarters of the new Royal Theatre, of which I am the lucky patron. Before throwing you on the mercy of the palace, I thought we'd spend our first night with friends."

"Friends?"

Before she'd even got the word out, the car door was whipped open and with the gust of icy air came a redhead in a pink beanie with a pom-pom on top.

"Hugo! You're late," she said in a lilting sing-song ac-cent that reminded Amber of Hugo's. "It had better be be-cause you stopped on the way for chocolate. Or wine. Or both." Then she leaned down to peer deeper into the car. As she spied Amber, her face broke out into a grin. "You must be Amber. I'm so happy you're here! Oh, Hugo, she's gorgeous. Why did you not tell us how gorgeous she was?"

"Maybe he doesn't think I'm gorgeous," Amber said, then regretted it instantly. "Forget I said that. Jet lag and catnaps, summer to winter—my brain has clearly not found its feet. Hi, I'm Amber."

"Sadie." Sadie grabbed her by the hand and all but dragged her out of the car, meaning she had to climb over Hugo, hands and elbows trying not to land anywhere precarious.

When their eyes locked for a split second he gave her the kind of smile that made thought scatter, bones melt, and strong women rethink their boundaries.

Amber spilled from the car and landed in a Sadie hug that squeezed the air from her lungs so fast it puffed out in a cloud of white. "I am so happy to meet you. You have no idea."

Sadie pulled back, looked into Amber's eyes and laughed. "Oh, no. What has Hugo said about me? It had better have been nice. For I have stories I can tell you—"

"Leo," said Hugo, now standing very close behind Amber. "It might surprise you to know that Amber and I haven't actually spent all our time together talking about you."

Sadie poked out her tongue and Hugo laughed.

Interesting. From the little that Amber had heard about this woman she hadn't imagined her to be so lovely, so charismatic and warm. Or for Hugo to be so easy with her after what she had done. But if Sadie was indeed a friend of Hugo's it only made sense.

Sadie looked from Amber to the man standing over her shoulder before a smile settled on her face. "You must be exhausted. Let's get you lovebirds inside. Prospero, you have the bags. Excellent. Follow me."

And then she was gone, Prospero in her wake.

"Wait," said Hugo when Amber went to follow. Taking her by the hand and drawing her close. "Don't let her run over the top of you."

"Excuse me?"

"I can see your mind ticking over. Trying to figure her out. Trying to figure *us* out. Leo—Sadie—is my very oldest friend. Which is why I am allowed to say that she is hyperactive, full of energy and opinions and a compulsive need to make everyone around her happy. I know you need your space, your quiet time. Don't be afraid to tell her to stop."

He knew she needed space. He knew she needed quiet time. He knew her.

Determined not to let him know how touched she was, how much that meant, Amber lifted her chin and said, "Do I look afraid?"

The hint of a smile. Then, "No."

"Okay, then."

"It's just... You got me to thinking on the plane. I don't want us to be like my aunt and uncle, so cold with one another they could barely make eye contact. I hope we can be better than that. Because we have a chance to do good here. Together. I am on your side, no matter what Sadie, or Will, or Aunt Marguerite, or the press, or ex-girlfriends who will no doubt come out of the woodwork have to say."

He reached up and pressed her hair behind her ear—a move that always sapped her breath.

Needing to hold on to her dignity before she did something stupid like fall for him, right then and there, in the moonlit darkness, she said, "You don't need a speechwriter, Hugo. You're a natural."

His face split into a smile. "Am I, now?"

"The way you put words together? I have chills."

"Then how's this for a speech? You know I think you're gorgeous, right?"

The cautious voice in her head threw its hands out in surrender. "Hugo, that was a stupid quip. Forget I ever said it."

"Can't. It's out there now. You are gorgeous. But above

and beyond that you are smart. Canny. And generous to a fault."

Amber pinched her leg to try to stop the trembles rocketing through her that had nothing to do with the cold. "You promised you wouldn't mess with me."

"On the contrary. If you were not aware of how much I appreciate your decision to accompany me, how much I appreciate you, then I have been remiss. And I apologise."

Desperate to get out of this conversation, she mumbled, "Apology accepted."

No such luck. Hugo moved closer, his voice dropping, the chill in the air nothing compared to his body heat, making her feel all warm and soft and molten. "Now it's your turn to say something nice about me. Quid pro quo."

She laughed despite herself. Better that than sighing, which was what her entire body was on the verge of doing. "My mother always said if I didn't have anything nice to say, not to say anything at all."

"From memory it's been quite some time since you've done anything your mother told you to do."

He was right. Damn him.

And as she looked into his eyes the memory of their first kiss swarmed over her. It had been inside her kitchen, mere moments after she'd invited him inside after finding him in her hammock. Like two lost souls desperate for warmth, for connection, finding recognition in one another's loneliness, they'd fallen together. After which they'd burned up the sheets.

Then something unexpected had happened over the days and weeks. The heat had expanded, allowing for warmth, loneliness giving way to comfort, to small acts of kindness and caring.

Whatever had gone down between them since—the white lies, the disagreements, the forced intimacy neither had asked for—that time had happened. It was a part of their story. A part of them.

Her hand fluttered to his chest to push him away. Or perhaps to give in to the feelings messing her up inside. To take a chance, and risk it all.

"Get a room!"

Hugo blinked, and came to, turning and smiling in the direction of the deep male voice behind Amber. "Will Darcy. Impeccable timing as always."

"Come on, mate. It's bloody freezing out here."

As the men bantered, relief and regret whirled inside of Amber, and she had to grip Hugo's shirt to keep herself from collapsing under the combined weight.

Once she felt able, she turned to meet Hugo's friend Will, a Clark Kent type, with curling dark hair, a cleft chin and bright, clever eyes.

He stepped forward. "You must be the famous Amber. Will Darcy. Pleasure to meet you."

She took his hand and was hit with a wave of familiarity. "Have we met?"

"I'm sure I'd remember." A smile. Neat white teeth. Dimple in one cheek. English accent. Again those bright, clever eyes.

Then it hit her. She clicked her fingers. "You spoke in a documentary I saw once. You're an astronomer, right?"

He nodded, and held out both hands as if to say, *Sprung*.

"I can't believe this. I was travelling at the time and you were so inspiring I actually decided on my next destination by following the Southern Cross. It's how I ended up in Serenity in the first place. Wow! Ha! This is amazing."

From behind her Hugo grumbled, "She was far less excited when she found out I was a prince."

Will laughed. "Smart woman." He then took her hand, placed it into the crook of his elbow and swept her away from Hugo, through a set of glass doors and inside the building, where they had to dodge drop-cloths and paint buckets.

In the low lamplight she saw crown mouldings, ancient wallpaper and more crumbling brick. It was like something out of a play.

They followed the sound of Sadie's voice to find her regaling Prospero with tales of refurbishment and *Much Ado About Nothing*.

Sadie looked up and saw Amber just as she yawned. "You poor love. Your rooms are right here. One each if you're sticklers for tradition, or share and share alike. Apologies that they are not yet finished. We are a work in progress."

Amber's thank-you was lost in another yawn.

Then Sadie's eyes darted to Amber's belly, before darting away.

And all the good, warm, mushy emotions she'd been feeling towards Hugo evaporated.

He'd told Sadie about the baby. Who else? Did the entire royal family know it was a shotgun wedding?

It doesn't matter, she tried to convince herself. *This was an arrangement, not a relationship.*

"Okay," said Sadie, "we'll head upstairs and leave you to it. Though I'll be fast asleep in two minutes flat, Will will be on the roof looking at his stars if you need anything. Oh, wait." She reached into the pocket of her gown and gave Hugo a small box. "That thing you wanted me to procure."

"Right. Thanks."

Will took Sadie by the hand and tucked her in behind him. "With that we'll take our leave. Goodnight. Sleep tight. See you when it's light." Then he pressed her ahead of him and into the darkness.

"If you don't have a preference I'll take the room on the left."

"Fine," said Hugo, spinning the box in his hand.

"Anyway, goodnight."

"Wait." Hugo put the box in his upturned palm and held it out to Amber, all remnants of playfulness gone. "I apologise in advance."

Amber took the box, opened it slowly and her jaw literally dropped when she saw what was inside.

It was a ring—a baguette half the size of her pinkie finger set with dozens of different-sized pink diamonds on a thick rose-gold band. "Is this for real?"

"I'm afraid it is. For that is the Ring of Vallemont. Handed down through the family for generations. My grandmother gave it to me after my father died. Quite contentious within the family, as usually it is given to the next in line to the throne. The woman was clearly psychic. When Reynaldo and Marguerite had the boys, I should have passed it on, but for some reason I couldn't. Funny, that."

"Well, it's big. And shiny. And very pink." She went to hand it back.

"No, Amber. It's yours."

"Excuse me?"

"It's your engagement ring."

She looked down at the ring again, this time with a different eye. It was huge. Cumbersome. Like something you saw in a museum, not something you wore for the rest of your married life. "But it must be worth millions."

"No. It's priceless."

She opened her mouth to protest but Hugo shut her down.

"Amber, I know my proposal was not…normal."

"Enough with the normal already."

"Yes. But no matter the circumstance, a woman should at least be given the respect of tradition."

In the near-darkness, it took a moment for Amber to

realise Hugo was making to get down on one knee. But Amber grabbed him by the shoulders and yanked him back to standing, her heart racing, blood rushing to her face.

Keeping her footing here meant not mistaking the situation even slightly. Their attraction was palpable, a constant hum that vibrated between them. Something might come of that. Who knew? But there was no room for *romance*. None.

"Look," she said, popping the ring out of the box and sliding it onto her finger. "All done."

And by gosh it fitted. Like a glove. The gold was warm and smooth, the pink the perfect tone for her skin. It didn't look nearly as big and gaudy on her finger as it had in the box. It looked pretty, elegant, right.

If she'd thought her heart was racing like a rogue train before, now it was about to jump the tracks.

"Amber," said Hugo, his voice rough, as if he'd noticed it too.

So she faked a yawn. "Sorry, but I really need some sleep."

Hugo nodded, moving into the open doorway of the unfinished room next to hers.

"What time is the thing in the morning?" she asked.

Hugo looked at his watch. "We thought about two in the afternoon. Give us time for a sleep-in and time to get ready. Do you need anything until then?"

"Someone to pinch me so I know this isn't all some strange dream."

"Sorry," he said, backing away. "I've had a dose of your reality; now it's time for you to get a dose of mine."

"Quid pro quo."

He smiled. "Exactly. I'll see you in the morning?"

Which was when Amber heard the question in his voice. No wonder. The last time Hugo had planned to marry he'd been the only one to turn up.

"I'll be there," she said, and meant it.

With a nod, and a furrow of the brow, Hugo slipped into his room and quietly shut the door.

Amber did the same. She glanced over her bag, then to the bed. It had been so long since she'd slept on a mattress that hadn't been handed down a thousand times, she crawled from the end to the pillows and sank onto her back, her entire body groaning in pleasure.

She wished Ned were here now. She could do with something to cuddle. But he was in quarantine, hurrying through the requisite vet checks, and would hopefully be with them within the month.

A gentle knock rapped at her door. She sat up, heart thumping, expecting Hugo.

"Come in," she said.

Her disappointment must have been obvious as Sadie's face dropped before she glanced towards the wall connecting the two rooms.

"Sorry," said Sadie. "I know you just want some privacy and sleep. But I was upstairs feeling awful about something... There was a moment earlier when I saw you touch your tummy, and you saw me see and..."

Sadie took the few steps into the room and sat next to Amber, before taking her by the hand. When she saw the ring she stopped, a smile tugging at the corners of her mouth. "Wow. I never thought that thing could suit anybody, but you rock the rock."

Then she looked up and said, "Hugo came to visit us briefly when he was here for Reynaldo's funeral. To tell us about you. And about the baby."

Amber breathed out hard. Sadie shook Amber's hands as if hoping to shake out the sigh.

"But not to embarrass you or make you feel uncomfortable. Only so that he could insist we were gentle with you. And so that we didn't force you to stay up late and chat and tell us all about yourself, which I'd really love to do. And so I didn't try to force prawns or wine down your throat. Why prawns I have no idea. I can't remember the last time I even ate a prawn. And because he's so excited. In fact, I've never heard him talk the way he talked about you; words tripping over themselves, so many adjectives. I was actually a tad worried he'd been hypnotised until I saw you. Or, more specifically, saw him with you."

Amber had no idea what to say.

Sadie clearly took it as a sign to keep talking. "He's usually so cool. Nothing fazes him. Not even being ditched at the altar. He understood, he moved on. He can be frustratingly enlightened that way. But he followed you in here like a lost puppy. It's actually hilarious. I'm going to enjoy this very, very much."

"Well, I'm not so enlightened, just so you know. I'm rather overwhelmed right now."

"I'd be more worried if you weren't." Sadie patted her on the hand. "Just trust in Hugo, love Hugo, and you'll be right as rain."

Trust? Love? She might as well be asked to run to the moon. Amber managed to say, "Thanks for putting us up here tonight. And for organising tomorrow."

"My pleasure." With a wink Sadie was gone, leaving Amber to fall back onto the bed, splaying out like a star.

She stared at the ceiling, her mind whirling, wondering if she'd sleep at all…and was gone to the world less than three minutes later.

The next day, at just after two on a chilly winter's afternoon, with Will and Sadie as witnesses, and their office manager, Janine, throwing peony petals at their feet, Amber and Hugo were married.

CHAPTER EIGHT

"PLEASE TELL ME you are not married!"

Hugo had been reading about the measures that would be put in place to protect the royal family at the coronation, when his aunt barged into his office in the palace.

Because she'd recently lost her husband—and that barging into any room in her palace used to be within her rights—he let it go.

"I could. But that would be a lie."

"Oh, Hugo. What were you thinking?"

"Better for worse. Richer for poorer. That kind of thing."

"Hugo…"

Hugo reclined in his chair, the very picture of laid-back. "Aunt Marguerite, we didn't see the point in starting my reign with a costly wedding followed by a costly coronation, so we married atop the roof of La Tulipe with a view of the palace and friends bearing witness."

And it had been fun, of all things, everyone in a festive mood. The ceremony was a blur but afterwards they'd talked, laughed, told stories. And after the tumult of the past several months, watching that group of people get along, he felt an uncommonly large swell of pride at knowing the lot of them.

"*We?*" Marguerite looked around as if his wife might be hiding under the table.

"Her name is Amber. And you will be nice to her. Kind. Helpful. In fact, you will be her fairy godmother."

Marguerite looked as pained by the idea as he'd hoped she might. "At least tell me she can string a sentence together. That she has some semblance of class."

While he itched to tell her Amber was all that and more, Hugo folded his arms and admitted nothing. Let her sweat.

Marguerite sighed. "I had a number of lovely girls from good families lined up ready to meet you. I'd even sent out invitations for an intimate dinner party for tonight."

"Probably best you cancel."

Another sigh. "And her name is truly *Amber*?"

"Amber Giordano, Princess of Vallemont, no less." A beat, then he threw her a bone. "It was Grantley."

"I'm not sure I know the family."

Hugo laughed. "I'm sure you don't. Amber's parents are very well-respected lawyers out of Canberra." Hugo didn't know why he was building them up because Amber's background mattered not a jot to him. But it would be of interest to others. Something he hadn't considered in his hot-headed decision to throw her over his shoulder and bring her back to his cave.

"She is *Australian*?" She pressed a hand to her forehead.

"So dramatic. If you're looking to spice things up, Sadie could give you a role in one of her plays."

Marguerite lifted her head and levelled him with a look. "You look more and more like your father every year, you know. And now you have found a girl in that hot, dusty, hippy outback town and brought her here and for some reason you expect a different result."

Hugo didn't even realise he was standing until his hands hit the desk top. While it took every ounce of diplomacy he had not to erupt, his voice was like ice chips as he said, "That's enough. Amber is my wife. This time next week she will be the wife of your Sovereign Prince. And even if none of that were true, she still deserves your respect. When you meet her you will see that she is bright, articulate and lovely. She is also resolute. If you try to push her she will push back because she does not take bull from anyone. Not even me."

Marguerite kept eye contact for a long while before glancing away. "At least tell me she is beautiful."

Hugo moved around the desk and held out two hands to lift his aunt out of the chair. "Very."

"Brunette?"

"Blonde."

She winced. "At least it's better than red. Our Sadie, with that red hair of hers, would have been much harder to dress."

"I wouldn't count on it. Now go away. I am a busy man. And you have a coronation to plan."

"At least there is that." Marguerite nodded, angling her cheek for a kiss, then left.

It left Hugo feeling on edge, though quite honestly he'd been feeling on edge all day. He hadn't seen Amber since the palace chef had insisted on feeding them a private wedding banquet in the dining hall the night before. Amber had nearly fallen asleep in her dessert.

He wondered where she was right now, whether she was coping, if she was content. Though he feared he knew her well enough to know that without focus, without someone or something to look after, she would be bored out of her mind.

"Prospero?"

The big guy was through the door in a flash.

"Can you check if the package has arrived?"

Amber sat on the balcony of her rooms in the palace, huddled under a blanket, drinking ginger and honey tea to keep her nausea at bay and staring out into the very un-Australian wilderness in the distance.

To say she felt antsy would be an understatement.

While Sadie called daily and Hugo checked in as often as he could, she was used to keeping busy. Tending her bees, working at the shop, keeping Sunflower company while she painted, or taking Johnno into town to make sure he made it back again. She missed her friends. She missed Serenity. But, knowing they were only a plane flight away, mostly she missed being of use. At least Sunflower was looking after her bees.

She glanced at the side table where the pile of books Hugo had left in her room one night sat; books about princesses past. From ex-movie stars to kindergarten teachers. Women who had used their new platform to highlight children's diseases, women's rights, science, the arts, mental health.

All wrapped in an ostentatious big pink ribbon with little tiaras imprinted all over it, the gift had been given with a wink, but also a nudge. The man knew her too well.

She sat forward to read the back cover blurb when out of the corner of her eye she saw movement below...

No. It couldn't be. He wasn't due to get through quarantine for another few weeks.

But it was Ned, bounding across the grass!

Throwing off the blanket, she leaned as far over the balcony as she could without tumbling over the side to see if he had anyone with him. But he seemed to be galumphing around happily on his own. She called his name as loud as she could. But he wouldn't have heard her anyway.

So she had to go down there, find her way out of the maze of halls and staircases and wings and—

Hand to her throat, she stifled a scream. A woman cast a shadow in her doorway.

Something about her, several things in fact—the chignon, the long neck, the lean frame, the pale, elegant skirt suit, the legs locked straight on prohibitively high heels—

made Amber think of her mother and she came out in an instant sweat.

Then the woman stepped out onto the balcony and Amber's panic eased.

"I startled you," said the stranger.

You think?

"I'm Princess Marguerite."

"Amber," said Amber. She held out a hand and the other woman took it, as if expecting her ring to be kissed. But Amber hadn't come this far to be kissing anyone's ring. Amber shook and let go.

"How are you settling in, my dear?"

"Gradually."

"Hmm. You're a long way from small-town Australia."

Suddenly Hugo's promise to be "on her side" had resonance. For while the Princess was being perfectly civil, Amber was fluent in the language of passive-aggressive disappointment.

Amber casually leant her backside against the brick balustrade and said, "A whole twenty-four hours by plane, in fact."

A quick smile came and went, along with a flash of surprise. "And what did you do in Serenity, Amber?"

"I was a beekeeper. And I co-ran a honey shop." She let that sit a moment before adding, "How about you, Marguerite? What do you do around here?"

The woman's eyes widened, before a smile lit her face. "My nephew warned me that if I pressed you, you would press back. I'm rather glad to see he was right."

Amber felt herself begin to relax.

"He also said you were beautiful, but he didn't tell me I had all of that to work with. The man has always underplayed his achievements."

Amber opened her mouth to protest being labelled an achievement.

But Princess Marguerite waved her hand, stopping her. "I had come in here merely to have a look at you, but now that I have I think I can skip forward a few steps and we can have an honest conversation."

"Okay."

"I stood where you are before you were even born. On the precipice of being the wife of a ruling prince." She glanced down at the pile of books on the side table next to Amber's chair and made no comment. "It's a position that requires grace, diplomacy, style, self-assurance and temerity."

Amber laughed softly. "One out of five ain't bad." Then she heard a bark and turned to look over the balcony.

Only to find Ned was not alone after all.

Hugo was there, striding across the grass in suit trousers and a dress shirt, the wind ruffling his hair and the wintry sun glinting down upon him as if he was made of gold.

He stopped, brought a hand to his mouth, and whistled loud enough for all the forest animals to hear. It worked. Ned pricked his good ear, before bounding back.

But then Hugo reached down. He threw a towel over his shoulder and picked up a bucket and a sponge. And Ned stopped so fast he practically laid down smoke.

It fast became a case of chicken. Ned, standing like a statue, waiting for Hugo to creep up on him, then bolting the moment he got close. Leaving Hugo to place hands on hips and breathe so as not to lose all patience.

Amber laughed at the ridiculousness of the sight, bringing her hands to her mouth to hold in the waves of emotion lifting and rising inside of her.

Oh, Hugo. That's not playing fair.

"What on earth is he doing?" Marguerite had joined her.

"Trying to wash my dog and failing heroically."

Amber felt Marguerite's curious gaze on her but she didn't care. No one was about to burst this bubble. Ned was here, and Hugo had made that happen. She wanted to hug them both so hard.

She cupped her hands around her mouth and called Hugo's name, but her voice didn't carry nearly far enough. So instead she held her arms tight about her and watched, smiling so hard her cheeks ached.

"Where is Prospero? Shall I summon help?"

"Nah," said Amber. "Let him figure it out himself. It's character building."

By the time Hugo managed to catch his quarry he had wet patches on his dress shirt and soap bubbles in his hair. His cheeks were pink from the cold air, and the exertion. And Ned looked so happy with all that land, the cool sunshine and the man who'd given it to him that Amber's heart clutched. Squeezing so tight she groaned.

She'd never felt anything like it in her life. As if she was filled with air and breathless all at once. It was too much. And she could no longer hold it back.

Like a stone tossed into a lake, she was falling for him. Tripping and tumbling and sinking deeper and deeper.

Not that she could ever tell him so.

She wouldn't have a clue where to start. She couldn't remember a single time her parents had told her they cared, much less used the magic word. Meaning she never had either—not once. Not even to Ned.

But mostly because the thought of putting herself out there like that terrified her to the centre of her very bones. He wouldn't laugh in her face. That wasn't Hugo's style. But what if he was ambivalent? She couldn't face that again.

No. There was no quid pro quo for this. This was a secret to keep.

She breathed out a sigh as Hugo knelt in the wet grass and Ned's muddy paws landed on his shoulders. He gave the wet dog a big rub about the ears, looking more relaxed than he had since arriving at the palace.

He was so busy, which was to be expected, but she had a new job to do too. Sure, it would be a challenge, but she thrived on challenge. And, so long as she had that man *on* her side and *at* her side, then it might well be the adventure of her life.

"Marguerite, can I ask you a favour?"

"Of course, my dear. What is it?"

"I have a pretty important event coming up and I think I might need a new dress."

"Oh, you dear girl. I thought you'd never ask."

Hugo stood behind the doors leading to the ceremonial balcony.

Marguerite had given him a kiss on the cheek before heading off to schmooze with the invited guests. His mother had even come by to wish him luck before disappearing back into the sanctuary of her rooms.

Leaving him to stare at the gap between the doors leading outside, alone.

Memories of his childhood flittered and faded; running these roads till he knew every fallen log, every hidden stream, every badger sett; slicing open a knee jumping a fence or two—he still had the scar; climbing those trees and dropping seedpods on the ancestors of the sheep that roamed there today.

Today he would officially become Sovereign Prince of all that and more. No longer merely a finance whizz, but a master of policy, of protection. Open to new ways while respecting the methods of governance and social life that had worked for generations. Beholden to the people of his country until the day he died.

He could not wait.

"Hugo?"

Hugo turned to find Amber strolling towards him. And whatever he'd been thinking about dissolved into dust motes in his mind.

For she was a vision in a sparkling pink dress that shimmered as she moved. The top hugged her curves, the skirt a feast of silk peonies swishing about her legs as she walked. A small diamond tiara nestled in her long, honey-gold hair, she looked like the Queen of the fairy folk.

Hugo swore beneath his breath. Or perhaps a little louder than that, as she shot him a quick smile.

"I know, right?" she said, giving a little twirl. "I scrubbed up well."

"Understatement of the millennium," he said, his heart thundering at the sight of her. "In fact, who cares about the coronation? I'm sure there's a broom cupboard somewhere if you'd care for a quick five minutes in heaven."

A smile quirked at the edge of her mouth and she moved closer and fussed with the brocade of his royal uniform on one shoulder. "From what I remember, you can do better than five minutes."

The world slowed to a complete stop. His wife was flirting with him.

Not that he was about to complain. In fact… He slid his hand around her waist, tugging her closer, and she let him. His voice grew low, intimate, as he said, "I wanted to thank you for my coronation gift. It was terribly thoughtful."

"What do you get for the man who has everything? I know your library is extensive, so I hoped you didn't have it."

"No. It is my very first edition of *Dog Washing for Dummies* and I will treasure it always."

She laughed then. Her soft pink mouth twisting into a smile that made his head spin.

Then the trumpets blared and the murmur of the crowd reached a crescendo. And there was no time for broom cupboards. Or flirting. Or mooning over his wife. There were more important things—

Screw it.

He pulled her in and kissed her before he could think about it. There was no hesitation; she sank into him, tipped onto her toes, her arms going around his neck as she kissed him back.

Then, far too few seconds later, she pulled back in a rush. Her gaze going to his mouth.

"Oh, no, no, no. My lipstick. You're all pink." She slid down his front, and it was all he could do not to groan. And she frantically rubbed the edge of his mouth using her thumb.

"It *is* one of our national colours. Perhaps the people might even appreciate it."

She laughed, though it was slightly hysterical.

Then the doors pressed open, letting in the wintry sunlight, the fresh Vallemontian air, and the voice and song of his people.

He let Amber go but only so far as he needed to in order to take her by the hand.

"But Marguerite said I was only to go this far."

"And do you care what Marguerite says?"

Her eyes sparked and she tucked her hand between his and looked out to the hills, tipping onto her toes to see the size of the crowd. Tens of thousands. More than the entire population of the country. She laughed. "This is insane."

"No," he said, walking her out onto the balcony, "this is us."

The coronation went without a hitch.

With the head of parliament taking Hugo's oath, tens of thousands of Vallemontian nationals as well as many tourists cheered and waved flags.

Once it was all over, Hugo and Amber retired once more

to the relative quiet of the anteroom. Their gazes caught and they both burst into laughter. Then Hugo reached out to Amber, gathered her up and twirled her about, her honey-blonde waves swinging behind her.

When he put her down she smacked her fists against his chest. "Was that as much of a rush for you as it was for me? It was like a million-person love-in. They adore you, Hugo."

"Of course they do. I am adorable," he said, taking off his gloves, then undoing the buttons on his jacket and passing the accoutrements to a valet. Then, catching her eye, he said the first thing that came into his head. "I want to kiss you again very badly."

Her laughter faded, but the light remained in her eyes. "It's the dress."

"It's the woman inside the dress."

No comeback for that one.

"One of these days I'm going to crack that crotchety exterior of yours, Amber Giordano, and I'm going to find that your centre is as soft and gooey as they come."

"Dream on," she said.

"I plan on it." Then, "Do you want to get out of here?"

"More than anything."

Within half an hour they were in the palace garage.

Instructed to change into something more comfortable, Amber had taken him at his word, changing into her old jeans, boots, a jumper and a beanie.

Amber looked wide-eyed over the royal car collection; at least a small part thereof.

Hugo pointed to a small Fiat, bright yellow, laughing at how disappointed she was. "The last kind of car people would expect to see their Prince driving, so get in."

"Yes, Your Highness," she said. When she saw Ned

sitting in the back seat, panting happily, she brightened. "Hey, boy. Are you coming too?"

And they were off, with Prospero and a bolstered security team discreetly on their tail.

Soon they were driving up into the foothills, heading towards the rugged landscape of Folly Cascades—the site of Vallemont's most infamous waterfall.

"This was once a primary timber area," he said, when he noticed Amber craning to see out of every window. "Prosperous from milling and hydro-power."

It was now the location of Cascade Cabins. They were small by the standards of the places he built today. Quaint and rustic, but still extremely popular. Except right now, the place was empty, the guests having been "upgraded" to the elegant Lake Glace resort over the next rise so that he would not be disturbed. So that the security team felt more comfortable too.

Hugo pulled up by a log cabin, its age evident in the ivy climbing the walls, the damp, mossy rocks lining the path and the forest that had regrown around it.

Ned hopped out of the car first and sniffed all the lovely woodsy smells.

Amber followed close behind, rolling her shoulders, breathing deeply. "What is this place?"

"The first resort I ever built."

Her eyes swung to him. "You built this?"

His hands went into his pockets and he swung up onto his toes. "Not with my own bare hands, but yes, it was my design. My idea, my funding, my project. Validation I could be successful at something other than just a spare prince-in-waiting."

This place had been the making of him. The planning battles, the down-to-the-wire negotiations, the extreme physicality required to get a place such as this to fruition, had given him grit, built his fortitude, shown him how to deal with failure. He would be a better prince for it.

"This is what you had in mind for Serenity?"

Hugo's gaze swung back to Amber. "My style has evolved since I built this place, as well as my budget. But I imagine a similar kind of 'grown out of the environment' feeling to the place. This, but with every modern luxury."

She breathed out hard through her nose, then looked with a fresh eye, taking in lush surroundings, the quiet overlaid with sounds of birdsong, of forest animals, the comfortably rustic aesthetic.

Hugo knew the moment she found the sign. A couple of days back he'd had it made, the words "The Shack" burned into a piece of wood. It was now attached to the front door of the small cabin ahead.

She walked slowly up onto the porch, barely noticing when Ned ran past chasing a butterfly.

Hugo followed. "If you ever need a time-out, a break from the crazy goings-on of the palace, this cabin can be your escape. There's a spare room, which I thought we could set up as a nursery. Perhaps get a fold-out couch in case of visitors. But I'll leave all that up to you, since it is your coronation gift."

"My...? But I gave you a book."

"Which I will read from cover to cover. Now back to my gift. I asked Maintenance to take the door off its hinges, and to put a hammer to a couple of the walls to make it feel more like home, but—"

"Shut up," she said, her voice ragged. "Just shut up."

And then she threw herself at him. Literally. Her feet left the ground and he wrapped her up tight, right as her lips found his.

The soft, sweet taste of her was like an elixir, scrambling his thoughts. But not so much that he couldn't find the door. He yanked it open, carrying her inside using one arm.

He kicked the front door closed—his security team was out there somewhere and there they could stay—and together they stumbled into the main room, where a fire crackled in the hearth.

They backed into the room, narrowly missing couches and end tables, and bumping into a lamp that threatened to topple. Then Amber's toes caught on the floor or the rug, acting as a brake, and Hugo twisted to take the brunt of the fall. He rolled so that she was beneath him, her hair splayed out across the fur.

Her chest rose to meet his as she breathed heavily, her dark eyes looked unblinking into his. He lowered his face, achingly slowly, and brushed his lips across hers.

Then suddenly she scrunched her eyes shut tight. "This is too much."

For Hugo it wasn't nearly enough.

"I can't take all this…this romance."

"Is that what this is?"

"Come on, Hugo. The cars, the sign, the fireplace. You're romancing me." She stuck her left hand in his face, showing off the ring. "At this point in time, it's pretty much moot."

Hugo took her hand, kissed her knuckles and then turned her hand over and kissed her palm. "I beg to differ. We did this all backwards, you see."

She blinked. He kissed the tips of her fingers one by one.

"We fell into bed together. And then we fell out. Then we fell pregnant. And then we eloped. We missed this part, you see. The drives, the dates, the romance."

She breathed and said nothing.

"Now, will you shut up and let me woo my wife?"

He let her hand drop back to her chest and looked into

her eyes, where he saw hope, timid and shy; emotion, ragged and true; desire and slow sexual unfurling.

"No more talk," she said, her voice barely a whisper. "I've had enough talk. From Sadie and Marguerite. From the protocol people and the ladies-in-waiting. Even Prospero has found his voice. Did you know he has a thing for insects? I've never answered so many questions about bees as I have this week."

"No more talk," Hugo promised.

"I'm a girl of action."

"Then let's get you some." Hugo ran a hand down her side, holding himself together by the skin of his teeth as her body undulated beneath his touch.

"More," she said, and he wondered how he had gone this long without touching her, tasting her, revelling in her beautiful abandon.

He kissed the bottom of her jaw and the soft spot below her ear.

He knew her tells—like the way she nibbled at her bottom lip. But there was something new here too. A new tension that had her in its grip.

"It's okay if you're nervous."

She flung her eyes open. "I'm not nervous."

"I'd understand," he said, taking advantage of her open mouth and tugging on her lower lip until her eyes near rolled back in her head. Then, "The last time we did this, I was merely a man. This time you'll be making love to a prince."

It took a moment for her to come back to him, but when she did she burst into laughter. "If you believe it makes a difference, prove it."

"As you wish," Hugo murmured, and set about doing just that.

It was agony taking it slow. The sweetest agony there was. But he took his time undressing her, caressing her, stretching out her pleasure. Until her breaths grew ragged, her hands clung to him and she rolled and writhed beneath the touch of his fingers, his mouth.

When he kissed her belly he did so with all the gentleness he could manage. He kissed to the right of her belly button, then the left, breathing in the scent of her skin, letting the knowledge that a part of him grew inside of her wash over him.

He rose to kiss her. She lifted to catch the kiss.

When he pulled back her eyes caught on his—dark, sensual, nearly lost to pleasure.

He stopped torturing her—torturing himself—and joined her. Neither looked away as they rocked together. As they made love.

Then Amber gasped, gripping him, her fingers digging into his arms. Heat and pleasure and emotion collected inside his core, before flooding through him like a lava flow.

While a single tear travelled down the edge of her cheek, manifesting the stunning emotion welling behind her eyes. No hiding. No pretending. No secrets. As if he could see all the way to her soul.

It was sumptuous. It was undefended.

It was his.

"What does *miele* mean?" she asked, her voice sleepy.

"Hmmm?"

"You call me that sometimes."

Did he? He hadn't noticed. But then, it did suit her. "It means honey."

Amber smiled up at him before rolling onto her side and taking his arm to place it over her like a cage. She snuggled into the cradle of his body. Within moments her breathing slowed.

While Amber drifted gently to sleep, Hugo had never felt so awake in his entire life.

* * *

An hour later, Hugo stood by the window, looking unsee-ingly into the forest beyond, his mind still freewheeling.

He was married to the most compelling woman he had ever known. They had a child on the way, and he had just been crowned Sovereign Prince of the country he loved.

It was a strange and unexpectedly difficult moment to realise he had everything he could ever want.

Philosophically, he knew that he should be crowing. Instead he felt as if he was careening towards the edge of a cliff.

He glanced back at Amber, who lay asleep on the fluffy rug by the fire, curled up in a ball beneath the throw he'd laid over her, not quite covering her dandelion tattoo. Her face was gentled in sleep.

As if the things he had to face—the security threats, the debilitating weight of overwhelming bureaucracy that remained after such a long reign—had nothing to do with her. But they did, as she was his wife. Making it far harder to make clear decisions when how it would affect her was never far from his mind.

He could no longer pretend that this was a mere mar-riage of convenience; a prince in need of a princess, a child in need of a father. There were feelings here—deep, broad, twisty, ingrained, developing, reaching feelings.

It would not have concerned him nearly as much if it had been one-sided. He had been stuck on Amber from the moment they had met.

But now he was certain Amber felt something for him too. He'd seen it in her eyes. Felt it in her touch. He'd tasted it as he'd kissed away the tear as she'd fallen asleep in his arms.

He could not offer any more than he already had—a beautiful home, the opportunity to do real good in the world, and as much help raising their child as she desired. But truly tender feelings? Love?

At thirty-two years of age his growing was all done. His heart was as big as it was ever going to get.

And yet making love to Amber, as her husband, had created a shift inside of him, allowing an aching kind of regret to bleed through the cracks. Only proving that, while he would not bend, he could still break.

As Sovereign Prince of the great nation of Vallemont, breaking was not an option. He would not make the mistakes his father had made and screw it all up.

He crouched down, pressing her hair away from her face, and forced himself to ignore the heat rushing through him. "Amber. *Miele*, wake up."

One eye opened, and then the other. Her hair was all messed up, her face pink with sleep, leaving him feeling disorientated with desire.

You can do this. You can resist. It's the only way.

"Did I snore?" she asked. "I dreamt I was snoring."

"Like an ogre," he lied.

She breathed sleepily. Then she ruffled her hair and yawned and Hugo felt such a heady mix of affection and bone-deep attraction it threatened to take his legs out from under him.

It seemed that decades of protocol would no longer be enough. He would have to keep his wife at arm's length in order not to slip again. It might well be the hardest thing he ever had to do, but it was the price he had to pay to take on the role for which he had prepared for his entire life.

"I just had the best dream," she said, her words sliding into a yawn. "The best part? Waking up and knowing real life was better."

Then she reached up to touch his face. Wound so tightly, he couldn't help but flinch, his entire body physically recoiling from her touch.

Amber saw it too. She suddenly went stiff, as if the blood had drained out of her extremities. "Hugo?"

He squared his shoulders and stood. "It's time to go."

"Already?"

"I'm needed back at the palace."

"Shortest honeymoon ever." She tried for a joke, her brow furrowing when he didn't smile. "But I guess the beauty of being married to the owner means we can come back any time."

It was. But it could never happen. Not if he had any chance of being the kind of prince he'd always wanted to be.

"Come on." He held out a hand. Hesitating, she took it, allowing him to help her to her feet.

Confusion flashed behind her eyes, as well it might. She searched his face for the reason for his reticence.

The urge to explain was near overwhelming. But confessing his feelings would only put the onus on her, which was entirely unfair.

In that moment, he found himself understanding his forebears. Keeping separate apartments wasn't a simple matter of conflicting social hours, or full closets, or accommodating separate staff; it was a necessary form of self-protection.

Then Amber straightened her shoulders, pulled the blanket around her and said, "Okay, then. I guess that's that. I'll collect my things."

He made to let her go, but then at the last—blaming the streak of self-destruction he could have inherited from either of his parents—he took her by the hand and twirled her into his arms and placed a gentle kiss on her lips.

She sank into him without hesitation, his beautiful, fierce, impossible Princess.

When she pulled back she looked into his eyes for a moment. And this time she pressed away. As if she was so used to being dismissed that closing herself off was the easier path for her too.

It was why he was sure this could work.

The both of them were so screwed up they would never let love get in the way of a good thing.

CHAPTER NINE

THE MORNING AFTER the coronation, Amber lay on the colossal bed in her private apartment feeling nothing.

Not sick. Not any more. The usual gnawing sensation had gone from her belly. She was simply...blank.

She stared at the canopy over her bed, her gaze skimming brocade and fringing, lace and...were those crystals? The workmanship was beautiful. Exquisite even. Sunflower would take one look at the detail and burst into happy tars.

But Amber couldn't seem to find the energy to care.

Perhaps it was because she'd grown up with money—with prestige, luxury, really nice bedding—and had turned her back on it.

That was the thing her friends had been so shocked about. Not the fact she felt misunderstood and overlooked to the point of legally emancipating herself, but that it had been enough for her to turn her back on the rewards.

Over the first few years she'd questioned her decision more than once—when she'd been hungry, broke, when she'd had every one of her meagre possessions stolen from a cheap motel.

Until she'd followed the Southern Cross and arrived in Serenity.

From the moment she'd looked up that hill, over that field of lavender, she'd felt vindicated in her choice to follow her own path. For she had found people who opened their arms to anyone. Heck, Hugo had planned to rearrange their entire existence and they'd welcomed him in and said, "Let's see what you have to say." Every decision they made came from a place of acceptance. Of love.

People were life's true reward. Having a community to rely on. Having a community rely on her.

She'd met Hugo while high on their goodness, in a single glance seeing him as worthy of her time, and over time finding him a man of honour and depth, of humour and heat. A man who truly seemed to value her, not for what she could do for him but because of the qualities he saw in her. The elusive something she'd been searching for her entire life.

It was their fault that she'd believed his promises.

Waking in front of the fire on their "honeymoon", she'd felt so happy. That a man as busy as he, with all the pressures he was under, had taken the time to create something private, something uniquely them. It had been a few seconds of pure and utter bliss.

And then she had opened her eyes.

There had been nothing in particular that she could put her finger on. Only that he'd seemed cool, detached; like a marble bust of a prince rather than flesh and blood.

On the drive back to the palace he'd asked her questions, answered hers; his hands had been relaxed on the wheel. But nothing was as it had seemed before. Nothing at all. Suddenly, the wintry cold outside was nothing compared to the chill within.

Which was when she'd realised it had all been in her head.

That she was so desperate for affection she'd believed the fairy tale. But it had been nothing but an illusion created by a broken, lonely girl.

Finding some deep reserve of energy, she pulled herself to sitting then padded over to the dressing table and sat.

The reflection in the mirror was of a woman she barely knew. Her hair was a mess, her eyes dark and sleepy; her cheeks a little leaner than usual, a result of barely keeping her food down for days. But that would change. She'd fill out, become smooth and rosy and plump.

The baby that had connected them in some quiet, magical way suddenly felt vulnerable. As if she hadn't been as diligent in her protection as she'd promised.

Amber put a hand over her belly and said, "Shh. It's all right. It's all going to be okay."

And then a knock came at the door.

Marguerite didn't wait for a response before entering. A plethora of strangers followed in her wake.

Amber grabbed the fine mohair throw from the back of the chair and wrapped it around her shoulders to cover her thin T-shirt and bare legs.

"Good morning, Your Highness."

"Good morning." She ran a quick hand over her bed hair and edged over to the Princess. "Marguerite? Who are these people?"

"My dear, I'd like to introduce you to your staff." One by one Marguerite pointed to the people in the line, listing hairdresser, make-up artist, stylist, linguists, personal planner, personal cook, and other positions she didn't quite catch.

She gave a double-take to the cook, who had the same wild strawberry-blonde waves as Sunflower, but the woman's smile was tight. Not like sunny Sunflower's at all.

So this was her new "community": a group of strangers whose job it was to tell her what to do, how to look, talk and dress, what to eat and where to go.

It didn't feel right. Not a bit. In fact, it felt horribly familiar.

She glanced towards the door, but what was she going to do? Complain to Hugo? He was so busy. And after the day before, she was no longer sure how firmly on her side he really was.

Instead, she turned to Marguerite, who looked positively buoyant as she pressed one last woman forward. In her fifties, with a tight grey bun and a stern countenance, she looked like the nasty principal from a Roald Dahl novel.

"Hi," said Amber as the woman loomed over her. "And you are…?"

"This," said Marguerite, "is Madame Brassard. She is the nanny."

Amber stilled. It took everything in Amber not to put a hand to her belly. "The what, now?"

"The nanny. For when the time comes, in the future, that you and Hugo are blessed with children, Madame Brassard will be assisting you in their day-to-day care. She has impeccable credentials, has worked with several important families, although non-disclosure agreements mean I cannot say who."

Having a breakdown was bad enough. Having one in front of a room full of strangers, some of whom probably didn't even understand a word she was saying, was a mortifying thought.

"Marguerite, may I please talk to you in private?"

"Dear girl, I'm afraid that the moment you become a Giordano there is no such thing as private any more. Especially from these good people."

"But I don't know these people."

"You will. In good time. They are your team, my dear."

Ah, no, she would not. Amber's hackles were now screaming.

"I actually prefer to build my own teams, if it's all right with you."

"Unfortunately, that is not possible. We have security to consider. Tradition. Royal protocol."

With every one of Marguerite's attempts to block her, Amber felt the walls closing in. She held up both hands in the international sign for stop. "I don't give a flying hoot about royal protocol. I truly don't."

Marguerite's eye twitched. "You married a prince, my dear. And not just any prince. The Sovereign Prince. It comes with responsibilities…"

Amber held up a finger to hush her, and the "team" all gasped in shock. But Amber's head was now buzzing so hard it might as well have been filled with bees. "Semantics aside, I did not marry a prince. I married a man. I married Hugo. A man who I may, one day, have children with. And if I do, it was made very clear that I will raise them myself." She added a belated, "With him."

Marguerite's expression was unreadable, though Amber could have sworn she saw a flicker of respect.

"Where's Hugo? I need Hugo."

Marguerite snapped her fingers, the lady-in-waiting leaping to her side. "Sofia, send word to the Prince that—"

"Wait! No. Thank you, Sofia, but you do not have to send word. I'm a smart woman with two feet and the ability to put one in front of the other. I can find the Prince myself."

With that she left her parody of a "commune" in her rooms. She tracked down Hugo in his apartment, which was down the hall and around a couple of bends. Seriously, who lived that way and called it a relationship? It was insane.

This whole thing was insane.

Her head spinning, her heart racing, she came to a halt in the open doorway when she saw Hugo was with his "team" too.

Prospero noticed her in an instant. "Your Highness?"

"Just a moment," said Hugo, sitting on the banquette at the end of his big bed, paper resting on his knee. Her heart squeezed at the sight of him, turning her into a mess of confusion and need.

"Hugo," Prospero said, his voice more insistent than Amber had ever heard it.

Hugo clearly felt the same way, as his gaze swung past his muscle man to Amber. Whatever he saw on her face brought him to his feet, eating up the floor and coming to her side.

"*Miele*, what is wrong? What happened? Is it—?"

His hands reached out to hold her before they stopped mid-air, as if a remote control had changed him from go to stop. The anxiety ramped from an eight to an eleven.

Then he stared at her belly as if an alien were about to explode out of her.

"No." She looked around at the half-dozen others in the room, each one looking out of the window or at their feet. "It's not that."

He breathed out hard. "Good. Excellent."

And then he took a step back and put his hands into his pockets, the disconnection as strong as if he had shut the door in her face.

And whatever anxiety she had felt at Marguerite's intrusion was nothing on the emotional wreck she became in that moment.

She somehow found words, saying, "I can see you are busy, but do you have a moment?"

He breathed out hard, and looked around at the dozen people all vying for his attention. He ran a hand through his hair and it stayed messy. He looked beleaguered. And it made her heart twist, just a smidge, to note that he was struggling too.

"Just one minute," she said, holding onto the very last hope that she was reading things wrong; giving him a chance to show her that she was wrong. That he *was* on her side. That he did care. That she could count on him as she'd thought.

Then he said, "Give me five minutes to finish up here and I'll come find you."

He hovered a hand near her back, ostensibly shooing her from the room. Once she was over the threshold he nodded at one of his lackeys, who closed the door in her face.

And something inside of her came away. Like a rowing boat snapping its moorings and drifting out to sea.

On numb feet she headed back to her room. Aware that, when it came down to it, it wasn't even really his fault. She'd never asked for affection. In fact, she'd made it clear she didn't want any of that kind of guff.

He'd given it anyway. And now she was used to it. To how it felt to be a part of something real, something warm. A community of two.

And she would never accept anything less than that again.

It was more like an hour before Hugo was finally able to drag himself away.

Unable to come up with a reason not to, he'd been forced to fire half the people on the board of the transport department for bad management bordering on state fraud. When he'd agreed to take on the position he'd never imagined his first week would be so onerous.

But it was compensated for by the security breakthrough. Prospero's compatriots had tracked down and rounded up the misanthropes who had orchestrated the attack on his uncle at the picnic all those months ago. The same ones who'd been causing strong headaches for Security since Hugo's return, a burr that had lived in the back of his head. And they were singing like canaries.

Still, starved and emotionally raw, his whole body felt like one big ache.

But he'd promised Amber some time. And the truth was, he could do with seeing her. Despite his best efforts at keeping his distance, for both their sakes, it turned out he couldn't function—not in the capacity he desired—without her keeping his head on straight.

His feet no longer dragged as he strode down the hall towards Amber's apartment.

"Amber?" he called from the open doorway.

No response.

He poked his head into her room to find it empty when he'd expected laughter and noise. And arguments, to be sure. For Marguerite had volunteered to get Amber acquainted with people who could guide her in the coming months. And, hoping to keep his aunt distracted from her woe, he'd agreed.

Where was everyone?

Where was Amber?

With security on his mind, he didn't like this one bit. "Amber?" he called more loudly this time, his ear straining, his heart thunderous.

"In here."

The sound of her voice, coming from her dressing room, brought a rush of relief.

But he pulled up short when he found her. She'd changed into warm clothes—boots, jeans, an oversized jumper that kept falling off one shoulder, and her hair fell in golden waves from beneath a beanie the colour of lavender that Sunflower had knitted for her before they'd left.

And she was folding clothes into a suitcase.

Ned sat at her feet, looking the way dogs looked when they thought they were in trouble. Only Hugo knew Ned wasn't the one Amber was mad at.

"Amber?"

She looked up. She seemed tired, fragile. He ached just looking at her.

"Amber, what's going on?"

"You said I could leave at any time."

The word *no* almost tore from deep inside, but he held it at bay. Just. He moved deeper into the room and said, "And I meant it."

He told his hands to go into his pockets so that he would not touch her, but one moved to her elbow, gently stopping her from packing. He turned her to face him, and she didn't even try to stop him. As if she was hollow. As if she had no fight left to give.

He placed a finger beneath her chin, lifting until he could see her face. As beautiful as the first time he'd seen her. More so now that he knew the mind that whirled behind it, the vast heart that held her together.

"Talk to me," he said, his voice raw.

She closed her eyes for a second before they fluttered open, hitting him with all that whisky-brown delight. "Do you need me here, Hugo?"

Hugo baulked. It wasn't what he'd been expecting. Or a side of her he'd ever seen before. She sounded almost brittle. It rang of Marguerite.

"Amber, please—"

"No. After meeting the vast number of people I apparently need to make me a palatable princess, I'm pretty sure I'll be nothing but a distraction." She threw a shirt into her bag. Then another. "A hindrance to your ability to do what you have to do. Especially in these early days of transitioning."

It was so close to what he'd been thinking the day before that he baulked again. Only she made it sound as if she was a burden when the truth was the polar opposite. "Amber, stop bloody packing, will you? I want you here. I would not have asked it of you unless I believed it was the

right decision. If I didn't know that my country would benefit from your…" Heart, soul, fierce upstanding goodness.

She stopped, some item of clothing scrunched in her
hand. "My what?"

"Your innate knack for ferreting out trouble."

Coward, his subconscious muttered.

No, he shot back. *The smart move.*

Because he knew what she wanted to know. He could
see it in the set of her shoulders; hear it in the raw scrape of
her voice. She wanted to know how he truly felt about her.

But he couldn't tell her what she wanted to hear. For,
while he wanted her, while he cared for her so deeply it
was disorienting, he didn't *need* anyone. He'd amputated
that part of himself when he was a younger man.

And yet, with Amber, he wasn't even half as afraid of
losing her as he was of loving her.

Which was how he managed to say, "I am married. I am
of age. I am crowned. I needed you to ensure all that was
possible. And for which I will be eternally grateful. But
hereon in, whatever you decide to do will not affect that."

She blinked at him then, like a puppy who'd been kicked
out of the house during a downpour. Marguerite had earned
a reprieve. Now he wanted to throttle himself instead.

Amber grabbed a pile of clothes and threw them into
the case without folding them, then she slammed the case
shut, zipping with all her might. "That's just great. I hope
you know how lucky you are, going through life so blithely
unaffected. I hope the people of Vallemont know what a
big-hearted leader they have."

She grabbed the bag, and hauled it past him into her
bedroom.

"And where exactly are you planning to go?"

"I'm not sure."

"You can't just walk out the front door."

"You think so?" She turned on him then. She had her

fight back—thank goodness—her spirit so strong it burned in her eyes. "Watch me."

Screw it, he thought. Screw holding back. Screw the job. Screw everything but this woman. He took the three steps to meet her and hauled her into his arms and kissed her.

She resisted for a fraction of a second, anger and hurt still raging inside her. Before tossing her suitcase to the floor and wrapping her arms about him and kissing him with such unbridled passion it took his breath away.

It felt like days since he'd touched her, not hours. All the energy spent thinking about keeping her at arm's length only making the abandon more intense.

She tasted like honey and sunshine and everything good as she sank into him, and he into her. Basking, exploring, until the world contracted to the size of her.

He might not need her, not in the way she needed him to, but God how he wanted her. In his arms, in his bed, in his life.

He spread his hands over her back, sliding his thumbs up her sides, catching her sweater until he reached skin. Silken soft, hot from the inside.

She gasped, her head falling away, leaving him scope to trail kisses along her jaw, down her neck. As her body melted against him, he feared he might tell her whatever the hell she wanted to hear. So he wrapped his arms more tightly around her; holding on for dear life.

When the backs of her knees pressed into the bed, he lowered her down and they fell together. Landing in a mass of twisted limbs. Their ragged breaths snagged against the silence.

And Amber looked into his eyes, deep, searching. Her hair splayed out around her like waves of sunlight, her lips pink from kissing.

Hugo ran his thumb down her cheek and she turned her cheek to rub into his touch.

Then she lifted a hand as if about to run it through his hair...

Only at the last she stopped, pressing against his chest with her other hand to push him away and disentangling her legs so fast she nearly fell off the bed.

And she split the heavy silence with a growl. That turned into a roar. That had even near-deaf Ned jogging out of the dressing room to make sure she was all right.

"I can't do this! I won't. I spent my entire childhood collecting the rare drops of attention from my parents and waiting in agony for the next. Do you know why I divorced them? Really why?"

Hugo hooked his feet over the edge of the bed and ran a hand down his face. Still trying to collect his wits, he shook his head.

"That paperwork was physical proof that my life was mine. No one else's. That it would, from that moment on, be lived on my terms. Those terms were hard for a really long time. Scary at times. But I got through it, because I knew that, no matter what, my choices were mine. I won't do hot and cold, Hugo. Not now. Not ever."

Hugo had never felt more like a grown-up than he did in that moment. And it wasn't as much fun as the brochures had made out. "Are you saying you want a divorce?"

"What? No. I don't think so." A beat went by then she shook her head. "We had a contract and I plan to honour that contract. But I need some time away to come to terms with what we are. What we *really* are. I think I've been stuck on those two lonely people who shared a small, lumpy bed and talked in ridiculous streams of consciousness until three in the morning. But that was the fairy tale."

Finally her hands went to her belly. "We have a baby coming, Hugo, and that's as real as it gets. To be ready for that I need to shake this off. This feeling..." She glanced at him—a flash of hurt, a flash of heat—and something squeezed deep inside his chest.

"How much time?"

"As much as it takes."

Hugo ran a hand over his face. To think he knew a dozen perfectly lovely women who would have fallen over themselves to be Princess. Women who could have led a civil, courteous, undramatic life by his side. And he'd have been bored out of his mind.

Amber had never been the safe choice, or even the smart choice, but she had been his only choice. Choice being the important word. For the choice was also hers. To stay or to go.

For all his faults, he was no bastard. He wouldn't keep her if she wanted to go. Even with the possible future of his country growing inside of her. But once he had a handle on this behemoth job of his, he'd track her down wherever in the world she landed and bring her home.

"All right," he said. His mind was set, but his voice was raw. "On the proviso you allow me to assign security."

Her expression grew thunderous. "Hugo—"

"That's non-negotiable. I know you, Amber. I know you'd take on a dragon if it looked sideways at someone you cared about. I need to know that you are safe."

She swallowed, her eyes giving nothing away. Then she nodded.

"You must also promise you'll find appropriate housing—heated, with walls that actually keep out the wind."

At mention of the shack her expression softened. "No buckets to catch the drips?"

"Stairs that don't crack when you walk on them. Railings that don't wobble. Working plumbing."

She glanced towards the bathroom with its double

shower and claw-footed bathtub. "I do like working plumbing."

His voice was rough as he said, "You will have a bank account at your disposal. And access to the best doctors. For the baby."

"Thank you. Any other demands, Your Highness?"

The only words that made their way out of his mouth were, "Come back soon."

Then, aware of how close he'd come to completely giving himself away, he added, "You can do good here, Amber. So much good. I hope, in time, you find that level of service reward enough."

She swallowed. Nodded. And picked up her suitcase.

Even while Hugo's head hurt with the effort not to command her to stay, he did as so many princes had done before him and leant on history, on convention, on duty and said, "So be it."

He moved to the side of the bed and pressed a button in the panel. A knock came at the door moments later. "Come in."

Prospero entered.

"Prospero, could you please organise a car for Amber?"

The big man glanced at Amber, then Hugo, at Amber's suitcase, concern lighting his stern, solid features. "Where shall I say the car is to take her?"

"The airport. From there the family plane will take her wherever she wishes to go."

"If that is her wish."

"It is," Amber said. "I'll call. Let you know when I'm settled. Don't worry about me. I'll be fine."

Hugo wasn't worried about her. He was worried about himself.

But it was too late to do anything about it as she gave Hugo one last long look, then walked out of the bedroom door. Gone. For how long, he did not know. Where to? He did not know that either. He couldn't remember ever feeling this ineffective.

"Your Highness." Prospero's voice was tight.

Hugo held up a hand—he didn't want to hear it. When he saw his hand was shaking he shoved it into a pocket.

"Your Highness," Prospero insisted. Then, breaking protocol for the first time since they'd known one another, said, "What the hell happened?"

"Stay with her. Keep her safe. She's…" *Important*, he'd been about to say, but it felt so cold compared with how much she meant to him. "She's wily. Even more so than I was."

"I will protect her as if she's my own." Prospero nodded and then was gone, leaving Hugo feeling more alone than he remembered feeling his entire life.

As if sensing his loss, Ned padded over to Hugo and sat on his foot, looking up at him with his strange mismatched eyes. Hugo sank his hand into the dog's soft fur. "I know, buddy. But this is life. People come, people go. And some make such an impact they leave a crater that never quite heals."

Hugo gave Ned one last rub before the dog harrumphed and left to follow his girl out of the door. Then he looked around Amber's apartment, the unmade bed, the open door to the wardrobe she'd never had the chance to fill.

Everyone he cared for left. Died. Ran. Or slowly slipped away.

But now was not the time to be morose. It was time to focus. He would be the best damn prince they had ever seen.

All he'd ever wanted, deep down, was to follow the family tradition, to be a true Giordano.

Now he was prince of all he surveyed. Even as his private life lay in tatters.

"Well, what do you know?" he said out loud. "You're a Giordano, through and through."

CHAPTER TEN

"TOLD YOU WE'D find him here. What is he wearing? Is he drunk? Give him the coffee."

Hugo had smelled the warm, hazy scent before he heard Sadie's voice. He opened one eye just enough to see Will shrug. Good man.

"I don't think I've ever actually seen him drunk. Is he allowed to get drunk, being the leader of the country? What if he has to decide on the blue wire or the red wire and he's too drunk to remember which is which?"

Will gave Sadie a look. "I'm not sure nuclear launch codes are something you need to be concerned about in Vallemont."

"True. I'm just worried. I've never seen him like this."

Will pressed forward, his face darkening. "I have. The last two times his world fell apart. Mate!" he said, giving Hugo a shake.

"I'm awake." Awake enough to feel the press of a rogue stone from the wall of the tallest turret in the castle wall pressing into his back. "And I'm not drunk. I'm merely exhausted."

For he had barely slept a night since Amber had walked out of his door.

He'd worked. And worked. And worked. Wrangling with parliament. Sweeping through government departments, cleaning house like an avenging angel. And dealing with the reason behind the security threat that had dogged his family for months.

When there was no other work to be done he'd spent his time in the garden. Washing Ned—for all its challenges—had been therapeutic. On a whim, he'd had his staff install a kind of modified greenhouse. And he worked in it daily. It was so physically demanding it was the only thing that could send him into a dead sleep when he needed it most.

In fact, he'd been working in there before he'd followed his feet and ended up here.

The staff called it his Zen Garden. He wondered if it might yet kill him.

Will added, "Then stop eavesdropping and get the hell up. You're worrying my woman."

Hugo gave Sadie a look, realised she was truly worried, then pulled himself to standing.

He held out his hand for the mug and Will handed it over. Sadie moved to stand beside him, crossing her arms but near enough to nudge with her elbow. She gave him a once-over, her gaze stopping a moment on his torn jeans, battered sneakers, holey beanie. "This is a new look for you."

"I've been gardening."

"You what, now?"

Hugo took a long sip, closing his eyes against the bliss of the bitter taste. Strong, black. Laced with something medicinal. No wonder Will was his oldest friend.

Thankfully Sadie changed the subject, though it wasn't any easier. "How is Amber?"

"Safe," he said, which was the most important thing.

"Have you heard from her?"

"Prospero has been sending updates."

Hourly at times, good man.

Amber wasn't sleeping well. The nausea seemed to have abated. She looked pale. She laughed at a joke. She was reading children's books, making lists. Baking. She wasn't good at it and he hoped she'd give it up.

"Is she okay?"

He sipped on his coffee again.

"Jeez," Sadie muttered, "it's like pulling teeth."

"If you are looking for news I can update you on the security issue."

"Fine. Do that."

"The group who attacked Reynaldo all those months ago was led by the husband of a woman Reynaldo had... befriended. The husband had found out, fallen into the waiting arms of a cuckolded husbands help group, and in a frenzy of misguided support together they made the bungled attack."

Sadie blinked. "For *that* I nearly married you? I could kill Reynaldo right now. You know, if he was still alive." Then her eyes narrowed. "So what does this have to do with Amber?"

His clever friend knew him all too well. "There has been chatter since I arrived back home that something else was in the planning. The leader, the man who'd lost his wife, got it into his head that—considering my father's infamous infidelity and now my uncle's—I would be next to have a go at his wife. So they were planning to have a go at mine."

Neither Sadie nor Will laughed.

"Oh, Hugo. You must have been terrified."

Terrified didn't even come close. The shake in Hugo's hand still came over him every now and then when he thought about it.

"The leader now realises how twisted his thinking had become and is all remorse and apology. It's over. Happy ending all round."

Sadie looked to Will and mouthed something Hugo didn't catch.

"I saw that," said Hugo.

"What?"

He put down the coffee, cleared his throat, ran hard hands through his hair and looked at Sadie. This place, this turret, had been their favourite spot as kids. The place they'd run to when feeling hard done by, or in need of some peace and quiet; to sort out their heads.

In the days since Amber had left he'd wanted to move into the turret. Maybe for ever.

"If it's such a happy ending, why are you hiding on our turret?"

Good question.

"Only one way to turn that frown upside down. Go get your girl."

"She's in Serenity." Probably. "Surrounded by lavender fields and stingless honey bees, where she belongs. And if Serenity makes her happy then I'm not about to take it away from her."

"Right. Because you're in love with her."

Hugo kept his trap shut. The strength of his feelings for his wife did not matter—how he acted on them did. That was the lesson to be learned from all this.

The problems his uncle had left behind were due to him making the easy choices over the right ones, leading to blackmail, extortion and leaving behind his wife and young family. Hugo planned to fix it all.

"Don't panic. It's quite normal to be in love with your wife. Right, Will?" Sadie asked.

"So I hear."

"What are you talking about?" Hugo asked.

"What are *you* talking about?" she shot back.

"How I can best serve Vallemont, redeem the family name and sleep at night."

"By being a loving husband and father first, of course."

"Leo, for Pete's sake. Leave it the hell alone."

"Fine!" She threw her hands in the air and paced to the other side of the turret. "But just one last thing. She knows how you feel, right? Before she left you told her you loved her and that's why you had to let her go?"

Hugo turned and gripped the rock wall, looked over verdant farmland, craggy mountains, the road he and Amber had travelled from the airport. And he said, "Not in so many words."

"Okay, but you told her when you proposed to her."

Hugo kept his mouth shut again.

"How did you propose, Hugo? We never heard the story. Knowing how you proposed to me, I'm assuming you learnt your lesson and did it right this time."

Hugo thought back to the words he had used. The offer he had made. He tried to pretty it up but in the end simply said, "I made it impossible for her to refuse."

Sadie's face sank into her hand, her laughter rueful. "Hugo, Hugo, Hugo!"

"She prides herself on being pragmatic."

"Then that's why she agreed to marry you. But did you tell her why you wanted to marry *her*?"

"I don't understand."

"Of course you don't. And maybe I wouldn't have either before I met Will. Hugo, you're *in love with her*."

"Yes, all right, I'm in love with her. I've been in love with her since I first laid eyes on her, looking down at me with those wild whisky eyes, telling me off for invading her hammock, all the while looking at me like I'm a hot lunch." Hugo pressed away from the wall and paced about the turret. "I've never met anyone who makes me feel like I'm floating an inch above the ground while also so grounded in my own reality I can see it, smell it, taste it fully for the first time in my life. Who makes me feel..." He thumped a fist against his chest. "She makes me feel. And not having her near, not knowing when I'll see her again… I can't sleep. I can't function. I'm running on automatic."

Sadie sighed. "Was that so hard?"

"That was more difficult than you can possibly imagine!"

She gave his arm a squeeze. "And it didn't occur to you to lead with all that, when you asked her to be yours?"

"She prides herself—"

"On being pragmatic. Yes, so you said. So do we all, unless we are given reason to believe in the alternative. She might *want* to be pragmatic, Hugo. But what she needs, what all of us need, is affection, consideration, love. Some of us also need a rockin' hot prince. Or a puppy. Will, can we get a puppy?"

"We live in a construction zone, so no."

"Okay."

Hugo only heard the last of it in his periphery, for he was onto something. His brain having switched from automatic to clear and present. "A phone. I need a phone."

Sadie looked to Will, who was way ahead of her. He handed it over then took Sadie by the wrist, drawing her away, murmuring to her about giving him space.

Hugo called Prospero. The big guy answered on the third ring. Didn't wait for a hello before asking, "Where is Ned?"

A beat, then, "Your Highness?"

"If she went back to Serenity, Ned would be in quarantine. She would never have put him through that twice in such a short space of time. So where is she?"

But Hugo knew before he'd even finished the question.

"If you tell me she's been staying in the shack just up the road all this time, while I've been out of my mind worried about her, trying to run the country without her, I will send you on a mission to Siberia."

"Then I won't tell you that."

Hugo tried.

"I do like what you've done with the garden, Your Highness. Very Zen."

Hugo hung up, paced towards the exit, then turned to give Will back his phone. Then he was off, running down the winding staircase before he even had any semblance of a destination.

"Go!" Sadie's voice followed him.

She might have said, "Get our girl and bring her back," but Hugo's mind was otherwise engaged with thoughts of Amber.

He'd made the mistake of thinking he was a man who had it all, but he wasn't even close.

Not without her. She was his counterweight. The yin to his yang. The uptight hippy to his laid-back royalty.

And he loved her. Deeply. Ferociously.

Not because of the baby. Her child, their child, was important. But right now, it was only a dream. A fairy tale he hoped would come true.

Amber was his reality.

With that as his touchstone, Hugo hit the bottom of the stairs, sweat sliding down his face, his heart like a runaway horse, and burst out into the light.

Amber sat in the back of the town car, Ned sitting in the footwell, Prospero in the back seat with her, a strange smile playing around his eyes.

They came out through a copse that hung over the bumpy country road and the palace came into view.

"Are you sure about this, Your Highness?" Prospero asked.

She shot him a look. "You're the one who said Hugo sounded strange."

"Very strange."

"If you're pulling my leg and I drive up there and find

him sitting in his office surrounded by lackeys, I will find out if I have the authority to send you to—"

"Siberia?"

She'd been about to say Mongolia, but Siberia was close enough.

Staying in the shack, sleeping, reading books that weren't about princesses—mostly about what to do when you were expecting—and snuggling with Ned and talking to Sunflower and Johnno on the phone had been exactly what she'd needed.

Too long feeling like a car in need of a service—clunky and misfiring—she was now a finely tuned machine. Waking at six, yoga by sunrise, nap at three, bed by nine. Eating clean, drinking water like it was going out of fashion. She was the picture of hippy health.

And she couldn't remember ever feeling so miserable in her life.

The truth was, when she'd heard Prospero answer the phone she'd known it was Hugo on the other end. She so wanted to hear his voice, to make sure he was all right, perhaps even to fight with him a little so as to get her blood sparking again, it was a miracle she didn't tear the phone from Prospero's grip.

When Prospero had murmured something about the Prince sounding strange on the phone she'd practically grabbed him by the collar and dragged him to the car.

She might not have figured out what she'd gone to the shack to figure out, but she had discovered something. That she missed him. Missed his humour, his work ethic, the way he looked at her as if he'd never seen anything quite like her.

And that in the grip of old fears, she may have judged him too harshly.

The only way to figure out what they were to one another was to figure it out together.

Minutes later, the car pulled through the front gates of the Palace of Vallemont. It hooked around the back, heading towards one of the huge garages.

Prospero helped her out of the car.

She stretched her legs, looking into the garden leading to the forest. The one she could see from her balcony, where she'd seen Hugo wash Ned with his own bare hands and whatever methods she'd used to deny her feelings had truly dissolved away.

Hang on a second. What was that? A big white tent-type structure had been put up on the lawn since the last time she was there.

Curious, she took a few steps that way, only to see Hugo striding inside the thing as if his life depended on it, wearing what looked like an old knit jumper, dirty jeans and gumboots. His nose was pink, his beanie ragged.

He looked like a right royal mess. And she loved him more than anything.

Maybe that was what she'd figured out in the shack: that she could love their little family enough for the both of them.

Then suddenly Hugo was back at the entrance, what looked like a pile of weeds in his hand.

She saw the moment he clocked her.

She wasn't sure how he might react, whether she would get warm Hugo, or cool Hugo, or a whole new beast. Perhaps the Hugo she had left in the lurch.

But then he mouthed her name and soon he was running.

And she was running too, her bag dumped by the car.

And then she was in his arms, wrapped tightly. His face was buried in her neck, tears sliding down her face.

And then they were kissing as if they hadn't seen one another in weeks rather than days. And maybe they hadn't. Not really.

Amber slowly slid down Hugo's body, her feet touching the ground before their lips came apart. Then she blinked up into his eyes and knew. Something had happened to him in their separation as it had happened to her. Something magical.

"Hi," she said.

"Hi to you too."

His gaze slid past her shoulder to where Prospero stood on edge of the hill. Once Hugo gave him the all-clear he slipped into the shadows and was gone.

"What are you doing here, *miele*? I was just about to come and find you. If I'd known you hadn't fled to the other side of the world I'd have been there sooner. I'd have been there every day and night. Doing whatever it took to convince you that I want you here. With me. I want you at my side. In my bed. In my damn apartment. Or I'll move into your sparkly pink monstrosity if that's what it will take to show you I mean it."

She laughed at the words pouring from his lips. "Slow down before you hurt yourself."

"Too late," he said, reaching up to swipe her hair from her face. Then, realising he still gripped the weeds, he stepped back and held them out to her. "These were for you."

"Thank you...?"

"They're lavender seedlings. Not yet flowering, clearly. But with the bees at play we should see a good crop that we can plant along this patch of grass so you can see them from our window. *Our* window."

"Hugo?"

"Hmmm."

"I have no idea what you are talking about." Not that it mattered. He could have been talking wheat prices and sheep farming for all she cared. For he had his hand in hers, and the look in his eye made her feel faint.

"Right," he said. "Of course. Come on."

He took her by the hand and dragged her down the grassy slope. Up close, the tent was huge. Taller than a tree and half the size of a soccer field. With a half-smile, Hugo opened the flap with a flourish.

What hit her first was the heat. It was a hothouse. As humid and warm as an Australian spring. To go with it, a small forest had been planted in her absence. Wattle trees and banksia, liquidambar saplings and pots and pots of lavender. And buzzing around the lot were tiny little stingless Australian bees.

"Hugo, what have you done?"

"It's not finished yet. Not by a long shot. But it's a start."

"A start of what? Turning this into Australia?"

"Just this patch. Just for you. I realised that I had torn you out of your natural environment and stuck you in a cage when I should have been nurturing you. Nurturing *us*. I somehow thought that if I built this, a little patch of home, it might be enough to tempt you back."

He took her by the shoulders and moved her.

In the far corner, two huge trees had been transplanted into the soil. Mature gum trees, no less. And between them swung a hammock.

Seeing it, Amber burst into tears.

Hugo spun her around, stooped to look into her eyes. "Oh, hell, Amber."

Hands on her shoulders, he hustled her out of the hothouse and into the fresh air. "I'm sorry. Has it made you homesick? I can take it down. I'm not good at this kind of thing."

"What kind of thing is that exactly?" she asked, knowing but wanting to hear him say it.

"Romance."

She burst into laughter. "You toss a priceless family heirloom at me as if it's a trinket." She wangled her hand at him to prove her point. "And you romance me with a hammock."

He felt for her hand, held it up to the light. "You're wearing the ring."

"Of course I'm wearing your ring, Hugo. I've never taken it off. You could have given me the pull ring from a soda can and I'd still be wearing it. Because you gave it to me."

She grabbed him by the front of the jumper, a light glinted in his eye and he smiled. It was enough to push her over her last great hurdle. And once she leapt she felt as if she could fly.

"I don't need romance, you great big lug. Or crown jewels. Or a staff. Or a huge apartment of my own. I just need you." She breathed in, not sure if the words would come. But then it was as easy as breathing out as she said, "I love you, Hugo. I love you so much I'm willing to put up with your odd bodyguard and your family's strange obsession with the colour pink. I don't need romance, Hugo, I just need you." And with that she pulled him in and kissed him until she was about to faint. Then just a little more because it felt that good.

When she pulled back she was woozy with lust, and lack of oxygen, so she wasn't quick enough to stop him when he sank to one knee. "Get up."

"No."

She looked around to see a couple of gardeners watching from the hedgerow. A band of maids had congregated by the laundry door. Marguerite stood watching from a balcony on the first floor, her hand to her mouth. From that distance, Amber could have sworn she saw tears. "Hugo, please. I don't need this."

"Amber Hartley Giordano."

Amber looked down at the Prince and the rest of the world faded to nothing. "Yes, Hugo?"

"You may think you don't need romance, but I'm afraid that you live in a palace now, and you are married to a prince. Romance will from this point on be a given. Because I am besotted. Fuelled by desire. I am crazy in love. With you. I'd convinced myself it was dangerous to love that hard. But the only danger was the possibility of losing you because I never let you know it."

Amber was speechless, overwhelmed and so happy her cheeks hurt from smiling. "Right back at you. Now please get up."

"Not until you agree to marry me."

"I already did."

"Again. In front of your friends and mine. In front of God and country. And the world."

He was too big for her to lift, and too stubborn to convince, so she sank to her knees as well. "Okay."

"Really?"

"Why not?"

He leaned down, kissed her gently. Pulled back. "You like the hammock?"

"I love the hammock. I can't wait till everyone's asleep and we can sneak out to the hammock and..." She leaned in, whispering her intentions in his ear.

"I can order them all to bed now, you know. I have that power."

"No, you don't."

"You're right, I don't. So later, then?"

"It's a date."

"A date. I don't believe we ever had one of those."

"Now seems like a fine time to start."

Two weeks later, Marguerite got the wedding she wanted. Hugo had insisted on a no-camera policy inside the chapel, but the guest list was extensive and the decor extravagant.

The bride wore pink, because it was tradition. She was even beginning to get used to the colour.

"You look edible."

Amber turned to find Hugo leaning in the doorway of the anteroom in which she was getting ready. Then Sadie leapt in between them, waving her arms like a mad thing.

"Get out! It's bad luck to see her before the wedding. Your mother's family was dripping in bad luck, remember, Your Highness. Should you really risk it?"

"Bad things happen," said Hugo. "We do what we must to fend them off. Protecting those we love. It's been the way of things since the time of cavemen. Fending off sabre-tooth tigers with big sticks. It's not all that different now. Besides, if you don't remember, we're already married. You were even there."

"Oh, right. So this is all…"

"For the good of the country."

"I've heard that before."

"Mmm," said Hugo before taking Sadie by the hips, spinning her and pushing her forcibly out of the door, which he locked behind her.

Amber simply kept on pinning a silk peony rose she had unpicked from her coronation gown into her hair.

He moved in behind her, placing his hands on her gently rounded belly and kissing her on the neck. "Morning, wife."

"Morning, husband."

"Nearly ready?"

"I was born ready."

"Yes, you were. I had a quick look at the crowd."

"And?"

"Hell of a crowd. Nearly as big as my last wedding."

She caught his eye in the mirror. "Funny man."

"I try. When you get out there don't forget to check out the first few rows."

"Why?"

"Just do it."

"Tell me why. Right now."

"Fine, but only because I can't resist you when you get all bossy on me. On the right we have my mother sitting in a better position than Marguerite and clearly loving it, while my aunt looks as pleased as if she sucked a lemon. And on the left of the chapel, in a sea of hemp formal wear, half of Serenity."

"What? How?"

"We flew them in on a chartered plane yesterday." Hugo held out both hands, smug as all get-out.

"You really are a powerful man."

"Handsome too, don't forget."

"So handsome," she said, her finger climbing up the front of his shirt before popping a button.

"Oops," Hugo said with a smile.

When his hand went to her back, unzipping her simple, floaty dress in one fell swoop, there was no time for "oops". For soon they were both undressed, their wedding clothes strewn on the floor, and both glad Hugo had locked the door.

When the wedding start time came and went, the crowd did wonder if they might be about to see another exciting non-wedding at the Palace of Vallemont. But when the bride and groom took one another down the aisle fifteen minutes later, it was clear to everyone present how smitten they both were.

And that a new day was dawning in the story of Vallemont.

EPILOGUE

"AAAARGH!"

The midwife gave Hugo a look.

"Sorry," he whispered. "I stubbed my toe."

Amber rolled her eyes. Which was quite a feat, considering she'd been in labour for six hours and didn't feel as if she had the energy to breathe, much less express sarcasm in any meaningful way.

"I never imagined His Highness to be so precious," the midwife said to Amber, loud enough for Hugo to hear.

"It's a new thing. He seems to think I am made of glass and, in response, his tiptoeing skills have become excellent."

The tingle in the base of her spine, and the encroaching red at the edges of her mind, heralded another contraction. Amber closed her eyes, breathed gently and counted to fifteen. When she reached the peak, she rode the relief counting back down to one.

The midwife pottered about, doing her wonderful, calming, capable, midwifey things, and, after a glance to be sure Amber was back, said, "So how did you two lovebirds meet?"

"You really don't know?"

The midwife shot her a look.

"Of course you know. You're just trying to distract me. It's a long and winding tale," said Amber.

"We have time," she said, glancing at her watch as she checked Amber's pulse. "Not much, but a little."

Hugo caught Amber's eye, panic swirling about the hazel depths. "How little?" he asked.

"That's up to the little Prince or Princess." The midwife threw him a smile. Before patting Amber on the hand. "You are doing great. Textbook."

"Hear that?" Amber said as another wave of pain ripped through her body. "I'm a natural."

"You are perfect."

The midwife scoffed. "Don't ever let him forget he said that."

Amber smiled as the pain ebbed.

At which point the midwife had a look and a feel. She held Amber's eyes. "Are you ready to have a baby, Your Highness?"

Amber nodded. After months of nausea, followed by months of baby bliss, then months of swollen feet and arguments with Marguerite as to the nursery colours, she was so ready to have a baby, this man's baby, she could barely hold herself together. Her joy was such she felt as if she might split into a thousand pieces.

Hugo, on the other hand, groaned as if he might not last.

"Perhaps His Highness could go to the desk, track down another heat pack?"

Hugo wagged a finger at the midwife. "Not happening. I've spoken to other fathers. I know the tricks you lot pull when you think we're not handling things. I am fine. I will not miss the birth of my daughter."

"Or son," Amber said through gritted teeth as she hit thirteen, fourteen, fifteen, sixteen, seventeen… The pain was different now—bigger, broader—and she gripped the edges of her subconscious as it tried to disintegrate. Thankfully her body seemed to know what to do even if her mind was shutting up shop; taking over, bearing down.

And then…relief.

"That's right," said Hugo, suddenly at her side, holding her hand. Though his knuckles looked strangely white—bloodless, in fact…because she was squeezing the life out of them.

Amber let go. Or tried. But Hugo wrapped his hand around hers.

"We had a summer affair in a beautiful little country town in Australia," he said, eyes on hers. "Which ended when she kicked me out of her bed for no reason whatsoever."

Amber tried to open her mouth to disagree, but reality had taken a hike. Her head was full of stars. Her body felt as if it was floating above the bed, no doubt trying to escape the pain.

Hugo's deep voice was like a balm. "After that we got to know one another and discovered we actually liked one another. Knowing then I'd never met a woman of her like—fierce and fearless, loyal and lovely, bright and bold—I found myself terrified I'd screw up the best thing that had ever happened to me, so I did my very best to screw it up just to make sure."

Amber heard it all through the spangled depths of her brain as she came out of her next contraction. The urge to scream was stoppered by the stronger need to hear Hugo's words.

"The rest was pretty textbook. We found out we were pregnant; we got married; I was crowned; she became a princess; she left me; I willed her back." With his spare hand, Hugo pushed damp hair from Amber's cheek, tucking it behind her ear. "And somewhere in there we fell in love."

"And then…?"

"I'm hoping the 'and then' will be born pretty soon. Healthy, whole, and as beautiful as my wife."

Amber felt a tear running down her cheek even as she fell into the mental abyss that was birthing a baby. No matter how much she wanted to look into Hugo's eyes, to tell him how deeply she loved him, her eyes closed, her breaths came hard and fast and she dug deep, knowing she'd need every bit of energy she had to get through this.

The midwife's voice came as if down a tunnel. "I like it. Very modern. Though I'm not sure there's a greetings card that covers it."

"I'd expect not."

"Your Highness? Amber?"

Amber opened her eyes to see a team of people now milling about the room. The midwife clicked her fingers to make sure Amber was looking into her eyes. "The baby's head is clear, Amber. One more good push and your baby will be born."

Amber looked to Hugo. A matching tear left a track down his cheek too.

"You ready for this?" she asked. "For all of this? For us?

Hugo's smile was slow. Warm. Genuine. "I was born ready."

And somehow, Amber found the strength to laugh.

Half an hour later, after weighing and measuring and the most fundamentally soulful moments of Hugo's life to date—watching his wife smile and coo and glow as she enjoyed skin-to-skin time with her child—Hugo held a bundle of snuggly swaddled baby in his arms.

He kept his voice low so as not to wake Amber as he said, "I know I said your mother was perfect, and she'll never let me forget it, but I do believe I was jumping the gun. You," he said, looking down at the face of his baby daughter, "you are perfect."

Amber stirred and settled. Hugo knew she'd wake up grumpy, having fallen asleep and missed this, but after witnessing what her body had put her through for the past several hours Hugo did not wake her. Not just yet.

His daughter was sleeping too, still too squishy from her own recent ordeal to look much like her mother, but he could see the potential in the lashes brushing her cheeks, in the shape of her chin, the tuft of fair hair. Lucky girl.

Give her a day to grow into her new world and Princess Lucinda Sadie Sunflower Giordano would be the most beautiful child that ever was. And the most loved.

Princess or no princess, she had two parents who wanted her and adored one another so very, very much. Add an adoring dog, a dozen already besotted honorary aunts and uncles on the other side of the world, and a mini-hammock he had secretly hung in the hothouse as a surprise and Hugo knew this kid was as lucky as they came.

If Hugo had his way in the next session of parliament— and if that was what she wanted to be—he was looking upon the face of the girl who could one day become the first Sovereign Princess of Vallemont.

Shifting gently on his chair, instinctively mindful that not waking the baby was going to be a big deal, he leaned towards his wife and kissed her on the cheek. Then the edge of her mouth. Then her lips.

Her eyes fluttered open in surprise, before softening as she kissed him back.

"Lucy?" she said.

And Hugo shifted so she could see her baby.

"She has your nose."

"Poor kid."

"I love your nose," Amber said with a frown, so loyal to those she cared for she wouldn't even let him make a joke about himself.

"As you should. For it is the nose of princes and princesses."

"It's the nose of Hugo; that's all I care about."

"You did good, kiddo."

"I did, didn't I?"

"Did it hurt as much as it seemed?"

"More."

"Want to do it again?"

"As soon as humanly possible."

Hugo gave Amber a nudge and with a wince she scooched over so that the entire family could fit on the big hospital bed.

"But first, I want to talk to you about the nurses. I got talking to one when you were on a phone call earlier, about their working conditions. I believe we can do better for them. Job share for those who are keen. Add a crèche. I want to know more about mandatory breaks. I might even have offered to represent them…"

Hugo laughed. "Please tell me you're not about to call me out in front of parliament."

"Do the right thing and I won't have to."

"It's a deal."

Amber snuggled deeper into the bed, wincing again as she moved, but looking happier than he had ever seen her. "I'm going to like this job, aren't I?"

"Told you so. Vallemont has no idea how lucky it is to have you on its side, *miele*."

"Right back at you, My Highness."

With his daughter secure in his arms, Hugo leaned down and kissed his Princess, his wife, his partner, his conscience, his love. And the rogue Prince of Vallemont had finally found his way home.

* * * * *

EXPECTING THE PRINCE'S BABY

REBECCA WINTERS

I dedicate this book to my angelic grandmother, Alice Vivia Driggs Brown, who made my childhood a constant enchantment. She was so romantic she called the home she and my grandfather had built 'Camelot.'

CHAPTER ONE

VINCENZO DI LAURENTIS, thirty-three-year-old crown prince of the Principality of Arancia, stood before the camera on the balcony of the royal palace overlooking the gardens to officially open the April Fifteenth Lemon and Orange Festival. This was his first public appearance since the funeral of his wife, Princess Michelina, six weeks ago. He waved to the crowds that had come out en masse.

His country was nestled between the borders of France and Italy on the coast of the Mediterranean. Eighty thousand people lived in the city of the same name. The other thirty thousand made up the population that lived in the smaller towns and villages. Besides tourism, it had depended on the lemon and orange industries for centuries.

For the next two weeks the country would celebrate the mainstay of their economy with marching bands in the streets, food fairs, floats and statuary in the parks decorated with lemons and other citrus fruit.

Vincenzo had just gotten back from a series of visits to three continents, doing business for the monarchy with other heads of state. It felt good to be with his father, King Guilio, again. On his return, he'd forgotten how beautiful Arancia could be in the spring with its orchards in full flower. He felt an air of excitement coming from the people that winter was over. As for himself, the darkness that had consumed him over the last six weeks since Michelina's death seemed to be dissipating.

Their marriage had never been a love match. Though betrothed at sixteen, they'd spent very little time together before their wedding fourteen years later. When he'd walked into their apartment earlier this afternoon, more than any other emotion, he was aware of a haunting sense of guilt for not having been able to love her the way she'd loved him.

Romantic love never grew on his part for her, only respect and admiration for her determination to keep up the image of a happily married couple. They'd suffered through three miscarriages hoping for a child, but it hadn't happened.

His passion had never been aroused when they'd made love because he hadn't been in love with her, but he'd done his best to show her tenderness. He'd known passion with other women before he'd married Michelina. But it had only been a physical response because he was never able to give his heart, knowing he was betrothed.

Vincenzo suspected Michelina's parents had undergone the same kind of unfulfilled marriage. He knew his own parents had struggled. It was the rare occurrence when a royal couple actually achieved marital happiness. Michelina had wanted their marriage to be different, and Vincenzo had tried. But you couldn't force love. That had to spring from a source all on its own.

However there was one thing he *had* been able to do that had brought them their first real happiness as man and wife. In fact it was the only thing that had gotten him through this dark period. Just a few days before she'd died, they'd learned they were pregnant again. Only this time they'd taken the necessary steps to prevent another miscarriage.

Relieved that his last duty for today was over, he left the balcony anxious to visit the woman who'd been willing to be a gestational surrogate for them. Abby Loretto, the American girl who'd become his *friend.* Since twelve years of age she'd been living on the palace grounds with her Italian father, who was chief of security.

Vincenzo had been eighteen, with his own set of friends and a few girlfriends his own age, when Abby had arrived on the scene. Yet Abby had become the constant in the background of his life, more like a younger sister flitting in and out of his daily life. It was almost like having a sibling. In a way he felt closer to Abby than he'd ever felt to his sister, Gianna, who was six years older.

The two of them had played in the sea or the swimming pool. She was fun and bright. He could be his real self around her, able to throw off his cares and relax with her in a way he couldn't with anyone else. Because she lived on the grounds and knew the inner workings of the palace, she already had the understanding of what it was to be a royal. They didn't have to talk about it.

When his mother had died, Abby had joined him on long walks, offering comfort. When he didn't want anyone else around, he wanted her. She'd lost her mother, too, and understood what he was going through. She asked nothing from him, wanted nothing but to be his friend and share small confidences. Because they'd been in each other's lives on a continual basis, he realized it was inevitable that they'd bonded and had developed a trust.

She'd been so woven into the fabric of his life that years later, when she'd offered to be a surrogate mother for him and Michelina, it all seemed part of the same piece. His wife had liked Abby a great deal. The three of them had been in consultation for several months before the procedure had been performed. They'd worked like a team until Michelina's unexpected death.

He'd gotten used to their meetings with the doctor and the psychologist. While he'd been away on business, it had felt like years instead of weeks since he'd seen or talked to Abby. Now that she was carrying Vincenzo's son or daughter, she was his lifeline from here on out. He needed to see her and be with her.

All he could think about was getting back to make certain she and the baby were doing well. But accompanying this need was an uncomfortable sense of guilt he couldn't shake. Less than two months ago he'd lost his wife. While still in mourning over the marriage that had been less than perfect, he now found himself concentrating on another woman, who was carrying the baby he and Michelina had made.

It was only natural he cared about Abby, who'd agreed to perform this miracle. Before long he was going to be a father, all because of her! Yet with Michelina gone, it didn't seem right.

But neither was it wrong.

While he'd been traveling, he hadn't had time to dig deep into his soul, but now that he was back, he didn't know how to deal with this new emotional dilemma facing him, and he left the balcony conflicted.

Abigail Loretto, known to her friends as Abby, sat alone on the couch in her apartment at the palace, drying her hair while she was glued to the television. She'd been watching the live broadcast of Prince Vincenzo opening the fruit festival from the balcony of the palace.

Abby hadn't known he was back. Her Italian-born father, Carlo Loretto, the chief of palace security, had been so busy, he obviously hadn't had time to inform her.

She'd first met Vincenzo sixteen years earlier, when her father had been made the head of palace security. The king had brought him and his American-born wife and young daughter from the Arancian Embassy in Washington, D.C., to live in the apartment on the palace grounds. She'd been twelve to his eighteen.

Most of her teenage years had been spent studying him, including his tall, hard-muscled physique. Instead of a film star or a famous rock star, she'd idolized Vincenzo. She'd even kept a scrapbook that followed his life, but she'd kept it hidden from her parents. Of course, that was a long time ago.

The crown prince, the most striking male Abby had ever met in her life, had many looks depending on his mood. From what she could see now, he appeared more rested since his trip.

Sometimes when he was aloof, those black eyes and furrowed brows that matched his glistening black hair made her afraid to approach him. Other times he could be charming and fun, even a tease. No one was immune from his masculine charisma. Michelina had been the most fortunate woman alive.

His picture was always on the cover of magazines and newspapers in Europe. The camera loved the handsome thirty-three-year-old son of Arancia, with his olive skin and aquiline features. Dogged by the press, he made the nightly news on television somewhere on the continent every day of the year.

The knowledge that he was home from his travels sent a wave of warmth through her body. Six weeks without seeing or talking to him about the baby had felt like an eternity. She knew he'd get in touch with her at some point. But after being away, he would have so much work to catch up on at home, it might be another week before she heard his voice on the phone.

Now that he'd left the balcony and had gone back inside the palace, the station began showing a segment of the funeral that had been televised on every channel throughout the kingdom and Europe six weeks ago.

She would never forget her father's phone call. "I have bad news. Before Vincenzo and Michelina were due to return to Arancia today, she went for an early-morning ride on her horse. Vincenzo rode with her. While she was galloping ahead of him, the horse stepped in a hole. It tossed her over end. When she hit the ground, she died on impact."

Abby froze.

Michelina was dead?

It was like déjà vu, sending Abby back to that horrific moment when she'd learned her own mother had died.

Poor Vincenzo. He'd seen the whole thing… She

couldn't stand it. "Oh, Dad—he's lost his wife. Their baby will never know its mother."

Before long she was driven to the hospital, where Dr. DeLuca had his office. "My dear Abby, what a terrible shock this has been. I'm glad your father brought you here. I'm going to keep you in the hospital overnight and possibly longer to make certain you're all right. The prince has enough pain to deal with. Knowing you're being looked after will be a great comfort to him. Excuse me while I arrange for a private room."

When he left, Abby turned to her father. "Vincenzo must be in absolute agony."

He kissed her forehead. "I know he is, but right now it's you I'm worried about. Your blood pressure is up. I plan to stay with you and will tell Signor Faustino you've caught a bad cold, but will be back to work in a few days."

"You can't stay with me here, Dad. Your place is at the palace. The king will want you there."

"Not tonight. My assistant is in charge, and Guilio wants to be there for his son. My daughter needs me, and I need you, so let that be the end of the discussion."

Her father's words had been final. Deep down she'd been glad he'd remained with her.

Abby kept watching the funeral she'd lived through once before. It was shocking to see how gaunt and shadowed Vincenzo's handsome features had been back then. His wife's death seemed to have aged him.

The most beautiful man she'd ever known in her life made a striking yet lonely figure in his mourning finery. Once again her soul shuddered to see his somber expression as he walked behind the funeral cortege toward the cathedral. He led Michelina's favorite horse from the palace stable alongside him. The chestnut mare was covered in a throw of his wife's favorite pink roses. The scene was so heart wrenching, Abby felt tears well up once again.

Behind him came the king, in his uniform of state, and his mother-in-law, dressed in a black mantilla and suit. They rode in the black-and-gold carriage with the siblings of both families. When the broadcast moved inside the cathedral, Abby listened once again to the scripture reading and remarks from the archbishop. When it was over and the bells from the cathedral rang out their mournful sound, she was once more a trembling mass of painful emotions.

"For those of you who've just tuned in, you're watching the funeral procession of Her Royal Highness Princess Michelina Cavelli, the wife of Crown Prince Vincenzo Di Laurentis of the Principality of Arancia. Earlier in the week she was killed in a tragic horse-riding accident on the grounds of the royal palace on the island kingdom of Gemelli.

"In the carriage is His Majesty Guilio Di Laurentis, King of Arancia, her father-in-law. His wife, Queen Annamaria, passed away two years ago. Seated next to him is his daughter, Princess Gianna Di Laurentis Roselli and her husband, Count Roselli of the Cinq Terres of Italy.

"Opposite them is Her Majesty Queen Bianca Cavelli, mother of Princess Michelina. Her husband, King Gregorio Cavelli of Gemelli, was recently deceased. Also seated in the royal carriage is His Royal Highness Crown Prince Valentino Cavelli of Gemelli and Prince Vitoli Cavelli, the brothers of Princess Michelina.

"On this day of great sadness for both royal houses,

one has to speculate on the future of the Principality of Arancia. The world has been waiting to hear that their Royal Highnesses were expecting a child after three miscarriages, but tragically the love match between Michelina and Vincenzo ended too soon.

"Should the Princess Gianna and her husband, Count Enzio Roselli, have offspring, then their child will be third in line to—"

Abby shut off the TV with the remote and got to her feet, unable to watch any more. She shouldn't have allowed herself to live through that funeral segment a second time. Vincenzo's trip appeared to have done him some good. It was better to leave the tragic past behind and concentrate on the future.

She walked into the den to do some work at her laptop. Her dinner would be arriving shortly. Except for the occasional meal out with her best friend, Carolena, Abby normally ate in while she worked on one of her law briefs. But she had little appetite tonight.

How hard for Vincenzo to come back to the palace with no wife to greet him. His loneliness had to be exquisite and her heart ached for him.

After receiving an urgent message from his father that couldn't have come at a worse moment, Vincenzo had been given another reason to visit Abby. As he rounded the corner to her suite, he saw Angelina leaving the apartment with the dinner tray.

Angelina was Abby's personal bodyguard, hired to keep an eye on Abby, virtually waiting on her. She was the one who fed Vincenzo information on a daily basis when he couldn't be there himself. He stopped her so he could lift the cover. Abby had only eaten a small portion of her dinner. That wasn't good. He put the cover back and thanked her before knocking on the door.

"Yes, Angelina?"

He opened it and walked through until he found Abby in the den, where he could see her at the desk working on her computer in her sweats and a cotton top. The lamp afforded the only light in the room, gilding the silvery-gold hair she must have just shampooed. He could smell the strong peach fragrance. It fell to her shoulders in a cloud.

Instead of the attorney-like persona she generally presented, she reminded Vincenzo of the lovely teenager who'd once flitted about the palace grounds on her long legs.

"Abby?"

She turned a face to him filled with the kind of sorrow he'd seen after her mother had died. "Your Highness," she whispered, obviously shocked to see him. A glint of purple showed through her tear-glazed blue eyes. She studied him for a long moment. "It's good to see you again."

Because of the extreme delicacy of their unique situation, it frustrated him that she'd addressed him that way, yet he could find no fault in her.

"Call me Vincenzo when the staff isn't around. That's what you used to shout at me when you were running around the gardens years ago."

"Children are known to get away with murder."

"So are surrogate mothers." There was something about being with Abby. "After such a long trip, I can't tell you how much I've been looking forward to talking to you in person."

"You look like you're feeling better."

Though he appreciated her words, he wished he could say the same about her. "What's wrong? I noticed you hardly ate your dinner. Are you ill?"

"No, no. Not at all." Abby got up from the chair, rubbing the palms of her hands against the sides of womanly hips. To his chagrin the gesture drew his attention to her figure. "Please don't think that finding me in this state has anything to do with the baby."

"That relieves me, but I'm still worried about you. Anything troubling you bothers me."

She let out a sigh. "After I watched your live television appearance a little while ago, they replayed a segment of the funeral. I shouldn't have watched it." Her gaze searched his eyes. "Your suffering was so terrible back then. I can't even imagine it."

Diavolo. The media never let up. "To say I was in shock wouldn't have begun to cover my state of mind," he said.

Abby hugged her arms to her chest, once again drawing his attention to her slender waist. So far the only proof that she was pregnant came from a blood test. She studied him for a moment. "Michelina loved you so much, she was willing to do anything to give you a baby. I daresay not every husband has had that kind of love from his spouse. It's something you'll always be able to cherish."

If he could just get past his guilt over the unhappy state of their marriage. His inability to return Michelina's affection the way she'd wanted weighed him down, but he appreciated Abby's words.

Little did Abby know how right she was. In public his wife had made no secret of her affection for him and he'd tried to return it to keep up the myth of a love match. But in private Vincenzo had cared for her the way he did a friend. She'd pushed so hard at the end to try surrogacy in order to save their marriage, he'd finally agreed to consider it.

Needing to change the subject, he said, "Why don't you sit down while we talk?"

"Thank you." She did as he asked.

He subsided into another of the chairs by her desk. "How are you really feeling?"

"Fine."

"Rest assured that during my trip I insisted on being given a daily report on your progress. It always came back 'fine.'"

"It doesn't surprise me you checked. Something tells me you're a helicopter father already," she quipped.

"If you mean I'm interested to the point of driving you crazy with questions, I'm afraid I'm guilty. Since you and I have known each other from the time you were twelve, it helps me to know I can have the inside track on the guardian of my baby. Dr. DeLuca said your blood pressure went up at the time of the funeral, but it's back to normal and he promises me you're in excellent health."

Abby had a teasing look in her eye. "They say only your doctor knows for sure, but never forget he's a man and has no clue."

Laughter broke from Vincenzo's lips. It felt good to laugh. He couldn't remember the last time it had happened. "I'll bear that in mind."

"So what does the crown prince's *personal* physician have to say about the state of the expectant father?"

He smiled. "I was disgustingly healthy at my last checkup."

"That's good news for your baby, who hopes to enjoy a long, rich life with his or her daddy."

Daddy was what he'd heard Abby call her father from the beginning. The two of them had the sort of close relationship any parent would envy. Vincenzo intended to be the kind of wonderful father his own had been.

"You're veering off the subject. I told you I want the unvarnished truth about your condition," he persisted.

"Unvarnished?" she said with a sudden hint of a smile that broke through to light up his insides. "Well. Let me see. I'm a lot sleepier lately, feel bloated and have finally been hit with the *mal di mare*."

The Italian expression for sea sickness. Trust Abby to come up with something clever. They both chuckled.

"Dr. DeLuca has given me medicine for that and says it will all pass. Then in the seventh month I'll get tired again."

"Has he been hovering as you feared?"

"Actually no. I check in at the clinic once a week before going to work. He says everything looks good and I'm right on schedule. Can you believe your baby is only one-fifth of an inch long?"

"That big?" he teased. Though it really was incredible, he found it astounding she was pregnant with a part of him. He wished he could shut off his awareness of her. Michelina's death had changed their world.

Vincenzo suspected Abby was also having to deal with the fact that the two of them were now forced to get through this pregnancy without his wife. No doubt she felt some guilt, too, because they were treading new ground neither of them could have imagined when they'd had the procedure done.

A laugh escaped her lips. "It's in the developmental stage. He gave me two identical booklets. This one is for you. Anatomy 101 for beginner fathers."

Abby...

She reached in the desk drawer and handed it to him. The title said *The Ten Stages of Pregnancy at a Glance.*

"Why ten, not nine?"

"A woman wrote it and knows these things."

He appreciated her little jokes more than she could imagine. Her normally lighthearted disposition was a balm to his soul. Vincenzo thumbed through the booklet before putting it in his pocket. When he went to bed tonight, he'd digest it.

"Thank you. Now tell me about your law cases." A safe subject that intrigued him. "Which one keeps you awake at night?"

"The Giordano case. I have a hunch someone's trying to block his initiative for political reasons."

"Run it by me."

Her arched brows lifted. "You'd be bored to tears."

"Try me." Nothing about Abby bored him.

She reached in one of the folders on her desk and handed him a printout on the case, which he perused.

As has been stated, major constraint to import into Arancia is nothing more than bureaucracy. Import certificates can take up to eight months to be released, and in some cases are not released at all. However, if the procedure is simplified, an increase of imports could particularly benefit Arancia, providing high-value high-season products.

That made even more sense to Vincenzo since talking to important exporters on his trip.

At present, the hyper/supermarket chains do not operate directly on the import market, but use the main wholesalers of oranges and lemons as intermediaries. Signor Giordano, representing the retailers, has entered the import market, thus changing some long-established import partnerships. He's following a different strategy, based on higher competition, initial entry fees and spot purchases, thus bringing more revenue to Arancia.

Vincenzo knew instinctively that Signor Giordano was really on to something.

Signor Masala, representing the importers, is trying to block this new initiative. He has favored cooperative producers and established medium-to long-term contracts, without requiring any entry fee. The figures included in this brief show a clear difference in revenue, favoring Signor Giordano's plan.

I'm filing this brief to the court to demonstrate that these high-quality products for fast-track approval would benefit the economy and unfortunately are not unavailable in the country at the present time.

Vincenzo handed her back the paper. Her knowledge and grasp of their country's economic problems impressed him no end. He cocked his head. "Giuseppe

Masala has a following and is known as a hard hitter on the trade commission."

Abby's brows met in a delicate frown. "Obviously he's from the old school. Signor Giordano's ideas are new and innovative. He's worked up statistics that show Arancia could increase its imports of fuel, motor vehicles, raw materials, chemicals, electronic devices and food by a big margin. His chart with historical data proves his ideas will work.

"I'd like to see him get his fast-track idea passed, but the lobby against it is powerful. Signor Masala's attorney is stalling to get back to me with an answer."

She had him fascinated. "So what's your next strategy?"

Abby put the paper back in the folder. "I'm taking him to court to show cause. But the docket is full and it could be awhile."

"Who's the judge?"

"Mascotti."

The judge was a good friend of Vincenzo's father. Keeping that in mind, he said, "Go on fighting the good fight, Abby. I have faith in you and know you'll get there."

"Your optimism means a lot to me."

She was friendly, yet kept their relationship at a professional distance the way she'd always done. To his dismay he discovered he wanted more, in different surroundings where they could be casual and spend time talking together like they used to. Her suite wasn't the right place.

Her bodyguard already knew he'd stopped by to see her and would know how long he stayed. He wanted to trust Angelina, but you never knew who your enemies were. Vincenzo's father had taught him that early on. So it was back to the business at hand. "The doctor's office faxed me a schedule of your appointments. I understand you're due for your eight weeks' checkup on Friday, May 1." She nodded. "I plan to join you at the clinic and have arranged for us to meet with the psychologist for our first session afterward."

"You mean you'll have time?" She looked surprised.

"I've done a lot of business since we last saw each other and have reported in to the king. At this juncture I'm due some time off and am ready to get serious about my duties as a father-in-waiting."

Laughter bubbled out of her. "You're very funny at times, Vincenzo."

No one had ever accused him of that except Abby. He hated bringing the fun to an end, but he needed to discuss more serious matters with her that couldn't be put off before he left.

"Your mention of the funeral reminds me of how compassionate you are, and how much you cared for Michelina. I've wanted to tell you why we decided against your attending the funeral."

She moistened her lips nervously. "My father already explained. Naturally, none of us wanted the slightest hint of gossip to mar your life in any way. Just between us, let me tell you how much I liked and admired Michelina. I've missed my daily talks with her and mourn her loss."

He felt her sincerity. "She cared for you, too."

"I—I wish there'd been a way to take your pain away—" her voice faltered "—but there wasn't. Only time can heal those wounds."

"Which is something you know all about, after losing your mother."

"I'll admit it was a bad time for Dad and me, but we got through it. There's no burning pain anymore."

When he'd seen Carlo Loretto's agony after losing his wife, Vincenzo had come to realize how lucky they'd been to know real love. Abby had grown up knowing her parents had been lovers in the true sense of the word. Obviously she could be forgiven for believing he and Michelina had that kind of marriage. *A marriage that had physically ended at the very moment there was new hope for them.*

"Did your father explain why I haven't phoned you in all these weeks?"

"Yes. Though you and Michelina had told me we could call each other back and forth if problems arose, Dad and I talked about that too. We decided it will be better if you and I always go through your personal assistant, Marcello."

"As do I."

It would definitely be better, Vincenzo mused. She understood everything. With Michelina gone, no unexplained private calls to him from Abby meant no calls to be traced by someone out to stir up trouble. They'd entered forbidden territory after going through with the surrogacy.

Vincenzo had to hope the gossip mill within the palace wouldn't get to the point that he could no longer trust in the staff's loyalty. But he knew it had happened in every royal house, no matter the measures taken, and so did she.

"I mustn't keep you, but before I go, I have a favor to ask."

"Anything."

"Michelina's mother and brothers flew in for the festival." It was an excuse for what the queen really wanted. "She would like to meet with you and me in the state drawing room at nine in the morning."

His concern over having to meet with his mother-in-law had less to do with the argument Michelina and the queen had gotten into before the fatal accident, and much more to do with the fact that he hadn't been able to love her daughter the way she'd loved him. He was filled with guilt and dreaded this audience for Abby's sake. But his mother-in-law had to be faced, and she had refused to be put off. "Your father will clear it with your boss so he'll understand why you'll be a little late for work."

"That's fine."

It wouldn't be fine, but he would be in the room to protect her. "Then I'll say good-night."

She nodded. "Welcome home, Vincenzo, and *buonanotte.*" Another smile broke out on her lovely face.

"Sogni d'oro."

CHAPTER TWO

THE PRINCE'S FINAL words, "sweet dreams," stayed with her all night. Seeing him again had caused an adrenaline rush she couldn't shut off. She awakened earlier than usual to get ready, knowing Michelina's mother would ask a lot of questions.

Abby always dressed up for work. Since the law firm of Faustino, Ruggeri, Duomo and Tonelli catered to a higher-class clientele, Signor Faustino, the senior partner, had impressed upon her and everyone else who worked there the need to look fashionable. Though her heart wasn't in it this morning, she took her antinausea pill with breakfast, then forced herself to go through the motions.

Everyone knew she was the daughter of the chief of security for the palace, so no one questioned the royal limo bringing her to and from work. Except for her boss and Carolena, her coworkers were clueless about Abby's specific situation. That's the way things needed to remain until she took a leave of absence.

After the delivery, the palace would issue a formal statement that a surrogate mother had successfully carried the baby of their Royal Highnesses, the new heir who would be second in line to the throne. At that time Abby would disappear. But it wouldn't be for a while.

Vincenzo had been a part of her life for so long, she couldn't imagine the time coming when she'd no longer see him. Once the baby was born, she would live in another part of the city and get on with her life as a full-time attorney. How strange that was going to be.

From the time she'd moved here with her family, he'd been around to show her everything the tourists never got to see. He'd taken her horseback riding on the grounds, or let her come with him when he took out his small sailboat. Vincenzo had taught her seamanship. There was nothing she loved more than sitting out in the middle of the sea while they fished and ate sweets from the palace kitchen. He had the run of the place and let her be his shadow.

Abby's friends from school had come over to her parents' apartment, and sometimes she'd gone to their houses. But she much preferred being with Vincenzo and had never missed an opportunity to tag along. Unlike the big brothers of a couple of her friends who didn't want the younger girls around, Vincenzo had always seemed to enjoy her company and invited her to accompany him when he had free time.

Memories flooded her mind as she walked over to the closet and pulled out one of her favorite Paoli dresses. When Abby had gone shopping with Carolena, they'd both agreed this one had the most luscious yellow print design on the body of the dress.

The tiny beige print on the capped sleeves and hem formed the contrast. Part of the beige print also drew the material that made tucks at the waist. Her friend had cried that it was stunning on Abby, with her silvery-blond hair color. Abby decided to wear it while she still could. The way she was growing, she would need to buy loose-fitting clothes this weekend.

After arranging her hair back in a simple low chignon with three pins, she put on her makeup, slipped on matching yellow shoes and started out of the bedroom. But she only made it to the hallway with her bone-colored handbag when her landline rang. Presuming it was her father calling to see how she was doing, she walked into the den to pick up and say hello.

"Signorina Loretto? This is Marcello. You are wanted in the king's drawing room. Are you ready?"

Her hand gripped the receiver tighter. It sounded urgent. During the night she'd worried about this meeting. It was only natural Michelina's mother would want to meet the woman who would be giving birth to her grandchild. But something about the look in Vincenzo's eyes had given her a sinking feeling in the pit of her stomach.

"Yes. I'll be right there."

"Then I'll inform His Highness, and meet you in the main corridor."

"Thank you."

Because of Vincenzo, Abby was familiar with every part of the palace except the royal apartments. He'd taken her to the main drawing room, where the king met with heads of state, several times. Vincenzo had gotten a kick out of watching her reaction as he related stories about foreign dignitaries that weren't public knowledge.

But her smile faded as she made her way across the magnificent edifice to meet Michelina's mother. She knew the queen was grieving. Marcello met her in the main hallway. "Follow me."

They went down the hall past frescoes and paintings, to another section where they turned a corner. She spied the country's flag draped outside an ornate pair of floor-to-ceiling doors. Marcello knocked on one of the panels and was told to enter. He opened the door, indicating she should go in.

The tall vaulted ceiling of the room was a living museum to the history of Arancia, and had known centuries of French and Italian rulers. But Abby's gaze fell on Vincenzo, who was wearing a somber midnight-blue suit. Opposite him sat Michelina's stylish sixty-five-year-old mother, who was brunette like her late daughter. She'd dressed in black, with a matching cloche hat, and sat on one of the brocade chairs.

"Come all the way in, Signorina Loretto. I'd like you to meet my mother-in-law, Her Majesty the Queen of Gemelli." Abby knew Gemelli—another citrus-producing country—was an island kingdom off the eastern coast of Sicily, facing the Ionian Sea.

She moved toward them and curtsied the way she'd been taught as a child after coming to the palace. "Your Majesty. It's a great honor, but my heart has been bleeding for you and the prince. I cared for your daughter very much."

The matriarch's eyes were a darker brown than Michelina's, more snapping. She gave what passed for a nod before Vincenzo told Abby to be seated on the love seat on the other side of the coffee table. Once she was comfortable, he said, "If you recall, Michelina and I flew to Gemelli so she could tell the queen we were pregnant."

"Yes."

"To my surprise, the unexpected nature of our news

came as a great shock to my mother-in-law, since my wife hadn't informed her of our decision to use a surrogate."

What?

"You mean your daughter never told you what she and the prince were contemplating?"

"No," came the answer through wooden lips.

Aghast, Abby averted her eyes, not knowing what to think. "I'm so sorry, Your Majesty."

"We're all sorry, because the queen and Michelina argued," Vincenzo explained. "Unfortunately before they could talk again, the accident happened. The queen would like to take this opportunity to hear from the woman who has dared to go against nature to perform a service for which she gets nothing in return."

CHAPTER THREE

ABBY REELED.

For Vincenzo to put it so bluntly meant he and his mother-in-law had exchanged harsh if not painfully bitter words. But he was a realist and had decided the only thing to do was meet this situation head-on. He expected Abby to handle it because of their long-standing friendship over the years.

"You haven't answered my question, Signorina Loretto."

At the queen's staccato voice, Abby struggled to catch her breath and remain calm. No wonder she'd felt tension from him last night when he'd brought up this morning's meeting. Michelina's omission when it came to her mother had put a pall over an event that was helping Vincenzo to get up in the morning.

He was counting on Abby being able to deal with his mother-in-law. She refused to let him down even if it killed her. More time passed while she formulated what to say before focusing on the queen.

"If I had a daughter who came to me in the same situation, I would ask her exactly the same question. In my case, I've done it for one reason only. Perhaps you didn't know that the prince rescued me from certain death when I was seventeen. I lost my mother in that same sailboat accident. Before I was swept to shore by the wind, I'd lost consciousness.

"When the prince found me, I was close to death but didn't know it." Abby's eyes glazed over with unshed tears. "If you could have heard the way my father wept after he discovered I'd been found and brought back to the living, you would realize what a miracle had happened that day, all because of the prince's quick thinking and intervention.

"From that time on, my father and I have felt the deepest gratitude to the prince. Over the years I've pondered many times how to pay the prince back for preventing what could have been an all-out catastrophe for my father."

The lines on the queen's face deepened, revealing her sorrow. Whether she was too immersed in her own grief to hear what Abby was saying, Abby didn't know.

"The prince and princess were the perfect couple," Abby continued. "When I heard that the princess had had a third miscarriage, it wounded me for their sake. They deserved happiness. Before Christmas I learned through my father that Dr. DeLuca had suggested a way for them to achieve their dream of a family."

Abby fought to prevent tears from falling. "After years of wishing there was something I could do, I realized that if I could qualify as a candidate, I could carry their child for them. You'll never know the joy it gave me at the thought of doing something so special for them. When I told my father what I wanted to do, he was surprised at first, and yet he supported my decision, too, otherwise he would never have approved."

She took a shuddering breath. "That's the reason

I'm doing this. A life for a life. What I'm going to get out of this is pure happiness to see the baby the prince and princess fought so hard for. When the doctor puts the baby in the prince's arms, Michelina will live on in their child, and the child will forever be a part of King Guilio and his wife, and a part of you and your husband, Your Majesty."

The queen's hands trembled on the arms of the chair. "You have no comprehension of what it's like to be a mother. How old are you?"

"I'm twenty-eight and it's true I've never been married or had a child. But I won't be its mother in the way you mean. I'm only supplying a safe haven for the baby until it's born. Yes, I'll go through the aches and pains of pregnancy, but I view this as a sacred trust."

Her features hardened. "You call this sacred?"

"I do. During my screening process, I met a dozen different parents and their surrogates who'd gone through the experience and now have beautiful children. They were all overjoyed and agreed it's a special partnership between them and God."

For the first time, the queen looked away.

"The prince is a full partner in this. He and the princess discussed it many times. He knows what she wanted and I'll cooperate in every way. If you have suggestions, I'll welcome them with all my heart."

Quiet reigned.

Realizing there was nothing more to say, Abby glanced at Vincenzo, waiting for him to dismiss her.

He read her mind with ease. "I'm aware the limo is waiting to drive you to your office."

"Yes, Your Highness."

At those words Michelina's mother lifted her head. "You intend to work?" She sounded shocked.

"I do. I am passionate about my career as an attorney. After the delivery, I will have my own life to lead and need to continue planning for it."

Vincenzo leaned forward. "She'll stop work when the time is right."

"Where will you live after the baby's born?" The pointed question told Abby exactly where the queen's thoughts had gone.

Nowhere near the prince.

She couldn't blame the older woman for that. How could Michelina's mother not suspect the worst? Her fears preyed on Abby's guilt, which was deepening because she'd found herself missing Vincenzo more than she should have while he'd been away. He shouldn't have been on her mind so much, but she couldn't seem to turn off her thoughts. Not when the baby growing inside her was a constant reminder of him.

For weeks now she'd played games of *what if?* during the night when she couldn't sleep. What if the baby were hers and Vincenzo's? What would he or she look like? Where would they create a nursery in the palace? When would they go shopping for a crib and all the things necessary? She wanted to make a special baby quilt and start a scrapbook.

But then she'd break out in a cold sweat of guilt and sit up in the bed, berating herself for having any of these thoughts. Michelina's death might have changed everything, but this royal baby still wasn't Abby's!

How could she even entertain such thoughts when Michelina had trusted her so implicitly? It was such a betrayal of the trust and regard the two women had for each other. They'd made a contract as binding as a blood oath. The second the baby was born, her job as surrogate would no longer be required and she'd return to her old life.

But Abby was aghast to discover that Michelina's death had thrown her into an abyss of fresh guilt. She needed to talk to the psychologist about finding strategies to cope with this new situation or go crazy.

Queen Bianca had asked her a question and was waiting for an answer.

"I plan to buy my own home in another part of the city in the same building as a friend of mine. My contract with the prince and princess includes living at the palace, and that ends the moment the baby is delivered."

Vincenzo's eyes narrowed on her face. "What friend?"

That was probably the only thing about her plans the three of them hadn't discussed over the last few months.

"You've heard me speak of Carolena Baretti and know she's my best friend, who works at the same law firm with me. We went through law school together at the University of Arancia before taking the bar."

If a woman could look gutted, the queen did. "This whole situation is unnatural."

"Not unnatural, Your Majesty, just different. Your daughter wanted a baby badly enough to think it all through and agree to it. I hope the day will come when you're reconciled to that decision."

"That day will never come," the older woman declared in an imperious voice. "I was thrilled each time she informed me she was pregnant and I suffered with her through each miscarriage. But I will never view surrogacy as ethically acceptable."

"But it's a gestational surrogacy," Abby argued quietly. "Dr. DeLuca says that several thousand women around the globe are gestational surrogates and it's becoming preferable to going with traditional surrogacy, because it ensures the genetic link to both parents. Think how many lives can be changed. Surely you can see what a miracle it is."

"Nevertheless, it's outside tradition. It interferes with a natural process in violation of God's will."

"Then how do you explain this world that God created, and all the new technology that helps people like your daughter and Vincenzo realize their dream to have a family?"

"It doesn't need an explanation. It's a form of adultery, because you are the third party outside their marriage. Some people regard that it could result in incest of a sort."

Tortured by her words, Abby exchanged an agonized glance with Vincenzo. "What do you mean?"

"As the priest reminded me, their child might one day marry another of *your* children. While there would be no genetic relationship, the two children would be siblings, after a fashion."

Naturally Abby hoped to marry one day and have children of her own, but never in a million years would she have jumped to such an improbable conclusion. By now Vincenzo's features had turned to granite.

"There's also the question of whether or not you'll be entitled to an inheritance and are actually out for one."

Abby was stunned. "When the prince saved my life, he gave me an inheritance more precious than anything earthly. If any money is involved, it's the one hundred and fifty thousand dollars or more the prince has paid the doctors and the hospital for this procedure to be done." She could feel herself getting worked up, but she couldn't stop.

"I've been given all the compensation I could ever wish for by being allowed to live here in the palace, where my every want and need is taken care of. I'm so sorry this situation has caused you so much grief. I can see you two need to discuss this further, alone. I must leave for the office."

Abby eyed the prince, silently asking him to please help her to go before the queen grew any more upset. He got the message and stood to his full imposing height, signaling she could stand.

"Thank you for joining us," he murmured. "Whatever my mother-in-law's reaction, it's too late for talk because you're pregnant with Michelina's and my child. Let's say no more. I promise that when the queen is presented with her first grandchild, she'll forget all these concerns."

The queen flashed him a look of disdain that wounded Abby. She couldn't walk out of here with everything so ugly and not say a few last words.

"It's been my privilege to meet you, Your Majesty. Michelina used to talk about you all the time. She loved you very much and was looking forward to you helping her through these coming months. I hope you know that. If you ever want to talk to me again, please call me. I don't have a mother anymore and would like to hear any advice you have to help me get through this."

It was getting harder and harder to clap with one hand and the prince knew it.

"Again, let me say how sorry I am about your loss. She was so lovely and accomplished. I have two of her watercolors hanging on the wall of my apartment. Everyone will miss her terribly, especially this baby.

"But thankfully it will have its grandmother to tell him or her all the things only you know about their mother."

The queen stared at Abby through dim eyes.

Abby could feel her pain. "Goodbye for now." She curtsied once more. Her gaze clung to Vincenzo's for a few seconds before she turned on her low-heeled sandals and left the room. The limo would be waiting for her. Though she wanted to run, she forced herself to stay in control so she wouldn't fall and do something to hurt herself.

The queen had put Abby on trial. No wonder Vincenzo's wife had been frightened to approach her mother with such an unconventional idea. Only now was Abby beginning to understand how desperate *and* courageous Michelina had been to consider allowing a third party to enter into the most intimate aspect of all their lives. Facing the queen had to be one of the worst moments Abby had ever known.

But this had to be an even more nightmarish experience for Vincenzo. Here he was trying to deal with his wife's death while at the same time having to defend the decision he and Michelina had made to use a surrogate. He had to be suffering guilt of his own.

Abby blamed no one for this, but she felt Vincenzo's pain. How he was going to get through this latest crisis, she couldn't imagine. Probably by working. That was how *she* planned to survive.

Twenty minutes later Abby entered the neoclassical building that housed her law firm and walked straight back to Carolena's office. Her friend was a patent attorney and had become as close to Abby as a sister. Unfortunately she was at court, so they'd have to talk later.

Both Carolena and Abby had been hired by the well-known Arancian law firm after they'd graduated. Abby had been thrilled when they'd both been taken on a year ago. She had planned for this career from her junior-high days, and had been hired not only for her specialty in international trade law, but because she was conversant in French, English, Italian and Mentonasc.

Since the Mentonasc dialect—somewhere between Nicard and a dialect of Ligurian, a Gallo-Romance language spoken in Northern Italy—was currently spoken by about 10 percent of the population living in Arancia and its border areas, it gave her an edge over other applicants for the position, which required her particular linguistic expertise.

Abby's parents had cleverly directed her studies from a very young age. Thanks to them her abilities had taken her to the head of the class. However, this morning Abby's mind wasn't on her latest cases.

She felt disturbed by the revelation that Michelina had kept her mother in the dark about one of the most important events in her life. Abby had done her research. Since the death of King Gregorio, Queen Bianca become the ruler of Gemelli and was known to be rigid and difficult. Abby had felt her disapproval and didn't envy Vincenzo's task of winning his mother-in-law over.

Hopefully something Abby had said would sink in and soften her heart. At the moment, Abby's own heart was breaking for all of them.

* * *

Six hours later, Abby finished dictating some memos to Bernardo and left the building for the limo. But when she walked outside, she noticed the palace secret service cars had parked both in front of and behind the limo. One of the security men got out of the front and opened the rear door for her. What was going on?

As she climbed inside and saw who was sitting there waiting for her—in sunglasses and a silky claret-colored sport shirt and cream trousers—the blood started to hammer in her ears.

"Vincenzo—"

His name slipped out by accident, proving to her more and more that he filled her conscious and unconscious mind.

The tremor in Abby's voice made its way to every cell of Vincenzo's body. After she'd bared her soul to his mother-in-law that morning, he'd realized not only at what price she'd sacrificed herself to make their dreams of a baby a reality, but he'd been flooded with memories of that day when she'd lost her mother.

Abby had been a great swimmer and handled herself well in the sea. As some of his friends had pointed out years ago when they'd seen her in the water offshore, she wasn't a woman yet, but she showed all the promise.

By the time she'd turned seventeen, he'd found himself looking at her a lot more than he should have. She was one of those natural-blond American girls with classic features, noted for their long, gorgeous legs. At that point in time Vincenzo had already been betrothed to Michelina. Since the marriage wouldn't be for at

least another ten years, he'd had the freedom to date
the women who attracted him.

Abby had been too young, of course, but pleasing
to the eye. She'd turned into a very beautiful girl who
was studious, intelligent and spoke Italian like a native.
He enjoyed every moment he spent with her; her enthusiasm for everything surprised and entertained him.

But even if he hadn't been betrothed, Abby had been
off-limits to Vincenzo for more reasons than her young
age or the fact that she wasn't a princess. Her parents
had become close friends with Vincenzo's parents. That
was a special friendship that demanded total respect.

Though her periwinkle-blue eyes always seemed
to smile at him with interest when they chanced upon
each other, there was an invisible boundary between
them she recognized, too. Neither of them ever crossed
it until the day of the squall…

As Abby had told Queen Bianca earlier, she and her
mother, Holly, had been out in a small sailboat off the
coast when the storm struck. Nothing could come on
as rapidly and give so little time for preparation as did
a white squall.

Vincenzo had been in his father's office before lunch
discussing a duty he needed to carry out when they'd
noticed the darkening sky. A cloudburst had descended,
making the day feel like night. They hadn't seen a storm
this ferocious in years and felt sorry for anyone who'd
been caught in it.

While they were commenting on the fierceness of
the wind, a call came through informing the king that
the Loretto sailboat was missing from its slip. Someone
thought they had seen Signora Loretto and her daugh-

ter out sailing earlier, but they hadn't come back in yet. Several boats were already out there looking for them.

Abby—

Vincenzo was aghast. *She* was out there?

The sweet girl who'd always been there for him was battling this storm with her mother, alone?

Fear like Vincenzo had never known before attacked his insides and he broke out in a cold sweat. "I've got to find them!"

"Wait, son! Let the coast guard deal with it!"

But he'd already reached the door and dashed from the room. Driven by fear, he raced through the palace. Once outside, he ran to the dock, where a group of men huddled. He grabbed one of them to come with him and they took off in his cruiser to face a churning sea.

The other man kept in radio contact with the rescue boats. Within a minute they heard that the sailboat had been spotted. Vincenzo headed toward the cited coordinates, oblivious to the elements.

The rescue boats were already on the scene as Vincenzo's cruiser came close to the sailboat. It was tossing like a cork, but he couldn't see anyone on board. "Have they already been rescued?"

"Signora Loretto was found floating unconscious in the water wearing her life preserver, but there's no sign of her daughter yet," replied his companion.

Vincenzo's heart almost failed him.

Abby had drowned?

It was as though his whole life passed before him. She *couldn't* have drowned! He couldn't lose her! Not his Abby…

"We've got to look for her! She knows to wear a life jacket. The wind will have pushed her body through the water. We're going to follow it. You steer while I search."

"It's too dangerous for you, Your Highness!"

"Danger be damned! Don't you understand?" he shouted. "There's a seventeen-year-old girl out there who needs help!"

"Tell me where to go."

He studied the direction of the wind. "Along the coastline near the caves!" Vincenzo knew this coastline like the back of his hand. When a low pressure over the Mediterranean approached the coast from the southeast, the weather could change quickly for the worse and its clear sky change to an east wind. If Abby had been knocked unconscious, too, she could have been swept into one of the caves further up the coast.

When they reached the opening of the largest cave, Vincenzo dove in and swam through to the three hidden grottoes, where he'd been many times with his friends. In the second one, his heart had leaped when he saw Abby's body floating lifelessly, like her mother's. Quickly he'd caught hold of her and swum her out to the boat, where he took off her life jacket and began giving her mouth-to-mouth resuscitation. At first there was no response. Her face was a pinched white. Though terrified she was too far gone, he kept up the CPR.

At the last second there came sounds of life, and her eyelids fluttered. He turned her on her side while she coughed and threw up water.

"That's it, my precious Abby. Get rid of it."

When she'd finished, she looked up at him, dazed. "Vincenzo?"

"Sì," he'd murmured in relief. "You were in a storm,

but I found you in one of the grottoes and you're all right now."

Abby blinked. "My mother?" she cried frantically. "Where is she?"

"With your father." It wasn't a lie, but since he didn't know the whole truth of her condition, he kept quiet.

"Thank God." Her eyes searched his. "I could have died in there. You saved my life," she whispered in awe. In a totally unexpected gesture, she'd thrown her arms around his neck and clung to him.

"Thank God," he'd whispered back and found himself rocking her in his arms while she sobbed.

Vincenzo had never felt that close to another human being in his life. She'd felt so right in his arms. When they took her to the hospital and she learned her mother had died of a blow from the mast, she'd flung herself into his arms once more.

That was the moment when he knew Abby meant more to him that he could put into words. Their relationship changed that day. His feelings for her ran much deeper than he'd realized. To imagine his life without her was anathema to him.

She'd been too inconsolable for him to do anything but let her pour out her pain and love for her mother. His only desire had been to comfort her. He'd held her for a long time because her father, overcome with grief, had to be sedated.

In front of the queen today, they'd both relived that moment. Abby's outpouring of her soul had endeared her to him in such a profound way, he could hardly find expression. Though he knew it was wrong, he'd decided to break one of his own rules and pick her up from work.

Bianca had put Abby through a torturous session.

Despite his guilt in seeking her out for a reason that wasn't a medical necessity, he couldn't let it go until he'd seen for himself that she was all right.

"I came to find out how well you survived the day."

The picture of her in that yellow dress when she'd walked in the room had made an indelible impression of femininity and sophistication in his mind. Bianca couldn't have helped but notice how lovely she was, along with her moving sincerity. It hadn't surprised him his mother-in-law had been so quiet after Abby had left the room to go to work.

"My worry has been for you." She sat down opposite him and fastened her seat belt. "For me, work is the great panacea. But it's evident the queen has been in absolute agony."

"She's flown back to Gemelli with a lot to think about."

"The poor thing. We have to hope she'll let go of her preconceived beliefs so she can enjoy this special time."

There was a sweetness in Abby that touched Vincenzo's heart. "You're the one I'm concerned about. It hurts me that you no longer have your mother to confide in." Until now he hadn't thought about how alone Abby must feel. Bianca's castigations had been like a dagger plunged into her, bringing out his protective instincts.

She flicked him a glance. "But I have my father, and I have you and the doctor. Who better than all of you to comfort me when I need it?" Except that Vincenzo wanted to do more than comfort her, God forgive him.

He held her gaze. "I'm sorry if anything the queen said has upset you, but I promise everything's going to be all right in time."

"I believe that, too. Did she say anything else?"

"No, but her son Valentino and I are good friends." When he'd gone with the queen and his brothers-in-law to visit Michelina's grave once, they'd eaten lunch before he'd accompanied them to their jet. "He's promised to keep in close touch. Now let's change the subject."

"You're taking too great a risk, Your Highness. We mustn't be seen out together like this."

"The limo protects us." Even as he said it, he was trying to tamp down his guilt over pressuring her when it was obvious she was afraid to be seen with him. He ought to be worried about that, too, but something had come over him.

"Please, Your Highness. The fact that there are so many security men will cause the locals to speculate about who is so important, driving around in the crowded streets. Have the car turn around and take me back to the office."

"It's too late for that." Vincenzo had no intention of letting her go yet.

"After my audience with the queen, surely you understand my fears."

"After the way she went after you, I have my own fears where you're concerned. You didn't deserve that and I want to make it up to you."

CHAPTER FOUR

"WE'RE GOING IN the wrong direction to the palace."

Vincenzo ignored Abby's comment. "Last night you didn't eat a full meal. This evening I intend to remedy that and take you to a very special place for dinner to celebrate the Lemon and Orange Festival. Don't worry," he said when he saw her eyes grow anxious. "We'll be arriving via a private entrance to a private dining room where my own people will be serving us. All you have to do is enjoy a meal free of caffeine and alcohol, with salt in moderation."

She kneaded her hands. "I know why you're doing this, Vincenzo, but it isn't necessary."

"Has being pregnant made you a mind reader?"

For once she couldn't tell if he was having fun with her or if her comment had irked him. "I only meant—"

"You only meant that you don't expect any special favors from me," he preempted her. "Tell me something I don't already know."

"I've annoyed you. I'm sorry."

"Abby—we need to have a little talk. Because of the sacrifice you've made for me and Michelina, any social life you would normally enjoy has been cut off until the baby's born. At this time in your life you should be out having a good time. I have no doubt there are any number of men who pass through your office wanting a relationship with you. Certainly I don't need to tell you that you're a very beautiful woman. My brother-in-law shared as much with me earlier."

"I've never met Michelina's brother."

"But he saw you this morning after you left the drawing room for the limo."

That was news to Abby. Vincenzo's words had shaken her. "Thank you for the compliment."

"Now you sound vexed with me."

"I'm not!"

"Good. Then try to understand that our relationship isn't one-sided, with me reaping all the benefits while you lie around like a beached whale, barefoot and pregnant, as you Americans tend to say."

Abby burst into laughter.

"I'm glad you think that's funny. We're making progress."

No one could be more amusing than Vincenzo when he revealed this exciting side of his nature. "I can't believe you've ever heard those expressions."

"I graduated in California Girls 101 during my vacation one summer in San Diego."

She rolled her eyes. "*That* school. I don't doubt it." She knew he'd traveled a lot in his twenties. "I guess you didn't need a booklet for the class."

He grinned, revealing a gorgeous white smile. "And the tuition was free. Why do you think most men congregate there when they get the chance?"

"Isn't it interesting that most women congregate in Arancia and Italy to attend Mediterranean Gods 101? They don't need booklets, either."

Vincenzo let go with a belly laugh that resonated throughout the interior of the limo. "You must be dynamite in the courtroom."

"Why don't you come up and see me some time?" she said in her best Mae West impersonation. *Why didn't he come to her apartment and stay...* It was a wicked thought, but she couldn't help it. The other night she hadn't wanted him to leave.

The corner of his mouth lifted. "Who were you imitating just now?"

"Someone you'd never know. She was in American films years ago. My mother loved her old movies."

"Tell me her name."

"I'll give you a hint. They named inflatable life jackets after her in the Second World War. If you still can't think of it, I'll do better and have a DVD sent to you so you can see for yourself."

"We'll watch it together."

No. They wouldn't watch it together. They'd done enough of that when she was much younger. He had his own theater in the palace, where she'd seen a lot of films and eaten marzipan with him. But that time was long gone and this idea of his had to be stopped right now. She was having too much fun and needed his company too much.

Thankfully they'd left the Promenade d'Or along the coast and were following a winding road up the hillsides above the city. In another minute they rounded a curve and pulled up to, of all things, a funicular railway.

Vincenzo got out of the limo and came around to help her. Together with some of his security people, they got on and sat on one of the benches. He told her to buckle up before it started climbing the steep mountain.

"There's a lovely little restaurant two kilometers higher that overlooks the Mediterranean. While we eat, we'll watch the festival fireworks being set off in town."

Once Abby was settled, Vincenzo had to talk to one of his security men, leaving her alone with her thoughts for a second. During her teenage years she'd had ridiculous daydreams about being alone with him, but none of them could match the wonder of such an evening. Without question this was the most thrilling moment in Abby's life.

However, there was one problem with reality intruding on this beautiful dream. While he was trying to give her a special night out to make up for her being denied a social life at present, Abby could never forget she was carrying the child he and Michelina had made. The wife he'd adored was gone, leaving him desolate, just like her father.

She remembered the night of Michelina's funeral, when she'd wandered out onto the patio of her apartment, not knowing where to go with her pain. Before her was the amazing sight of dozens of sailboats and yachts anchored offshore from up and down the Riviera with Arancian flags flying at half-mast in the breeze to pay respect to the prince.

While she stood there, her cell phone had rung, causing her to jump. She hurried inside to check the caller ID, hardly able to see through the tears.

"Carolena?" she'd cried after clicking on.

"Abby? When the announcer started speculating on the future of the monarchy, I had to call and see if you're all right."

She breathed in deeply. "Yes," she'd murmured, wiping the moisture off her cheeks with her hand.

"No, you're not. I don't know how you're handling this."

"Truthfully, not very well."

"Talk to me. I know you told me you can't leave the palace until tomorrow and I can't come over there today, so the phone will have to do. Have you even talked to Vincenzo since the accident?"

"Yes. He came for a minute last evening, worried about my welfare, if you can imagine."

"Actually, I can. To know you're carrying his child is probably the only thing keeping him from going under. I never witnessed anything more touching in my life than the sight of the horse covered in her favorite flowers walking alongside that incredible-looking man. Already I've seen one of the tabloids out in the kiosk bearing the headline The Prince of Every Woman's Dreams in Mourning."

Abby had closed her eyes tightly. "The media will make a circus of this." She could hear it all now: *Who will be the next princess? Will she be foreign? Will he wait a year, or will he break with tradition and take a new bride in the next few months?* Abby had a question of her own: *How will the next woman he chooses feel about the surrogacy situation?* All those thoughts and more had bombarded her.

"You really shouldn't be alone."

"All I have to do is get through tonight, Carolena. Tomorrow I can start living a normal life."

Now, seven weeks later, here Abby was with the prince of every woman's dreams, riding to the top of the mountain. But there was nothing normal about his life or hers. When she and her father had gone through all the *what if*s before she'd made her decision to be a surrogate, the idea of either Michelina or Vincenzo dying had only been mentioned in passing. But she couldn't have imagined anything so horrible and never thought about it again.

"Shall we go in?" sounded the deep, velvety male voice next to her.

"Oh—yes!" Abby had been so immersed in thought she hadn't realized they'd arrived. Night had fallen during their journey here. Vincenzo led her off the funicular and walked her through a hallway to another set of doors. They opened onto a terrace with a candlelit table and flowers set for two.

A small gasp of pleasure escaped her lips when she realized she was looking out over the same view she could see from her own patio at the palace. But they were much higher up, so she could take in the whole city of Arancia alive with lights for the nightly festival celebration.

"What an incredible vista."

"I agree," he murmured as he helped her to sit. Of course it was an accident that his hand brushed her shoulder, but she felt his touch as if she'd just come in contact with an electric current. This was so wrong; she was terrified.

Grape juice from the surrounding vineyard came first, followed by hors d'oeuvres and then a luscious rack of lamb and fresh green peas from the restaurant's garden. Abby knew the chef had prepared food to the prince's specifications.

She ate everything. "This meal is fabulous!"

His black eyes smiled at her. "Tonight you have an appetite. That's good. We'll have to do this more often."

No, no, no.

"If I were to eat here every night, I'd be as big as that whale you referred to earlier."

He chuckled. "You think?"

"I know."

While Abby enjoyed the house's lemon tart specialty for dessert, Vincenzo drank coffee. "Mind if I ask you a personal question?"

How personal? She was on dangerous ground, fearing he could see right through her, to her chaotic innermost thoughts. "What would you like to know?"

"Has there been an important man in your life? And if so, why didn't you marry him?"

Yes. I'm looking at him.

Heat filled her cheeks. "I had my share of boyfriends, but by college I got serious about my studies. Law school doesn't leave time for much of a social life when you're clerking for a judge who expects you to put in one hundred and twenty hours a week."

"Sounds like one of my normal days," he remarked.

She knew he wasn't kidding. "You and I never discussed this before, but I'm curious about something. Didn't you ever want to be a mother to your own child first?"

Abby stifled her moan. If he only knew how during her teenage years she'd dreamed about being married to him and having his baby. Since that time, history had been made and she was carrying his baby in real life. But it wasn't hers and that dream had come with a price. How could she be feeling like this when he was forbidden to her?

"Well—" She swallowed hard. "The desire to be a mother has always been rooted in me. I've never doubted my ability to be a good one. Despite the fact that Mother died early, I had a charmed and happy childhood. She was a wonderful mom. Warm and charming. Funny. Still, I never saw raising a child as my only goal.

"I'd always envisioned motherhood as the result of a loving relationship with a man, like my parents had. Carolena has told me many times that it's just an excuse because no man has ever lived up to my father. She said the umbilical cord should have been cut years ago. With hindsight I think she's probably right, but there's no one like him."

In truth, there was no one like Vincenzo and never would be. *He* was the reason she hadn't been able to get interested in another man.

"Your father has been a lucky man to have inspired such fierce love from his wife and daughter."

The comment sounded mournful. "Michelina loved you the same way."

"Yes."

"So will your child."

His eyes grew veiled without him saying anything.

The fireworks had started, lighting up the night sky in a barrage of colors, but she couldn't appreciate the display because of a certain tension between them that hadn't been there earlier. She was walking such a tightrope around him, her body was a mass of nerves.

"Maybe coming out to dinner wasn't a very good idea for you, Your Highness."

"What happened to *Vincenzo?*"

Again she had the feeling she'd angered him, the last thing she wanted to do. But it was imperative she keep emotional distance from him. "You're still mourning your wife. I appreciate this evening more than you know, but it's too soon for you to be out doing the things you used to do with her." *And too hard on me.*

She wiped her mouth with the napkin. "When was the last time you brought her here? Do you want to talk about it?"

That dark, remote expression he could get had returned. "Michelina never came here with me."

She swallowed hard. "I see." She wondered why. "Nevertheless, being out on a night like this has to bring back memories."

His fingers ran over the stem of the wineglass that was still full. "Today as I opened the festival, you could feel spring in the air. You can feel it tonight. It calls for a new beginning." His gaze swerved to hers, piercing through to her insides. "You and I are together on a journey that neither of us has ever taken. I want to put the past behind us and enjoy the future that is opening up."

"With your baby to be born soon, it will be a glorious future."

"There are a few months to go yet, months you should be able to enjoy. I want to help you. How does that sound?"

It sounded as though he didn't want to be reminded of his wife again because it hurt him too much and he needed a diversion. Naturally, he did, but Abby couldn't fill that need! She didn't dare.

"I'm already having a wonderful time enjoying this meal with you. Thank you for a very memorable evening."

"You're welcome. I want us to enjoy more."

"We can't, Vincenzo. The people close to you will notice and there will be gossip. If I've angered you again, I'm sorry."

Silence followed her remarks. They watched the fireworks for a while longer before leaving. The ride down the mountain was much faster than the ride up. It was much like the sensation when Dr. DeLuca had said, "Congratulations, Signorina Loretto. The blood test we did revealed the presence of the HCG hormone. You're pregnant!"

Abby hadn't believed it. Even though she'd wanted to be a surrogate mother and had done everything possible to make it happen, for the doctor to tell her the procedure had worked was like the first time she rode the Ferris wheel at a theme park. The bar had locked her in the chair, filling her with excitement. Then the wheel had turned and lifted her high in the air. That was the way she felt now, high in the air over Arancia. She didn't know if she wanted this descent to continue, but it was too late to get off. She had to go with it and just hang on. Only this time she wasn't on the Ferris wheel or the funicular and this ride would continue for the next thirty-odd weeks.

Abby hadn't been able to tell anyone about her pregnancy except Carolena. But she knew she could trust her best friend with her life, and that news hadn't been something she could keep to herself on that day of all days.

When she went to work on the day she'd found out she was pregnant, Abby visited with her gorgeous, fashionable Italian friend, who stopped traffic when she stepped outside. Carolena had worn her chestnut hair on top of her head in a loose knot. Though she didn't need glasses, she put on a pair with large frames to give her a more professional appearance.

She looked up when she saw Abby and smiled. "*Fantastico!* I've been needing a break from the Bonelli case."

"I'm so happy you said that because I've got something to tell you I can't hold in any longer. If I don't talk to you about it, I'll go crazy." She closed and locked the door behind her before sitting down in the chair opposite the desk.

"This has to be serious. You looked flushed. Have you settled the Giordano case already? Shall we break out the champagne?"

"Don't I wish! No, this has nothing to do with the law." She moved restlessly in the leather chair. In fact there'd be no champagne for her for the next nine months. "What I say to you can't ever leave this room."

Carolena's smile faded before she crossed herself.

Abby leaned forward. "I'm going to have a baby," she whispered.

Her friend's stunned expression said it all before she removed her glasses and walked around the desk in her fabulous designer sling-back high heels to hunker down in front of her. She shook her head. "Who?" was all she could manage to say.

The question was a legitimate one. Though Abby had been asked out by quite a few men since joining the firm, she hadn't accepted any dates. No on-site romances for her. Besides, she wanted to make her place in the firm and that meant studying when she wasn't in the office so she could stay on top of every case.

"Their Royal Highnesses."

Carolena's beautifully shaped dark brows met together in a frown. "You mean…as in…"

"Prince Vincenzo and Princess Michelina."

There was a palpable silence in the room. Then, "Abby—"

"I realize it's a lot to swallow."

A look of deep concern broke out on Carolena's expressive face. "But you—"

"I know what you're going to say," she broke in hurriedly. "It's true that I'll always love him for saving me from drowning, but that was eleven years ago when I was seventeen. Since then he has married and they've suffered through three miscarriages. The doctor suggested they look for a gestational surrogate mother for them."

"What?"

"His logic made total sense. Gestational surrogacy, unlike adoption, would allow both Vincenzo and Michelina to be genetically related to their child. Even better, they would be involved in the baby's conception and throughout the pregnancy, so they'd feel a total part of the whole experience."

"But you can't be a surrogate because you've never had a baby before."

"There are a few exceptions, and I'm one of them."

Carolena put a hand on Abby's arm. "So you just nominated yourself for the position without any thought of what it would really mean and threw yourself into the ring?" She sounded aghast at the idea.

Abby had hoped for a happier response from her friend. "Of course not. But I wasn't able to stop thinking about it. I even dreamed about it. The answer of how to repay him for saving my life came to me like a revelation. *A life for a life.*"

"Oh, Abby—despite the fact that you push men away, you're such a romantic! What if midway through the pregnancy you become deathly ill and it ruins your life? I can't even imagine how awful that would be."

"Nothing's going to happen to me. I've always been

healthy as a horse. I want to give them this gift. I didn't make the decision lightly. Though I had a crush on him from the time I was twelve, it had nothing to do with reality and I got over it after I found out he was already betrothed to Michelina."

Those famous last words she'd thrown out so recklessly had a choke hold on Abby now. She adored him, but had to hide her feelings if it killed her.

By the time she and Vincenzo had climbed in the limousine, she realized her due date was coming closer. In one regard she wanted it to get here as quickly as possible. But in another, she needed to hug the precious months left to her, because when it was over, she wouldn't see Vincenzo again. She couldn't bear the thought.

When Abby's eight-week checkup was over, Dr. De-Luca showed her into another consulting room, where she saw Vincenzo talking with the psychologist, Dr. Greco. Both men stood when she entered. The prince topped him by at least three inches.

Her vital signs had been in the normal range during her exam, but she doubted they were now. Vincenzo possessed an aura that had never made him look more princely. He wore a cream-colored suit with a silky brown sport shirt, the picture of royal affluence and casual sophistication no other man could pull off with the same elegance.

The balding doctor winked at her. "How is Signorina Loretto today, besides being pregnant?" She liked him a lot because he had a great sense of humor.

"Heavier."

Both men chuckled before they all sat down.

The doctor lounged back in his chair. "You do have a certain…how do you say it in English? A certain bloom?"

"That's as good an English term as I know of to cover what's really obvious. I actually prefer it to the Italian term *grassoccia*."

"No one would ever accuse you of looking chubby, my dear."

Vincenzo's black eyes had been playing over her and were smiling by now. The way he looked at her turned her insides to mush. She felt frumpy in the new maternity clothes she'd bought. This morning she'd chosen to wear a khaki skirt with an elastic waist and a short-sleeved black linen blouse she left loose fitting.

The outfit was dressy enough, yet comfortable for work. Her little belly had definitely enlarged, but Carolena said you wouldn't know it with the blouse hanging over the waist.

Dr. Greco leaned forward with a more serious expression. "A fundamental change in both your lives has occurred since you learned the embryo transfer was successful. We have a lot to talk about. One moment while I scroll to the notes I took the last time we were together."

Abby avoided looking at Vincenzo. She didn't know if she could discuss some of the things bothering her in front of the doctor. Up to the moment of Michelina's death, when she'd been through a grueling screening with so many tests, hormones and shots and felt like a scientific experiment, she'd thought she'd arrived at the second part of her journey. The first part had been the months of preparation leading up to that moment.

Abby recalled the smiles on the faces of the hopeful royal couple, yet she knew of their uncertainty that made them feel vulnerable. The three of them had seen the embryo in the incubator just before the transfer.

It was perfect and had been inserted in exactly the right place. The reproductive endocrinologist hugged Michelina and tears fell from her eyes. Vincenzo's eyes had misted over, too. Seeing their reaction, Abby's face had grown wet from moisture. The moment had been indescribable. From that time on, the four of them were a team working for the same goal.

For the eleven days while she'd waited for news one way or the other, Abby had tried to push away any thoughts of failure. She wanted to be an unwavering, constant source of encouragement and support.

When the shock that she was pregnant had worn off and she realized she was carrying their child, it didn't matter to her at all that the little baby growing inside of her wasn't genetically hers. Abby only felt supreme happiness for the couple who'd suffered too many miscarriages.

Especially *their* baby, who would one day be heir to the throne of the Principality of Arancia. Vincenzo's older sister, Gianna, was married to a count and lived in Italy. They hadn't had children yet. The honor of doing this service of love for the crown prince and his wife superseded any other considerations Abby might have had.

But her world had exploded when she'd learned of Michelina's sudden death. The news sent her on a third journey outside her universe of experience. Vincenzo had been tossed into that black void, too.

"Before you came in, Vincenzo told me about the meeting with you and his mother-in-law," said the doctor. "He knows she made you very uncomfortable and feels you should talk about it rather than keep it bottled up."

She bit her lip. "*Uncomfortable* isn't the right word. Though I had no idea the queen had such strong moral, ethical and religious reservations against it, my overall feeling was one of sadness for Vincenzo."

"He feels it goes deeper than that."

Abby glanced at Vincenzo. "In what way?"

The doctor nodded to him. "Go ahead."

Vincenzo had an alarming way of eyeing her frankly. "When we went out to dinner the other night, you weren't your usual self. Why was that?"

She prayed the blood wouldn't run to her face. "Months ago we decided to be as discreet as possible. Since your wife's death I've feared people would see us together and come to the wrong conclusion. But you already know that."

"The queen put that fear in you without coming right out and saying it, didn't she?"

This was a moment for brutal honesty. "Yes."

"Abby—our situation has changed, but my intention to go through this pregnancy with you is stronger than ever. You shouldn't have to feel alone in this. I intend to do all the things Michelina would have done with you and provide companionship. I don't want you to be afraid, even if people start to gossip about us."

She shuddered. "Your mother-in-law is terrified of scandal. I could see it in her eyes. It's evident that's why Michelina was afraid to tell her the truth. The other morning I sensed the queen's shock once she heard you'd saved my life, and that I'd lived on the palace grounds since the age of twelve.

"It wouldn't be much of a stretch for her to believe that not only am I after an inheritance, but that I'm after you. I even feared she believes I've been your mistress and that the baby isn't her grandchild."

"I *knew* that's what you were worried about the other night," Vincenzo whispered.

"I wish Michelina had talked to her mother before the decision was made to choose a surrogate, Your Highness."

"So do I. It grieves me that my wife was always intimidated by her and couldn't admit she hadn't told her mother first, but what's done is done and there's no going back."

Abby was in turmoil. "Vincenzo and Michelina have broken new royal ground with my help, Dr. Greco. Unfortunately it's ground that Queen Bianca isn't able to condone. I'm half-afraid she's going to demand that the pregnancy be…terminated." The thought sickened Abby to the point that she broke out in a cold sweat.

"Never," Vincenzo bit out fiercely. "She wouldn't go that far, not even in her mind, but she's going to have to deal with it since the time's coming when people will know you're the surrogate."

The doctor looked at both of them with concern. "Vincenzo is right. I think it's good you've already felt the fire by dealing with Michelina's mother first. To my knowledge no other royal couple in the known world has undergone the same procedure. The situation involving the two of you is an unprecedented case, but a wonderful one since it means preserving the royal line."

"Here's my dilemma." Vincenzo spoke up once more. "Before Michelina's death I'd planned to keep a lower profile around you, Abby, but that's impossible now and I can't have you feeling guilty. Of course we'll try to be careful, but only within reason. Otherwise I'll be worried about the stress on you and the baby."

"Vincenzo makes a valid point, Abby," the doctor inserted.

She lowered her head. "I know he's right. The moment I decided to go through with this, I realized it would be a risk, but I felt helping them was worth it. But with the princess gone…"

"Yes. She's gone, but you still need to keep that noble goal uppermost in your mind. One day soon you'll be free to live your own life again and the gossip will be a nine-day wonder. Do you have any other issues you'd like to discuss with me in this session?"

Yes. How did she keep her emotional distance from Vincenzo when he'd just stated that he intended to be fully involved with her?

"I can't think of any right now."

"You, Vincenzo?"

He shook his dark, handsome head. "Thank you for meeting with us. I'm sure we'll be talking to you again." Vincenzo got to his feet. "Abby needs to get back to work and so do I."

The three of them shook hands before they left his office and walked out of the building to the limousine. Abby's office wasn't that far away from the hospital. When the limo pulled up in front of the entrance, Vincenzo reached over to open the door for her.

"Have you made plans for the evening, Abby?"

"Yes," she lied. "Carolena and I are going to enjoy the festival before it ends."

"Good. Be careful not to tire yourself out."

She didn't dare ask him what he was doing tonight.

It was none of her business. How on earth was she going to get through seven more months of this?

Vincenzo watched until Abby hurried inside before he closed the door and told his driver to head for the palace. For the moment he had an important meeting with the minister of agriculture. That would keep him occupied until Abby got off work.

If she'd been telling the truth and had plans with her friend, then he was in for a night he'd rather not think about. But she didn't make a good liar. He'd known her too long. He had the strongest hunch she would go straight back to the palace after work and dig into one of her law cases. If he was right—and he would find out later—he'd take her for a walk along the surf.

Incredible to believe that the girl he'd saved from drowning eleven years ago had become a gorgeous woman in every sense of the word, *and* was carrying his child. Even though Michelina had been the biological mother, Abby was now the birth mother.

Though there'd been other candidates, the second he'd heard that Abby was one of them, his mind was made up on the spot. Because she'd always lived on the grounds and they'd developed a special bond, he knew her in all those important little ways you could never know about another person without having had that advantage.

Abby was smart, kind, polite, thoughtful, intelligent, fun. In fact, he knew that he would never have gone through with the surrogacy process if she hadn't been on the list. Michelina had been determined to go through with it because she was desperate to fix their marriage. After her incessant pleading, his guilt finally caused him to cave about turning to the procedure for the answer.

No matter how hard they'd tried, theirs had been a joyless union they'd undergone to perform a duty imposed by being born into royalty. He'd driven himself with work, she with her hobbies and horseback riding. Part of each month she spent time in Gemelli, riding with her friends. They had been counting on a child to bring happiness to their lives.

Thanks to the pregnant woman who'd just left the limo, his baby would be born in November. It would have been the miracle baby his arranged marriage had needed to survive. Now that he was alone, he needed that miracle more than ever. His eyes closed tightly. But he needed Abby, too…

CHAPTER FIVE

"ABBY?"

"Yes, Bernardo?"

"You just received a message from Judge Mascotti's court. Your case for Signor Giordano has been put on the docket for June 4."

"So soon?"

"It surprised me, too."

"Wonderful. I'll call my client."

That kind of good news helped her get through the rest of the afternoon. At five-thirty Abby said good-night to Carolena, who was going out on a date with a friend of her cousin, and hurried out to the limousine. She needed to let go of any unwanted feeling of guilt for lying to Vincenzo over her plans for the evening.

Once she reached the palace, she walked to her suite with its exposure to the water. In her opinion, her new temporary home, set in the heart of the coastal city, was the jewel in the crown of the Principality of Arancia.

At a much younger age, Vincenzo had shown her around most of the palace and she'd adored the older parts. Nine weeks ago she'd been moved from her dad's apartment to the palace and installed in one of the renovated fourteenth-century rooms, with every convenience she could imagine. It thrilled her that Vincenzo had remembered this one was her favorite.

The maid had told her he'd had it filled with fresh flowers, just for her. When she heard those words Abby's eyes smarted, but she didn't dare let the tears come in front of the staff.

Her bedroom had a coffered ceiling and was painted in white with lemon walls up to the moldings. The color matched the lemons of the trees clumped with the orange trees in the gardens below. This paradise would be hers until the baby was born. Vincenzo had told her she had the run of the palace and grounds until then.

She'd marveled at his generosity, but then, he'd always been generous. Years earlier, when she'd mentioned that she wanted a bike to get around sometimes and hoped her parents would get her one for Christmas, he'd provided one for her the very next day.

They did a lot of bike riding on the extensive grounds and had races. He let her win sometimes. She wondered what the doctor would say if she went for a bike ride now. If he gave her permission, would Vincenzo join her? It was a heady thought, one she needed to squelch.

After a snack, Abby decided to take a swim in the pool at the back of the palace and told Angelina she wouldn't want dinner until later. She was supposed to get some exercise every day and preferred swimming to anything else in order to unwind.

Once she'd put her hair in a braid and pinned it to the top of her head, she threw on a beach robe over her bikini and headed out wearing thonged sandals. When she reached the patio, she noticed Piero Gabberino pulling weeds in the flower bed.

"Ciao, Piero!"

"*Ehi*, Abby!"

The chief gardener's nice-looking son, who would be getting married shortly, had always been friendly with her. They'd known each other for several years and usually chatted for a while when they saw each other.

When she'd found out he was going to college, she took an interest in his plans. Three weeks ago Saturday she'd invited him to bring his fiancée and have lunch with her on the patio. The young couple were so excited about the coming marriage, it was fun to be around them.

"Only a week until the wedding, right?"

He grinned. "*Sì.*"

She removed her robe and got in the pool. The water felt good. She swam to the side so she could talk to Piero. "I'm very happy for you. Thank you for the invitation. I plan to come to the church to see you married." Both she and her father had been invited, but she didn't know if her dad would be able to take the time off.

Piero walked over to the edge of the pool and hunkered down. "Thank you again for the lunch. Isabella always wanted to come to the palace and see where I work."

"It's a beautiful place because you and your father's crew keep the grounds in exquisite condition."

"*Grazie.*"

"Aren't you working a little late this evening?"

"I had classes all day today."

"I know what that's like. Have you and Isabella found an apartment yet?"

"Two days ago. One day soon you will have to come over for dinner."

"That would be lovely."

"*Buonasera,* Piero!"

At the sound of Vincenzo's deep voice, Abby's heart thudded. She flung herself around in the water at the same time Piero got to his feet.

"Your Highness! It's good to see you again. Welcome home."

"Thank you. You look well."

"So do you. May I take this moment now to tell you how sorry I am about the princess. We've all been very sad."

"I appreciate those kind words."

As long as Abby had known Vincenzo, he'd almost always gone swimming in the sea in the evenings and did his early-morning workouts in the pool. Now she'd been caught in the act of lying.

He looked incredible in a pair of black swim trunks with a towel thrown around his broad shoulders. Mediterranean Gods 101 could have used him for their model.

Vincenzo eyed both of them. "Don't let me disturb the two of you."

"I was just leaving. *Scusi,* Your Highness." He gave a slight bow to Vincenzo and walked back to the plot of flowers to get his things before leaving the patio.

Abby shoved off for the other side of the rectangular pool while she thought up an excuse why she hadn't gone out with Carolena. She heard a splash and in seconds Vincenzo's dark head emerged from the surface of the water next to her.

His unreadable black eyes trapped hers. "Why did you tell me you had plans with Carolena when it's obvious you wanted to rush home after work to be with Piero? My apologies if I interrupted something between the two of you. You both looked like you were enjoying yourselves."

Her heart fluttered out of rhythm. Coming from any other man, Abby could be forgiven for thinking he was jealous. But that was absurd.

"Before work was over, Carolena told me she'd been lined up with her cousin's friend, so we decided to do something tomorrow evening instead." That was partially a lie, too, but she would turn it into a truth if at all possible.

She could hear his brilliant wheels turning. "Have you and Piero been friends long?"

"Quite a few years. He speaks Mentonasc and has been a great teacher for me. I, in turn, have been coaching him in one of his first-year law classes, but he doesn't really need help."

His black brows lifted in surprise. "He's going to be an attorney?"

"That's been his hope since he was young. He has been influenced by his father to get a good education. Some kind of business law, probably. I've been helping him review appellate court decisions and analyze the judges' reasoning and findings. He's very bright."

Vincenzo looked stunned. "I'm impressed."

"Six months ago he got himself engaged and is going to be getting married next week. I met his fiancée the other day and we had lunch together out here. They've invited me to the wedding next week. I'm thrilled for them."

Vincenzo raked a hand through his wet black hair. "Apparently a lot has been going on around here, under my nose, that I've known nothing about."

"You have so much to do running the country. How could you possibly know everything? Don't forget I've lived on the grounds for years and am friends with everyone employed here. When I was young the gardeners helped me find my mom's cat, who went out prowling at night and never wanted to come home."

Vincenzo's smile was back, reminding her of what a sensational-looking male he was.

"Sometimes they brought me a tiny wounded animal or a bird with a broken wing to tend. Piero's father used to call me 'little nurse.'"

His gaze played over her features and hair. She saw a tenderness in his eyes she'd never noticed before. "All the same, I should have been more observant."

"Need I remind you that your royal nose has much greater worries, like dealing with your country's welfare?" He chuckled. "The word *multitask* could have been coined on your work ethic alone. Don't you remember the dead starling I found and you helped me plan a funeral for it?"

He nodded. "You were so broken up about it, I had to do something."

"It was a wonderful funeral." Her voice started to tremble. "You even said a prayer. I'll never forget. You said that some angels watched over the birds, but if they couldn't save them, then they helped take away the child's sorrow."

His black brows lifted. "I said that?"

"Yes. It was a great comfort to me." *You've always been a great comfort to me.*

"Your praise is misplaced, but like any man I admit to enjoying a little flattery."

"It's the truth. I have a scrapbook to prove it." Her confession was out before she could prevent it. Feeling herself go crimson, she did a somersault and swam to the deep end of the pool to cool down. When she came up gasping for air, he was right there, without a sign of being winded. If her heart didn't stop racing pretty soon, she was afraid she'd pass out. "Haven't you learned it's impolite to race a woman with a handicap, and win?"

His eyes grew shuttered. "Haven't you learned it's not nice to tease and then run?"

Touché.

"When am I going to see this scrapbook?"

Making a split-second decision, she said, "I plan to send it to you when your child is christened." She couldn't help searching his striking features for a moment. "The pictures showing you and your wife will be especially precious. I can promise that he or she will treasure it."

Abby heard his sharp intake of breath. "How long have you been making it?"

"Since soon after we arrived from the States."

"Clear back then?"

"Don't you know every girl grows up dreaming about palaces and princes and princesses? But my dream became real. I decided I would record everything so that one day I could show my own little girl or boy that I once lived a fairy-tale life.

"But now that you're going to have a little girl or boy, *they* should be the one in possession of it. The story of your life will mean everything in the world to them. If they're like me when I was young and poured over my parents' picture albums for hours and hours, they'll do the same thing."

Vincenzo was dumbfounded. Evening had crept over the palace, bringing out the purity of her bone structure, but he saw more than that. An inward beauty that radiated. It was that same innocent beauty he'd seen in her teens, but the added years had turned her into a breathtaking woman.

He wondered what she'd say if he told her that....

Of course he couldn't, but something earth-shattering was happening to him. As if he was coming awake from a hundred-year sleep. Vincenzo was starting to come alive from a different source, with feelings and emotions completely new to him. Not even his guilt could suppress them.

"I'm looking forward to that day, Abby."

"You're not the only one." But she said it with a charming smile. He liked her hair up in a braid. She wore it in all kinds of ways, each style intriguing.

"Shall we swim a couple of laps before we have dinner? When I talked to Angelina and she told me you hadn't eaten yet, I arranged for us to be served out here on the patio." While she was forming an answer he said, "I promise to let you set the pace."

"Thank you for taking pity on me." On that note, she started for the other side of the pool.

Vincenzo swam beside her, loving this alone time with her. There was no tension. A feeling of contentment stole through him. At the moment he was feeling guilty for *not* feeling guilty. He asked himself if he would feel this way if she weren't pregnant, but it wasn't a fair question. With Michelina gone, he naturally felt more protective toward Abby, who no longer had a female mentor to turn to for support.

To his surprise, he'd been disturbed to find her talking and laughing with Piero. *Why* had he felt that way? Was it the helicopter father coming out in him, as she'd suggested? Vincenzo frowned. Was he already becoming possessive?

Her comment about never finding a man who measured up to her father had been on his mind since they'd eaten at the mountain restaurant. He wondered if she'd ever been intimate with any of her boyfriends. If the answer was no, then in one respect he understood his mother-in-law's remark about the pregnancy being unnatural.

Just how would Vincenzo feel when Abby did get married, knowing she'd carried his child for nine months before she'd known another man? When she did get married one day—he had no doubt about that—how would the man she loved feel to know she'd given birth to Vincenzo's baby? Would that man feel robbed in some way?

His thoughts kept going. What if Vincenzo wanted to marry a woman who'd already given birth through surrogacy? It would mean she'd already gone through a whole history with some other man and his wife. Would that change the way he felt about her?

The more he pondered the subject, the more he couldn't answer his own questions.

While he succeeded in tying himself up in knots, Abby climbed the steps to leave the pool. For a moment he caught a side view of her lovely body. His heart clapped with force to see her stomach wasn't quite as flat as he remembered, but at this stage you wouldn't know she was pregnant. Dr. DeLuca had said that since this was her first pregnancy, it might be awhile.

That didn't matter. *Vincenzo knew.*

The day Abby had given him that pamphlet, he'd studied it and learned she would probably start showing by twelve weeks. Michelina had lost their three babies by that point, so he'd never seen his wife looking pregnant.

His excitement grew to imagine Abby in another month. Since he wasn't the most patient man, the waiting was going to be hard on him. And what about her? She was the one going through the travail that brought a woman close to death. Her patience had to be infinite.

He found himself asking the same question as the queen: What *did* Abby get out of this?

Vincenzo had listened to her explanation many times, but right now he was in a different place than he'd been at Christmas when they'd talked about surrogacy as an answer. His focus hadn't been the same back then. Now that he was no longer desperate for himself and Michelina, he had a hard time imagining this remarkable woman, who could have any man she wanted, being willing to go through this.

How did any surrogate mother who wasn't already a mother or who had never given birth leave the hospital and go back to her old life without experiencing changes, psychologically and emotionally? He could understand why it was illegal in many parts of the world for someone like Abby. He and Michelina must have been so blinded by their own unhappiness that they'd agreed to let Abby go through with this.

Though they'd discussed everything before the procedure, nothing had seemed quite real back then. Those same questions were haunting him now in new, profound ways. A fresh wave of guilt attacked him. He needed to explore his feelings in depth with Dr. Greco, because he was concerned for Abby's welfare. She was having to put off being with other men until the baby was born. That meant putting off any possible marriage. To his dismay, the thought of her getting married brought him no joy. What was wrong with him?

Abby put on her white beach robe over her green bikini and they sat down to dinner. "This cantaloupe is so sweet I can't believe it."

"I hear it's especially good for you."

"You're spoiling me, you know."

He gripped his water glass tighter. "That's the idea. You're doing something no one should expect you to do."

A wounded look entered her eyes. "I didn't *have* to do anything, Vincenzo. It was my choice."

"But you've never been pregnant before. My wife and I were entirely selfish."

Michelina because she'd wanted so much to have a child. Vincenzo because he'd wanted Abby to be the woman if they did decide to go through with it. The perfect storm...

After drinking the rest of his water, he darted her another glance. "Though I know you would never admit it to me, you've probably regretted your decision every day since the procedure was done."

She put down her fork. "Stop it, Vincenzo!" It pleased him she'd said his name again.

"You know the reason I did this and you couldn't be more wrong about my feelings now. Why don't we take Dr. Greco's advice and drop all the guilt? Let's agree that though this is an unprecedented case, it's a wonderful one that's going to give you a son or daughter. We need to keep that goal foremost in our minds."

Vincenzo sucked in a deep breath. "So be it! But I

have to tell you that you're the bravest, most courageous soul I've ever known."

"You mean after you. Let's not forget *you* were the one who dove into that cave looking for my body during the most ferocious storm I'd ever seen after moving to Arancia. It wasn't the men in the coast guard who'd performed that deed.

"Their first duty was to protect you. Instead they let you risk your life to save me. If Father hadn't been so devastated over losing Mother at the time, those men would have faced severe penalties, so I'd say we're equal."

There was no one like Abby when her back got up. "All right." He lifted his water glass.

"Truce?"

She did likewise. "Truce." They touched glasses.

After she drank a little and put her glass on the table, he could tell there was something else on her mind. "What were you going to say?"

"How did you know?" she asked, bemused.

"A feeling."

She was quiet for a moment. "Today a minor miracle occurred when I received word that Judge Mascotti is going to hear the Giordano case in less than a month. I was expecting it to be six at the earliest." She eyed him with blue eyes that sparkled with purple glints in the candlelight. "Who do you suppose was responsible?"

"I have no idea," he said in a deadpan voice.

"Liar." No one had ever dared call him that, but then, no one was like Abby. "I'm very grateful, you know. It's my biggest case so far with the firm."

"You've got a good one. My bet is on you to win it in the end."

"Please don't hold your breath."

He smiled. "In my line of work I'm used to doing it. Don't forget I have to face our constitutional assembly on a weekly basis, and they're *all* stars." Laughter bubbled out of her, but he noticed she'd drawn her beach robe closer around her. "It's cooling off, Abby. Since you have another workday tomorrow, I mustn't keep you up any longer."

She got up from the table before he could help her. "I've enjoyed the company and dinner very much. After your good deed in getting my law case heard sooner, I have to hope my side will prevail. *Buonanotte,* Vincenzo."

Her disappearance left him at a loss. As he walked swiftly to his apartment, Vincenzo phoned Marcello. "My mail included an invitation for the wedding of Luigi Gabberino's son. Can you give me the particulars?"

"Momento." Vincenzo headed for the bathroom to take a shower while he waited.

"Friday at four o'clock, San Pietro Church."

"Grazie. Put that date on my calendar. I intend to go."

"I'm afraid there's a conflict. You'll be in a meeting with the education minister at that time."

"I'll cut it short."

"Bene, Your Highness."

On Friday Abby left work at three-thirty in order to get to the church and be seated by four. She'd worn a new designer dress in Dresden-blue silk to the office. The top of the square-necked two-piece outfit shot with silver threads draped below the waistline. The sleeves were stylishly ruched above the elbow. On her feet she wore low-heeled silver sandals.

She'd caught her hair back in a twist with pins. Once she'd bid her latest client goodbye, she retouched her makeup before pulling the new floppy broad-brimmed hat with the silvery-blue rose from her closet. After putting it on, she grabbed her silver bag and left the office with a trail of colleagues gawking in her wake. Carolena had been with her when she'd bought the outfit, and now gave her the thumbs-up.

Outside the building she heard whistles and shouts of *bellissima* from the ever-appreciative male population of Arancia. She chuckled. What a gorgeous, sunny day for a wedding! There was a delightful breeze off the Mediterranean.

The limo wound through the streets until it came to a piazza fronting the church of San Pietro, where she was let out. Abby followed a group of people inside and found a seat in the assembled crowd of friends and extended family. She recognized several employees from the palace, and of course Piero's immediately family.

Before the Mass began, heads turned as a side door opened. When she saw Vincenzo enter surrounded by his bodyguards, she started to feel light-headed. The exquisitely groomed prince of Arancia wore a dove-gray suit. He was heartbreakingly handsome and took her breath away, along with everyone else's.

He sat off to the side. Piero's parents had to feel so honored. This was the second time Vincenzo had gone out of his way to perform a service that hadn't been on his agenda—the first, of course, being a word put in Judge Mascotti's ear to hasten Abby's court case hearing.

The prince was an amazingly thoughtful man. She'd

worked around a lot of men. No man of her acquaintance could touch him. Abby knew deep in her heart he was so grateful for her being willing to carry his baby, there wasn't enough he could do for her. It was something she would have to get used to. When he dedicated himself to a project, he went all out.

For the next hour Abby sat there eyeing him with covert glances while Piero and his bride took their vows. When the service was over, Vincenzo went out the side exit while she followed the crowd outside to the piazza to give the radiant couple a hug. But when she was ready to walk to her limousine, one of the security men touched her elbow.

"Signorina Loretto? If you would come with me, please."

With heart thumping, she followed him around the side of the church to another limousine, where she knew Vincenzo was waiting inside. The breeze was a little stronger now. As she started to climb in, she had to put her hand on her hat to keep it in place. At the same time, her skirt rode up her thighs. She fought madly with her other hand to push it down.

Vincenzo's dark eyes, filled with male admiration, missed nothing in the process, causing her to get a suffocating feeling in her chest. The hint of a smile hovered at the corners of his compelling mouth. After she sat down opposite him, he handed her the silver bag she'd accidentally dropped.

"Thank you," she said in a feverish whisper.

"Anyone could be forgiven for thinking *you* are the bride. That color is very becoming on you. We can't let such a stunning outfit go to waste. What is your pleasure?"

Her pleasure… She didn't dare think about that, let alone take him up on his offer.

"To be honest, it's been a long day. I'm anxious to get back to the palace and put my feet up. If that sounds ungracious, I don't mean for it to be."

"Then that's what we'll do." He let his driver know and the limo started to move out to the street. His arms rested along the back of the seat. He looked relaxed. "I enjoyed the wedding."

"So did I. Piero was beaming. I know he was a happy groom, but your presence made it the red-letter day in all their lives. That was very kind of you, Vincenzo."

"I have you to thank for reminding me of my duty. Now that it's over, we'll concentrate on taking care of you. When we get back to the palace we'll have dinner in your apartment and watch a movie I ordered."

Ordered? Her pulse raced. "I'm sure you have other things to do."

His black eyes glinted with a strange light. "Not tonight. It will feel good to relax. Tomorrow my father and I are leaving to visit my mother's sister in the French Savoie. We'll be attending another wedding and taking a vacation at the same time."

"That's right. Your father usually goes away this time of year."

He nodded. "I'm not sure how soon we'll be back, but I promise I'll be here for your June appointment with the doctor."

June… He'd be gone several weeks at least. She fought to keep her expression from showing her devastating disappointment.

The limo drove up to his private entrance to the palace. "I'll come to your apartment in a half hour, unless you need more time."

"Knowing that you have a healthy appetite, thirty minutes is probably all you should have to wait for dinner."

The flash of a satisfied white smile was the last thing she saw before he exited the limo. It stayed with her all the way to her suite. Her hands trembled as she removed her hat and put it on the closet shelf. Next came the dress and her shoes.

After Abby had put on jeans with an elastic waist band and a pink short-sleeved top, she redid her hair. While she fastened it with a tortoiseshell clip, she was assailed by the memory of Vincenzo's eyes as she'd climbed in the limo. They'd been alive and there was a throbbing moment when...

No. She was mistaken. The prince was a man, after all, and couldn't have helped looking while she was at a disadvantage. Furious with herself for ascribing more to the moment than was there, she lifted the phone to ring Angelina for her dinner tray, then thought the better of it. Vincenzo had made it clear he was orchestrating the rest of this evening.

If she wasn't careful, she could get used to this kind of attention. But once she'd had the baby, her association with the prince would be over. By November he could easily be involved with another woman, who had the right credentials for another marriage.

Her thoughts darted ahead to his trip with the king. Since Vincenzo had recently returned from a trip that had lasted weeks, she doubted he'd be accompanying his father because he needed another vacation.

In all probability there was someone the king and

his aunt wanted him to meet. With a baby on the way, he needed a suitable wife who was already situated at the palace to take over the duties of a mother the minute Abby delivered. But the thought of another woman being a mother to Abby's baby killed her.

This baby was Abby's baby. She couldn't possibly separate herself from it now. She'd been imagining the day she held it in her arms, the clothes she'd buy, the nursery she'd create. No other woman would love this baby as fiercely as the way Abby already did.

But Vincenzo was the father and he'd been born to fulfill his duties. One of them at the moment was to make certain Abby felt secure while she was pregnant with the next royal heir of Arancia. She knew better than to read anything more into what was going on. He was doing his best while trying to cope with the pain of his loss. There was only one way for her to handle this and keep her sanity at the same time.

He needs a friend, Abby. Be one to him.

A half hour later Vincenzo arrived at her apartment. He'd changed out of his suit into chinos and a polo shirt. He looked so fabulous, she tried not stare at him. He'd tucked a DVD under his arm. She flashed him her friendliest smile. "You're right on time."

"In the business I'm in, you have to be."

A quiet laugh escaped her lips. "Well, tonight you can forget business for once. Come right in and make yourself at home."

"If it's all right with you, I'll put this in the machine."

She closed the door after him and folded her arms. "Aren't you going to show me the cover?"

"I'd rather surprise you." In a minute he'd inserted it

so they could watch it on the living room couch when they were ready.

"All I have to offer you is soda from the fridge in the kitchen."

"I'll drink what you're drinking."

"It's boring lemonade."

"Sounds good."

She didn't call him a liar again. He was probably used to some kind of alcohol at the end of the day, but was going out of his way to make her comfortable. This man was spoiling her rotten.

"Excuse me while I get it." When she came out of the kitchen, she found him on her terrace leaning against the balustrade. "In the States we say 'a penny for them.'" She handed him a can.

He straightened and took it from her. "I'll give you one guess." He popped the lid and drank the contents in one go. Abby was thirsty, too, and followed suit, but could only drink half of hers before needing a breath.

"A name for your baby."

"It has already been picked, whether it's a boy or a girl. Actually, I was thinking about your plans after the baby's born," he said on a more serious note.

So had she... Since that terrible morning with the queen, she'd decided that living anywhere in Arancia wouldn't be a good idea after all. "You're giving me a complex, you know."

A frown marred his handsome features. "In what way?"

"You worry too much about everything, so maybe what I tell you will help. The other night my father came over and we had a long talk. Before Christmas, in fact, before I even knew you were looking for a surrogate,

Dad was planning to resign his position here and move back to the States. He says his assistant, Ernesto, is more than ready to take over."

Stillness enveloped Vincenzo for an overly long moment. "Does my father know about this?"

"Not yet. He plans to tell him soon. We have extended family in Rhode Island, where I was born."

"But your father has family here in Arancia, too."

"That's true, but he's been offered a position at a private firm there I know he will enjoy. He won't leave until after I have the baby. Though I had thoughts of living in Arancia and working at the firm with Carolena, I can't abide the idea of him being so far away. Therefore I'll be moving back with him and plan to study for the Rhode Island and New York bar exams. So you see? That's one worry you can cross off your long list."

During the quiet that followed, she heard a knock on the door. He moved before she did to answer it. Angelina had arrived with their dinner. Vincenzo thanked her and pushed the cart to the terrace, where they could sit to enjoy their meal while they looked out over the view.

Once they started eating, he focused his attention on her. "Are you close with family there?"

"We've all kept in touch. Mom took me for visits several times a year."

"I remember. The grounds seemed emptier then."

Abby wished he hadn't said that. Though it was nice to see family, she lived to get back to Vincenzo.

"After she died, Dad always sent me to stay with my mother's sister and her husband at Easter. I have a couple of fun cousins close to my age. It will be wonderful to live around all of them again. My aunt's a lot like my mom, so nice and kindhearted."

That part was the truth, as far as it went. These years in Arancia were a dream that had to end, but she wouldn't allow herself to think about leaving the country, about leaving *him*. Not yet.

"If you've finished," he said all of a sudden, "shall we go inside and start the movie?"

"Marvelous idea. I can't wait to see what you picked out. Something American and silly, I presume, like *Back to the Beach*."

A mysterious smile appeared to chase away his earlier somber look. She got up from the chair before he could help her and walked in the living room to turn it on.

CHAPTER SIX

ABBY'S REVELATION HAD put Vincenzo off the last of his dinner. He'd meant it when he'd told her he missed her presence during her vacations out of the country. Because of their situation, Abby had always been natural with him and treated him like a friend. No artifice. Though he'd been six years older, she'd been there in the background of his life for years. But when she went away next time, she wouldn't be returning.

The sense of loss was already hitting him. He was staggered by the depth of his feelings. When she'd opened the door to him awhile ago, he'd discovered her in yet another new maternity outfit. This time she wore flattering casual attire. Yet no matter how she played down her assets, nothing could disguise the fact that she was a very desirable woman.

Now that she was carrying his child, how could he not notice her or stop certain thoughts from creeping into his mind without his volition? Abby had become as precious to him as the little life growing inside of her.

Earlier, once he'd entered the church and scanned the guests, he'd spotted the hat and the face beneath it. For the rest of the ceremony he couldn't take his eyes off her. She'd lit up the interior like an exotic orchid among the greenery.

"My Little Chickadee?" The excitement in her voice was all he could have hoped for. She swung around to face him with a brilliant smile. "Trust you to manage getting hold of a copy of it. This was Mom's favorite Mae West film. W.C. Fields is in it, too. This movie is hilarious."

"While you stretch out on the couch and put your legs up, I'll sit in the chair with the ottoman."

"Vincenzo—I didn't literally mean I needed to do that. My feet aren't swollen yet!"

He took his place in the chair anyway. "From what I saw as you got in the limo, I couldn't detect any problem in that department, either, but as you reminded me a week ago, I'm only a man and don't have a clue about a woman."

While the film got underway, she curled up on the end of the couch. He saw her shoulders shaking with silent laughter. "You'll never let me live that down. Apparently you have a photographic memory. I bet Gianna could tell me what a maddening brother you were at times."

He grinned at her. "It's a good thing she's not here to reveal my secrets."

Abby flicked him a narrowed gaze. "Oh, I heard a few."

"Like what, for instance?"

"Like the time you and your friends brought some girls to the palace and sneaked them into the pool at three in the morning to go skinny-dipping. I know it's true because I heard about it from my father later. He'd been awakened in the middle of the night by some of the security men."

He spread his hands. "What can I say? My life has been an open book in more ways than one. Were you scandalized?"

"I was only fifteen at the time and wondered how any girl could be so daring."

"But not the guys?"

"No. It's in your nature, which has been written into your Roman mythology. Wasn't it the goddess Diana, Jupiter's favorite daughter, to whom he swore he wouldn't make her marry and allowed her to hunt by the light of the moon? She loved skinny-dipping, and naturally all the young men came to watch."

The laughter rolled out of Vincenzo. He couldn't help it.

Abby kept a straight face. "But sadly for them, when she caught them, she turned them into stags. Of course, that was centuries ago. Today it's the other way around. The teenaged girls are scandalized by prudes like me."

When he could find his voice, he said, "You mean I couldn't have talked you into it?"

"Not on your life!"

She could always make him laugh, and the film *was* hilarious. He'd been waiting for the famous line she'd impersonated. When it came, he realized Abby had sounded just like the legendary actress.

After the film ended, she got up and turned off the machine. "I wish I'd had an older brother. You and Gianna were lucky to grow up together. One day when you marry again, hopefully you'll be able to have another baby so your first one won't grow up to be an only child."

The thought of taking another wife sent a chill through him. He knew when his father had insisted Vincenzo accompany him on this next trip it had been motivated by an agenda that had little to do with the need for a vacation.

"Were you ever lonely, Abby?"

"Not in the sense you mean, because being the brightest light on my parents' horizon was my only reality. I knew nothing else. But when I think of you and Gianna, especially the two of you growing up in a royal household, I can see how great that would have been for you. She told me she went to bat for you when you got into trouble with your father. There's nothing like the power of sibling love."

With pure grace she curled her leg underneath her again and sat down. "Did you ever have to help her out of a spot?"

"Many times. She wanted money. When I didn't feel like carrying out some official function, I'd bribe her to do it for me."

Abby laughed. "At what cost?"

"Pocket money. Our parents kept us both on a strict allowance."

"Good for them! I always liked them, but that admission puts them on an even higher level in—"

Vincenzo's cell phone rang, breaking in on her. "Sorry." He pulled it out of his pocket and checked the caller ID. "Excuse me for a moment, Abby. I have to take this."

"Of course."

He moved to the terrace, out of earshot. *"Pronto?"*

"I'm sorry to disturb you, but the queen was insistent you call her back immediately."

"Do you have any idea why, Marcello?"

"No, except that she'd been talking to the king first."

He had an idea what this might be about. Something told him he needed to put out another fire, but first he needed to talk to his father. "I'll take care of it. *Grazie.*"

When he walked back inside, Abby was waiting for him near the front door. "Duty calls, right?" She'd given him no choice but to leave. "Thank you for this lovely and unexpected evening."

"I enjoyed it, too. Keep the DVD as a reminder of your mother," he said when she was about to hand it him.

"You're too generous, but I'll treasure it."

"That's the idea," he murmured.

She put a hand to her throat. "As soon as you came in from the terrace, I could tell by your face something was wrong. I hope it's nothing too serious."

If his hunch was right, then it *was* serious. But for once, this had nothing to do with Abby. He could thank the Roman gods for that, at least.

Too bad he couldn't get rid of a certain dangerous vision in his mind of joining Abby the Huntress in that forest pool and making love to her before her father discovered them and *he* turned Vincenzo into a stag.

He ground his teeth absently. "So do I, Abby. I'll see you at the clinic for your next appointment. Though I know you'll follow the doctor's orders, I have to say this anyway. Take meticulous care of yourself." June sounded an eternity away.

Her eyes had gone a smoky blue. "You, too, Your Highness. Your baby's going to need you."

Vincenzo turned from her before he couldn't and took off for the other region of the palace at a fast clip.

When he reached his apartment, he decided it wouldn't do any good to call his father first. Without hesitation he phoned Michelina's mother to get this over with.

"Thank you for returning my call, Vincenzo."

"Of course. How are you getting along, Bianca?"

"How do you think? My world has fallen apart. I didn't believe it could get worse until I talked with your father. He informed me you're going on vacation tomorrow to stay with the *duc de Chambery*. If you hadn't chosen Michelina, you would have married his granddaughter Odile, who's still single. That would be a humiliation for our family if you choose her now. I'm telling you I won't—"

"Bianca?" he broke in on her. He had it in his heart to feel sorry for this woman who was grieving over her daughter. "You don't need to say another word. I know exactly how Michelina felt about her. I never considered marriage to Odile and I'll make you a solemn vow now that I never will. Does that answer your question?"

Her weeping finally stopped and all he heard was sniffing. "But you'll take another bride."

He'd braced his back against the door to his den and closed his eyes. "To be frank with you, I don't plan on marrying again. When Father is no longer alive, I may step down so Gianna can take over the business of ruling Arancia. My first duty is going to be to Michelina's and my child."

Her gasp came over the phone loud and clear. "I don't believe you."

"Which part?" he bit out.

"You don't fool me. We both know the only reason why you'd give up the throne..."

Her insinuation was perfectly clear. She'd all but accused Abby of going after Vincenzo. He'd been waiting for her to start in on him. This was just the first volley.

He heard the click, severing their connection.

"Congratulations, Signorina Loretto. You show no problems so far. It means you've been following directions to the letter." Abby could thank Vincenzo for that. "How is the nausea?"

"I hardly ever notice it anymore."

"Good. Your measurements are fine. Be sure to keep your feet up for a little each day after work."

"I will. How big is the baby by now?"

"Um, three inches. You're growing."

"I know. I already prefer lying on my side."

The doctor smiled. "I'll let the prince know that at your sixteen-weeks' checkup we'll do an ultrasound, which should reveal the gender of that special baby."

Abby didn't know if Vincenzo wanted to be surprised and wait until after the baby was delivered, or if he was anxious to know right away. But it was his business, not hers.

"You can get dressed now and I'll see you in another month. Be sure you keep coming in on a weekly basis for your blood pressure check. I'll give Vincenzo the full report when he's back. He'll be delighted. As for Dr. Greco, he said for you to call him when the two of you can come in."

"Thank you, Doctor."

Abby put on her white sundress with the brown-trimmed white bolero top and left for the office. Her father had told her the king had returned to the palace three days ago. That meant Vincenzo was still in France.

With a woman who might possibly take Michelina's place one day?

Abby was used to him honoring every commitment to her. The fact that he hadn't come today shouldn't have mattered, but it did. She missed him and would be lying if she didn't admit that to herself.

The show-cause hearing at the court yesterday had persuaded the judge to hear the Giordano case in August. Abby was thrilled with the outcome and knew his decision had frustrated Signor Masala's attorney. She wanted to share the good news with Vincenzo and thank him, but it would have to wait.

She was starting to get a taste of what it would be like when he wasn't in her life anymore. Not liking that he'd become the focal point of her thoughts, she phoned her father after she got in the limo and invited him to a home-cooked dinner at her apartment that evening. She planned to fry chicken and make scones, the kind her mom always made. He loved them. But to her disappointment, he couldn't come until the following night.

Once she got to work, she invited Carolena to the palace to have dinner with her at the pool. Abby would lend her one of the bikinis she hadn't worn yet. Thankfully her friend was thrilled to be invited and they rode home together in the limo at the end of the day.

"Am I in heaven or what?"

They'd finished eating and had spent time in the pool. Now they were treading water. Abby laughed at her friend. "I've been asking myself that same question since we moved here years ago." She was tempted to tell Carolena her future plans, but thought the better of it until closer to the delivery date. "I think I'll do one more lap and then I'll be done for the night."

She pushed off, doing the backstroke. When she reached the other side and turned to hold on to the side, she saw blood and let out a small cry.

"What's wrong?" Carolena swam over to her. "Oh—you've got a nosebleed."

"I don't know why." She pinched her nose with her thumb and index finger.

"I'll get a towel."

Abby followed her to the steps and got out.

"Sit on the chair." She handed Abby her beach towel.

After a minute she said, "It's not stopping."

"Keep holding while I call your doctor. Is his number programmed in your cell phone?"

"Yes. Press three."

Angelina came out on the patio to clear the table, but let out an alarmed sound the second she saw the blood on the towel and hurried away.

By now Carolena was off the phone. "The doctor wants you to lean forward on the chair and keep pressing your nostrils together for ten or fifteen minutes. Breathe through your mouth. It should stop. Apparently pregnant women get nosebleeds, so not to worry. If it doesn't stop soon, we'll call him back."

"Okay." Before another minute passed, Vincenzo came running toward her. He was back!

"Abby—" Without hesitation he hunkered down next to her. The fear in his eyes was a revelation to her.

"I'm all right, Vincenzo. My nose started to bleed, but I think it has stopped now."

He reached for his cell phone. "I'm calling Dr. DeLuca."

"Carolena already contacted him for me. I'm fine, honestly!"

She removed the towel to show him the episode was over. Already she felt like a fraud.

"Don't move." He got up to get her beach robe and put it around her shoulders. His touch sent fingers of delight through her body. "It's cooler out here now."

"Thank you. I don't believe you've been introduced to my friend, Carolena Baretti. Carolena, this is His Royal Highness Prince Vincenzo."

"Thank heaven you were here for her, Signorina Baretti. I'm very pleased to meet you."

"The pleasure is mine, Your Highness. Dr. DeLuca said the increased blood flow with pregnancy sometimes produces nosebleeds. She's supposed to stay put for a few minutes so she won't get light-headed when she stands. He'll be relieved to know the bleeding has stopped."

"I'll call him and tell him right now."

While Vincenzo walked out of earshot to make the phone call, Carolena moved closer to Abby. Her brows lifted as she stared at her. "When he saw you holding that towel to your face, I thought he was going to have a heart attack."

"I know he was afraid something had happened to the baby."

Carolena shook her head. "From the look in his eyes, it wasn't the baby he was worried about," she whispered. "If a man ever looked at me like that..."

Abby's heart thudded against her ribs. "You're imagining things." But inwardly she was shaken by the look in his eyes. It was that same look he'd given her after she'd recovered on the boat that black day, as if she'd meant the world to him.

What a time for him to return from his trip! She looked an utter mess.

Vincenzo walked toward her. "If you feel all right, I'll help you get back to your apartment."

"I'm fine. Carolena will help me."

"We'll both help." The authority in his voice silenced her.

Together the three of them left the pool. Carolena brought all their things while Vincenzo stayed at Abby's side. When they reached her suite, her friend changed her clothes and announced she was leaving.

"I'll have a limousine waiting for you at the entrance, *Signorina.* Again, my thanks for your help."

"Abby's the best."

"So are you." Abby hugged her friend.

"Thanks for dinner. See you at work tomorrow."

The minute the door closed, Abby glanced at Vincenzo. "If you'll excuse me, I'll take a quick shower."

"Don't hurry on my account. I'm not going anywhere."

That fluttery sensation in her stomach had taken over again. It happened whenever he came near. She rushed into the bathroom and got busy making herself presentable once more. After drying her hair with a clean towel, she brushed it the best she could and put on a clean blouse and skirt.

The nosebleed had definitely stopped. Just one of the surprises brought on by the pregnancy. She couldn't complain. So far she'd been very lucky.

Again she found him out on the terrace, which was her favorite place, too, especially at night. He looked sensational in anything he wore. Tonight it was a silky blue shirt and khakis. "Did the doctor reassure you?"

He turned and put his hands on his hips, the ultimate male. "To a point. I'm much more relieved now that I see you walking around without further problem."

"Don't do it," she warned him.

Those black brows furrowed. "Do what?"

"Start feeling guilty again because I'm in this situation."

"If you want to know the stark, staring truth, guilt is the last thing on my mind. I'm worrying about the next time you get another one. What if Carolena hadn't been with you?"

"I had the usual nosebleed here and there growing up. They've always stopped on their own, as this one did tonight, even though she was with me. But if I'd been alone and needed help, I would have called out for Angelina. Don't forget that at work I'm never alone."

Her logic finally sank in and his frown disappeared. "I'm sorry I didn't make it back in time for our appointment with Dr. Greco. If I hadn't been detained, I would have been in the pool with you when this happened."

A thrill of forbidden excitement shot through her body to hear that.

"Everything's fine. We'll reschedule when it's convenient for you."

His dark gaze wandered over her. "Dr. DeLuca says you're in excellent health."

"You see?" She smiled.

"He's going to do an ultrasound on you next month."

"Is the helicopter daddy anxious to know if he's going to have a boy or a girl?"

"I'm not sure yet. For the moment all I care about is that you and the baby stay healthy."

"That's my prime concern, too. But maybe by then you'll have made up your mind and want to know if the kingdom can expect a prince or a princess."

"Maybe. Let's go back inside where it's warmer so you'll stay well."

When Abby had told her father that Vincenzo was a worrywart, he'd laughed his head off. If he could see them now...

She did his bidding and walked through to the kitchen, where she opened the fridge. He followed her. "Orange juice all right?" she asked.

"Sounds good."

Abby chuckled. "No, it doesn't. Why don't you have some wine from the cupboard? You look like it might do you some good."

"Soda is fine."

"A warrior to the end. That's you." She pulled out two cans and took them over to the table, where he helped her before sitting down. They popped their lids at the same time. The noise was so loud they both let out a laugh, the first she'd heard come from him tonight. A smiling Vincenzo was a glorious sight. "How was your trip?"

"Which one are you talking about?"

She almost choked on her drink. "You took two trips?"

He nodded. "I only flew in an hour ago from Gemelli."

Abby blinked. "I didn't realize you were going there."

"It wasn't on the schedule, but Bianca slipped on a stair in the palace and broke her hip."

"Oh, no—"

"Valentino phoned me after it happened. It was the day Father and I were scheduled to come home. We agreed I should fly to Gemelli to be with her."

Whatever Abby had been thinking about the reason for his absence, she'd been wrong and promised herself to stop speculating about anything to do with him from now on.

"Is she in terrible pain?"

"At first, but she's going to be fine with therapy. We had several long talks. If there can be any good in her getting hurt, it seems to have softened her somewhat in her attitude about the coming event. Despite her misgivings, the idea of a grandchild has taken hold."

"That's wonderful, Vincenzo."

"She's missing Michelina."

"Of course." Abby took another long drink. "You must be so relieved to be on better terms with her."

He stared at her through veiled eyes. "I am. But when Angelina told me about you—"

"You thought you were facing another crisis," she finished for him. "Well, as you can see, all is well. Did your father have a good vacation?"

Vincenzo finished off his soda before answering her. "No."

"I'm sorry to hear that."

"He brought his troubles on himself."

"Is he ill?"

"If only it were that simple."

"Vincenzo—" She didn't know whether to laugh or cry. "What a thing to say."

"Before I was betrothed, my parents arranged for me

to meet the princesses on their short list of candidates, carefully chosen by the extended family."

Abby lowered her head.

"It came down to two, Michelina Cavelli and Odile Levallier, the granddaughter of the *duc de Chambery*. Both were nice-looking at their age, but of the two, I preferred Michelina, who wasn't as headstrong or spoiled."

"I can't imagine being in your situation."

"When you're born into a royal family, it's just the way it is. You don't know anything else. If I'd had a different personality, perhaps I would have rebelled and run away. I was still a royal teenager at the time and knew I had years before I needed to think about getting married, so I didn't let it bother me too much."

Her head came up and she eyed him soberly. "Were you ever in love?"

"At least four times that I recall."

"You're serious."

"Deadly so. In fact it might have been seven or eight times."

Seven or eight?

"Those poor women who'd loved you, knowing they didn't stand a chance of becoming your wife. Did you spend time with Michelina over the years, too?"

"Some. When my father decided it was time for me to marry, I saw her more often. She had always been good-looking and smart. We enjoyed riding horses and playing tennis. She was a great athlete, and loved the water. I could see myself married to her."

"When did you actually fall in love with her?"

He cocked his head. "Would it shock you if I told you never?"

Never?

Shaken to the core, Abby got up from the table and put their cans in the wastebasket.

"I can see that I have."

She whirled around. "But she loved you so much—"

Quiet surrounded them before he nodded. "Now you're disillusioned."

Abby leaned against the counter so she wouldn't fall down. "The loving way you treated her, no one would ever have guessed."

He got up from the table and walked over to her. "Except Michelina, her mother, my parents and now you... We both wanted a baby to make our marriage work."

She couldn't believe it had never worked, not in the sense he meant. Talk about a shocking revelation....

So *that* was the real reason they'd gone so far as to find a surrogate and flaunt convention. It explained Michelina's desperation and her decision not to tell the queen until it was too late to stop it. No wonder Bianca feared another woman coming into Vincenzo's life. The pieces of the puzzle were starting to come together. She could hardly breathe.

"Obviously we were willing to do anything. Again we were presented with a short list. This time it had the names and histories of the women available and suitable to carry our child."

She lifted pleading eyes to him. "Will you tell me the truth about something, Vincenzo?" Her voice throbbed. "Did Michelina want me?"

"Of course. She'd always liked you. She said you had a wonderful sense of humor and found you charming. When she learned you were on that list of possible surrogates who'd passed all the physical tests, like me she was surprised, but happy, too. Our choice was unanimous."

Unable to be this close to him, she left the kitchen for the living room and sat down on the end of the couch. He again chose the chair with the ottoman. They were like an old married couple sitting around before they went to bed.

Abby wished that particular thought hadn't entered her mind. With Vincenzo's revelation, the world as she'd known it had changed, and nothing would ever be the same again. All these years and he hadn't been in love with his wife? He'd been in love seven or eight times, but they didn't count because they weren't royal. She needed to move the conversation onto another subject.

"You were telling me about your father."

Vincenzo let out a sigh. "He wants me to marry again before the baby is born." He came out with it bluntly, rocking her world once more.

"In the beginning Odile was his first choice, only because of his close association with the *duc*. It would be advantageous to both our countries. She hasn't married yet and he feels she would make a fine mother. If she's there from the moment the baby is born, then she'll bond with it."

Abby sucked in her breath. "Does Odile still care for you?" It was a stupid question. The fact that she was still single was glaring proof, but she'd had to say it.

"She thinks she does, but that's because no one else has come along yet whom her grandfather finds suitable. I told Father I couldn't possibly marry Odile because I don't have the slightest feeling for her."

Unable to stand it, she jumped up from the couch.

"This is like a chess game, moving kings and queens around without any regard for human feeling!"

One black brow lifted. "That's where you're wrong. My mother-in-law certainly has a lot of feelings on the subject."

"She knows why you went to France?"

He sat forward. "Every royal household has its spies. That's why she phoned me before I left to tell me she wouldn't stand for it if I ended up marrying Odile. Michelina had been frightened I'd choose Odile over her in the first place."

Incredible. "What did you tell the queen?"

"That there was no chance of it because I don't plan to marry again. For once I'm going to do what my heart dictates and be a good father to my child, period."

Abby started trembling. "I'm sure she didn't believe you." Abby didn't believe it either. He was too young to live out the rest of his life alone. But if he had to marry another royal he didn't love...

"No, but it doesn't matter, because I've made my decision."

"Don't you have to be married to be king?"

"That has been the tradition over the centuries, but Father's still very much alive. If the time comes when someone else must rule, my sister will do it. So in answer to your question, *that's* how my father's trip went. Why don't we get onto another subject and talk about your court case? How did it go?"

She sat back down, still trying to get her head around everything he'd told her. "You know very well how it went. The judge had it put on his calendar for mid-August."

"Excellent. That relieves some of your stress, which

can only be good for the baby. What other cases are you dealing with?"

"I don't know. I—I can't think right now," Abby stammered. She honestly couldn't.

"Let's watch a little television. There's usually a movie on this time of night." He got up from the chair and reached for the remote on the coffee table.

"You don't need to stay with me, Vincenzo. The doctor assured you I'm all right. I know you must be exhausted after being in Gemelli. Please go."

A fierce look marred his features. "You want me to?"

A small gasp escaped. She'd offended him again. "Of course not. It's just that I don't want you to feel you have to babysit me."

"There's nothing I'd rather do. Everything I care about is in this room, and I've been away for weeks."

Shaken again by his honesty, Abby felt his frustration and understood it before he turned on the TV and sat back down again. One glance and she saw that the prince was a channel grazer. Nothing seemed to suit him. On impulse she got up from the couch.

"I'll be right back. I've got something for you." She made a stop at the bathroom, a frequent habit these days. Then she went to the bedroom and pulled her thick scrapbook out of the bottom dresser drawer. She'd had the leather cover engraved in gold letters: *The Prince of Arancia.* She hoped this might brighten his mood.

"Here." She walked over to him. "I'll trade you this for the remote."

He eyed her in surprise. When he got a look at the cover, he let out an exclamation. "I thought this was going to be a gift for the christening."

"I've changed my mind." Abby had compassion for

him and his father, who wanted his son to be happily married and was trying to make it happen in the only way he could think of as king. "You need to see what an impact you've made on the life of your subjects."

Maybe this album would make Vincenzo realize what an important man he was. To live out his life alone wasn't natural or healthy.

"I know the court has a historian who records everything, but this is more personal, with some of my own photos and articles I've found interesting from various magazines and newspapers coming from the U.S. Dad's been receiving the Stateside news for years and I read everything right along with him."

From the moment Vincenzo opened the cover, he went away from her mentally. While she watched the news, he turned page after page, thoughtfully perusing each one. No sound came out of him for at least an hour.

Eventually he closed it and looked over at her. "For the first time in my life, I know what it feels like to have your life flash before your eyes. I don't know what to say, Abby. I'm speechless."

"You're probably tired from viewing all the good works you've done over the years. I hope you realize you've *never* received negative press. Do you have any idea what a great accomplishment that is?"

He studied her as if he'd never seen her before. "I hope *you* realize I've never received a gift like this. You've touched me beyond my ability to express," he said in a husky voice she felt all the way to her toes.

"I'm glad if you're pleased. I consider it an honor to be a friend of yours, and an even greater honor to be the person you and Michelina chose to carry your child. Only a few more months before he or she is here."

She had the impression he wasn't listening to her. "All these photos of yours. I wasn't aware you'd taken them."

"While I was darting around on the grounds with my little camera, I took a lot of pictures and sometimes you were there."

"You got me on my motorcycle!"

"If you have a boy, he'll be thrilled to find out you didn't always behave with perfect decorum. I daresay he'll love it that you were a daredevil. The skinny-dipping I missed, because I had to be in bed and asleep by eleven."

Low laughter rumbled out of him. "I can be thankful your father was the head of security and made sure his daughter minded him."

She smiled. "Do you think you'll be a strict father if you have a girl?"

He got up from the chair and put the album on the coffee table before staring at her. "Probably."

"But since kindness is part of your nature, she won't mind."

He rubbed the back of his neck, looking tired. "Have you had any feelings yet whether you might be having a boy or a girl, Abby? I understand some women instinctively know."

"I've heard that, too, but since I'm not the mother, that's not going to happen to me." Secretly she didn't want him to know how involved she really was with this baby and that she thought about it all the time. "However, there's no law that says the father can't feel inspiration about his own unborn child."

He shook his head. "No indication yet."

"Well, you've got a month before there's the possibility of your finding out. That is, if you want to."

"If it's a girl, Michelina wanted to name her Julietta after her grandmother on her mother's side."

"That's beautiful. And if it's a boy?"

Their gazes held for a moment. "Maximilliano, after three kings in the Di Laurentis line. I'll call him Max."

"I love that name!" she cried. "We had a wonderful Irish setter named Max. He died before we moved here."

Vincenzo looked surprised. "I didn't know that. Why didn't your father get another one when you settled in your apartment?"

"The loss was so great, neither he nor Mom could think about getting another one. They kept saying maybe one day, but that moment never came. Did your family have a pet?"

He nodded. "Several, but by my later teens I was gone so much, my mother was the one who took care of them and they worshipped her."

"That's sweet."

"Whether I have a boy or a girl, I'll make certain they grow up with a dog. It's important."

"I couldn't agree more. Whether you've had a good or bad day, they're always there for you and so loving. My cousin and I liked little creatures. I once kept a cockatoo, a turtle, a snake and a hamster. When each of them died—not all at the same time, of course," she said with a laugh, "Max helped me get through their funerals. Daddy used to say the best psychiatrist is a puppy licking your face."

"Abby..." There was a world of warmth when he said her name. "No wonder Piero's father called you the little nurse."

"It's a good thing he didn't get together with my father to compare notes. If you got him alone, Daddy would tell you I probably killed them all off without meaning to."

She loved the sound of his laughter so much, Abby never wanted it to stop. But for the sake of her sanity and her heart, it was imperative he leave. Quickly she got up from the couch and handed him the scrapbook.

"This is yours to keep. You once saved my life, and now you're taking such good care of me, my thanks will never be enough. Now it's time someone took care of you. Please don't be mad at me if I tell you to go to bed. You look exhausted." She walked to the door and opened it. If he didn't leave, she was on the verge of begging him to stay the night.

"Good night, Your Highness."

In the weeks that followed, Vincenzo made certain his schedule was packed so tight with work he wouldn't be tempted to spend every free moment at Abby's apartment. Though he phoned her every morning before she went to work to know how she felt, he stayed away from her.

The night she'd given him the album, she'd shown him the door before he was ready to leave. When he'd told her the true situation that had existed between him and Michelina, there'd been a definite shift in the universe. He didn't regret his decision to tell her. At this point in the pregnancy, they shared an intimacy that demanded she understand what his marriage had been like so there'd be honesty between them.

The day of the ultrasound was here. His greatest concern was the health of the baby. If something was wrong, then he'd deal with it. Vincenzo had gone back and forth in his mind on the subject of gender and finally decided he didn't want to know. That way both sides of his family would have to go on speculating until the delivery. As for himself, he preferred to be surprised.

He had the limousine pulled around to his private entrance. When Abby appeared in a kelly-green dress with flowing sleeves and a high waist, he lost his breath for a moment. She was finally looking pregnant and more beautiful than she knew with her silvery-gold hair upswept and caught with a comb.

Dr. DeLuca met them in his office first and smiled. "This is the big day. Are you ready for it?"

"It's very exciting," Abby answered. Though she seemed calm, Vincenzo knew she had to be nervous.

"Will you come in to watch the ultrasound, Vincenzo?"

"Yes!"

Abby looked stunned. "You really want to?"

Vincenzo caught her blue gaze. "I've been waiting for this from the moment we found out you were pregnant."

"I—I'm excited, too," she stammered, rather breathlessly, he thought.

"Excellent," the doctor said. "If you'll come this way with me. It won't take long."

They followed him through another door to the ultrasound room. The doctor told Vincenzo to sit at the side of the bed while Abby lay down. His heart picked up speed to realize this moment had come. He didn't intend to miss a second of this whole process.

Abby's face had blushed when he'd said yes. He knew she'd been trying her hardest to keep her professional distance, but at this point in the pregnancy that was impossible. Having a baby was an intimate experience and she'd never been "just a surrogate" to him.

Over the last few months she'd come to be his whole world. It was miraculous that a sonogram could see inside her gorgeous body, where his baby was growing. The body he'd once rescued from the sea. How could he have known that one day she'd carry his child? He couldn't think about anything else.

Michelina was the mother of his child, but right now his focus was on Abby while the doctor put special gel on her stomach. For several nights he'd had trouble sleeping while his mind thought of all the things that might be wrong with the baby.

She shared a searching glance with Vincenzo as the doctor moved the transducer around her belly. Suddenly they both heard a heartbeat coming from the monitor. The doctor pointed to the screen. "There's your baby. The heart sounds perfect."

"Oh, Vincenzo—our baby! There it is!" In the moment of truth, her guard had come down, thrilling him with her honesty. As for himself, he couldn't believe what he was seeing and reached for her hand. She squeezed it hard. "It looks like it's praying."

The doctor nodded with a smile. "Nice size, coming along beautifully. No abnormalities I can see. So far everything looks good. This test can't detect all birth defects, but it's a wonderful diagnostic tool and tells me the pregnancy and your baby are both on the right track."

Relief poured off Vincenzo in waves. He looked into her tear-filled eyes. Without conscious thought he leaned over and kissed her mouth. "You're a wonder, Abby," he whispered. "You're giving me the world."

"I'm so thankful everything's all right."

The doctor cleared his throat. "Do you two want to know the gender?"

"That's up to Vincenzo," she said first.

He'd already made up his mind. "I'd rather wait and be surprised."

"Very well. Here are some pictures for you to keep." The doctor explained what Vincenzo was seeing, but he didn't have to, because the shape of the baby was self-evident and filled him with awe. If Michelina were here, the tears would be overflowing. "The fetus is four and half inches long and developing well."

Vincenzo put them in his jacket pocket. "Doctor? How's Abby?"

He removed his glasses. "As you can see, she's fine. No more nosebleeds?" She shook her head. "I'd say Abby is in perfect health. If she continues to do what I told her and rest a little more often after her swims, she should get through this pregnancy in great shape."

That was all Vincenzo wanted to hear, though it didn't take away his guilt that she was risking her life to give him this baby. "Thank you, Dr. DeLuca."

After the older man left the room, Abby got up off the table to fix her dress. "Can you believe it? Our baby's fine."

"I'm glad to hear you say *our* baby. It is our baby now, Abby. And I'm overjoyed to know you're fine, too." He got up from the chair. "This calls for a major celebration." As they walked out of the hospital to the waiting limo, he said, "After work, we're leaving for a weekend aboard the yacht. The doctor wants you to rest and swim and do whatever you like. I'll let you decide our destination once we leave port."

She looked startled. "How can you get away?"

"Very easily."

Once inside the limo, she turned to him. "Vincenzo? Do you think this would be wise?"

A dark frown broke out on his face, erasing his earlier happiness. "Obviously you don't."

"When I tell my father where we're going, he'll tell me it's not a good idea. Already he's talking about our move back to the States. I can tell he's getting nervous about you and me spending any more time together that isn't absolutely necessary."

Vincenzo's jaw hardened. "Has he spoken to my father yet about leaving?"

"Yes. Last night."

That was news to Vincenzo. "How did he take it?"

"He wanted to know the reasons and asked him about our extended family back home."

"Was my father upset?"

"No. He said he'd been expecting it for some time."

Vincenzo grimaced. "Then he didn't try to dissuade your father from leaving."

"No, and we both know why." Her voice trembled. "You and I have shared a unique relationship for many years. The baby's on the way and Michelina is gone. Guilio wants you to take a wife ASAP."

Vincenzo's dark head reared. "Father knows my feelings on the subject. I'm not planning to get married again and am already looking into finding a full-time nanny to help me with the baby."

"You're serious—"

His mouth tightened. "Do you think I would make that up? If so, then you don't know me at all."

"I don't think Guilio has any idea you mean it. The situation is even worse than I'd feared," she muttered.

"What situation?"

"You know exactly what I'm talking about. The only reason I felt all right about becoming a surrogate was because you and Michelina were a team. But she's not here anymore and *I* am."

He sat forward. "I still don't understand you."

"Yes, you do, even if you won't admit it."

"Admit what?"

"You and I have shared a unique relationship over the years. With Michelina gone and me carrying your child, our friendship is now suspect. The fact that your father isn't begging Dad to stay on tells me it will please him once we've left Arancia for good. He wants you to take Odile on the yacht, not me."

"You haven't been listening to me," he ground out.

Her heart thudded harder, because she could feel how upset he'd become. "Vincenzo, you're in a very rocky place right now and grabbing at what is easy and familiar because I've always been around. But you're not thinking straight. For us to go on the yacht could spell disaster. That's why I'm not going with you."

He said nothing while her guilt was warring with her heart, but her guilt won. "Your wife has only been gone a few months. Of course you haven't been able to figure out your future yet. You're in a state of limbo and will be until the baby is born."

"Have you finished?" came his icy question.

"Not quite yet." As long as she'd been this brave, she needed to get it all said. When she felt her lips, they still tingled from Vincenzo's warm kiss. She'd felt it to the very marrow of her bones. If the doctor hadn't been in the room, she would have kissed him back and never stopped.

"If you recall, Michelina was the one who wanted me to live at the palace, but without her there, it will be better if I move back home with Dad until I have the baby." It was true she and Vincenzo felt too comfortable together. To her chagrin she knew his visits and plans involving her were a distraction that kept him from doing some of his normal functions. All of it needed to stop. A change of residence was the key.

His next comment surprised her. "I was going to suggest it after we got back from our cruise."

"I'm glad we're in agreement about that. I'll still be living on the grounds and can get room service whenever I want. Living with my father will put the kind of distance needed to ease the king's mind." To ease her own mind.

Abby had been thinking of the baby as *their* baby. When he'd kissed her after the sonogram, it had felt so right. She couldn't delude herself any longer. Abby was painfully in love with Vincenzo and felt as if his baby was her baby, too.

"In that case I'll ask some of my security people to move your things back this evening."

"I don't have anything except my clothes, really."

They'd reached the law firm. Vincenzo opened the door for her. She stepped outside, aware that the good news from the ultrasound had been swallowed up in the tension that had plagued them since Michelina's death.

"I'll see you this evening, Abby. Take care."

* * *

After putting in a full day's work, Vincenzo grabbed his phone and left for a run in the palace gym to work off his nervous energy. After a heavy workout, he returned to his suite to shower and shave. His phone rang while he was putting on a polo shirt over cargo pants. He'd asked the sentry guard to alert him when Abby got home from work.

Moving fast, he reached the door to her suite before she did. He wanted to catch her off guard. The second she came around the corner and saw him she stopped, causing the fetching green dress to wrap around her long legs for a moment.

"H-How long have you been waiting here?" Her voice faltered.

"Not more than a minute. I'll help you get packed and we'll have a last dinner here on your terrace. In a little while some of the security men will be here to take your things over."

"No, Vincenzo. I—"

"No?"

She looked conflicted. "What I meant to say is that I'm virtually halfway through this pregnancy and everything has gone fine so far. You don't need to wait on me hand and foot anymore!"

"I *want* to. There *is* a difference, you know. Since you're the only person on this planet who's going to make my dreams come true, would you deny me the privilege of showing my gratitude?"

"But you do it constantly."

He sucked in his breath. "Three-quarters of the time I've been out of the country or occupied with business, so that argument won't wash. All you have to do is tell me that you don't want my company and I'll stay away."

Her eyes flashed purple sparks. "I've always enjoyed your company, but—"

"But what?" he demanded.

"We talked about it in the limo. For the time being, it's best if you and I stay away from each other."

"Best for you, or for me?"

"Best for everyone! From the beginning we knew there'd be gossip. With Michelina's death everything has changed and I'm sure the king is wary of it. You have to know that, Vincenzo." Damn if she wasn't speaking truth. "My going back to live with Father will quiet a situation that's building, but you shouldn't be here helping."

"We've already covered that ground."

"And we'll keep covering it for as long as I'm underfoot here or on the royal yacht!" she cried.

"You *do* have a temper." He smiled. "This is the first time I've ever seen it."

Her face filled with color. "I…didn't mean to snap at you."

He gave an elegant shrug of his shoulders. "Instead of us standing around arguing, why don't you open the door and we'll get started on moving you—baggage and all—out of sight."

She drew closer to him. "Be reasonable."

"I'm offering my services to help. What's more reasonable than that?"

"Because it's not your job!"

The only person who'd ever dared talk to him like this was his father. Abby was even more alluring when she showed this side of her. "What do you think my job is? To sit on my golden throne all day long and order my subjects to fetch and carry for me?"

"Yes!"

But the minute she said it, he could tell she was embarrassed and he burst into laughter that filled the hallway. In another second she started laughing with him. "You're outrageous, Vincenzo."

"My mother used to tell me the same thing. Come on and let me in. After a workout in my golden gym, I'm dying for a cold lemonade."

"The door's open," she said in a quiet voice. "I only lock it at night, but there's really no need to do it, because you've assigned bodyguards who are as far away as my shadow."

CHAPTER SEVEN

Vincenzo opened the door and waited for Abby to pass before he entered. But when he saw the sway of her hips, he had to fight the urge to wrap her in his arms and pull her body into him.

Never in his marriage with Michelina, let alone with the other women in his earlier years, had he known such an intense attack of desire, and without the slightest hint of provocation on Abby's part. She'd done nothing to bring out this response in him.

Somewhere along the way his feelings for her as a friend had turned into something entirely different. Perhaps it was the knowledge that she was leaving the palace tonight that had unleashed the carnal side of his nature. Maybe it was the reality of the baby now that he had the pictures in his possession, knowing it lived inside her body.

Her father was a red-blooded man who'd probably warned her ages ago not to go out on the yacht with him. Vincenzo's own father, a man with several quiet affairs in his background, had no doubt made it easy for Abby's father to leave his service to be certain no misstep was taken.

Vincenzo got it. He got it in spades. But the ache and

longing for her had grown so acute, it actually frightened him.

While she was in her bedroom, he phoned the kitchen to have some sandwiches and salad brought up to the room. "This is Signorina Loretto's last evening in the palace. Tonight she's moving back to Signor Loretto's apartment on the grounds. You'll be delivering her meals there from now on when she requests them."

"Very good, Your Highness."

Having quieted that source of gossip for the moment, Vincenzo hung up and went looking for Abby. "I ordered some sandwiches to be brought. While we're waiting, what can I do to help?"

She had several suitcases on the bed and had already emptied her dresser drawers. "Well…there's not much to take. I left most of my things at Dad's. Maybe if you would empty my CDs and DVDs from the entertainment center. I'll clean out the things in the den myself. The men will have to bring some boxes to pack all my books and Michelina's paintings." She handed him an empty shoulder bag.

She had an impressive collection of operas, from *Madame Butterfly* to *Tosca.* Her choice of movies was as varied as the different traits of her personality. He packed all but one of them and went back to the bedroom. "You enjoyed this?"

Abby glanced at the cover. "*24?* I absolutely love that series. Have you seen it?"

"Yes, and I found it riveting from beginning to end."

Her eyes exploded with light. "Me, too! Did you see the series about the signing of the peace accord?" He nodded. "That was my favorite. Even my father thought it was good, and that's saying a lot considering the kind of work he's in. He only picked apart half of the things in it that bothered him."

A chuckle escaped Vincenzo's lips. "Shall we watch a few episodes of it tonight while we eat and direct traffic?"

"That sounds wonderful."

"Bene."

"Oh—someone's knocking."

"I'll get it."

He opened the door and set the dinner tray on the coffee table.

After she'd emptied the bathroom of her cosmetics, she started on the den. Abby worked fast and it didn't take long. "There!" She came back in the living room. "It's done. Now all your poor slaves can move everything to Dad's."

With a smile he told her to sit in the chair and put her feet up on the ottoman. It pleased him that he got no argument out of her. With a flick of the switch, he sat back on the couch and they began watching *24*.

Again it gratified him that she was hungry and ate her sandwich with more relish than usual. He'd been afraid their little scuffle in the hall had put her off her food, but it seemed that wasn't the case.

The thought came into his head that she was probably excited to live with her father again and enjoy his company. Which left Vincenzo nowhere.

He craved Abby's company. During his trip to France she was all he ever thought about. To his surprise, it wasn't because of the baby. Perhaps in the beginning the two had seemed inseparable, but no longer.

Abby was her own entity. Lovely, desirable. Her companionship brought him nothing but pleasure.

"Don't you think the queen is fantastic in this series? She was the perfect person to be cast in that part. How could the king want that other woman when he had a wife like her?" Abby was glued to the set. Vincenzo didn't think her remark was prompted by any other thought than the story itself, but it pressed his guilt button.

In his own way he'd been faithful to Michelina, but it hadn't been passionate love. This need for Abby had only come full force recently. His amorous feelings for her had crept up on him without his being aware.

"She's very beautiful in an exotic way," Vincenzo agreed, but his mind was elsewhere.

"How would it be to have been born that exotically beautiful? I can't even imagine it."

He slanted her a glance. "You have your own attributes. There's only one Abby Loretto."

"What a gentleman you are, Vincenzo. No wonder your subjects adore you."

"Abby—"

"No, no." She sat up straight. "Let me finish. All you have to do is look through that scrapbook again to see it."

A burst of anger flared inside him for his impossible situation.

"If you're trying to convince me to continue playing the role I was born to in life, it's not working. I'm no longer a baby who happened to be the child of a king. I've grown into a man with a man's needs. If I've shocked you once again, I'm sorry."

"I'm not a fool," she said quietly. "I can understand why you balk at the idea of marrying someone you don't love, even if it is your royal duty. After your experience with Michelina, it makes more sense than ever. But I can't believe that someday a woman with a royal background won't come along who sweeps you off your feet so you can take over for your father."

The program had ended. Abby got up from the chair to take the disk out of the machine and put it in the shoulder bag with the others.

He eyed her moodily. "Perhaps that miracle will occur. But we're getting ahead of ourselves. At this point, the birth of our child is the only event of importance in my life. It's all I can think about."

"That event isn't far off now."

No... He had less than six months before she left for the States. Getting to his feet he said, "The men should be here shortly. Come with me. If you're up to a walk, I'll escort you back to your old stomping grounds."

A happy laugh, like one from childhood, came out of her. "That sounds like a plan. I ate an extra sandwich half. The doctor would say that's a no-no. Otherwise at my next appointment I'll weigh in like—"

"Don't say it," he warned her. "I prefer my own vision of you."

She was turned away from him so he couldn't see her reaction. "I'll leave a note to tell them everything is here in the living room ready to go."

Vincenzo waited, then led her down another hall outside her apartment that came out at the side of the palace. They passed various staff as they walked down the steps and out the doors into an early evening.

July could be hot, but the breeze off the Mediterranean kept them cool enough to be comfortable. He'd crossed these grounds hundreds of times before, and many of those times with Abby. But this was different.

If he wasn't fearful of giving her a minor heart attack, he'd reach for her hand and hold it tight while they strolled through the gardens. Her father's apartment was in one of the outbuildings erected in the same style and structure as the palace. At one time it had housed certain members of the staff, but that was a century ago and it had since been renovated.

On impulse he stopped by a bed of hydrangea shrubs in full bloom to pick some flowers. "These are for you." He put them in her arms. "The petals are the color of your eyes. Not blue, not lavender, just somewhere in between."

"Their scent is heavenly." She buried her face in them, then lifted her head. "Thank you," she whispered. "You have no idea how many times over the years I've longed to pick these. Mother called them mop heads. These were her favorite flower and color."

"Maybe it's because she was reminded of them every time she looked into her only baby's eyes." Abby now averted them. "Abby, was there a reason your parents didn't have more children?"

She nodded. "Mom and Dad had me five years after they were married, because he'd been in the military. Two years later they decided to get pregnant again, but by that time Dad had been shot while on duty and it turned out he'd been rendered sterile. They weren't keen on adopting right away. I think it's one of the reasons they decided to move to Arancia, where they could make new memories."

Vincenzo was aghast. "I didn't know. Your father was so devastated when he lost her. I'll never forget."

"No. They were very much in love, but they had a great life all the same."

"And they had you." He was beginning to understand why she and her father were so close.

"Their inability to increase the family size was probably another motivating reason for my wanting to be a surrogate for you and Michelina. It's crazy, isn't it? So many women and men, whether in wedlock or not, seem to have little difficulty producing offspring while others…" Abby didn't finish the rest. She didn't have to.

They continued walking until they reached the apartment where she would live until the baby came. She left him long enough to put the flowers in water and bring the vase into the living room. He watched her look around after she'd set it on the coffee table.

This was the first time Vincenzo had been inside Carlo's suite. Family pictures were spread everywhere. He saw books and magazines her father must have read.

"Is it good to be home, Abby?"

She turned to him. "Yes and no. The apartment at the palace has been like home to me for quite a while. Both Dad and I can be semireclusive without meaning to be. We're both insatiable readers and like our privacy on occasion. He's going to have to put up with me invading his space again."

"Oh, I think he can handle it." Vincenzo happened to know her father had been on a countdown to get Abby out of the country from the time Michelina had died. "I'll stay until the men arrive with your things."

Abby sat down on one of the love seats, eyeing him with some anxiety. "I hope you didn't go to too much trouble to get the yacht ready."

"My father pays the captain a good salary to make certain it's able to sail at any time."

She shook her head. "I don't mean the money."

He let out a sigh. "I know you didn't. Frankly, the only person put out is yours truly, because I had my heart set on taking you to Barcaggio, on the northern tip of Corsica."

"I've never been there. You think I'm not disappointed, too?"

Abby sounded as though she meant it. Her response went a long way toward calming the savage beast within him.

"With your love of history, you'd find it fascinating. They had a unique warning system, with sixty guard towers dating from the fifteenth century, to keep the island safe. At least three towers in sight of each other would light fires to give a warning signal of pirates approaching. The Tower of Barcaggio is one of the best conserved and the water around it is clear like the tropics."

"Don't tell me anything more or I'll go into a deep depression."

A rap on the door prevented him from responding. He was glad the men had come. The sooner they left, the sooner he could be alone with her for a while longer. "I'll answer it."

For the next few minutes, a line of security people walked in with bags and boxes. Vincenzo helped to carry some of her law books into the library. What he saw on the desk gave him an idea. After he'd thanked them and they'd left, he called to Abby.

"Is there something wrong?" She hurried in, sounding a little out of breath.

"I think I've found a way we can be together for meals without leaving our suites."

She looked at him with those fabulous eyes. "How?"

"We'll coordinate our meals for the same time every evening and talk on Skype while we eat. That way I can check on you and know if you're lying when you tell me you're feeling fine."

Her lips twitched. "That works both ways. I'll know if you're in a mood."

"Exactly. Is it a deal?"

"Be serious, Vincenzo."

His heart beat skidded off the charts. "When I get back to my apartment, I'll Skype you to make sure everything's working properly."

"You don't mean every night?"

"Why not? Whether I'm away on business, out of the country or in the palace, we both have to stop for food, and we're usually alone. At the end of a hectic day, I'd rather unwind with you than anyone else. It'll save me having to go through Angelina to find out your condition for the day. Shall we say seven?"

"That'll last about two minutes before you're called away to something you can't get out of."

He decided he'd better leave before her father showed up. Together they walked to the entrance of the apartment. "Shall we find out? How about we give this a thirty-day trial? That should keep the gossips quiet. Whoever misses will have to face the consequences."

Amusement lit up her eyes. "You're on, but a prince has so many commitments, methinks *you'll* be the one who will wish you hadn't started this."

Vincenzo opened the door. "Don't count on it. I'll be seeing you as soon as I get back to my apartment." He glanced at his watch. "Say, twenty minutes?"

"I won't believe it till I see you."

With that challenge, he left at a run for the quick trip

back to his suite. There was more than one way to storm the citadel for the rest of her pregnancy without physically touching her. He didn't dare touch her.

It disturbed him that though he'd been in a loveless marriage, he could fall for another woman this fast. He was actually shocked by the strength of his feelings. To get into a relationship was one thing, but for Abby to be the woman, Vincenzo needed to slow down so he wouldn't alarm her. He knew she was attracted to him. It wasn't something she could hide, but she never let herself go.

Because of her control, he had to hold back, but they couldn't exist teetering on the brink much longer. Thanks to cybertechnology, he'd found a way to assuage some of his guilt. Without others knowing, he could be with her every night for as long as he wanted to satisfy his need to see and talk to her while he focused on the baby.

Vincenzo intended to be a good father, but he was struggling with the fact that he'd fallen for the woman who was carrying his child. What did that say about him?

Abby hurriedly put away her clothes and got settled as best she could before heading for the library. Passing through the living room, she picked up the vase of flowers and carried it with her.

After putting it on the desk, she sat down at her dad's computer, ready to answer Vincenzo's call. The big screen rather than her laptop screen would be perfect to see him, *if* he did make contact. She didn't doubt his good intentions, but she knew from her father that the prince followed a tight schedule, one that often ran late into the evenings.

In her heart she knew the decision to move home had been the right one, but when Vincenzo had walked out the door a little while ago, a feeling of desolation swept through her. Her move from the palace had marked the end of the third journey. Now she was embarking on the fourth into the unknown and had the impression it would try her mettle.

She'd lost Michelina, who'd provided the interference. Now it was all on Vincenzo to support her, but he'd made the wise decision to stay at a distance. So had she, yet already she felt herself in free fall.

Trust that clever mind of his to dream up Skyping as a way to stay in touch without distressing their fathers or the queen. As she was coming to find out, Vincenzo's resourcefulness knew no bounds.

Unable to resist, she leaned over to smell the hydrangeas. She'd never see one again without remembering how he'd just stopped and picked an armload for her.

The way to a woman's heart... Vincenzo knew them all, she admitted to herself in an honest moment. He was in there so tightly, she was dying from the ache. There'd never be room for anyone else. The video-call tone rang out, making her jump.

"Good evening, Abby." She'd put the speaker on full volume to make certain she could hear him. The sound of his deep, velvety voice brought her out of her trance-like state.

His looks went beyond handsome. Adrenaline rushed through her veins. "Good evening, Your Highness."

"You've become very formal since I left you."

"I've got stage fright." It was the truth. No one

in Arancia would believe what she was doing, and with whom.

"Our connection is good. We should have no problem communicating tomorrow evening."

"I might have one problem with the time. Dad is going to be home early for a dinner I'm cooking. Would you mind if we said eight-thirty?"

"I'll make a note on my agenda," he teased.

She smiled. "This is fun, Vincenzo."

"It's not the same as being with you in person, but I'm not complaining. Would you answer a question for me?"

"If I can."

"Did Dr. DeLuca let you know the gender of the baby?"

Her lungs froze. "No. He wanted to obey your wishes. I think you're wise not to know yet. Then your father and the queen would either be planning on a future king or future princess. This way everyone's still in the dark."

He chuckled. "I love the way you think, especially when you read my mind so easily. However, there is one thing I'm curious about. You never talk about the baby."

Pain stabbed at her heart. "I've been taking Dr. Greco's advice—don't think about the actual baby too much. Better to stay focused on taking care of yourself rather than dwelling on a child that won't be yours."

His face sobered. "How's that advice working out for you?"

She took a deep breath. "I'm finding it's very hard to carry out. I have to admit that if you hadn't asked me that question just now, I would know you had a stone for a heart."

"Abby," his voice grated, "you've accepted to do the impossible for me. You wouldn't be human if you weren't thinking about the baby day and night."

"You're right. During the talks I had with you and Michelina before I underwent the procedure, I made a decision to be like the postman who delivers the mail without knowing what's inside the letters.

"If a postman were to open one, he'd probably be so affected he would never make it to the next destination. Getting the ultrasound today was a lot like opening that first letter. I can't not think about the baby, whether it's a boy or a girl, if it will look like you or Michelina or someone else in your families."

Vincenzo turned solemn. "I've told you before, but I'll say it again. I'm in awe of you, Abby. You've taken on a weight too heavy to bear."

"You took on a weight, too. Not every man would trust a stranger with the life of his unborn child."

"You're no stranger," he answered in a smoky tone.

"You know what I mean."

"I don't think you know what *I* mean. You were never a stranger to me. A child in the beginning, of course, but from the beginning always a friend. I feel like I've known you all my life. It seemed a natural thing that you became our baby's surrogate mother."

She moistened her lips. "Depending on when the baby decides to come, we could be halfway home right now." Abby didn't want to think about the big event because of what it would mean. The thought of permanent separation was killing her. "Have you bought any things for the baby yet?"

"I'm glad you brought that up. In a few days I'm

going to go shopping and would like your help to set up the well-furnished nursery."

He couldn't know how his comment thrilled her. "I'd love to be involved."

"I'll send you pictures online and we'll decide on things together."

"Do you know where you're putting the nursery?"

"Either in my apartment or the room down the hall next to it."

"What did Michelina want?"

"We never got that far in our thinking. Her concerns over telling Bianca about the pregnancy overshadowed the fun."

Of course. "Well, it's fun to think about it now. If it's in your apartment, you'll have a nanny coming and going out of your inner sanctum." His low chuckle thrilled her. "When you're up all hours of the night with a baby with colic, will you be glad it's near at hand or not?"

"I'll have to think on that one."

"While you do that, what's on your schedule for to-morrow?"

"You really don't want to know."

"Why don't you let *me* decide?"

His smile was wicked. "Remember that you asked. First I'll do a workout in the pool when I get up, then I'll get dressed and eat breakfast with my father, who will tell me what's on his mind. I'll scan a dozen or so newspapers on certain situations in the world.

"At ten I'll visit the Esposito social enterprise to meet the staff and disadvantaged young people working on a building project at Esposito Ricci.

"At eleven-thirty I'll meet representatives of the San

Giovani Churches Trust, the National Churches Trust and restoration workers at Gallo-Conti.

"At noon I'll meet with the different faith communities at Gravina, where I'll be served lunch.

"At one-thirty, in my capacity as president of business, I'll visit the Hotel Domenico, which has been participating in my initiative to promote the meet-and-greet program in all the hotels. I'll visit the shop, which has been created in the meet-and-greet center, and chat with locals.

"At ten to three, as patron of the Toffoli Association, I'll meet staff and residents working at San Lucca Hospital. At four I'll meet pupils and staff at Chiatti Endowed Schools, where I'll tour the school hall and chapel. The pupils have prepared a brief performance for me.

"At ten to five I'll meet local community groups at the town hall in Cozza, as well as some members of the town council.

"At five-thirty, as president and founder of the Prince's Trust, I'll meet with young people who have participated in programs run by the trust, particularly the team program at the Moreno Hotel in Lanz."

Abby tried to take it in, but couldn't. "You made that up."

He crossed himself. "I swear I didn't."

"You mean that's all? That's it? You didn't have time to ride around in your made-for-the-prince sports car?" she exclaimed. "You're right, Vincenzo. I really didn't want to know and never want to think about it again."

Coming over the Skype, his laughter was so infectious she laughed until she had tears, which was how her father found her when he walked in the den. He could see Vincenzo in all his glory on the screen.

"Abby? Why aren't you talking?"

Her father had leaned over to smell the hydrangeas. "I have company."

Vincenzo didn't blink an eye. "Tell your father good evening."

"I will. *Buonanotte,* Your Highness."

She turned off the Skype. Nervous, she looked over at her dad, who had the strangest look on his face.

"Guilio told me his son has always been perfectly behaved. I wonder what could have happened to him."

Abby got up from the desk, needing to think of something quick. "He's going to be a father."

Carlo gave her a hug. "That must be the reason. Welcome home, sweetheart."

CHAPTER EIGHT

REPORTERS BESIEGED ABBY as she and Signor Giordano came out of the Palazzo di Giustizia in downtown Arancia. She'd won the case for him and it meant some big changes for the country's trade policies. Judge Mascotti had summoned her to the bench after announcing his ruling.

"I realize the palace was interested in this case, but I want you to know I made my decision based on the merits you presented."

Abby couldn't have been more pleased to hear those words.

For court she'd pulled her hair back to her nape and used pins to hold a few coils in place.

She'd worn a navy designer maternity outfit with a smart white jacket. The dress draped from a high waistline and fell to the knee. Her bump seemed quite big to her already, but the jacket camouflaged it well. On her feet she wore strappy white sandals.

Mid-August meant she was into her twenty-third week of pregnancy. Two days ago she'd had her first episode of Braxton-Hicks contractions, but the doctor said it was normal because her body was getting ready.

When Vincenzo found out, he had a talk with Dr. De-Luca and they both decided she should quit work.

Abby wasn't ready to stay home yet. Without work to do she'd go crazy, but she'd made an agreement in the beginning and had to honor it. When she got back to her office there was a celebration with champagne, not only because this case was important to their firm, but because it was her last day at work.

Everyone thought she was going back to the States, so she let them think it. Carolena poured white grape juice into her champagne glass when no one was looking. That was how she got through the party. If some of them realized she was pregnant, no one said anything.

After Skyping with Vincenzo every night from the start, except for the night she'd gone to the hospital about her false contractions, she told Carolena to Skype her at the apartment. Until the birth of the baby, Abby planned to do research for her friend to help pass the time. Carolena had a backlog of work and had gone crazy over the idea.

They drank to their plan and Abby left the office in brighter spirits than before. She walked out to the limo pretty much depleted energywise after her court appearance. Once settled inside, she rested her head against the back of the seat and closed her eyes, still thinking about what the judge had said to her.

She worked hard on every case, but that one had special meaning because it would benefit Arancia. After listening to Vincenzo's schedule for one day, she realized he'd spent his whole adult life promoting the welfare of his country. It felt good to know she'd made a tiny contribution toward his goals.

"Signorina?" She opened her eyes to discover they'd

arrived at the harbor. "Your presence is requested aboard the yacht. If you'll step this way, please."

Her heart thundered in her chest as she climbed out and walked with a security man up the gangplank into the gleaming white royal craft. Angelina was there to meet her.

"The palace heard of your victory in court and wishes to honor you with an overnight cruise. A few of your personal things are on board. Come with me and I'll show you to your cabin. Your orders are to relax, swim, eat and wander the deck at will."

"Thanks, Angelina," she murmured, too overcome to manage any more words and followed her. Strange as it was, this meant she'd miss her nightly conversation with Vincenzo. How crazy was that, when anyone else would be jumping out of their skin with joy at such a privilege?

But she'd lived on the palace grounds for years and inside the palace for four months of that time. She'd learned that if Vincenzo wasn't there, it didn't matter if the whole place was paved in gold. Since the judge's ruling, she'd been living to talk to him about everything tonight. Now she'd have to wait until tomorrow night.

"Is there anything else I can do for you?" Angelina asked from the doorway. The separate cabins were on the main deck, with a glorious view of the sea.

"I'm fine, thanks. Right now I just want to lie down. It's been a long day." She checked her watch. Five to six.

"Of course. If you need something, pick up the phone and the person on the other end will contact me. There's food and drink already on the table for you."

She nodded and closed the door after her. The queen-size bed looked good. After closing the shutters over the windows, Abby went to the bathroom, then removed her jacket and sandals. She ate half her club sandwich and some fruit salad before walking over to the bed. She'd undress all the way later. For the moment she was too tired to take off the sleeveless dress before she simply lay down to close her eyes for a little while.

The last thing Abby remembered before she lost consciousness was the movement of the yacht. When she heard someone calling her name, she thought it was the prince talking to her through Skype. She stirred.

"Vincenzo?"

"I'm right here."

"Oh, good. I wanted to talk to you and was afraid we wouldn't be able to until tomorrow night." But as she sat up in the semidark room, she realized something wasn't right. Abby wasn't at the desk. She was on the yacht and there was Vincenzo standing right in front of her in jeans and a sport shirt.

Her pulse raced. "You're here! I mean, you're *really* here."

"I knocked, but you didn't hear me, so I came in the room to check up on you. You didn't eat a lot of the dinner Angelina brought in."

"I was too tired to eat very much when I reached the room." Abby's hair had come unpinned and fell around her shoulders. "How did you get here?"

"I flew aboard on the helicopter. Are you all right?"

No. She wasn't! Abby hadn't seen him in person in about six weeks. The shock was too much and she was totally disoriented.

"Abby?" he prodded.

"Yes," she said too loudly, sounding cross. He was

much too close. She smoothed the hair out of her eyes. "You're not supposed to be here."

"Don't get up," he admonished gently, but she felt at a disadvantage sitting there and stood up anyway. "You're the loser in our contest, remember? This is the penalty I've chosen to inflict, so you're stuck with me until morning."

Her body couldn't stop trembling. "I confess I didn't think you could stick to it."

"Is that all you have to say?"

She'd been caught off guard and didn't know if she could handle this. A whole night together? "What do you want me to say?"

"That you're happy to see me."

"Well, of course I am." But the words came out grouchy.

"You really do look pregnant now. Will you let me feel you?"

If he'd shot her, she couldn't have been more astonished. That's why he kept standing there? It was a perfectly understandable request. It was his baby, after all. But this was one time when she didn't know what to do. To say no to him didn't seem right. But to say yes...

On instinct she reached for his hand and put it on her bump, to make it easier for both of them. It wasn't as if he hadn't touched her before. Heavens, he'd saved her life. She'd sobbed in his arms.

But there had been a whole new situation since then. The warmth of his fingers seeped through the material of her dress, sending a charge of electricity through her body. She held her breath while he explored.

"Have you felt it move?" he asked in a husky voice.

"I've had quickenings, kind of like flutters. At first I

wasn't sure. They only started a few days ago. But when I lay down a few hours ago, I felt a definite movement and knew it wasn't hunger pains."

"It's miraculous, isn't it?" His face was so close to hers, she could feel his breath on her cheek. He kept feeling, shaping his hand against her swollen belly. "I'm glad you're through working and can stay home, where you and the baby are safe."

She bowed her head. "No place is perfectly safe, Vincenzo."

"True, but you were on television today in front of the courthouse. I saw all those steps and a vision of you falling. It ruined the segment for me."

"Signor Giordano had hold of my arm."

"I noticed. He's recently divorced from his wife."

How did Vincenzo know that? But the minute she asked herself the question, she realized how foolish she was. He always checked out everything she did and everyone she worked with.

"I found him very nice and very committed to his fast-track proposal."

"Has he asked you to go out with him?"

Why did Vincenzo want to know? It couldn't be of any importance to him. "He did when he put me in the limo."

His hand stopped roving. "What did you tell him?"

"What I told everyone at my goodbye party. I'm moving back to the States." If she said it long and hard enough, she'd believe it, but his tension heightened. Being barefoot, Abby felt shorter next to his well-honed physique. She took the opportunity to ease away from him before turning on the switch that lit the lamps on either side of the bed.

He gazed at her across the expanse. "Are you still exhausted?"

No. His exploration of her belly had brought her senses alive and no doubt had raised her blood pressure. If he was asking her if she wanted to go up on deck and enjoy the night, the answer was yes. But she could hear her father saying, "I wouldn't advise it."

They'd both crossed a line tonight. His wish to feel the baby was one thing, but she'd sensed his desire for her. Since her own desire for him had been steadily growing for months, there was no point in denying its existence. Once you felt its power and knew what it was, all the excuses in the world couldn't take that knowledge away. Could you die of guilt? She wondered...

But to give in to it to satisfy a carnal urge would cheapen the gift. She'd told the queen this was a sacred trust. So she smiled at him.

"Maybe not exhausted, but pleasantly tired. I need a shower and then plan to turn in. Why don't we have breakfast in the morning on deck and enjoy a swim? That I would love." *Keep him away from you, Abby.*

"We'll be along the coast of Corsica at dawn. If you're up by seven-thirty, you'll see the water at its clearest."

Part of her had been hoping he'd tell her he didn't want her to go to bed yet, but he was a highly principled man and had made a promise to get her safely through this experience. "I'll set my alarm for that time and join you."

"Good night, then." As Vincenzo turned to leave she called his name.

"Thank you for this unexpected surprise."

"You won the court case and deserve a treat. Everyone in the country will benefit."

"Thank you. But I'm talking about more than a night on this fabulous yacht. I want to thank you for our nightly video sessions. I looked forward to every one of them."

His brows lifted. "They're not over."

"I'm so glad to hear that."

"They've saved my life, too, Abby." On that confession, he left her cabin and shut the door.

To read more into those words would be Abby's downfall. They were both waiting out this pregnancy on tenterhooks in a cage no one else could see. It was an unnatural time under the most unnatural circumstances a prince and a commoner could be in. The closer they got to the delivery date, the more amazed she was that she and Vincenzo had made things work this far.

During the early-morning hours, the sun burned a hole through clouds over the Mediterranean. The ray of light penetrated the turquoise water near the guard tower he'd told her about. Abby had thrown on a beach robe and leaned over the yacht's railing to see how far down it went, causing her braid to dangle.

Vincenzo had done several dives and wore his black trunks, so she could see his hard-muscled body clearly. The dramatically rugged landscape continued underwater in the form of more mountains, canyons, needles, peaks and rocky masses. He clung to some huge rocks below the waterline, then moved downward until he was almost out of sight.

Though he swam like a fish, she was nervous until she saw him come up for air. Abby wished she'd brought a camera to capture him on film, but when she'd left the courthouse yesterday, she could never have imagined where she'd end up.

"I'm envious of you!" she shouted to him. Even though it was August, she'd bet the water was cold this morning, but he seemed impervious to any discomfort.

"One day soon you'll be able to do this," he called back to her.

Not this. Not here. Not with him.

"Is there anything dangerous lurking down there?"

"Only a big white."

"Vincenzo!"

A grin appeared on his striking face. With his black hair slicked back, he was the stuff women's fantasies were made of. "Is breakfast ready?"

She giggled. "Have I told you how funny you are sometimes? You know very well your food is always ready!"

"Well, I'm starving!"

"So am I!"

He swam with expertise to the transom of the fifty-two-foot luxury yacht and came aboard. In a minute they were seated around the pool being served a fantastic meal. Once they'd eaten, Abby took off her robe to sunbathe for a little while. Their loungers were placed side by side. Talk about heaven!

The yacht was moving again, this time around the island. By tomorrow evening her idyll would be over, but she refused to think about that yet.

After the intimacy they'd shared last night when he'd reached out to feel the baby, she decided it didn't matter that he could see her pregnant with only her bikini on. Those black eyes slid over her from time to time, but he never made her feel uncomfortable.

The deck steward brought them reading material in case they wanted it. Vincenzo propped himself on one elbow to scan the newspaper. "You made the front page yesterday. I quote, 'A new star has risen in the legal firmament of Arancia.

"'One might take her for a film star, but Signorina Abigail Loretto, a stunning blonde with the law firm of Faustino, Ruggeri, Duomo and Tonelli, has a brain and pulled off a coup for import trade in Judge Mascotti's court that had the attorney for Signor Masala already filing an appeal.'"

Vincenzo handed it to her so she could have a look. "Have I told you how proud I am of you?"

Her body filled with warmth that had nothing to do with the sun. "Am I lying here on the royal yacht being treated like a princess by none other than His Royal Highness?"

"I think we need to start a scrapbook for you."

"It will be a pitiful one, since I quit work yesterday. This was it. My one meteoric rise to fame that came and went in a flash. I hope it's all right with you if I help do research for Carolena at the apartment."

"Your life is your own, Abby. My only concern is that you keep your stress level to a minimum, for your sake as well as the baby's."

"Agreed."

His eyes played over her. "You're picking up a lot of sun, but it's hard to feel it with the breeze."

"You're right. I'll cover up in a minute."

"Abby—" She could tell he had something serious on his mind.

"What is it?"

"When you hear what I have to tell you, it will cause you some stress, but it has to be said."

"Go on."

"We've told Gianna about the situation."

Alarmed, she sat up in the lounger and reached for the beach towel to throw over her. "How long has she known?"

"My sister saw you on the evening news. Since she's known you for years, too, she phoned me about it. I was with Father when her call came through. Now that you've been identified to the public, so to speak, we decided it was time she knew about the baby in case word got out and she hadn't heard it first."

"That makes sense, Vincenzo. She'd be hurt if you hadn't told her." Her heart pounded so hard, it was painful. "Did she have the same reaction as your mother-in-law?"

He sat up to talk. "No. She thinks it's terribly modern of all of us—her exact words—but couldn't believe Michelina would go along with the idea."

"Because of the queen?"

"No," he murmured, sounding far away. Abby supposed she knew the real answer deep down.

"Then it was because *I'm* the surrogate."

Vincenzo's silence for the next minute told its own tale. "It's nothing personal," he said in a grating voice.

"I know that."

"She's afraid of how it's going to look when the news gets out. You and I have already discussed this at length, but I wanted you to be prepared when she and her husband come for a visit."

"How soon?"

"Tonight."

Abby's breath caught.

"If she weren't coming, we could have stayed out another night. You don't have to meet with her if you don't want to, Abby. This is none of her business."

"But it is, Vincenzo. She's going to be your baby's aunt. We'll face her together like we faced the queen. Was she good friends with Michelina?"

He nodded. "They were very close. I know for a fact Gianna's hurt because Michelina never confided in her about this."

"Some matters aren't for anyone's ears except your own spouse. Surely she understands that."

"You would think so." He threw a towel around his shoulders and got up from the lounger. "Come on. You need to get out of the sun."

She pulled on her robe and they walked to the covered bar laid out with cocktail tables and padded chairs. Soft rock played through the speakers. One of the stewards brought them iced lime drinks.

"I'm sorry your sister is upset, but I'm not worried about it, if that's what you're thinking. I had my trial of fire with the queen." A smile slowly broke from her.

Vincenzo saw it and covered her free hand with his own. "Then I won't take on that worry." He squeezed it, then let her go with reluctance and sat back. But she still felt the warmth and pressure of his after it had been removed.

"How long will it take us to get back to port?"

"For you, about five hours."

She groaned inside. "But not you."

"No. Another helicopter will be arriving in a half hour to take me back." The yacht had everything, including a landing pad. "Before I leave, I want to dance with you."

Ignoring her slight gasp, he reached for her and drew her into his arms. He moved them around slowly, pressing her against him.

"Do you know how incredible it is to be holding you in my arms while our baby is nestled right here between us?"

Abby couldn't breathe.

"I've needed to feel you like this for a long time. Don't fight me, Abby." He kissed her cheek and neck, her hair.

She felt as if she would faint from ecstasy. The last thing she wanted to do was push him away. For a little while she let herself go and clung to him. "I wish you didn't have to leave," she whispered.

"It's the last thing I want to do." While she was trying to recover from her severe disappointment that he had to go, he brushed his lips against hers before giving her a man's kiss, hot with desire. It spiked through her like electricity.

Close to a faint, she heard the sound of rotors and saw a speck in the sky coming their way. As it grew larger, she felt her heart being chopped into little pieces. Vincenzo had given her a fantastic surprise, but she wished he hadn't. She couldn't handle being around him like this and being kissed like this, only for him to be whisked away. This was torture.

"I'm afraid it will be better if no one sees us arriving together. The paparazzi will be out in full force. Angelina's going to help you leave with some of the staff from the yacht."

"You've had to go to a lot of trouble for me."

"How could it possibly compare with what you're doing for me?" She averted her eyes. "I'll send for you when it's time. We'll meet in the state drawing room as before. It's the only neutral ground in the palace, if you understand my meaning."

She knew what he meant. They couldn't talk to his sister in either of their apartments or his father's.

Though it was painful, she slowly eased out of his arms. "You need to get ready to go, so I'll say goodbye now and take a shower in my cabin."

He moved fast and accompanied her along the deck to open the door for her. But when she went inside and started to shut it, he stood there so she couldn't. His eyes stared at her. The desire in those black depths was unmistakable. She went weak at the knees. A small nerve throbbed at the corner of the mouth she was dying to taste over and over again.

"I'll see you tonight," he whispered in a raw-sounding voice she hardly recognized.

"Stay safe, Vincenzo. Don't let anything happen to you in that helicopter. Your child's going to need you."

"Abby—the last thing I want to do is leave you."

Then don't! she wanted to cry out. "With family coming, you have to."

His face darkened with lines. "Promise me you won't let Gianna get to you."

"She couldn't."

Abby had the feeling he wanted to warn her about something, then changed his mind.

"It'll be all right, Vincenzo."

His jaw hardened. "I'll Skype you at ten tonight."

She'd be living for it. *"A presto."*

Abby shut the door. After the passion in that kiss, this time it had to be goodbye for good.

When Marcello ushered Abby, wearing her jacketed white dress with the brown trim, into the drawing room, she glowed from the sun she'd picked up on her one day cruise. Her blond hair had been caught back with a dark comb. The newspaper had been right. She was stunning. Vincenzo had never seen her looking so beautiful.

"Gianna and I are glad you're here, Abby," he said, welcoming her to come in and sit down.

"I am, too. It's wonderful to see you again, Gianna." Since they'd all known each other for years, Vincenzo had dispensed with the pretense of formality, hoping to put Abby at ease. But he needn't have worried. She had incredible poise. Her self-possession came naturally to her and served her well in her profession.

Gianna, a tall brunette, smiled at her. "Pregnancy becomes you. You look well."

Vincenzo cringed. His sister wasn't pregnant yet and had gone straight for the jugular. So far the two women in his life who'd insisted on talking to Abby since Michelina's death had managed to show a side that couldn't help but hurt her, though she would deny it.

"Thank you. I feel fine."

His sister crossed her slim legs. "I told Vincenzo I wanted a private word with you. Do you mind?"

"Of course not."

He took that as his cue. "I'll be outside," he told Abby before leaving the room. For the next ten minutes he paced before she came out of the double doors. Despite her newly acquired tan, she'd lost a little color. He was furious with Gianna, but since their father had insisted she be allowed to talk with Abby, Vincenzo had given in, knowing it wouldn't go well.

"Are you all right?"

"I'm fine."

"I'll walk you back to your father's apartment."

"Please don't." It was the first time in their lives she'd ever spoken to him in a cold tone. Gianna had to have been brutal.

"I'll call you as soon as I know you're home." When Abby didn't respond he said, "We have to talk. I want your promise that you'll answer, otherwise I'll show up at your door."

"I—I need to go." Her voice faltered before she hurried down the hall and disappeared around the corner.

Tamping down his fury, he went back inside the drawing room. Gianna was waiting for him. He knew that look. "What in the hell did you say to her?"

Ten minutes later he started for the doors.

"Don't you dare walk out on me!"

Vincenzo wheeled around. "I already did." He strode rapidly through the corridors to the east entrance of the palace and raced across the grounds to Carlo's apartment. Once he arrived, he knocked on the door and didn't stop until Abby answered. After closing the door, he took one glance at her wan face and pulled her into his arms.

"Gianna told me what she unleashed on you. I'm so sorry." He cupped the back of her head and pressed it into his shoulder, kissing her hair. "You have to know it was her pain talking. She had to marry a man she didn't love and so far she hasn't conceived. Though she's attractive, she's not a beauty like you and never was. Her jealousy of you and your association with Michelina finally reared its ugly head."

It was like déjà vu with Abby sobbing quietly against him, the way she'd done after she'd been rescued.

"She used scare tactics on you so you'll leave, but don't you know I'd never let you go?"

After she went quiet, she pulled away from him. Her eyes resembled drenched violets. "Maybe I should."

"Abby—how can you even say that?"

She stared at him, looking broken. "The issues she brought up I've already faced in my mind, except for one."

"Which one?"

"Your child. The thought of it growing up with doubts about who its mother really is breaks my heart."

Vincenzo didn't think he could ever forgive Gianna for planting that absurd fear in Abby's mind. "The baby will be a part of Michelina. Michelina had distinctive genes, like her mother and brother. They don't lie, remember?"

She took a shuddering breath. "You're right. How silly of me."

"Not silly, only human in the face of behavior I haven't seen come out of my sister since she was a teenager and threw a tantrum because she couldn't get her own way. But she'll calm down in time, just like the queen. I left her with the prospect that when Father steps down, she'll be the new ruler of Arancia.

"As Dr. DeLuca reminded us, this is a nine-day wonder that will be over for her soon. The good news is, you've walked through your last fire. From now on, we wait until our baby sends you into labor. Does the prospect make you nervous?"

She nodded and put on a smile for him. "Yes, but I'm not frightened, exactly. How could I be, when hundreds of thousands of babies are born every day? It's just that this baby is special."

"After finding out what it's like to be an expectant father, I've learned every baby is special if it's yours, royal or not. If Gianna had given me the chance, I would have told her you've been a blessing to Michelina and me. She would say the same thing if she were here, so never forget it."

"I won't."

"Do you believe me, Abby? It's imperative you believe it."

Her eyes searched his. "Of course I do."

"Thank you for that." Without conscious thought, he brushed his lips against hers. "I have to go and we'll see each other tomorrow night at seven o'clock. Right?"

"Yes."

Before he went back to the palace, he hurried down to their private beach. After ripping off his clothes, he lunged into the water and swam until he had no more strength before returning to his suite.

His phone registered four messages, from Marcello, his father, Gianna, and Gianna's husband, Enzio.

Not tonight.

Normally he didn't drink except on certain occasions. But right now he needed one or he'd never get to sleep. However, even the alcohol couldn't quiet the adrenaline gushing through his system since he'd held Abby. He'd felt every curve of her body.

Tonight he'd felt the baby move against him, igniting a spark that brought him to life in a brand-new way. It was something he'd never expected to feel. The last thing he remembered before oblivion took over was the sweet, innocent taste of her lips. *Abby, Abby.*

CHAPTER NINE

WHEN ABBY COULDN'T reach her father, she left him a message.

"Hi, Dad. I'm just leaving the doctor's office and wanted to report that my checkup went fine. Can you believe my pregnancy is almost over? I'm meeting Carolena for dinner at Emilio's, then we're going to the concert hall to see Aida. Be sure and eat your dinner. It's in the fridge."

This was one night she wouldn't be Skyping with Vincenzo. Last night she'd told him her plans. He wasn't too happy about her sitting through an opera all evening, but she promised to take it easy during the day.

Since the night when everything had come to a head because of Gianna, he hadn't surprised her by showing up unexpectedly. For the last little while he'd been treating her like a friend. She was doing the same. No contact except for technology. It was much easier this way and relieved her of a lot of guilt.

Gianna had forced Abby to face up to the fact that she was desperately in love with Vincenzo. When he'd kissed her before leaving the apartment, it had taken every ounce of her will not to return it. That kiss from him had been one of affection, not passion. It was his way of trying to comfort her.

She loved him for it.

She loved him to the depth of her soul.

During the last scene of *Aida,* she came close to falling apart. Radamès had been taken into the lower part of the temple to be sealed in a dark vault. Aida was hidden there so she could die with him.

When the tenor cried that he'd never see the light of day again, never see Aida again, she told him she was there to die with him. As they fell into each other's arms, Abby choked up. Tears dripped off her chin onto her program because she could imagine a love like that. It was the way she felt about Vincenzo. Before long she'd have the baby and then she'd be gone for good. Thinking of that goodbye was excruciating.

On the way home in the limousine, Carolena teased her that she was full of hormones. Abby attributed her breakdown to the glorious music and voices, but they both knew it was much more than that.

Her dad was at the computer when she walked in the apartment. He lifted his head. "How was the opera?"

"Fantastic."

"You look like you've been crying."

She smiled at him. "Come on, Dad. You know *Aida* is a real tearjerker." They both loved opera.

"Your aunt phoned me today. They've found a house for us near them and sent an email with pictures. Take a look and see what you think. I like it more than any of the others she's sent."

Abby wandered over and stood next to him to check it out. "That's a darling house. I love the Cape Cod style. Let's do it."

Her response seemed to satisfy him. He turned to look at her. "Did you tell Dr. DeLuca about our plans?"

"Yes. He says he has no problem about my flying back to the States within a week of the delivery, provided I'm not having complications. Since Vincenzo is having us flown on the royal jet with a doctor on standby, Dr. DeLuca is fine with it."

"Good."

"He told me something else. Though he hopes I'll go full-term, I shouldn't worry if I start into labor sooner. The baby has dropped and could be born any time now. He says it would be fine. I was glad for that reassurance. My pregnancy has been so free of problems, it's comforting to know that if there's a complication now, the baby will be all right."

"That reassures me, too."

"Dad? Are you having second thoughts about leaving Arancia?"

Their gazes connected. "Absolutely not. There comes a time when you know you're done. How about you?"

"Naturally I'm going to miss it. I've spent more than half my life here, but we have family in Rhode Island and you'll be there. Once I'm settled in a law practice and take the bar, I know I'll be happy."

"I do, too. You'd better get to bed now, honey."

"I'm going. Good night." She kissed his forehead and left for her bedroom.

While she got ready, her mind was on her father. Abby knew he'd had relationships with several women since her mother died, but he seemed eager to leave Arancia. Since she didn't think it was all because of the situation with Vincenzo, she wondered if there was someone back home he'd known before and was anxious to see again.

Once she got under the covers, there was no comfortable position anymore. Then she got hot and threw them off. She'd had backache for the last week and looked like that beached whale. The doctor said she was a good size. Though she'd tried not to think about having to give up the baby, it had kicked her a lot since her sixth month and made her wonder if it was a boy with Vincenzo's great legs.

Abby knew he would have loved to feel it kicking, but by tacit agreement they'd stayed away from each other. She went swimming when he didn't. He didn't pick her up in the limo. Being able to Skype made it possible for them to talk to each other face-to-face and design the nursery, but that was it. Those days would soon be over.

Everything was planned out. Once Abby delivered, she'd be taken to a private place away from any staff or media before the flight back to the States. The contract she'd made in the beginning was specific: no contact with the baby or the parents. Abby's job would be done. That would be it, the end of her association with Vincenzo.

No meetings, no Skyping, no technology to connect them. It had to be that way for the rest of their lives, for the good of the kingdom, for all of them. Vincenzo would be the prince she couldn't forget, but he could never be a part of her life again.

Carolena was getting ready to go to court with a big law case. The work she'd asked Abby to do while she waited out these last few weeks was heaven-sent. Every time she started thinking about the little life getting ready to come into the world, she'd get busy doing more research. But she couldn't turn off her mind in the middle of the night.

Like Vincenzo, this child would be born into that world never knowing anything else. He'd make a marvelous father. She was excited for him, because his whole world was going to change once the doctor put the baby in his arms.

But to never see the baby, to never see Vincenzo again. She sobbed until oblivion took over.

Dr. DeLuca had given her the phone numbers of several former surrogates, but she hadn't felt the need to talk to them. No matter what, every surrogate's experience giving up a baby was different. Hers most of all, since she loved this royal heir and its father with every fiber of her being.

About five in the morning she woke up with lower-back pain. This was a little stronger than usual. She knew it could mean the onset of labor. Then again, it might be because she'd been to the opera last evening and it had been too much for her poor back.

She went to the bathroom and walked around the apartment for a few minutes. The ache subsided. Instead of going back to bed, she sat on the couch with her legs outstretched to watch a Godzilla film in Italian. Her feet were swollen. So were her fingers.

The film put her to sleep, but pain woke her up again. Whoa. She got up to go to the bathroom. Um. It hurt. It hurt a lot.

She went into her father's bedroom. "Dad? Did Mom have a bad backache before I came?"

He shot up in bed. "She sure did. The pain came around to the front."

"Yup. That's what I've got."

"I'll call the doctor."

"Tell him not to alert Vincenzo and tell him no one at the hospital is to leak this to him on the threat of death!"

"You can't ask him that, honey."

"Yes, I can!" She yelled at him for the first time in her life. "I'm the one having this baby and I'm not Vincenzo's wife. This isn't my child." Tears rolled down her hot cheeks. "If something goes wrong, I don't want him there until it's all over. He's been through enough suffering in his life. If everything's fine, then he ca— O-o-h. Wow. That was a sharp pain.

"Dad? Promise me you'll tell the doctor exactly what I said! I've been good about everything, but I want my way in this one thing!

"And make Angelina swear to keep quiet. If she breathes one word of this to Vincenzo, then—oh, my gosh—you'll fire her without pay and she'll never get another job for as long as she lives. I'm depending on you, Dad. Don't let me down."

He put a hand on her cheek. "Honey, I promise to take care of everything." Then he pressed the digit on his phone.

Vincenzo's life had become a ritual of staying alive to hear about Abby's day, but he was slowly losing his mind.

After a grueling session with parliament, he hurried to his apartment for a shower, then rang for some sandwiches and headed for the computer. It was time for his nightly call to Abby. With the baby's time coming soon, he couldn't settle down to anything. The only moments of peace were when he could see her and they'd talk.

Tonight he was surprised because he had to wait for her to tune in. One minute grew to two, then five. He gave her another five in case she was held up. Still no response.

The phone rang. It was Angelina. He broke out in a cold sweat, sensing something was wrong before he clicked on. "Angelina?"

"I wasn't supposed to let you know, but I think you have the right. You're about to become a father, Vincenzo."

What? "Isn't it too soon?"

"Not according to Abby's timetable. She didn't want you to worry, so she didn't want you to come to the hospital until after the delivery, but I know you want to be there. The limo is waiting downstairs to take you to the hospital."

His heart gave a great thump. "I owe you, Angelina! I'm on my way down."

Vincenzo flew out of the apartment and reached the entrance in record time. "Giovanni? Take me to the hospital, stat!"

Everything became a big blur before one of his security men said, "Come this way, Vincenzo." They took the elevator to the fourth floor, past the nursery to one of the rooms in the maternity wing.

"When did she go into labor?"

"Awhile ago," came the vague response. Vincenzo wanted to know more, but a nurse appeared and told him to wash his hands. Then she put a mask and gown on him before helping him into plastic gloves. He couldn't believe this was finally happening.

"Wait here."

As she opened the door, he saw Dr. DeLuca working with Abby. He was telling her to push. His beautiful Abby was struggling with all her might. "Push again, Abby."

"I'm trying, but I can't do this alone. I need Vincenzo. Where is he?" Her cry rang in the air. "I want him here!"

That was all Vincenzo needed to hear. He hurried into the operating room. The doctor saw him and nodded. "He's arrived."

"I'm here, Abby."

She turned her head. "Vincenzo!" He heard joy in her voice. "Our baby's coming! I should have called you."

"I'm here now. Keep pushing. You can do it."

After she pushed for another ten minutes, before his very eyes he saw the baby emerge and heard the gurgle before it let out a cry. Dr. DeLuca lifted it in the air. "Congratulations, Abby and Vincenzo. You have a beautiful boy." He laid the baby across her stomach and cut the cord.

"A *son,* Vincenzo!" Abby was sobbing for joy. "We did it."

"No, you did it." He leaned over and brushed her mouth.

The staff took over to clean the baby. In a minute the pediatrician announced, "The next heir to the throne is seven pounds, twenty-two inches long and looks perfect!"

He brought the bundled baby over and would have placed it in his arms, but Vincenzo said, "Let Abby hold him first."

The moment was surreal for Vincenzo as together

they looked down into the face of the child he and Michelina had created, the child Abby had carried. His heart melted at the sight.

"*Buonasera,* Maximilliano," she said with tears running down her cheeks. "Oh, he's so adorable."

Vincenzo could only agree. He leaned down to kiss the baby's cheeks and finger the dark hair. Carefully he unwrapped their little Max, who *was* perfect, with Michelina's eyes and ears.

"Look, Vincenzo. He has your jaw and the Di Laurentis body shape."

All the parts and pieces were there in all the right places. Vincenzo was overwhelmed.

Dr. DeLuca patted his shoulder. "You should go with the pediatrician, who's taking the baby to the nursery. I need to take care of Abby."

"All right." He leaned down again, this time to kiss her hot cheek. "I'll be back."

An hour later he left the nursery to be with Abby, but was told she was still in recovery. He could wait in the anteroom until she was ready to be moved to a private room. But the wait turned out to be too long and he knew something was terribly wrong.

He hurried to the nursing station. "Where's Signorina Loretto?" He was desperate to see the woman who'd made all this possible. She'd done all the work. She and the baby were inseparable in his mind and heart.

"She's not here, Vincenzo." Dr. DeLuca's voice.

He spun around. "What do you mean? To hell with the agreement, Doctor!"

Vincenzo felt another squeeze on his shoulder and looked up into Carlo's eyes staring at him above the mask he'd put on. "We all knew this was going to be the hard part. Abby's out of your life now, remember?

"Your boy needs you. Concentrate on him. You have all the help you need and a kingdom waiting to hear the marvelous news about the young prince, especially this bambino's grandfather and grandmother."

Vincenzo didn't feel complete without her. "Where is she, Carlo?"

"Asleep. She had back pain around five in the morning. In total she was in labor about fifteen hours. All went well and now that the delivery is over, she's doing fine."

"Tell me where she is," Vincenzo demanded.

"For her protection as well as yours, she's in a safe place to avoid the media."

He felt the onset of rage. "You mean she's been put in a witness protection program?"

"Of a sort. She fulfilled her part of the bargain to the letter and is in excellent health. You once saved her life. Now she's given you a son. Let it be enough."

Carlo's words penetrated through to his soul. What was the Spanish proverb? *Be careful for what you wish, for you just might get it.*

Vincenzo stood there helpless as hot tears trickled down his cheeks.

"Good morning, honey."

"Dad—"

"I'm here."

"This is a different room."

"That's right. You're in a different hospital. You were transported in an ambulance after the delivery."

"I'm so thankful it's over and Vincenzo has his baby."

"Yes. He's overjoyed. I'll turn on the TV so you can see for yourself." Carlo raised the head of the bed a little for her to see without straining.

Abby saw the flash, "breaking news," at the bottom of the screen. "For those of you who are just waking up, this is indeed a morning like none other in the history of the world. There's a new royal heir to the throne of Arancia. Last night at six-fifteen p.m., a baby boy was born to Crown Prince Vincenzo and the deceased Princess Michelina Cavelli by a gestational surrogate mother who we are told is doing well. The new young prince has been named Maximilliano Guilio Cavelli Di Laurentis."

Vincenzo...

"The seven-pound prince is twenty-two inches long."

"Max is beautiful, Daddy." The tears just kept flowing. "He'll be tall and handsome like Vincenzo!"

"According to the proud grandparents, their majesties King Guilio Di Laurentis and Queen Bianca Cavelli of Gemelli, the baby is the image of both royal families.

"We're outside the hospital now, awaiting the appearance of Prince Vincenzo, who will be taking his son home to the royal palace any minute. A nanny is already standing by with a team to ease Prince Vincenzo into this new role of fatherhood.

"Yes. The doors are opening. Here comes the new father holding his son. We've been told he's not going to make a statement, but he's holding up the baby so everyone can see before he gets in the royal limousine."

Darling. Abby sobbed in joy and anguish.

"This must be a bittersweet moment for him without Princess Michelina at his side. But rumor has it that sometime next year the king will be stepping down and the Principality of Arancia will see another wedding and the coronation of Prince Vincenzo."

Abby was dying for Vincenzo, who was being forced to face this. "I can't stand the media, Dad. Couldn't they let him enjoy this one sacred moment he and Michelina had planned for without bringing up the future?"

"Speculation is the nature of that particular beast. But we can be thankful that for this opening announcement, they played down your part in all this. For such forbearance we can thank the king, who told me to tell you that you have his undying gratitude."

Abby's hungry eyes watched the limo as it pulled away from the hospital escorted by security. The roar of the ecstatic crowds filled the streets. Her father shut off the TV.

She lay there, numb. "It's the end of the fairy tale." Abby looked at him. "I can't bear it. I love him, Dad, but he's gone out of my life."

He grasped her hands. "I'm proud to be your father. You laid down your life for him and Michelina and he has his prize. Now it's time for you to close the cover of that scrapbook and start to live your own life."

"You knew about that?"

Her father just smiled. He wasn't the head of palace security for nothing.

Abby brushed the tears off her face. "I gave it to him months ago when he told me he didn't want to be king. I wanted him to look through it and see all his accomplishments."

Her father's eyes grew suspiciously bright. "You've

been his helpmate all along and it obviously did the trick."

She kissed his hand. "Thank you for keeping him away as long as you could. I didn't want him to have to go through any more grief, not after losing Michelina. Forgive me for yelling at you at the apartment?"

"That's when I knew you meant business. As it so happens, I agreed with you, but a man should be at the bedside of the woman who's giving birth to his baby. Evidently Angelina thought so, too. She's the one who told him to get to the hospital quick."

"Bless her. I needed him there."

"Of course you did."

"Lucky for me I was blessed to have you there, too, Daddy."

"Someday you'll get married to a very lucky man, who will be there when the time comes for your own child to be born. I look forward to that day."

Abby loved her father, but he could have no conception of how she felt. Vincenzo was the great love of her life. There would never be anyone else and she would never have a baby of her own. But she'd had this one and had been watched over by Vincenzo every second of the whole experience.

Through the years she would watch Max in secret, because he was her son and Vincenzo's as surely as the sun ruled the day and the moon the night. No one could ever take that away from her.

"Honey? The nurse has brought your breakfast." He wheeled over the bed table so they could eat together. "Do you feel like eating?"

Abby felt too much pain and was too drugged to have

an appetite yet, but to please her father she reached for the juice.

"We haven't talked about you for a long time." She smiled at him. "I want to know the real reason you decided to step down and move back to Rhode Island. Is there a woman in the picture you haven't told me about? I hope there is."

He drank his coffee. "There has been one, but it was complicated, so I never talked about it."

"You can talk to me about it now." Because if there wasn't, then it meant she and her father had both been cursed in this life to love only one person. Now that she'd lost Vincenzo, both she and her dad would be destined to live out the rest of their lives with memories.

"Can't you guess? There's only been one woman in my life besides your mom. It's been you."

"Don't tease me."

"I'm not."

She frowned. "Then why did you decide you wanted to leave Arancia?"

"Because I could see the hold Vincenzo has had on you. Otherwise you would never have offered yourself as a surrogate. If you hope to get on with your life, it has to be away from here."

Abby lowered her head. "I'm afraid he'll always have a hold on me."

"That's my fear, too. It's why we're getting out of Arancia the moment you're ready to travel."

CHAPTER TEN

VINCENZO HAD SUMMONED Angelina to his apartment as soon as he'd returned to the palace with his son. He'd spent time examining Max from head to toe. After feeding him the way the nurse had showed him, and changing his diaper, Vincenzo gave Max to the nanny, who put him to bed in the nursery down the hall. Now there was no time to lose.

"Tell me what you know of Abby's whereabouts, Angelina."

"I can't, Your Highness. Please don't ask me. I've been sworn to secrecy."

"By whom? Carlo?"

"No."

"The king?"

"No."

"Abby?"

She nodded.

He knew it!

"Tell me which hospital they took her to."

Angelina squeezed her eyes tightly. "I don't dare."

"All right. I'm going to name every hospital in Arancia." He knew them all and served on their boards. "All you have to do is wink when I say the right one. That way you never said a word."

"She'll hate me forever."

"Abby doesn't have a hateful bone in her body. She carried my son for nine months and gave me the greatest gift a man could have. Surely you wouldn't deny me the right to tell her thank you in person."

"But she's trying to honor her contract."

"Contract be damned! She's fulfilled it beyond my wildest dreams. If another person had done for you what she's done for me, wouldn't you want to thank them?"

"Yes, but—"

"But nothing. That may have been the rule when Michelina and I signed on with her, but the baby has arrived. There's no more contract. You're free of any obligation. What if I tell you I won't approach her in the hospital?"

After more silence he said, "I'll wait until she leaves. Surely that isn't asking too much. I swear on my mother's grave she'll never know you told me anything."

Still more silence. He started naming hospitals while holding his breath at the same time. Halfway down the list she winked. His body sagged with relief. San Marco Hospital, five miles away in Lanz. Near the airport and several luxury hotels. It all fit.

"Bless you, Angelina. One day soon you'll know my gratitude with a bonus that will set you up for life."

As she rushed away, he phoned his personal driver. *"Giovanni?"*

"Congratulations on your son, Your Highness."

"Thank you. I need you to perform a special service for me immediately."

"Anything."

He'd been doing a lot of undercover services for Vincenzo since the pregnancy. "I hope you mean that. My red sportscar is yours if you do as I say."

His driver laughed. Giovanni came from a poor family.

"You think I'm kidding?"

"You are serious?"

"Do as I say and you'll find out. I want you to round up all your cousins *pronto* and have them drive to San Marco Hospital in Lanz. Signorina Loretto is there recovering from the delivery. She's being watched by her father's security people. Fortunately they don't know your cousins.

"I want them to cover all the hospital exits leading outside. She'll be leaving there by private limousine. I suspect it will happen by this evening if not sooner. When your cousins spot the limousine, they'll follow and report to you when her limo reaches its destination, which I believe will be a hotel, possibly the Splendido or the Moreno. Then you'll phone me and drive me there. Any questions?"

"No, Your Highness. You can count on me."

"There's a healthy bonus waiting for each of them. My life depends on your finding her, Giovanni."

"Capisci."

Vincenzo hung up and hurried down to the nursery to spend time with his precious son before his father and sister arrived. He had to stop Abby from leaving the country. If she got away, he'd track her down, but it would be much more difficult with the baby. He wanted her here. *Now!*

He played with his baby and took pictures with his phone. While the family took turns inspecting the new arrival, he took a catnap. Bianca and Valentino would be flying in tomorrow morning.

At five in the afternoon, his phone rang. He saw the caller ID and picked up. "Giovanni?"

"We've done as you asked. She was driven to the Moreno under heavy guard."

"I'll be right down." After telling Marcello his life wouldn't be worth living if he told anyone where Vincenzo was going, he put on sunglasses and rushed down to the limo in a Hawaiian shirt, khaki shorts, sandals and a droopy straw hat.

Giovanni took off like a rocket. "You look like all the rich American businessmen walking around the gardens. No one would recognize you in a million years, Your Highness," he said through the speaker.

He bit down hard. "If I can make it to her room before someone stops me, it won't matter."

Carlo had made Abby comfortable on the couch in their hotel suite. This would be their home for a few more days before they left the country. The painkillers they'd given her were working.

"Is there anything you want, honey?"

She kept watching the news on TV to see Vincenzo and the baby. "Would you mind picking up a few magazines for me to look at?"

"I'll get them. Anything else?"

"A bag of dark chocolate bocci balls and a pack of cashews." She'd been starving for foods she couldn't eat during the pregnancy. They wouldn't take away her depression, but she needed to give in to her cravings for some sweets or she'd never make it through the next few days.

"I'll have to go down the street for those."

"Dad—take your time. I'm fine and you need a break. Thank you."

A few minutes after Abby's father left, there was a knock on the door. "Room service."

She hadn't ordered anything, but maybe her father had. "Come in."

"Grazie, Signorina."

Abby knew that deep male voice and started to tremble. She turned her head in his direction, afraid she was hallucinating on the medicine. The sight she saw was so incredible, she burst into laughter and couldn't stop.

Vincenzo walked around the couch to stand in front of her. "What do you think?" he asked with a grin, showing those gorgeous white teeth in that gorgeous smile. "Would you recognize me on the street?"

She shook her head. "Take off the glasses." She was still laughing.

He flung them away and hunkered down next to her. His eyes blazed black fire. "Do you know me now?"

Her heart flew to her throat. "Wh-what are you doing here? How did you find me?"

"You'd be surprised what I had to go through. Giovanni's my man when I need him. Did you really think I was going to let you go?"

Tears stung her eyes. "Don't do this, Vincenzo."

"Do what? Come to see the woman who has changed my entire life?"

She looked away. "You have a beautiful son now. We had an agreement."

"I hate agreements when they don't give me the advantage."

Abby couldn't help chuckling, despite her chaotic emotions. "Is he wonderful?"

"I'll let you decide." He pulled out his cell phone to show her the roll of pictures.

"Oh, Vincenzo—he's adorable!"

He put the phone on the floor. "So are you. I love you, heart and soul, Abby."

The next thing she knew, his hands slid to her shoulders and he covered her mouth with his own. The driving force of his kiss pressed her head back against the pillow. His hunger was so shocking in its intensity a moan escaped her throat in surrender.

A dam had burst as they drank deeper and deeper, but Abby's need for him was out of control. She had no thought of holding back. She couldn't.

"For all my sins, I love and want you to the depth of my being, Vincenzo, but you already know that, don't you? I tried not to love you, but it didn't work. Everything your sister said to me that day in the drawing room was true."

His lips roved with increased urgency over her features and down the side of her neck to her throat. "I fell for you years ago when you almost drowned, but I would never admit it to myself because a relationship with you was out of the question. No matter how hard I tried not to think about you, you were there, everywhere I looked. You're in my blood, *bellissima*."

They kissed back and forth, each one growing more passionate. "It seems like I've been waiting for this all my life," she admitted when he let her up for breath.

"We've paid the price for our forbearance, but that time is over. I'm not letting you go."

Abby groaned aloud and tore her lips from his. "I can't stay in Arancia."

"There's no such word in my vocabulary. Not anymore."

"She's right, Vincenzo."

Her father had just walked in the hotel room, carrying some bags. Her breath caught as she eyed him over Vincenzo's shoulder.

"Carlo." He pressed another kiss to her mouth and got to his feet. "I'm glad you're here so I can ask your permission to marry Abby. She's my heart's blood."

Rarely in her life had she seen her father look defeated. He put the bags on the table and stared at the two of them.

"I don't want an affair with her. I want her for my wife. Since you and I met when I was eighteen, you can't say you don't know me well enough."

Her father moved closer. "That's certainly true." He looked at Abby. "Is this what you want?"

"Yes." Her answer was loud and instantaneous.

Vincenzo reached for her hand and squeezed it. "I have no idea if the parliament will allow my marriage to a commoner and still let me remain crown prince. If not, then I don't intend to be in line for the crown and my sister will take over when the time comes."

"Are you prepared to be the targets of malicious gossip for the rest of your lives?"

"If necessary we'll move to the States with our son. He *is* our son. One way or another, she and I have been in communication whether in person or skyping. Max is every bit a part of her as he is of me and Michelina."

Carlo swallowed hard.

"I love Abby the way you loved your wife. The state

you were in when you lost her altered my view of what a real marriage could be. If Abby leaves me, I'll be as lost as you were."

Vincenzo was speaking to her father's heart. She could tell he'd gotten to him.

"I know the king's feelings on the subject, Vincenzo. He was hoping you would follow after him."

"I was hoping I would fall in love with Michelina. But we don't always get what we hope for. If it's any consolation, Gianna always wished she'd been born a boy so she'd be first in line. She'll make a great ruler when the day comes."

"Are you two prepared to face the wrath of your mother-in-law?"

Vincenzo glanced at Abby. "We'll deal with her. When she sees Michelina's likeness in Max, her heart will melt. I know she'll secretly be full of gratitude to Abby, who put her life on the line for Michelina and me to give her a grandson."

"Dad?" Abby's eyes pleaded with him. "What do you think Mom would say if she were here?"

He let out a strange sound. "She always did say it was sinful that Prince Vincenzo had been born with every physical trait and virtue any red-blooded woman could want. Since she loved films so much, she would probably say yours is one of the greatest love stories of this generation and should be made into a movie. Then she'd give you her blessing, as I give you mine."

"Carlo..."

Vincenzo was as moved as Abby, who broke down weeping. He finally cleared his throat. "I want her to move back into the palace tonight in her old room until we're married. Max needs his mother tonight, not a nanny or a nurse."

"In that case a quiet, private marriage in the palace chapel needs to be arranged within a week or two. Just as soon as you've talked to the king."

"I don't want you to take that job back in Rhode Island, Dad."

He broke into a happy smile. "Since I'm going to be a grandpa, I guess I'm stuck here."

"That'll be music to my father's ears." Vincenzo put his hands on his hips. "Do you feel well enough for the trip back to the palace now?" he asked Abby.

She stared at him. "I feel so wonderful, I'm floating. I want to see our baby."

"Do what you need to do while I help your father get everything packed up. Then we'll go out to my limo for the drive back."

"I'll just run to the restroom and grab my purse." Except she walked slowly and looked back at Vincenzo. "I'm waddling like a goose."

His laughter resonated off the walls.

In a few minutes she was ready. When she came back into the room, she found he'd donned his hat and sunglasses. When she thought he would take hold of her hand, he picked her up like a bride, as if she were weightless.

"You and I have done things differently than most of the world. Now we're about to cross the threshold the other way."

"And me looking such a mess." She didn't have on makeup and her hair hung loose, without being brushed.

"You're the most beautiful sight I ever saw in my life." He gave her a husband's kiss, hot with desire.

"So are you," she murmured, resting her head against his shoulder.

Her father opened the door. "The men have the hallway closed off to the exit. Let's go."

After leaving his stunned father and sister in the king's private living room, where he'd announced he was getting married, Vincenzo headed for the nursery. He found Max sleeping and gathered him in his arms. The nanny left for Abby's apartment, wheeling the bassinet on its rollers down the hall. He followed and carried his son through the corridors of the palace. One day their little boy would run on these marble floors.

The staff all wanted to steal a look at Max, but Vincenzo was careful not to let them get too close. Dr. De-Luca had warned him to keep Max away from people during the next few weeks. He found Abby on top of the bed with her eyes closed. After fifteen hours in labor, she had to be exhausted. She was wearing a blue nightgown and robe and had fastened her gilt hair back at the nape.

Their nanny put the bassinet with everything they would need to one side of the queen-size bed and left the apartment. Since both were asleep, Vincenzo put the baby in the little crib on his back. Then he got on the other side of the bed and lay down facing Abby.

It felt so marvelous to put his arm around her. He'd wanted to do this on the yacht and had been aching for her ever since. While she slept he studied the exquisite oval mold of her face. Her lips had the most luscious curve. He had to pinch himself this was really happening. To have his heart's desire like this was all he could ever ask of life.

Abby sighed and started to turn, but must have felt the weight of Vincenzo's arm. Her eyes flickered open.

"Good evening, Sleeping Beauty." The famous fairy-tale character had nothing on his bride-to-be.

Her eyes looked dazed. "How long have you been here?"

"Just a little while. *Viene qui tesoro.*" She *was* his darling.

He pulled her closer and began kissing her. Abby's response was more thrilling than anything he'd ever dreamed about the two of them. Vincenzo had promised himself to be careful with her. The kind of intimacy he longed for wouldn't happen until her six-week checkup, but he already knew she was an exciting lover.

They didn't need words right now. There'd been enough words expressed to last months, years. The kind of rapture they derived from each other had to come from touch, from her fragrance, from the sounds of her breathing when she grew excited, from the way she fit in his arms as if she were made for him. She was the fire, giving off life-giving warmth. He couldn't get close enough.

In the throes of ecstasy, he heard newborn sounds coming from the other side of the bed. He planted one more kiss to her throat. "Someone's waking up and wants to meet his mama."

With reluctance, he rolled away from her and walked around to the crib. "I've got a surprise for you, *piccolo,* but let's change your diaper first." Practice made perfect.

Abby sat up higher on the bed, her eyes glued to the baby he placed in her arms. "Oh—" she crooned, bending over to kiss his face. "You darling little thing.

You're already a kicker, aren't you? I've been feeling your father's legs for several months and thought you had to be a boy. Are you hungry? Is that why you're getting all worked up?" Her soft laughter thrilled Vincenzo's heart.

He handed her a bottle. She knew what to do. It fascinated him to watch her feed him as if she'd been doing it every day. A mother's instinct. Deep down he knew she'd been thinking about it from the moment she found out she was pregnant.

"Give him about two ounces, then burp him. Here's a cloth."

What took him awhile to learn she seemed to know instinctively. When she raised Max to her shoulder, their little boy cooperated and they both chuckled. She raised a beaming face to him. "I'm too happy."

"I know what you mean," he murmured emotionally.

"I hope you realize I wanted to talk about the baby for the whole nine months, but I didn't dare."

"You think I don't understand?" He sat down on the side of the bed next to her and watched a miracle happening before his eyes. "We'll take care of Max all night and feed him every time he wakes up."

"I can't wait to bathe him in the morning. I want to examine every square inch of him."

Vincenzo leaned over to kiss her irresistible mouth. "Once the doctor gives you the go-ahead, I'm going to do the same thing to *you*."

Blood rushed to her cheeks. "Darling—"

Abby had just put the baby down in the nursery when her cell phone rang. She hurried out of the room, clutching her robe around her, and slipped back in the bedroom she shared with her husband to answer it. "Carolena!"

"You're a sly one."

Her heart pounded in anxiety. "I was just going to call you. I guess the news is officially out."

"Out? It's alive and has gone around the world. I've got the Arancian morning news in front of my eyes. I quote, 'Crown Prince Vincenzo Di Laurentis marries commoner surrogate mother Abigail Sanderson Loretto in private chapel ceremony with only members of the immediate family in attendance. The question of the prince stepping down is still being debated by the parliament.

'The twenty-eight-year-old first-time mother, an American citizen born in Rhode Island, attained Arancian citizenship six years ago. At present she's an *avvocata* with Faustino, Ruggeri, Duomo and Tonelli.

'Her father, Carlo Antonio Loretto, a native of Arancia who served in the Arancian Embassy in Washington, D.C., for a time, is chief of security for the royal palace. His American-born wife, Holly Sanderson Loretto, is deceased due to a tragic sailboat accident eleven years ago on the Mediterranean.

'Prince Maximilliano Guilio Cavelli Di Laurentis, the son of deceased Princess Michelina Agostino Cavelli of the Kingdom of Gemelli, is second in line to the throne.

'The spokesman for the palace reports that Prince Vincenzo's wife and child are doing well.'"

Abby gripped the phone tighter. "This day had to come, the one the three of us talked about a year ago, when I first met with Michelina and Vincenzo.

But I didn't know then that she would die." Her voice throbbed before breaking down in tears.

"I know this is hard, Abby, but you might take heart in the fact that the paper didn't do a hatchet job on you and your husband. They presented the facts without making judgments, something that is so rare in the media world, I found myself blinking."

"That's because of the publisher's long-standing friendship with the king. I shudder to think what the other newspapers have printed."

"I haven't read anything else except the story in one magazine. Do you remember the one after Michelina's death that said The Prince of Every Woman's Dreams in Mourning?"

"Yes." She'd never forget.

"The quote now reads, 'Hopeful royal women around the world in mourning over prince's marriage to American beauty.'"

Abby groaned. "The truth is, that magazine would have been writing about me if he'd decided to marry Princess Odile."

"But he didn't!" Carolena cried out ecstatically. "Listen to this article from that same magazine. 'Enrico Rozzo, a sailor in the coast guard who was at the scene of the terrible death of Holly Loretto, the mother of then seventeen-year-old Abigail Loretto, said, "Prince Vincenzo thought nothing of his own life when he went in search of Signorina Loretto during the fierce storm. He found her body floating lifeless in a grotto and brought her back to life. His bravery, skill and quick thinking will never be forgotten by the coast guard."'"

Abby's body froze. "How did they get hold of that story?"

"How do they always do it? It's a glowing testimonial to your husband, Abby. He's well loved."

"I know." *By me most of all.* She was blinded by tears, still euphoric after knowing Vincenzo's possession for the first time.

"Just think—he married *you* under threat of losing the throne. Talk about Helen of Troy!"

A chuckle escaped despite Abby's angst. "Will you stop?"

"I always thought you were the most romantic person I ever knew. After what you went through to get that baby here, no one deserves a happier ending more than you."

"I'm not looking very romantic right now." She wiped her eyes. "At my six-week checkup yesterday morning, the doctor told me I'm fifteen pounds overweight. I won't be able to wear that gorgeous yellow dress for at least two months! I look like an albatross!" Carolena's laughter came through the phone.

"A stunning albatross," Vincenzo whispered, sliding his arms around her from behind. She hadn't heard him come in. He was in his robe.

At his touch Abby could hardly swallow, let alone think. "Carolena? Forgive me. I have to go, but I promise to call you soon. You've got to come to the palace and see the baby."

"I can't wait!"

He was kissing the side of her neck, so she couldn't talk.

"Your time is coming."

"When the moon turns blue."

"Carolena, you're being ridiculous."

"A presto."

The second Abby clicked off, Vincenzo took the phone and tossed it onto one of the velvet chairs. He pivoted her around and crushed her against him. "Do you have any idea how wonderful it is to walk into a room, any room, day or night, and know I can do anything I want to you?"

She clung fiercely to him, burying her face in his hair. "I found out how wonderful it was yesterday after you brought me home from my checkup." Heat filled her body as she remembered their lovemaking. She'd responded to him with an abandon that would have been embarrassing if he hadn't been such an insatiable lover. They'd cried out their love for each other over and over during the rapture-filled hours of the night.

"I told the nanny we'd look in on the baby tonight, but for the next eight hours, we're not to be disturbed unless there's an emergency."

"We've got eight hours?" Her voice shook.

His smile looked devilish; he rubbed her arms as a prelude to making love. "What's the matter? It *is* our honeymoon. Are you scared to be alone with me already?"

Her heart was racing. "Maybe."

"Innamorata—" He looked crushed. "Why would you say that?"

She tried to ease away from him, but he wouldn't let her. "I guess it's because the news has gone public about us at last. I don't want you to regret marrying me. What if the parliament votes for you to step down? It's all because of me."

He let out a deep sigh. "Obviously you need more

convincing that I've done exactly what I wanted. Whether I become king one day or not means nothing to me without your love to get me through this life." He kissed her mouth. "Sit on the bed. There's something I want to show you."

While she did his bidding, he pulled the scrapbook from one of his dresser drawers. "I've been busy filling the pages that hadn't been used yet. Take a good long look, and then never again accuse me of regretting the decision I've made."

With trembling hands she turned to the place where she'd put her last entry. On the opposite page were the two ultrasound pictures of the baby. Beneath them was a news clipping of her on the steps of the courthouse the day she'd won the case for Signor Giordano. A quiet gasp escaped her throat as she turned the pages.

Someone had taken pictures of her coming and going from the palace. Pictures of her on the funicular, at the restaurant, the swimming pool, the yacht, the church where she'd worn the hat, pictures on the screen while they'd Skyped. But she cried out when she saw a close up of herself at the opera. The photo had caught her in a moment of abject grief at the thought of a permanent separation from Vincenzo.

He'd always found a way to her...

Abby could hardly breathe for the love enveloping her. "Darling—" She put the album on the bedside table and turned in his arms. He pulled her on top of him.

"You're the love of my life and the mother of my child. How can you doubt it?" he asked in that low, velvety voice she felt travel through her body like lava, igniting fires everywhere it went.

"I don't doubt you, sweet prince," she whispered

against his lips. "I just want you to know I'll never take this precious love for granted."

"I'm glad to hear it. Now love me, Abby. I need you desperately. Never stop," he cried.

As if she could.

* * * * *

LET'S TALK
Romance

For exclusive extracts, competitions
and special offers, find us online:

 facebook.com/millsandboon

@MillsandBoon

@MillsandBoonUK

Get in touch on 01413 063232

For all the latest titles coming soon, visit
millsandboon.co.uk/nextmonth

JOIN THE
MILLS & BOON
BOOKCLUB

* **FREE** delivery direct to your door

* **EXCLUSIVE** offers every month

* **EXCITING** rewards programme

50% OFF
YOUR FIRST
PARCEL

Join today at
Millsandboon.co.uk/Bookclub

MILLS & BOON
MODERN
Power and Passion

Prepare to be swept off your feet by sophisticated, sexy and seductive heroes, in some of the world's most glamourous and romantic locations, where power and passion collide.